Lyn Andrews is one of the UK's top one hundred best-selling authors, reaching No. 1 on the *Sunday Times* paperback bestseller list. Born and brought up in Liverpool, she is the daughter of a policeman and also married a policeman. After becoming the mother of triplets, she took some time off from her writing whilst she raised her children. Shortlisted for the Romantic Novelists' Association Award in 1993, she has now written twenty-seven hugely successful novels. Lyn Andrews divides her time between Merseyside and Ireland.

lyn andrews

Ellan Vannin

headline

First published in 1991 by Corgi Books
an imprint of Transworld Publishers

First published in this paperback edition in 2008
by HEADLINE PUBLISHING GROUP

5

ISBN 978 0 7553 4186 3

Typeset in Janson by Avon DataSet Ltd,
Bidford-on-Avon, Warwickshire

Printed and bound in the UK by
CPI Antony Rowe, Chippenham, Wiltshire

Headline's policy is to use papers that are natural, renewable and
recyclable products and made from wood grown in sustainable
forests. The logging and manufacturing processes are expected to
conform to the environmental regulations of the country of origin.

HEADLINE PUBLISHING GROUP
An Hachette Livre UK Company
338 Euston Road
London NW1 3BH

www.headline.co.uk
www.hachettelivre.co.uk

For my daughter, Helen

Prologue

1901

———•———

THE SHIVER STARTED AT the nape of George Vannin's neck and ran down his spine like a trickle of ice-water. He looked down at the ten-year-old child trudging along beside him and his dark eyes clouded. His expression became troubled. The lines etched on his thin, pale face, caused by fatigue and anxiety, deepened and the cold tingling started again. It was as though he already knew what lay ahead for them both, he thought with a dull sadness.

He stopped as they came to the stile set into the stone wall that marked the boundary of the fields, lifted the child effortlessly and sat her on the wooden spar. His gaze wandered over the familiar scene and his troubled spirit lightened a little. He was of pure Manx stock and he loved every inch of this island that lay off the north-west coast of England: the wide, sandy sweep of the bay, his home village of Peel nestling around the harbour where the fishing fleet anchored. In the distance was the mountainous backbone of the island with Snaefell to the north, its peak in the clouds: the patchwork of fields and meadows, woodlands and heathlands and the slopes of Tynwald Hill where the members of the House of Keyes met in high summer. Officially the Isle of Man was a part of Great Britain but they had their own parliament, made their own laws and spoke their own language as they had done from time immemorial.

On a clear day, from this vantage point, you could see the Welsh coastline, but this evening it was obscured by a hazy mist; like the mist that had been clogging his mind, holding in its depths a fear he didn't understand, he thought morosely.

The child seemed to sense his mood. 'What's the matter, Pa?'

His rounded shoulders beneath the old tweed jacket moved upwards in a half shrug and his expression altered. The lines eased and he smiled. 'Nothing, Ellan. Should there be something amiss, lass?'

'Then why are we going to see Aunt Maud tonight? It's not Sunday,' she said, truculently. Ellan didn't like Maud Quirk very much and was secretly glad that she was not her real aunt. She was only the wife of her pa's friend Amos Quirk whom she had never minded calling Uncle. It was very easy to say 'Uncle Amos', it was much harder to say 'Aunt Maud' but her pa had said she must be respectful to them both and that Aunt Maud in particular had been good to them over the years. Ellan did not think that going to Chapel twice on Sunday, sharing the Sabbath meal with them, running errands and being taught how to keep a 'decent and respectable' house constituted being good to them. In the domestic tasks she was often sharply rebuked and just as cutting were the comments on her character and appearance. She had the feeling that Maud didn't really approve of her or of the fact that her pa worked all the hours God sent to keep her in decent clothes and at school so that she wouldn't grow up ragged and ignorant. Young as she was she knew how much of a struggle that was.

She didn't mind the three Quirk boys. John and Mathew were so much older than her that she classed them as adults and as such she had a disinterested respect for them. Andrew was different. He was only two years older than herself and although he had now joined his brothers on the short fishing trips, during the autumn and winter he stayed at home and helped on the croft. There were times when he teased and tormented her, but she usually got her own back.

George smiled down into the eyes that were a mirror of his own and passed a work-worn hand over the long, blue-black hair. She was a bonny lass, was his Ellan. She had the striking good looks of her poor ma, dead two hours after giving birth to his still-born son. But he'd never become bitter inside at the loss of his young wife. It was as though all the love he'd had for Sarah had been transferred to his four-year-old daughter.

They'd managed all right these past six years, just the two of them, with the help of Maud and other neighbours before Ellan had gone to school. They were a clannish community, that was their strength in times of sorrow and hardship. Ellan was a bright, intelligent child which was why he'd resisted all Maud's attempts to persuade him to keep her at home. He wanted better things for Ellan. Nothing too grand, he was realistic enough to know that dreams must have limitations. A grim smile hovered about his lips as he remembered Maud's arguments about Ellan's future.

'And what good will all that learning do her, George Vannin? As long as she can write her name and read from the Bible that's enough for any girl. Her place is at home looking after you!'

'But I want more than that for Ellan,' he'd replied.

'More? Have you some daft notion in that skull of yours to pass her off as the "Quality"?'

'I'm no fool, Maud! I'm not aiming for the impossible. Just a decent home of her own and a well set-up husband so she'll never want.'

Maud had tutted and placed both hands on her hips and stared at him with barely concealed triumph. 'Then she'd better learn how to keep a good table and an orderly house for this "well set-up" husband she's to have!'

He'd shaken his head and sighed. Maud would never understand what he meant. Her vision was too narrow, her outlook on life restricted by the dourness of her nature. 'I'll never be able to make you understand, Maud, not in a thousand years.'

She'd tutted again, her mouth puckered with disapproval and annoyance as she'd begun to set the table. 'Maybe not, but there are times when I don't understand you either! For all you're a working man there's something foolish, aye, even fey, about you.'

'That's a strange word to use.'

'But a fitting one. For all your common sense you're a dreamer. And what possessed you to give the lass a

4

name that isn't really a name, I'll never know. She's not a "someone" she's a "something"!' She'd leaned on the table, facing him squarely.

He'd felt the colour suffuse his cheeks. 'Vannin is my name and it's as old as the cliffs of Bradda Head and well you know it!' he'd retorted.

'I'm not denying it, but to call her Ellan . . . what kind of a name is that to go with Vannin?'

'It's a Manx name.'

'Oh, it's that all right! "Ellan Vannin", "Isle of Man", couldn't you have spelled it ELLEN?' She laughed derisively. 'And it's the name of one of the Steam Packet boats, too!'

'Well, then, if it's good enough for a ship it's good enough for my lass!' he'd shot back.

'You go putting ideas like that in her head and you're storing up a bushel of trouble for yourself and her, you mark my words.'

Only the entry of Ellan herself into the room had ended that conversation. Aye, Maud was a narrow, unbending woman with no vision, no dreams or ambitions, but she was a good wife and mother and he trusted her. She was the only person he would trust with the most precious thing he had, Ellan.

Ellan tugging at his sleeve brought him out of his reverie. 'Do we have to go? Can't we stay here and watch the boats coming in?' she asked, petulantly.

He shook his head. The sun was beginning to set, slipping away down behind St Patrick's Isle, throwing shadows over the ruined castle and turning the sea the colour of copper. Great draperies of scarlet and gold drifted across a sky the colour of a duck's egg. It was as pleasant an evening as a man could wish for and it was tempting to stand and watch the sunset, to breathe deeply of the evening air and feel the clean, salt breeze on your face. They were all rare luxuries for him. He sighed heavily. 'I have something I have to give Aunt Maud. It's important. It won't wait. Come on, I'll race you as far as the house and I'll give you a bit of a start, just to be fair.'

She jumped down, tossing her head back and laughing up at him, the rays of the dying sun giving her skin a golden, luminous glow. 'I'll still beat you, Pa! I can run faster than you! I can run faster than anyone!'

He laughed with her. 'Aye, it will have to be a quick man to catch you, Ellan.' But as he watched her hitch up her skirt and begin to run across the short, springy grass on which the dew was already beginning to form, his smile died. The feeling that had held him in its grip for days was back. That dark foreboding that had made him sit down and laboriously write the short note to Maud Quirk, giving into her care and hers alone, his daughter, Ellan. Maybe it was just another of his foolish, fey moods, he thought, but try as he might he couldn't shake off the premonition. He began to run and his long legs were as ungainly in this unaccustomed exercise as they were a hindrance in his work.

Amos Quirk was leaning against the stone wall that surrounded the small croft, smoking his pipe. He grinned at the two approaching figures: the child with her dark hair streaming out behind her like a veil, her skirt drawn up to her knees and determination stamped on her small, animated face. Behind her came his old friend, a tall, thin, gangling man prematurely aged, as they all were by grinding hard work and the constant struggle to make ends meet. As they drew closer he laughed. 'Eh, but you're an awkward sod, George! All legs and spindly shanks at that, like a new born colt! Come on in with you, man, and get your breath back.'

Ellan stood beside him laughing up into George's face. 'I told you I'd beat you, Pa.'

'And I said it would have to be a quick man to catch you and it looks as though I'm not that man.'

Amos laughed again as he led them inside the cottage.

Maud looked up as they entered. She was in her mid-thirties but looked older. Her thin, mousy hair, peppered liberally with grey, was drawn back in a bun. Her long, thin features were constantly set in a disapproving manner so that there were deep lines across her forehead and the corners of her mouth drooped downwards. Everything about Maud was angular, she seemed to have no soft curves. Her shoulder blades stuck out sharply beneath the plain brown dress, as did her elbows. Even her white apron was so stiffly starched that it, too, seemed to be all jutting angles and corners. In her bony hands she held a large, brown stewpot which she placed on the range.

'What's brought you up here?' she asked, her grey eyes moving quickly from George's face to that of her husband, with a look that obviously blamed him for this intrusion.

'That's a nice greeting, I must say, Maud!' Amos rebuked her.

She ignored him and cocked her head to one side, waiting for an explanation. Ellan moved closer to her pa's side and Maud noticed.

'Have you wiped your boots, Ellan?'

Ellan nodded.

Seeing that his wife was not going to extend the invitation, Amos indicated the ladder-backed chair beside the range. 'Sit down, man. Make yourself at home.'

Maud picked up her mending basket and placed it on the table, shooting a guarded look at George. There was something on his mind, she surmised. Something important enough to bring him here mid-week and this late in the evening when that child should be in bed. She picked up a sock and her needle.

George felt awkward and rather foolish, doubting his actions for the first time. He cleared his throat. 'It's . . . it's you I've come to see, Maud.'

Ellan moved closer to her father, suddenly afraid. She'd noticed how quiet and preoccupied he'd been lately. He'd hardly spoken to her after their supper and when she'd asked the reason for his silence, all he'd said was, 'I'm thinking, lass. Thinking about the future.' She felt sick as a terrible thought struck her. Suppose he'd come to ask Aunt Maud to keep her? To stay here with them? But surely he would have said something to her about it, tried to explain, as he usually did. Sometimes he spoke to her as though she were grown up. She tugged at the sleeve of his jacket but he just patted her hand and as Maud's gaze was now fixed on her, she was afraid to speak.

The three adults exchanged glances as George pulled a creased envelope from his pocket. Amos looked puzzled but then, seeing something in his friend's face, he smiled broadly and jovially at Ellan. 'Did you know that old Floss has had her pups? Four of them. Come on and I'll show you them,' and clasping her tightly by the hand he guided her towards the door, giving her no time to protest or hang back.

'Don't you go bringing them in here, nor Floss either,' Maud called after them. When the door had closed she turned to George. 'What's all this about and what have you got there?'

George leaned forward and held out the envelope. 'I want you to keep this, Maud, please? I don't want you to open it . . . not yet.'

'What is it?'

'My Will,' he muttered.

'Your Will!' she echoed. 'What's got into you, man? What need have you for a Will?'

'Every man should leave one. It stops a lot of trouble when . . .' he shrugged.

She placed the note on the table with obvious irritation. 'Why don't you give it to Amos then – why me?'

He twisted his hands together. 'Because I trust you, Maud. Oh, I'm not saying I don't trust Amos, but I know that you being a God-fearing, Christian woman would never go back on your word or on a request. I know Amos wouldn't either but . . .' The more he tried to explain the more confused he got and the worse it all sounded. 'Oh, I just wanted you to have it, that's all.'

She picked it up and turned it over in her hand, then she nodded curtly and, getting up, crossed to the dresser. Taking down a blue glazed teapot that was lacking its spout, she took off the lid and pushed the envelope inside.

George let out a sigh of relief. That old teapot was her 'strongbox' and no-one dared pry into its contents without first asking permission. Not even Amos.

She replaced the teapot, shaking her head. His brain was getting befuddled, she thought, and no wonder. Sitting in that cottage every night, scheming and spinning all kinds of outlandish dreams. He'd have done both himself and the child a power of good if he'd married again. There had been a couple of girls who would have been willing, too. But no, he worked all day and then sat gazing into the fire all night and now this foolishness about a Will of all things. Lord above! He had nothing to leave except a few sticks of furniture and his Sunday suit. 'I suppose you'll be wanting a cup of tea before you go?' she offered grudgingly.

He leaned back in the chair, more relieved than he had felt for days. 'If it's not too much trouble.'

She reached for the painted tea caddy and pushed the kettle on to the hob. 'It'll be no trouble, the lads will be in before long.'

'Work is never done, is it, Maud?'

The ghost of a smile flitted across her face. 'Mine never is, but I thank the Lord for giving me the strength to do it. That's all any of us can ask.'

He nodded his agreement slowly and then smiled as he heard Amos coming across the yard, calling to his sons who had finished tying up the boats. He heard the excited barking of the dogs and Ellan's laughter and he smiled again at Maud. 'You're a good woman, Maud Quirk, and you've taken a weight off my mind.'

She jerked her head in the direction of the door. 'I wish you'd tell them that. Take everything for granted, they do!'

'Well, a prophet is never recognized in his own country, isn't that what the Bible says?'

For the first time her features softened. 'Aye, it does. Bring your chair up to the table before the starving hordes descend on us and sit the lass on your knee or she'll be crushed in the stampede. They've no manners when it comes to food, though I'm worn out with telling them. It's an uphill struggle all the way, that's what it is.'

He smiled to himself. To get her point of view across Maud often exaggerated. 'Oh, come on out of that, they're grand lads. Fine fishermen all of them and you know it.'

'I'll not deny it. They've justified all my arguments about not following Amos down the mine. It's not natural that, men burrowing like moles in the darkness. Not natural at all.'

'There's not much choice, Maud.'

'Aye, well, we'll not start up that argument again.'

George grinned as the kitchen suddenly became crowded with Amos, John, Mathew and Andrew and in the middle of them all stood his pretty, dark-haired daughter and she, too, was smiling.

The following day in the golden light of early evening, Ellan stood silently beside Maud and her three sons as they watched the men being brought to the surface. Around them stood groups of men, women and children and there was a strange, silent tension hanging over them all. Despite new pumping equipment, the shaft at the Foxdale mine had collapsed and George Vannin and Amos Quirk were two of the last to be got out and both were dead.

Part One

1908

———•———

Chapter One

E LLAN LEANED ON THE stile and looked down the winding path that led into the village, down to the jetty and the harbour. She loved these summer mornings. The dawn light was soft. Fingers of mist clung to the trees and hedgerows and the sea took on the rose-tinted glow of the rising sun. The long shadows over the battlements of Peel Castle became dark purple and then blue until the sun burst over the edge of the sea and bathed everything in a shower of gold.

She had lived with Aunt Maud for seven years but it seemed longer, far longer. Every evening at prayers both her pa and Uncle Amos were formally remembered, and twice on Sundays, but she had no need for Aunt Maud's formalities. There wasn't a day that passed when she didn't think about her pa and when she was worried or in a quandary, she asked him to guide her, speaking to him as though he were in the same room instead of in the churchyard on the hill. Nor was there a day when she didn't lean against this stile, the very one he'd sat her on the night before the accident, and look down towards her old home and remember the happy days before the disaster in the Foxdale mine.

There had been a time when she wouldn't go near the stile; she'd taken the long way back to the croft, cutting across the common grazing land and the copse. She could still remember vividly the day when it had really dawned on her with dreadful clarity, that her pa was dead, that she would never see him again. From habit, or subconsciously, her steps had taken her back to the cottage by the harbour wall and she had stood staring, in wild disbelief, at the two small children playing in the open doorway and the sounds of a heated argument that came from within. Then, as though she had been slapped hard across the face, came the realization that it wasn't 'her' cottage any more. Another family had moved in. She'd never see her pa's tall figure in the doorway, stooping so as not to bang his head on the lintel. She'd turned and run, sobbing, back to the croft. Back to Aunt Maud with her quick temper and her sour looks for that was her home now and for ever.

She had cried that night as though her heart would break in two and not even all Maud's scolding or the boys' attempts to put aside their own grief to comfort her could stop the flood of tears. At last she'd fallen into an exhausted sleep and the next day it was as though she'd left her childhood behind and had grown up.

From then on she'd helped Aunt Maud in the house and in the fields with a grinding, monotonous routine that had gradually dulled the ache of her grief until there were nights when she fell into a deep sleep that had not been preceded by an hour of sobbing. 'Children adapt and accept loss,' she'd heard the minister say once and as she'd grown up she'd realized there was truth in his words.

When she was eleven she had learned how to gut and clean the fish that was so vital a part of their meagre existence. There had been no mention of her returning to school and when she thought about it, she had no real desire to go back. School belonged to the old life. With Uncle Amos gone, Andrew accompanied his brothers on the long fishing trips; it was the only source of income they had. They lived on what the croft produced, although there were things that had to be bought. No-one was totally self-sufficient.

She had no money of her own, her pa had had nothing left to leave, and she worked for her keep. That fact had been cruelly revealed to her one day when Miss Evans, the school teacher, came to see Aunt Maud to try to persuade her to send Ellan back to school. She'd been bringing in the washing, the wicker basket clutched to her for it was an awkward thing for a young girl to carry, but stopped outside the back door when she heard voices inside.

'She's a very bright child, Mrs Quirk,' she heard Miss Evans say.

'She doesn't want to go back and even if she did I couldn't spare her. There's enough work here for at least three people and seeing as how I'm a widow, my lads have to fish. There's no money to spare in this house. Ellan works for her keep. I can't afford to feed and clothe her, she has to pay for things like that in kind.'

That exchange prompted the first real outburst of temper, a temper and a resolve she never knew existed within herself. She faced Aunt Maud defiantly, her chin jutting forward, her dark eyes blazing. 'I want to earn money of my own! I don't want to be kept by you!'

Maud was astounded. 'Would you listen to her, the ungrateful little madam!' she cried, looking for support from her elder sons. She got none.

'I want to earn money so I can pay you,' she'd persisted.

'You don't need to pay us, Ellan, you know that. You're part of this family now,' John intervened.

'I'm not! I'm not! She told Miss Evans I have to earn my keep! I have to pay in kind!'

John shot a piercing look at his mother. 'I'll tell you what, Ellan, it's your birthday soon. Me and Mat will buy you some chickens of your own.'

'Chickens?' she repeated, puzzled.

'You can sell the eggs in Douglas. With all those hotels and guest houses springing up like mushrooms, they'll pay well for fresh eggs, then you'll have some money.'

As quickly as it had come her anger died. She laughed and threw her arms around John and he whirled her around the kitchen and they all laughed. Even Aunt Maud smiled for a second. And so her small enterprise started. Once a week she went to Douglas. She either walked or hitched a ride: if she got the train it cost money. Sometimes it didn't pay much when there was no great demand for eggs or there was a glut – for other people had seized on the same idea – or when the hens went broody. But it was something of her own. She felt a certain amount of satisfaction and independence when she handed over to Aunt Maud the sixpence that somehow she always managed to find by Saturday.

She narrowed her eyes as she peered at the distant horizon where two small black dots, as yet indistinguishable as shapes or objects, were visible, but she knew what they were. The boats were coming back after a night's fishing. She climbed over the stile and skirted the field of ripening corn swaying gently in the breeze. When she reached the wall she stopped and smiled as she caught sight of Lizzie Killip coming up the lane. Lizzie was the same age as herself and was as close to being a friend as anyone she knew. They'd been in the same class at school but Lizzie now worked as a parlour maid at Glentrammon, the big house owned by Thomas Costain who seemed to own most of the island and had his finger in several pies, including the mines and the shipping company.

'Going back, Lizzie?' Ellan called and the girl stopped and waved.

Lizzie was plump with a round, open face, hazel eyes and light brown curly hair, hair that was swept up in a tight roll around her head and on top of which was perched a straw hat with a blue ribbon around it.

'Come down on to the road. I'm not climbing that wall, I'll ruin my skirt on the brambles,' Lizzie called back.

Ellan climbed over the wall and down the slight, grassy incline, avoiding the brambles. Lizzie smiled, wondering how Ellan could bear to be stuck with that sour-faced, sharp-tongued, old besom all day and still remain so pleasant. And a dart of envy struck her. Ellan was turning into a real beauty, she had to admit that. Given the right clothes she could pass for a lady while Miss Mary Costain, who was a lady and had all the clothes she could wish for, looked like a drab little wren.

'Going back?' Ellan repeated.

Lizzie nodded. 'I stayed at home last night. Our Billy's got the colic and Ma's worn out, so I asked could I sleep over, to give her a break. You waiting for the boats?'

'Yes. They're on the way in now.'

They both looked out to sea to where two more shapes had appeared on the horizon and the first boats were drawing closer to land.

'There'll be plenty of work, the day, if the catch has been good,' Ellan remarked and Lizzie looked at the faded cotton skirt, the print blouse with the frayed collar and the rolled up sleeves, the old straw hat perched on the back of Ellan's head. Then she looked down at her own cotton challis dress and short linen jacket. Ellan deserved better than working down at the harbour, gutting and cleaning stinking fish in all weathers and working on the croft, too. Yet she'd never heard her complain.

Lizzie snapped off a piece of rye grass and twisted it between her fingers, turning over in her mind an idea that had just come to her. 'Do you think your Aunt Maud would let you come and work with me at Glentrammon? Molly Yourston has given in her notice. She's leaving, going to Liverpool to her sister. Better wages and opportunities. So they're going to need a Tweenie.'

'What's that?'

'A maid who works between the kitchen and the parlour and does more or less whatever's needed. Between, Tweenie. Get it? It's better than killing yourself for her and no thanks for it either.'

'She's given me a home,' Ellan answered, trying to be loyal.

'Not of her own free will, so my ma says. Only because your pa asked her to.' A look of pain crossed Ellan's face and Lizzie felt contrite.

'She'll only say she can't manage without me. She would be all on her own when the lads are away fishing.'

'She can pay someone, like a lot of people do. There's plenty of youngsters would be glad to earn a penny helping out after school and at weekends and don't tell me she can't afford it, Ellan Vannin! John and Mat were telling my pa they are hoping to buy a bigger boat soon.'

'Your ma's certainly well informed about everyone's business!'

Lizzie shrugged. Her ma was the village gossip and she'd become used to this kind of reaction. 'Ask her. You can give her some of your wages, that should keep her quiet about not being able to manage and she'll have someone else to boss around instead of you. You'll get your keep and your work dresses. Every third Sunday off and a half day every other week. He's not a bad old stick and Miss Mary is quiet and easy pleased and the other two lads are off at school.'

'What do they need so many servants for then, if there's only the two of them?'

Lizzie tossed her head. 'Position. He's got to keep up appearances, he's an important man. Molly's going come Friday, so if I tell Miss Mary that I know of someone who is very interested she'll at least see you.' And she'll think more highly of me, Lizzie reasoned to herself. 'Ask her, no harm in that, you've nothing to lose, have you?'

Ellan made up her mind. 'All right, I'll ask.' It was too good an opportunity to miss. A chance to get away from Aunt Maud's constant carping, to live in a lovely house, surrounded by beautiful things, and have real money of her own.

'Good. You've got to take the opportunities offered in life, Miss Mary says, never let them pass you by.' Lizzie shifted the basket on her arm and leaned against a tree whose branches shaded the lane but drooped low over the grassy bank on which they stood. She cocked her head to one side like a curious bird. 'What do you want for the rest of your life, Ellan?'

'What?'

'Oh, you know what I mean. Don't look at me as though I was speaking a foreign language. What plans have you got? You must have some. You surely don't intend to stay with *her* for ever?'

Ellan had broken off a twig from a low branch and regarded it thoughtfully, her brow furrowed. 'I've not really thought about it. I suppose . . . I suppose I'll get married one day.'

'Who to?'

Ellan shrugged and threw away the twig. 'I don't know.'

'Ma says you'll probably end up with Andrew Quirk – the others are too old for you. That will keep it all in the family, so to speak. Though you're not really family.'

Ellan felt her cheeks burn. 'Your ma should watch her tongue, Lizzie, it'll be the death of her one day! Andrew is . . . well, he's just Andrew. He's like a brother to me, always has been. You can tell your ma there's nothing between me and Andrew Quirk and if I were to tell Aunt Maud . . .' she rolled her eyes expressively.

'Oh, all right. Don't get a bee in your bonnet about it. I was only asking. Anyway, I don't intend to stay here, it's the back of beyond. Nothing ever happens here.'

Ellan forgot her annoyance. 'And what great plans have you got in mind?'

Lizzie looked seriously thoughtful. 'I intend to get a proper training. I'll stay on with the Costains for another year, then I'll go to Liverpool and get a better position and then maybe I'll even go to London. Get a job with a titled family that has an estate in the country as well as a London town house.'

'You've certainly thought it all out, Lizzie. No plans to get married?'

'Not until I'm really old and have met a "suitable" match. You get a better class of people working for the gentry.'

Ellan laughed. 'You snob, Lizzie Killip!'

'I'm not. I know my place, I'm working class, always will be, but I'm just saying that there's working class and . . . well, working class.' She was becoming flustered and she had the distinct feeling that Ellan was making fun of her, though it was hard to tell with Ellan.

'A sort of upper-working class as opposed to a lower-working class, like us?'

Lizzie shot her a suspicious look. Sometimes Ellan came out with some very long words. It was probably due to the fact that she had stayed on at school longer than most of them and Miss Evans had lent her books to read even after she'd left. She decided to abandon the subject of class and futures altogether. 'I'd best be on my way. Shall I put in a word for you with Miss Mary?'

Ellan's gaze shifted to where the roof of the cottage was just visible above the rise. 'Yes. You'll have to tell her I've never done work like that before but that I'm eager to learn and I'm a hard worker.'

'Of course you've done work like that, haven't you been doing it since you were knee high? It's only cleaning and preparing vegetables and things for Cook. Any fool could do it.'

Ellan grimaced. 'Thanks for the compliment, Lizzie!'

'I didn't mean it to sound like that. Oh, sometimes, Ellan, you're so . . . so . . .'

'Perverse?'

Lizzie sucked in her breath, more long words. 'Yes, perverse, but don't you go using words like that to Miss Mary or she'll wonder if you're fish or fowl and maybe too well-educated for the job.' Lizzie tucked a few wisps of hair that had escaped back beneath her hat and smoothed down her skirt. 'I'll be off then.'

'How will I know if she wants to see me?'

'I'll get word to you.' And with a small wave, Lizzie resumed her journey.

Ellan stared at the now empty, sun-dappled lane. Oh, it would be good to get away from Aunt Maud. Nothing ever suited her; there was hardly a good word from her these days. There would be an argument, of course. Aunt Maud would say she couldn't manage without her, that she was ungrateful, that she couldn't afford to pay the younger children a few pence to help out. And what about the fish? She hated that job, especially in winter when her fingers became swollen and painful with chilblains. She thought about what Lizzie had said about herself and Andrew and wondered what everyone thought. Oh, Dora Killip had a bad mind to think there was anything other than friendship between them. She did look on him as a brother, she did!

She looked out to sea and noticed that the gulls had

become more numerous and more raucous in their cries and she saw that the first of the 'nobbies' as the smaller boats were called, had almost reached the harbour. She smiled, her good humour restored. She'd go and meet them. She'd need Andrew's help and possibly that of John and Mat as well, if she were to have any hope of becoming a Tweenie at Glentrammon.

The breeze coming in off the sea had freshened and blew wisps of dark hair around her face. She raised her hand to brush them away and then began to wave as she saw the *Cockleshell* manoeuvring her way alongside the jetty. She ran and caught the rope that John threw to her.

'You're out early again, Ellan.' Andrew Quirk laughed as he jumped from the boat on to the jetty with an agility that belied his stature. The deep blue eyes in the tanned face smiled down at her, for although she was tall, he was well over six feet. His brown hair curled around the neck of his thick jersey and had been blown into disarray by the breeze and for the first time she felt a little shy, almost embarrassed in his presence. Oh, damn Lizzie! she thought, smiling back.

'I came to meet you. Good catch?' she indicated the writhing, silvery mass in the nets on the deck of the boat.

'Good enough. Have to get it gutted and out to smoke though in this weather,' Mat answered.

'But not before breakfast. Aunt Maud had the porridge on before I left. The gutting will keep for an hour.'

She let John and Mat walk on ahead and fell into step beside Andrew wondering how to broach the subject. Oh, better to come out with it than beat around the bush. 'I saw Lizzie in the lane. They're going to need another maid up at the house. Lizzie asked me should she put a word in for me and I said yes.' He didn't look at her, just kept on walking, his hands in his pockets. 'Well?' she asked, tentatively.

'Well, what?'

'You know how your ma will carry on!'

He nodded. 'I suppose she will, she's as prickly as a thicket of brambles these days.'

'Will you back me up?'

He stopped and looked down at her. 'Do you want the job so much?'

'Yes, I do. Lizzie set me thinking about . . . things.'

He moved off again. 'What kind of things?'

She shrugged. 'Oh, life and the future, things like that.'

'Aren't you happy, Ellan? I know it's not been easy for you, but we've tried.'

'I know that and I'm happy enough, it's just that I'd like to get away, to work with other people.' She bit her lip. It sounded so ungrateful. 'I don't mean you or . . .'

'I know what you mean, Ellan,' he interrupted. 'I'm not blind or deaf. You'd be paid for working there, paid well. Money of your own, and your keep and I suppose more . . . well, you'd be seeing a different way of life, seeing other people.' There was an edge to his voice and somehow his reassurance did nothing to alleviate the feeling of guilt that had arisen in her.

'I have my money from the eggs.'

'It's not the same, is it?'

She sighed, wondering what kind of a hornet's nest she was stirring up, but the more she thought about it the more she realized just how much she wanted that job.

'You know I'll back you up, as long as it's what you want. So will John and Mat.'

She smiled up at him. 'It is. It is! And I'll send money home so she can afford to pay for help when she needs it.'

He grinned. 'Send money home! You'll only be up the road a bit, not halfway around the world,' he joked, but as he looked down at her it struck him that she'd grown up and he hadn't even noticed it. It must be the fact that she now wanted to leave the croft that had drawn attention to the fact. He hadn't realized either that she was a bonny lass. A very bonny lass indeed with those huge, dark eyes fringed with thick, sooty lashes and that dazzling smile. The realization caused him to feel uncomfortable and strangely uneasy in her presence. Emotions he had never felt before.

Any other time Ellan would have slipped her arm through his and they would have walked back laughing and joking, but now he seemed preoccupied and Lizzie's words came back to her. She wondered if he'd heard the gossip, for she felt that something had changed between them.

Mary Costain was sitting at the table in the morning room, a pot of tea at her elbow. The household account books, various scraps of paper, bills and receipts were laid out in front of her. Lizzie had described her as plain and that was what she was. At twenty-nine she had already assumed the mantle of a confirmed spinster and her mode of dress heightened the fact. The cream blouse with the high neck and the leg-o'-mutton sleeves made her look prim and did nothing for her rather sallow complexion. The wide skirt of navy blue bombazine did not disguise her thinness. Her reddish-gold hair, which was her most attractive feature, was piled up on top of her head. Her pale, plain features were fixed in a frown as she scanned the neat rows of figures.

She hated this job and the figures never seemed to balance. It was no use telling her father that no matter how many times she went over and over things, the totals never agreed. Thomas Costain was a man with an agile mind that grasped all things mathematical in a few seconds while she . . . Not for the first time did she fume at the crass stupidity of the education deemed necessary for a young lady of her station in life. Needlework, painting in watercolours, playing the piano and of course reading and all the endless rules of social etiquette, but not how to balance ledgers. And after you had spent years appearing to be a brainless butterfly and had got married, you were quite suddenly expected to run a household and its accounts efficiently! In one aspect she did consider herself lucky: the household she had to run was very small compared to those of some of her friends. She sighed. They of course could always fall back in desperation on mothers and older sisters. She only had her father, who grew impatient with her frequent mistakes.

She sipped her tea and glanced out of the window, across the lawns with their carefully tended flower beds. It was going to be another hot day and the way things were going she'd have a raging headache by the end of the morning. She totted up a column of figures again and then threw down the pen. There was only one thing for it and that was to supervise the buying in of the groceries and other household items they purchased. The home farm did not supply everything. That was officially the province of Mrs Portree, the housekeeper, and although she trusted the woman, she didn't like her.

To the gentle tapping on the door she called, 'Come in,' and Lizzie came slowly into the room.

Thankful for the diversion Mary leaned back in her chair. 'You're back then, Lizzie,' she said before she realized how stupid a remark that was. Of course the girl was back, she was standing in front of her for heaven's sake!

Lizzie dipped a bow. 'Yes, miss, and thank you for letting me stay over. Ma said I was to thank you, too. There's not many ladies with such Christian goodness like yourself, Miss Mary.'

Mary ignored the flowery rhetoric. 'How is your brother?'

'Better. Much better, and now that Ma's had a good night's rest she'll be able to cope.'

Mary sighed deeply, her eyes following the direction of Lizzie's gaze to the cluttered table. 'I only wish I could,' she muttered softly, confident the girl hadn't heard her. 'Was there something else, Lizzie?' Lizzie began to pluck at the hem of her clean apron. Mary became more attentive. 'What is it?'

'Well, seeing as how Molly is leaving an' all, I suppose you'll be looking for someone else?'

'I will.'

'I was wondering . . . I know someone, miss. She's the same age as me and she's hard working. She's been doing chores since she first came to school and she's honest and steady.'

Mary smiled. 'And who is this paragon?'

Lizzie didn't know what a paragon was but obviously Miss Mary thought she did. 'Who?' she echoed.

'What's her name?'

'Oh, her name. Ellan Vannin, miss. She's lived with the Quirks ever since her pa was . . .' Lizzie fell silent remembering that Mr Costain was a part owner of the Laxey and Foxdale mines.

Mary understood. 'Ah, yes. Ellan Vannin. Poor child. But she's never been in service before, has she?'

'No, miss, but she's a fast learner. She stayed on at school long after me.'

Mary considered the matter. 'And she is definitely interested?'

Lizzie nodded emphatically.

'Well, it seems only fair that I at least see her. I'll send a message down for her to come here at three this afternoon.'

Lizzie bobbed another curtsey. 'Oh, thank you, miss. I know you'll find no fault with her.'

'I haven't said I'll engage her, Lizzie.'

'No. No, of course.' Lizzie was backing towards the door. 'Shall I tell Jamie Corlett to go down, miss?'

'Later,' Mary said and a flushed Lizzie left, closing the door quietly behind her.

Again Mary looked out across the manicured lawns and sighed. She'd seen the girl on occasions, a pretty, dark-haired child, motherless like herself, and then fatherless too. Her brow darkened as she remembered Maud Quirk. A harridan of a woman who'd actually come to the house, to the front door, and demanded to see her father. When she'd been told he was away in Liverpool, which was the truth, she'd flung the gold sovereigns on the polished floor of the hall and told her in no uncertain terms, what Thomas Costain and his cronies could do with their compensation money. A few guineas for the life of a man! She'd almost screamed the words at her. Oh, she remembered Maud Quirk right enough.

She'd put that outburst down to the woman's grief but time had not improved Maud and on every occasion she had had the misfortune to see the woman, cutting remarks were passed in a voice loud enough for half of Peel to hear, remarks which she of course ignored. And it was with Maud Quirk that Ellan Vannin had lived ever since the accident. No wonder the girl wanted to get out. Picking up her pen again, Mary Costain resolved that if Ellan Vannin was suitable she'd employ her. If only to get back at Maud Quirk for all the insults.

Chapter Two

———◆———

ELLAN WAS WALKING BACK from the village, a basket of fish wrapped in damp paper on her arm. She was hot and tired and felt as though she must reek of fish. As soon as she got home she'd sluice herself down at the pump and change her clothes. The overhanging trees gave some shade from the blazing sun but she looked up as she heard the sound of hooves on the road ahead. It was Jamie Corlett. Jamie was a groom at Glentrammon. He was the same age as Andrew and was a pleasant, rather quiet lad with hair and eyes almost as dark as her own. He'd been in service with the Costains since he'd left school and she didn't know him nearly as well as she knew Andrew's other associates. At the sight of him she stopped and self-consciously tried to tidy her hair.

'Have you come from Miss Costain?'

He nodded. 'She said you're to come back with me if you're interested in the position.'

'I am but I can't come looking like this, can I? You'll have to wait while I get changed. It won't take me long.'

His gaze flitted over the stained and damp blouse and

the faded skirt covered by a rough apron made from sacking. They moved in different circles so he'd never really had much occasion to speak to her. Even dressed like that he was suddenly attracted to her. She was beautiful, he thought and that thought itself intensified the attraction. 'I'll wait.'

'Could you wait by the stile?'

'You haven't told her then?' Lizzie had mentioned the fact that there might be some opposition, but he knew Maud's reputation.

'No.'

'How will I know if you're coming back with me? That she'll let you come?'

She squared her shoulders and her chin jerked up. 'She will. I want this job.'

'Then I'll wait by the stile for a quarter of an hour.' He admired her determination and his estimation of her rose. She wasn't just a pretty face as he'd first thought. He also felt sorry for her, left an orphan, living with Maud all these years. He was an orphan himself but Maggie, his elder sister, had brought him up and Maggie was just the opposite of Maud Quirk. But Ellan was better off than some, he mused. Whenever tragedy struck, be it in the mines, or a ship lost or a man drowned, if there were no relations willing to take the children it was off to the Orphanage or worse, the workhouse.

He watched her walk on ahead of him. The shafts of sunlight that pierced the canopy of branches played on her dark hair and the colour and sheen reminded him of a raven's wing. She'd taken off her hat and was wafting it to and fro as if it were a fan. Her step was light and lithe and her skirt swung alluringly from side to side. When she reached the wall and had clambered over it, she turned and smiled at him and he raised his hand in reply, feeling a stirring of emotion for her. Beauty and the Beast, he thought wryly. Still, he hoped she would get the job. Somehow he knew he wanted to see her every day.

Maud pounded and kneaded the dough for the round, flat loaves of bread. The rectangular wooden trough used for this practice was set in the middle of the scrubbed deal table in the centre of the kitchen. The fire in the hearth burned brightly and heated the oven built into the wall beside it but added to the stifling heat in the room.

Both doors were open to catch any breath of air there might be. Above the fireplace, on a wooden mantel shelf, reposed a few ornaments: a pair of base metal candlesticks; a pottery spill holder; two crudely made and garishly painted dogs; and a pottery replica of the Laxey Wheel. The wheel itself was becoming quite a tourist attraction but Maud had bought the cheap souvenir as a reminder to them all of the loss of their fathers, the blame for which she placed squarely on the shoulders of the owners of the Laxey and Foxdale mines.

Wooden spoons and cooking implements hung on the whitewashed walls. The leather bellows and iron poker lay on the hearth. A wooden chest stood beneath the window and a carved rocker was placed in the corner between the window and the hearth. In the other corner were two ladder-backed chairs and a long bench on which was a pile of freshly ironed linen. The flat iron still rested on its stand beside the bellows. From the beams that ran across the ceiling hung bunches of herbs and a ham joint, well out of reach of thieving dogs and cats.

John and Mat were poring over the *Manx Mercury* and

John was smoking a clay pipe, a habit Maud didn't approve of.

'That pipe stinks the whole house out. Even the bread will smell of it!' she complained. He ignored her. 'Maybe I'll get some help around here now the off-shore fishing is almost finished. I'm not getting any younger and it's small wonder there's so little wheat left in the barn with only myself and Ellan to harvest it.'

'It can't be helped, Ma. It's not our fault the fishing always clashes with the harvest. You know there's more money to be made from the fish. Enough to buy in to see us over the winter.'

Maud glared at John. 'I wouldn't need to buy in if just one of you stayed at home. It's a sinful waste of money!'

The brothers exchanged glances. Every year it was the same. The herring season lasted from July to October but they started early in March, going to Kinsale off the south-east coast of Ireland after the mackerel. And that hadn't pleased her either. It was as though she took a delight in being a martyr, refusing all offers of paid help. They needed every penny, she would state. Nets, sailcloth, repairs, clothes didn't come free or cheap.

'Where is that girl? Always dawdling and stopping to talk to all and sundry, never a thought about the time and me with so much to do, it being the Sabbath tomorrow.'

They exchanged glances again. She almost worked herself into the ground every Saturday, for being of the Independent Methodist persuasion she insisted on keeping the Sabbath rigidly. There was never a hot meal on a Sunday, for cooking she viewed as a desecration of the Lord's Day. It was Chapel in the morning, a cold lunch followed by an afternoon of reading and stilted conversation and then Chapel again in the evening. They occasionally managed to escape for an hour or two to walk across the fields and talk more openly, John managing to smoke his pipe, for she would allow no smoking on a Sunday either. It wasn't that they objected to their religion, for they had all been brought up on Chapel and good 'hellfire and brimstone' sermons, but things hadn't been always quite so strict. It was only after the death of their father that she had turned so strongly and resolutely to religion, with a devotion that bordered on the fanatical, John said at times.

Ellan came in followed by the yard dog, one of old Floss's pups.

'Get that animal out of my clean kitchen and where've you been until now?'

Ellan pushed the dog outside gently with the toe of her boot. 'You know where I've been, Aunt Maud, helping to gut the catch. Here, this is for supper.'

'Go and put them in a pan and cover them with cold water. They'll have to wait until the loaves are done before I bake them.'

John folded the newspaper and knocked out his pipe against the hearth. 'Come November we've been thinking of following the herring up to Stornaway and Lerwick this year, Ma. A bit more money and we'll have enough for a bigger boat.'

Maud stopped kneading, her head twisting towards her eldest son. 'In a nobbie? Have you taken leave of your senses, lad? You'd not last a week up there in the winter gales. Do you want me to be left with no-one? Do you want me to end my days in the workhouse?'

'Don't talk like that, Ma. We're not going alone, there's seven nickies going with us.'

She laughed cuttingly. 'You know as well as I do that even a fifty-foot boat can be lost up there.'

Andrew sat in the corner chair studying his brothers. They had agreed to tell her but he hadn't expected John to announce their plans so soon and there was truth in her words. In the November gales off Stornaway even the bigger boats known as 'nickies' could be swamped, let alone their thirty-foot little 'nobbie'. He looked up and saw Ellan standing by the scullery door, a stricken look in her eyes and he cursed. He should have told John and Mat about the job up at Glentrammon.

'Do we need the money that badly? Can't we wait a bit longer before buying a nickie?' He saw the look that passed between them. They hated the long, dark winter nights cooped up in the small cottage.

'Of course it can wait. I'll hear no more about chasing the herring!' Maud banged the flat loaves down hard on the floured surface of the table and a little cloud of white dust arose around her. Then she picked them up and placed them deftly on a baking tray and, using her apron, opened the oven door and shot the tray in expertly.

Ellan's resolve plummeted. She couldn't have picked a worse time to voice her intention of leaving. Why hadn't Andrew told her this morning of their plans? Perhaps he hadn't known. He had tried to placate his ma. But, taking a deep breath, she determined to try. It was now or never. She glanced at Andrew. 'I met Lizzie Killip this morning, she told me they need another maid. Molly Yourston's leaving on Friday. She asked me was I interested and I said I was and Miss Costain has sent for me. Jamie

Corlett is waiting.' It all came out in a rush.

Maud's face, already flushed from the heat of the oven and her exertions, became puce. 'Is he now? Then you can just go and tell him he's wasted his time and energy, and he can tell Miss High and Mighty Costain that you're *not* interested!'

'Why can't I go?' Ellan cried.

Maud turned on her. 'Have you no self-respect, girl? Have you no respect for your pa's memory? You want to go and slave for that man who had a hand in your pa's death?'

'He didn't. Not personally he didn't!'

'He's a part owner, isn't he? And to offer me his filthy money as compensation and not a penny for you! That's the kind of man you want to go and skivvy for?' Maud shook with outrage.

Ellan felt the tears prick her eyes but she stubbornly told herself she wasn't going to cry. Nor was she going to give up so easily. 'It's no different from skivvying here.' She took a step backwards, thinking Maud was going to strike her and Andrew and John stood up.

'You don't skivvy in this house. We all work for our daily bread, as the good Lord intended us to do. We don't sit back and let others do the work, face the dangers, then take the profits of their labours like they do! They don't go out facing the storms or burrow in the ground like moles. Oh, not them!'

Ellan tried a different approach. 'It's just a job, Aunt Maud. I just want to earn some decent money.'

'What's wrong with that, Ma?' Andrew asked.

'You keep out of this.'

'Why?' he challenged, angrily.

'Because it's got nothing to do with you, any of you. Her pa asked me in his Will, which was a sacred trust, to bring her up. Not you, nor John nor our Mat. Me. He trusted me to do right by her and he'd not want you working up there, Ellan Vannin. He'd turn in his grave! He wanted better things for you.'

She seized on Maud's last words. 'I know he did and it could lead to better things, it could.'

'Parlour maid or housekeeper if you're lucky, when you're about forty and worn out waiting on them hand and foot.'

Ellan began to feel confused and her determination was ebbing. She gazed pleadingly at Andrew.

He tried again. 'It could lead to better things, Ma, and like I said, she wants to earn money of her own – is that so much to ask?'

'And I could give you some of it each week, a lot more than I've been able to give you, for help when you need it.'

'I'd sooner drop with exhaustion than take help, paid for with *his* money. It's tainted. Tainted with the blood of the men who drowned in his mine and I'll hear no more of this! Your pa gave you into my care. Are you so set against his sacred, dying wish that you'll go running off up there?'

Ellan knew she'd lost. She couldn't refute her father's wishes. Aunt Maud had unerringly used the one argument she knew would stop her working at Glentrammon. She tossed her head, determined at least to have the last word. 'Then I'll go back with Jamie Corlett and tell Miss Costain herself, that's only fair.'

'You'll do no such thing. We owe "them" no explanations!'

'I will!' and before Maud could utter another word, she'd run out through the door.

An oppressive silence hung on the air until John spoke. 'You satisfied now, Ma? Satisfied you've upset the lass? Bye, but I've got to hand it to you, you're clever. What you just said to Ellan was little better than blackmail – and we're going to Stornaway! I'd rather the lashing of the sea and the wind to the lashing of your tongue all winter. For someone who goes to Chapel so often there's not much Christian charity in you, is there?' And with that he went out, followed by his brothers.

Maud sat down by the fire. Oh, why did she say such things? She hadn't always been like this, so bitter, she was sure she hadn't. Grudgingly she admitted that John was right. There wasn't much Christian charity in her these days, no matter how hard she strove for it. It had been different when Amos had been alive, but ever since the day of the accident she seemed to have had nothing but worry, work and hardship to contend with. Now she had driven them to chase the herring up the coast of Scotland. Had she driven them to their graves? She rested her aching head on her arm. It was all their fault, the Costains. Trying to lure Ellan away to work for them. Trying to touch everyone's life and poison it. Their long tentacles spread all over the island with a power obtained by their wealth, wealth they'd built on the blood, sweat and tears of others.

Ellan looked at the boy leaning against the grazing horse through a mist of tears. She'd wanted so much to get away, but the way Aunt Maud had put it she couldn't go. She couldn't let her pa down.

'Ready?' Jamie asked, ignoring the fact that she still

wore her dirty working clothes and looked flushed.

'I'm coming with you but . . . but not for the job.' She brushed away a traitorous tear from her cheek, feeling miserable, hurt, humiliated and yet angry all at the same time.

'Come on then, get up behind me.' And reaching down he helped her up. 'Put your arms around my waist or you'll fall off,' he said, not unkindly. Even at this distance, on the still afternoon air, he'd heard the raised voices, mainly Maud's. There'd obviously been a fight. God but she was a shrew of a woman if ever there was one, was Maud Quirk. He felt sorry for Ellan and at the same time protective. He wanted to tell her not to be upset, that Maud hated anyone to get on or be happy.

Ellan leaned her head against his shoulder, it was comforting, and the gentle swaying gait of the animal soothed her.

'What are you going to say to Miss Mary?' Jamie asked at length, when he felt he could no longer bear the silence.

'I don't know. The truth, I suppose, though I'll not be rude about it.'

'You wanted that job, didn't you?'

A muffled sob was his reply and he patted the clasped hands around his waist. 'You'll get away one day, Ellan, I know you will.'

There was another sob and again he patted her hands. He felt so helpless but the gesture seemed to comfort her and they rode the rest of the way in silence.

Only when they turned into the wide drive and Jamie said, 'We're here,' did she raise her head and look at the house that she would never work in. She'd passed it many times and had looked through the wrought-iron gates up the drive. Now it was as though she were seeing it for the first time. Set on a rise, sheltered by tall elder trees, was a three-storied imposing house of weathered grey stone. Its name in the Manx tongue meant the Glen of the Elder Trees. Its facade faced the sea, its outbuildings and stables formed two sides of a square at the back. The long, sash windows gleamed in the sunlight and the bright hues of the Virginia Creeper that twisted around the pillars supporting the porch gave it a gracious, yet welcoming look. The gravel drive was banked by neatly trimmed lawns and carefully tended flower beds and shrubberies that eventually merged with the clumps of gnarled elders that obscured the paddock from view. Ellan felt dejected and apprehensive as Jamie directed the horse around to the stables at the back.

Lizzie announced her, a Lizzie who bit her lip and cast her sympathetic glances.

Mary was surprised to see the girl in what were obviously her working clothes, and despite herself she wrinkled her nose as the faint odour of fish drifted towards her. She also noticed that the girl's eyes were over-bright and a little puffy.

'Miss Costain, I . . . came to thank you for sending for me.' Ellan tried to pick her words carefully.

'Is there something wrong?' Mary asked.

Ellan nodded and fiddled with the top button of her blouse.

'What is it?'

'I . . . I can't consider coming to work for you, miss.'

Mary's eyebrows rose but her voice was gentle. 'Why not?'

'It's . . . Aunt Maud. She said I . . . can't. It wouldn't be . . . fitting.'

Yes, Maud Quirk would say just that and quite a lot more besides, Mary surmised grimly. 'But would you like to, Ellan?'

'Yes, miss, I would.' Ellan's voice was barely audible.

'How old are you, Ellan?'

'Seventeen. Eighteen come November.'

Mary nodded. 'And Mrs Quirk is your legal guardian?'

'My pa asked her to take care of me, in his Will, so I suppose she is. I'm sorry, miss, to have wasted your time but I just wanted you to know the reason. I didn't want you to think I was being bad-mannered or ungracious.' The last word slipped out, a half-remembered word from her schooldays.

Mary looked at her with renewed interest. She spoke well, but then hadn't Lizzie said she'd stayed on at school. And she was a beautiful girl, she thought with a stab of envy. If she had looked like Ellan Vannin at seventeen there would have been an army of suitors beating their way to the door and fighting over her hand. But Mary Costain wasn't possessed of a jealous or vindictive nature and she smiled. 'That was kind and thoughtful of you and I'm sure you have risked your aunt's displeasure by coming here.'

Ellan bowed her head so that Mary couldn't see the incipient tears that had welled up again. She was so nice, so kind, she wished with all her heart that she could have worked for her. She was sure, too, that if her pa had known Miss Mary he wouldn't have objected. She was certain that Mary sympathized with her predicament, but she couldn't work here and that was the end of it. 'I'd better get back. I've work to do.'

Mary stood up. 'If there is ever anything I can do, Ellan, to . . . to help you in any way.'

'Thank you, miss, you're very kind.' And before her control broke and the tears coursed down her cheeks, she turned and left.

Mary walked to the window of the small, back parlour that overlooked the rear courtyard and wondered why she had been so touched by the girl, why she had made that offer to help her. It wasn't entirely due to the fact that she disliked Maud Quirk intensely. There was just something about the girl. She felt she deserved better from life. In Ellan Vannin she had sensed a depth of character, a strength and integrity as yet undiscovered. She was different from the other village girls. She was unusual, even her name was unusual. Ellan Vannin in the Manx tongue literally meant 'Isle of Man'. One of her father's own ships carried that name, one of the smaller ones, for bigger and faster ships like the *Douglas* and the *Mona's Queen* had been built and *L'il Daisy* as the seamen called the S.S. *Ellan Vannin* was now a sort of fleet mascot. The little steamer braved all weathers and some of the worst storms to reach Liverpool and Whitehaven, when even ocean-going ships sought out the shelter of Douglas Bay. *L'il Daisy* was plucky and so, too, she suspected was the dark-haired girl who bore the same name. It took courage to come and tell her that she was unable even to be considered for a job. That harridan of a woman that she called aunt had obviously forbidden her to take up employment here, probably on pain of some dire threat that she wouldn't hesitate to carry out. She felt Ellan deserved better from life. It was very unfair, but who ever said life was supposed to be fair? If it had been, she would have been married long ago.

Jamie was waiting by the door of the stables and when he saw Ellan come out through the kitchen he walked across. 'I'll give you a ride back. The master's in Douglas and Miss Mary isn't going out and I've finished here for an hour or so.'

She attempted a smile. 'I can walk. I don't want you to get into trouble.'

'It's no trouble,' he called as he went to fetch the chestnut gelding.

'What did she say?' he asked, after he'd helped her up and her arms were once more around his waist.

'She was very nice about it.'

'I thought she would be. She's a dream to work for is Miss Mary. "Jamie, I will take the trap into the village later. Will ten o'clock be suitable?" She asks me if it's "suitable" and me only a groom! Sometimes I don't think she realizes just what she's saying. It's as though she's talking to her pa or one of her friends, although it doesn't do to over-step the mark with her. Molly found that out once, but I don't think I've ever seen her in a temper, not even when Master William and Master David are home, and do they try her patience!'

'She said if there was anything she could ever do to help me, I've to ask. I wonder did she mean about Aunt Maud?'

'She could help you, too.'

Ellan was feeling a little less miserable. 'I wonder why she never got married?'

'I don't suppose anyone asked her. She's . . . well,

you've got to admit she's a bit plain, in a nice sort of way.'

'I didn't think she was plain and anyway, what have looks got to do with it?'

'That's easy for you to say, Ellan, you're the bonniest lass this side of Douglas.'

Suddenly she forgot about Aunt Maud and Mary Costain and became conscious that her arms were around his waist and that she'd been leaning her cheek against his broad shoulder and that now he was saying she was bonny. She blushed, glad that she didn't have to look him in the face, yet pleased by the compliment. She felt a strange sensation creeping over her, a kind of warm, prickly feeling and although the sun was high in the sky she felt goose bumps break out on her skin.

'Oh, there's others more bonny than I am,' she murmured.

He twisted around in the saddle and stared at her, feeling a little abashed. 'Not to me. Can I see you again, Ellan? We could go for a walk or a sail, one of the lads will lend me a boat and we could take a picnic.' He was surprised at the way the words just tumbled from his mouth, but she was smiling.

'I'd like that, Jamie.'

'And no-one could object to it as you're seventeen.'

'Eighteen in November.' Her spirits lifted, the disappointment fell away and when they reached the cottage and he helped her down, the grip around her waist was firm and she smiled shyly at him again. 'It hasn't been such a bad day after all, has it, Jamie?'

Chapter Three

———— ◆ ————

IT WASN'T UNTIL THE middle of August that they had gone for the sail and the picnic Jamie had promised.

On her return from Glentrammon Ellan went about her chores in silence and Maud, too, held her tongue. On Sunday afternoon Jamie came to the cottage in his best suit, a tweed cap covering his dark hair, a cap that was instantly removed when Maud opened the door, annoyed at the disturbance of her silent ruminations about how much she'd changed since Amos's death. She was taken aback to see Jamie Corlett standing on her doorstep.

'Is Ellan in, Mrs Quirk, please?' he asked.

'It's the Sabbath, of course she's in. Where else would she be?'

'May I see her, please?'

Maud was suspicious. 'What for? Is there another message from *them*?' She jerked her head in the general direction from which he'd come.

'No. Nothing like that. I came to see if she would like to take a walk with me . . . Er, if you don't mind, that is?' He ran his finger around the edge of his stiff collar. He felt foolish and the way she was staring at him made him thankful that he worked for the Costains and had had Maggie to bring him up. The look on her face reminded him of a picture he'd seen of the Avenging Angel in a book of Bible stories Miss Mary had once lent Lizzie.

He smiled though when Ellan appeared behind Maud. A very different looking Ellan with her dark hair swept up neatly, her pale skin and dark eyes enhanced by the white blouse with its high collar that emphasized her slender neck, and the maroon-coloured skirt that showed off a tiny waist.

'He's come to ask you to take a walk with him,' Maud informed her, disapproval evident in both her voice and manner.

John also appeared behind Ellan to see what diversion had presented itself to relieve the tedium of the day. 'Jamie, lad, come on in! It must be a month or more since we last had a real chat. Come in!'

Maud had no option but to go back into the room, followed by Ellan and Jamie.

Jamie nodded to both Mat and Andrew. Surely to heaven he wasn't going to have to ask her to go out with him in front of them all, he thought.

'I'll get my hat,' Ellan said firmly before she went up to her tiny room.

Jamie twisted his cap between his hands and looked to Andrew to rescue him from his predicament but Andrew was unusually reticent. So he stood and made small talk with John and Mat until Ellan reappeared.

'I'm ready,' she announced, refusing to look at Maud, placing a wide-brimmed straw hat trimmed with a pink ribbon over her shining, coiled hair.

'I'll be seeing you then and good luck with the fishing,' Jamie had said thankfully, moving towards the door.

'You see you're back in time for Chapel, miss,' Maud called but they had both gone and she shut the door.

They walked down the lane and out along the perimeter of the fields to the narrow path on the edge of the cliffs and they talked about the fishing and the crops and the weather until Ellan sat down and took off her hat.

He sat beside her. 'You didn't mind me calling, did you? She wasn't too pleased by the look on her face.'

'She wasn't but I don't care and I didn't mind you calling. I . . . I'd hoped you would, but I didn't expect you to come so soon. Well, not today anyway.'

'Did she say anything to you when you got back? Was there another row?'

'No, she didn't say a word. I think John had said something to her. She takes notice of him. In fact she's hardly opened her mouth at all to any of us all day.' She looked out across the expanse of sea that shimmered in the sunlight.

'At least she let you come out.'

'There wasn't a lot she could do to stop me. After all, your name isn't Costain, is it?'

'Would it matter to you if it was?'

'No, I don't think it would but if it were you would never have given me a second glance. You'd have been a gentleman like Master William and Master David and I'd still be what I am. A miner's daughter.' She leaned back, supporting herself on her elbows. 'What would you do if you had as much money as Mr Costain?'

'Me? I don't rightly know. Be just like him I suppose.'

'That's not very adventurous! Wouldn't you like to go

off and see all the countries of the Empire and America?'

'I might. What would you do if you had the money Miss Mary has?'

'I'd leave here to start with. I'd go to London and see all the sights and I'd buy lovely clothes in the fine shops and meet interesting people.'

'And then?'

'I'd probably meet someone and get married.'

'Miss Mary hasn't and she has been to London and to Paris.'

Ellan looked thoughtful. 'Then maybe she should travel further afield. She could go to America, she would be bound to find a husband there.'

He laughed. 'I'll tell her that, next time I'm talking to her.'

She pushed him backwards and playfully beat him with her hat. 'Don't you dare, Jamie Corlett! Don't you dare tell her I said anything like that! What would she think of me?'

He laughed with her, trying to grab the hat, rather ineffectually, until suddenly they were both lying on the grass laughing. At least, she had been laughing. He had been leaning over her and looking down at her, his eyes serious. Then he bent his head and kissed her gently on the lips and the goose bumps had broken out all over her again. Just as gently she pushed him away and sat up.

'I'm sorry, Ellan. I couldn't help it!' Self-consciously, he started to brush bits of dried bracken from the sleeve of his jacket.

She felt a little dizzy. 'There's no need to be sorry, Jamie. I . . . I liked it. I know it's very forward of me, but I can't tell a lie, not on the Sabbath.'

'Then you're not angry with me?' He tried to keep the emotion out of his voice. He wanted to gather her to him and kiss her again, to go on kissing her until . . .

'No. But I think we'd better go back now just the same.'

They got to their feet and he helped brush off the bits of grass from her skirt and watched her as she replaced her hat. He reached out to straighten the pink ribbon band. 'Then you do like me, Ellan?'

She nodded.

He took her hand in his and they began to walk slowly back, loath to reach the lane again when they would have to walk side by side demurely as convention demanded. Convention was very strong on the island.

When they left the village and the speculative stares behind them, he looked quickly around, then kissed her again. 'Shall I come next Sunday, if the master doesn't need me?'

'I'd like that, Jamie. I really would,' she answered quietly.

'I'll come about the same time then.'

'I'll be ready.' And on an impulse she reached up and kissed him on the cheek. It was only a peck but she felt very bold and turned quickly away and began to walk rapidly up the lane. She felt as though she were floating, not walking. Everything looked new and bright and different and she wondered if she had fallen in love. She'd never felt like this before.

Every Sunday after that, bar two, he called and they walked and talked and laughed and he always kissed her gently before they parted at the bend in the lane. She came back so full of happiness that even Aunt Maud's sour looks and barbed remarks couldn't dim that wonderful feeling.

It was that Sunday afternoon in late August when she knew for certain that she loved him and that he loved her. She'd had a lecture from Aunt Maud about how it looked, her going off alone with him in Albert Killip's boat. A lecture she'd listened to with bent head and lips tightly pressed together, for she knew that it would only take one word and Aunt Maud would absolutely forbid her to go.

There were just the two of them in the house for the boys were off fishing, but she knew John had spoken to his mother about her meeting with Jamie. Maud had grudgingly agreed that he was a decent enough lad and that he could be trusted, in so far as any lad could be trusted not to let his base and carnal desires get the better of him. It was up to a girl to keep that side of men's nature in check.

'I want no trouble brought to this house, do you understand me, Ellan? I've enough to bear as it is.'

'I'll bring no trouble or disgrace to you, Aunt Maud, you should know that. I promise to be back in time for Chapel,' she answered demurely.

'Don't let him take liberties with you and don't get those clothes ruined with salt water.'

'I won't.' She gritted her teeth, impatient to make her escape. She had some cheese and bread and hard boiled eggs tied up in a cloth and she clutched them to her, holding on to her hat with the other hand as she ran down the lane, through the village and towards the jetty.

It was a perfect day for a trip. The sea was calm and there was no wind to speak of. The sun was high in the bright, azure sky where only a few cirrus clouds floated.

He was waiting and when he saw her he waved his cap in the air.

'I thought I'd never get out!' she said breathlessly. 'She went on and on. Is that safe?' She pointed at the small rowing boat that was rocking gently on the swell.

'Of course it is. Bert goes out for lobsters and crabs in it. You wait there, I'll go in first and steady it.'

She eyed it askance as he climbed down the steps, wet and slippery with seaweed. She should have put an old skirt on, she thought ruefully.

'Give me your hand and mind the steps.'

With his help she climbed down and he guided her to the wooden slat that served as a seat. She tucked her skirt carefully around her and held the bundle on her knee. 'I brought a picnic.'

'I brought something, too. Some cold veal pie Cook gave me and a flagon of apple cider.'

She watched him as he expertly manoeuvred the boat away from the jetty and pulled strongly on the oars. Any doubts she had disappeared. He was obviously used to handling a boat, but she should have known that. Every lad in the village was adept at it though, oddly, few of them could swim.

'I'd thought of going down to Nairbyl Bay.'

She looked startled. 'That's almost as far as Bradda Head and Port Erin! It's miles away and I have to be back in time for Chapel.' Then seeing the look in his eyes and the twitch at the corner of his mouth, she laughed. 'You're teasing me.'

'It doesn't take much to set you off, does it?'

'Sometimes, Jamie Corlett, I could hit you! If I wasn't

53

afraid of upsetting the boat I would,' she laughed.

As they pulled out of the harbour she fell silent and pensive. She leaned cautiously over the side and let her hand trail across the top of the water. It was clear and calm and where her fingers had displaced the water, a thin silver ribbon of sunlight furrowed the wavelets. She loved the sea. She supposed that it came from living so close to it, but she also feared it and admired the men who risked their lives wresting a living from it, and she shared the sorrow when a man or a boat was lost. She felt as though the sea were extracting a price for giving so plentifully of its bounty. Chasing the herring, they called it, and more and more herring were needed to be smoked, for the kipper was becoming a favourite breakfast dish not only on the island, with its ever-increasing invasion of holiday-makers, but on the mainland, too.

She looked up at the greyish-white cliffs with their cracked, craggy faces, like wise and wizened old men looking out across the expanse of water that was constantly eroding their very existence. Her gaze followed the sea birds as they drifted on the air currents or came to rest on the tiny projections and narrow ledges.

The cove was deserted and to save her boots and skirt, Jamie carried her ashore, having taken off his own boots and rolled up his trousers. Then he went back and pulled the boat up out of the water while she found a sheltered spot at the base of the cliffs. She felt hungry and spread out the contents of both bundles on the cloths and they sat and ate, taking turns at sipping the sweet drink. For a while they watched the sea and the birds, then he leaned back against the cliff and pulled her to him so that her head was resting on his shoulder.

'I wish we could stay here for ever,' she said, wistfully.

'So do I. Away from everyone.'

She fell silent as the familiar heady feeling crept over her as he stroked her hair.

'What will we do when winter comes, Ellan? Where will we go?'

'I don't know. Oh, Jamie, I don't want to think about winter! I hate winter!'

He cupped her chin in his hand. 'I wish you had come to work at Glentrammon, Ellan. You'd have been warm and dry. You wouldn't have to work in the freezing cold, gutting fish.'

'Don't keep reminding me, Jamie.'

'I wish there was something I could do,' he said, feeling resentment at the injustice of it burn inside him.

'There is.'

'What?'

'Just keep on wanting to see me.'

He held her close. 'I'll always want to see you, Ellan. I love you. Don't you know that by now?'

Waves of pure happiness washed over her and she buried her head against his shoulder and clung to him. 'I love you, too, Jamie. I think I've loved you ever since the day I went to Glentrammon.'

He kissed her forehead and then she turned her face towards him and he pressed his lips against hers, gently at first as he'd always done, then with more urgency and passion. She clasped her arms around his neck and kissed him back, feeling as though her senses were swimming and that the earth was spinning and above her the sky was reeling. This was such a different feeling to those she had previously experienced. Her skin burned at his touch, her blood quickened and her heart was racing. She gave a little cry as his hand gently slid down her shoulders and touched her breast and she heard his voice repeating her name over and over.

She was slipping into a world of warmth and excitement. He loved her! He loved her! They would always feel like this. No-one would come between them. No-one would condemn them or trouble them. The word rang like a warning bell in her mind – *trouble*. Trouble! She pulled away from him, remembering Aunt Maud's words and realizing that she was standing on the brink of the abyss that would lead to that trouble.

'Jamie! Jamie! Stop! Please, stop!'

'Oh, Ellan, I love you so much.'

Sanity was returning. 'Jamie, she'll kill me. She will!'

He fought down his desire. She looked so frightened, so beautiful, yet so afraid and with good cause. 'Ellan, I'm sorry. I didn't mean . . .'

She cut off his words with her fingers, placed across his lips. 'I know. It was as much my fault. I wanted you to go on. I know it was wrong of me, sinful, but I wanted you to go on.' He leaned towards her but she drew away. 'I'm sorry. Do . . . do you still love me?'

He caught her hands and pulled them towards his lips. 'Of course I do, Ellan. What kind of a man do you take me for? It hasn't changed anything between us. It's just not the right time . . . yet, but I love you.'

She felt the tears prick her eyes, tears of happiness and yet tears with a taste of sadness. She had wanted him so much.

He smiled ruefully. 'I think we'd better get back. I don't trust myself. It's safer to be around people.'

Reluctantly she nodded and began to fold up the cloths and brush the sand from her skirt while he again took off his boots and prepared to carry her to the boat.

The sun had lost some of its warmth and brilliance, she thought as they headed for home. The cries of the gulls seemed mournful and she felt sad, but her spirits lifted when after he'd tied up the boat and they'd walked back through the village, he said, 'I love you, Ellan, but I think we'd better stick to walks for the future, don't you?'

They grew closer as the weeks went by and they had a whole glorious day blackberrying in late September, after the harvest was in. In the first week of October the fishing fleet returned home but she soon noticed a change in Andrew. He'd become moody and sometimes he snapped at both herself and his brothers.

Maud made some caustic comments on his changed attitude and that led to more cross words. Ellan hated to see such discord and determined to find out the cause.

She found him alone one afternoon, sitting on the yard wall and staring out to sea. Aunt Maud had gone into the village and John and Mat had gone to Douglas to see a man who had a boat for sale.

'Why are you out here alone?'

'No particular reason. Can't a man be on his own once in a while without everyone wanting to know the reason why?'

She bit her lip. 'There's no need to snap at me. I was only asking.'

He smiled, but she noticed that the smile never reached his eyes. 'I'm sorry,' he muttered.

She moved closer to him. 'What's the matter? Don't you want to go to Stornaway? Have you fallen out with

John or Mat? I thought you would have gone to Douglas with them.'

'We haven't exactly fallen out. Of course I want to go to Stornaway, if any of us can say we really "want" to go. It's more a case of having to go. Having to go where the fish are.'

'I know it's hard.'

'No, you don't know, Ellan!'

'What did you mean by "not exactly falling out"?'

'We have words, now and then. It's being cooped up together on a small boat that does it.' And being away from you, he added to himself. He'd had words with both his brothers over his feelings for her, after Mat had finally dragged out of him the reason for his surliness one night, when there was nothing to do but wait and watch the nets; a night like dozens of others when he had hours to think of her with Jamie Corlett and jealousy had gnawed at his insides, fanned by his desire and love for her.

'Don't be such a damned fool, Andy. She looks on you as a brother, like she does us! She's smitten with young Corlett and he with her and why not? She's young and bonny . . .'

'Too bonny for him. And he's there all the time, isn't he? A couple of miles up the road, not stuck out here in the middle of the Irish Sea!'

Mat had shaken his head ruefully. 'There's not much any of us can do about that, but she might get over him, and even if she doesn't there's not much you can do about it. Like I said, she looks on you as a brother. Try to forget how you feel, find another lass.'

'I don't want another lass!'

'Then you'd better go to Liverpool and sign on a

whaler, that's the only solution I can see,' John had advised. 'Three or four months in the Arctic should kill or cure you.'

Grudgingly he'd admitted they were right but it hadn't helped, he had no stomach for a life at sea for months at a time, but whenever he heard her mention Jamie Corlett the knife twisted deeper in his guts and his mood reflected his torment.

'Is it a girl?' she asked in all innocence, for she'd long forgotten Lizzie's words.

He clenched his hands over the stones until the knuckles were white. 'No! It's got nothing to do with a lass!'

'Something has changed you. Can't you tell me what it is? You always used to.'

'There were a lot of things I used to do. I'm saying no more. I'm going down to the harbour.' And jumping down he thrust his balled fists into the pockets of his trousers and strode away.

Ellan stared after him, hurt and bewildered. What had he meant by that? Was it something she'd done or said? Aunt Maud often shot her venomous looks after Andrew had ignored her comments and questions or had abruptly left the house. Was it because of Jamie? No, it couldn't be that. He was courteous enough with Jamie, the same as he'd always been. He couldn't be jealous of herself and Jamie, there must be another reason. Maybe there was a girl, someone he wouldn't admit to loving or couldn't admit to. Maybe she was spoken for or even married to someone else. It happened.

Ellan went back inside the cottage. Perhaps it was best that he was going to Stornaway soon.

After their conversation he tried to appear more like his old self. When he'd left her he'd cursed himself for a fool. Mat and John were right. She looked on him as a brother. She cared for him, that much was obvious in her eyes and her voice, but as a brother. He'd have to pull himself together, put her out of his mind and his heart. Maybe he would ask some other lass to walk out with him. Lizzie Killip wasn't a bad looking girl, although she chattered on like a dozen magpies. Perhaps he'd ask her out, at least it would keep his ma from making pointedly cutting remarks. Despite all her failings his ma was no fool and she suspected what was wrong with him. He kicked a pebble out of his path. That's what he'd do, he'd ask Lizzie out. That would show them all that he'd stopped mooning like a calf over Ellan. It would show Ellan that he didn't care, but the black despair returned as he realized that Ellan didn't even know he loved her. He kicked out at another stone. And that's the way it would remain. He wasn't going to become the laughing stock of the village.

Maud wasn't happy to see her youngest son walking out with Dora Killip's daughter. The woman was an idle gossip and Lizzie wasn't much better in her opinion, though lazy she wasn't. But the blackest mark against Lizzie was that she worked for the Costains. At least he seemed to have given up on Ellan, not that she would have had any objection to that match. Ellan was a good girl most of the time. After all, she'd brought her up, hadn't she? No, she would have had no complaints there but Ellan was moonstruck with young Corlett. What she saw in him was a mystery, unless it was something to do with the fact that he always seemed to have the use of one

60

of the Costains' horses and had more money in his pocket than Andrew had. She saw to it that he bought Ellan no fancy presents, that wasn't fitting. But he had no-one to support. His only sister was married to 'that' man's gamekeeper which was how he'd got his job, first as a stable lad then as a groom; he'd end up as coachman or even a driver if the 'important Mr Costain' ever bought himself one of those new-fangled horseless carriages they called motor cars. Andrew had to use his money to support both herself and Ellan.

She looked sideways at the girl standing at the stile beside her, a shawl pulled over her head and shoulders against the biting wind. They stood watching the three brothers walking down to the harbour to join the other men setting off for the coast of Scotland. They'd be away for over a month, making Lerwick their base.

She uttered a prayer for their protection. 'God keep them safe in His hand.'

Ellan added the 'Amen' and then followed Maud back towards the warmth of the kitchen. There were just the two of them again to face the short, cold days and the long, dark nights. She intended to ask Aunt Maud if Jamie could come and sit with them when the weather was too bad for walking. They would have no privacy and conversation would be strained, but the only alternative was for her to go to Glentrammon to sit in the kitchen there, which he'd told her she was perfectly welcome to do. But she dare not do that, not if she wanted any peace at all. It was going to be a long time until Christmas, she thought dejectedly.

Chapter Four

———— ⋅◆⋅ ————

THE WEEK BEFORE CHRISTMAS the boats came home.
Ellan was bringing their one cow back from the
common grazing to be milked and stalled for the night.
Already, the winter twilight was falling and it was no later
than four o'clock, she thought. The weather had been
dismal with needle-fine rain and sea fogs that soaked
through clothes in no time, and for the last two Sunday
afternoons she and Jamie had sat almost in silence staring
at each other in Aunt Maud's kitchen. She'd longed to
feel his arms around her, his lips on hers, but all that was
denied them. Aunt Maud never left the room and
watched them like a hawk.

The last faint streaks of red spread like long, thin
fingers out towards the sea, the feathered remains of the
brief, half-hour reign of the sun. The wind was strong
and coming in off the sea, a cold north wind that
promised early sleet or snow. She pulled the shawl closer
around her head and shoulders. The field sloped
downwards towards the croft and beyond the circle of St
Patrick's Isle, grey sea merged with grey sky. She shaded

her eyes with her hand. Just to the north, almost on the edge of the horizon were small, black shapes. She tapped the cow's rump sharply with the stick she carried to hurry it onwards and as soon as she reached the croft she called to Maud, pushing the animal towards the byre. 'Aunt Maud! Aunt Maud, they're back! I've just seen them. They're a good way out but it's them all right and with this wind they'll soon be in.'

Maud wiped her hands on her apron and grabbed her own shawl from its hook behind the door. 'She'll have to wait to be milked. Shut her in, Ellan!' she called as she hurried towards the lane.

Ellan caught up with her halfway down the lane. From all the cottages and crofts people were appearing; women, children, old men and boys too young as yet to join their fathers and brothers. Shawled figures like themselves, some with babies wrapped tightly in them, all hurried down towards the harbour, calling to each other.

They joined the group already standing on the jetty, and squinting into the wind Ellan searched for the familiar lines of the *Cockleshell*. As they drew closer she began to count them. Yes, they were all there!

The crowd around them grew larger as the small craft drew closer. Among the crowd was the minister; it was his custom to be the first to greet the fleet as it anchored, to bless their labours and give thanks for their safe return, although at times he was there to console, when not all the boats came back. He turned towards them, his long, black coat flapping in the wind, the Bible held firmly under one arm. He had a deep baritone voice that carried despite the wind. One by one they all joined in the seaman's hymn and Ellan added her clear soprano to the anthem. Beside her Maud, too, was singing in a fine contralto that in other circumstances would have been loudly applauded. The singing seemed to have quieted the howling wind as they finished,

> *Oh, hear us when we cry to Thee,*
> *For those in peril on the sea.*

They were closer now and women began to wave and shout, children to jump up and down. As the first hauser was thrown on to the jetty the minister raised his hand in the old blessing and when the first man stepped ashore it was the minister's hand he gripped.

The group began to mill around as one by one the boats anchored and John, then Mat, and finally Andrew stepped ashore to be given hugs by both Maud and Ellan.

'Did you do well? Was it worth it?'

'Now that's a fine greeting, Ma! But it *was* worth it and we're safely home in time for Christmas.'

'The catches were good, the nets full to breaking and the prices were good, too. They eat fish all year round on the mainland and they'll pay for it. We've enough now to buy that "nickie" and enough for you to buy in, Ma. No more working your fingers to the bone, nor you either, Ellan. And, no fish to gut, the women in Lerwick did it. Aye, and glad of the work!'

'There's a good hot stew in the pot, come on home.' Maud was actually smiling as she led the way back.

'Ah, meat. That sounds good. Dry tack and bloody fish is all we've had for weeks. Sorry, Ma.' John grinned.

'When will you have the new boat?' Ellan asked.

'Before Christmas. Johnny Kewin over in Douglas

more or less promised her to us, if we could come up with the money, and we have.'

'Oh, it's going to be a wonderful Christmas, I know it is!' Ellan cried, for she was as thankful as Aunt Maud that all three were safely home and it would be March before they ventured far from the coastal waters again.

Andrew smiled at her animated face. He'd missed her. How he'd missed her. But he refused to think of her and Jamie Corlett now, he wasn't going to let anything spoil this homecoming and he even dared to hope that she might have fallen out of love.

His hopes were dashed but Christmas for Ellan was wonderful. She and Aunt Maud had baked and cooked and cleaned and decorated the cottage with boughs of holly and evergreens. John had bought a small Christmas tree in Douglas and Ellan decorated it with paper chains and little candles, also bought in Douglas.

With what she had managed to save from her egg money, she'd bought a length of cherry-red worsted and with Lizzie's help had spent hours sewing and cutting, often late into the night. Of course, Aunt Maud had strongly disapproved of the colour, calling it cheap and common, something a painted hussy would wear, but it had been bought and paid for and besides, Ellan didn't care. Lizzie had gone with her to choose it and Lizzie had said it was a wonderful colour for her, her being so dark-haired. Besides, red was a festive colour, wasn't it? Lizzie was hoping that Andrew would call to see her soon for she intended to ask him to the Boxing Day supper that Miss Mary always laid on for the servants, and to which they could bring a friend.

'I wouldn't raise your hopes, Lizzie. Oh, I don't mean

that he wouldn't want to go with you, he would. Didn't he take you out before he went away. But you know what Aunt Maud is like about "them" and having two in the family going would be just too much.'

'Have you told her you're going with Jamie?'

'No.'

Lizzie rolled her eyes and grimaced.

'I'm going to have a word with John. He'll make her see reason. After all, I've been walking out with Jamie for months.'

'Then why won't Andrew come with me?' Lizzie persisted.

'It's different for him. I'm only a girl, I don't matter so much, but with Andrew . . . losing his pa forced him to go on the long trips. Forced him to grow up.'

'Losing your pa forced you to grow up and forced you to live with her!' Lizzie pointed out sharply.

'I know, but it's different for me.'

Lizzie was disappointed when Ellan's prediction was proved accurate. Andrew refused point blank to go to the servants' supper. And it was nothing to do with his ma or even herself, he told her. He would take no charity from Thomas Costain. He wanted to use the same argument to stop Ellan going, too, but John and Mat had both overruled him. The true reason he didn't want to go was that he could not bear to see Ellan with Jamie.

There had been a row, for Maud's hatred of the Costains appeared to be in danger of turning into an obsession.

'You sly, little liar! You knew all about this supper when you went to Douglas and bought that gaudy material.'

'I'm not a liar, Aunt Maud. I did buy it for a new dress for Christmas.'

'What are you trying to do, disgrace us all by hanging on Jamie Corlett's arm dressed like a trollop!' Maud shouted. 'Or are you trying to copy *them*? Trying to be something you'll never be – a lady?' The venom in Maud's voice brought tears to Ellan's eyes.

'Ma, that's enough!' John thundered. 'Ellan can go if she wants to, there's no disgrace in it. She's been walking out with the lad for months, it's all open and above board. It's only a supper, not a bloody Royal banquet and she's entitled to some enjoyment. And I'm not apologizing for my language either. You'd try the patience of Job. She's not a child, she's eighteen and many lasses are married and have bairns at her age. She's earned the right to go and she probably won't see hide nor hair of the Costains.'

'You're taking a lot on your shoulders,' Maud shouted back. 'She's my responsibility!'

'So you keep telling everyone and she's a good lass, you've done a good job, so why spoil it all? Let her go and let folk see what a credit she is to you, to us all. Don't have folk saying what a mean-minded woman you are to spoil her bit of pleasure or that you don't trust her enough to let her go. That would say a lot about how well you've brought her up, wouldn't it? Oh, Dora Killip would have a field day on that, especially as their Lizzie will be there.'

That did it. There was no way Maud would give Dora Killip room to gossip and speculate about whether Ellan could be trusted or not.

When Ellan had gone to get ready for the evening, Andrew went out on the pretext of checking on the few animals they owned. John and Mat exchanged glances and Maud pursed her lips with annoyance but kept on hemming her new aprons, stabbing the needle in and out like a small rapier.

Jamie was calling for her at half past seven and would have her back home before half past eleven. When she came down the narrow stairs with her hair swept up in a shining coil and in the neat-fitting, but plain scarlet dress, her appearance drew admiring nods from John and Mat.

'Eh, you look bonny, Ellan. As fine as a lady.'

She blushed with pleasure.

'Your pa would have been proud of you, the night, lass,' Mat added.

'And even prouder if she'd stayed at home,' Maud muttered but they all ignored her.

'Better wrap up well, though, it's a bitter night. Clear and frosty but bitter,' John urged.

Behind her back, concealed by her hand and the folds of her skirt she held a small object. With her right hand she took her shawl off the hook and deftly draped it over her head and waited with excited anticipation until she heard the sound of hooves in the yard. 'He's here,' she breathed.

'Off you go and enjoy yourself,' Mat urged.

'Aye, off to the ball, Cinderella, and be back here on time or you'll be turned into a pumpkin.' John winked at her and jerked his head in the direction of his mother.

Maud, with her head studiously bent over her sewing, did not catch the humour in her son's remark.

Jamie could see her clearly in the bright moonlight and he stood as though transfixed. 'Oh, Ellan!'

68

'Do you like it, Jamie?' she asked shyly, lifting her shawl away so the dress could be seen more clearly.

'You look beautiful. More beautiful than I've ever seen you look before. I'm so lucky, Ellan.'

She hugged him as he lifted her up into the saddle. 'Would you put this in your pocket? I might drop it.'

'What is it?'

'It's something for Miss Mary. It's some of the jam I made from the blackberries we picked. I wanted to give her something and I had nothing else. I made the cover from a bit of material in Aunt Maud's scrap bag she keeps for making patchwork.'

'She probably won't come down.'

'I know, but I can leave it with Lizzie.'

He pressed her close to him, for he'd sat her in front of him. 'I'll be the envy of everyone when they see you, Ellan.'

'Oh, give over, Jamie, or you'll have me swell headed.'

When she entered the kitchen at Glentrammon all eyes turned towards her and Lizzie's gaze was openly envious. Ellan felt embarrassed and moved closer to Jamie, looking quickly around the large room equipped with everything a household like Glentrammon should have. The overmantel above the huge range was decorated with holly and a large table was set in the middle of the room. There were pies and pastries, cooked joints of meat, pickles and sauces, jellies and mince pies and a chocolate Yule log. For the girls and women there was a large glass punch bowl filled with a fruit and cordial concoction and for the men bottles of ale and porter.

Mrs Portree, the housekeeper, beamed at them all. 'Well, now that everyone is here, let's sit down and eat.

Cook has excelled herself, despite being rushed off her feet all day with visitors.' Her manner was a little patronizing for she took her position very seriously and thought herself a cut above the other servants. She would only remain for the meal, then she and Stewart, the butler, would retire to his pantry to enjoy a quiet drink. Her title, Mrs, was a courtesy one as was Mrs Pearson's, the cook. Neither was married.

Cook was different. 'Bye, you've grown into a fine lass, Ellan Vannin, that you have. Come and sit here next to me and Lizzie. Jamie, you can sit there, opposite your lady friend.' She winked knowingly. 'He never stops talking about you and I can see why now. The image of your ma. We went to school together in Port Erin, did you know that? Lovely she was too. I remember her well.'

Lizzie grinned and behind Cook's back made a silent pantomime of someone tossing back drinks. Ellan smiled, feeling more at ease.

The conversation rose and fell and was interspersed with laughter and giggles as the evening wore on and Mrs Portree and Stewart left. They moved away from the table and Cook produced a bottle of sherry that she'd hidden earlier.

'Come on now, Will Sanford, give us a song. He's got a fine voice has our Will. Give us one of your Scottish songs. "I Love a Lassie" or "Bonny Mary".'

The coachman originally hailed from Argyllshire and after a few drinks could always be prevailed upon to sing.

After the first verse they all joined in and those who didn't know the words hummed along. Jamie held Ellan's hand tightly. He'd never taken his eyes off her all night.

'Oh, Jamie, this is grand. I've never enjoyed myself so much,' Ellan laughed when the song finished and there were great deliberations about what Will would render next. 'It's the happiest night of my whole life.'

'I wanted it to be, Ellan, and it's going to be even better, I promise.'

Suddenly the level of noise fell and turning, Ellan saw Mary Costain standing in the doorway, smiling. Ellan got to her feet as they all did.

'You sounded as though you were having such a good time that I had to come and see for myself,' Mary said, coming into the kitchen.

'Oh, we are, Miss Mary,' Cook gushed. 'Would you take a glass of punch with us? We'd be honoured.'

Mary hesitated, conscious of her position, yet tempted. Upstairs it had been so quiet. The last callers had departed at four o'clock and she and her father and brothers had taken an early supper to allow the servants their annual few hours of enjoyment. Then the boys had ridden over to St John's to the Bartons for the evening. She and her father had sat in the drawing room and talked for a while, until he'd excused himself and gone to his library. She'd tried to read but the sounds of merriment from belowstairs had tempted her to join them. 'Well, just this once, Cook, and just a small glass.'

As Cook moved away Mary's gaze fell upon Ellan and her eyes widened. She'd heard that Jamie was walking out with her but how she'd changed, how grown up and radiant she looked. The material of her dress was cheap and the cut simple, but it made her look . . . exotic was the word that sprang to her mind. 'Why, Ellan, how nice to see you.'

Ellan dipped a bob. 'Thank you, Miss Costain, and thank you for allowing Jamie to invite me.'

Still the same quiet, well modulated tone, the well chosen words, Mary thought. 'And how is . . . your, er . . . family?'

'Very well, miss, thank you. All the boats came home safely and the catches were good.'

Mary nodded and took the glass Cook offered and raised it. 'Here's health and happiness to you all.'

They all raised whatever drinking vessel was to hand and wished her well.

Mary finished her drink and turned to go. 'I'll leave you to enjoy the rest of the evening,' she said rather wistfully. Then she shook herself. What was she thinking of, wishing she could stay with them? That would never do and besides, they would be embarrassed by her presence. The evening would be spoiled for them and the whole object defeated. As she reached the door Ellan touched her gently on the arm and she turned. The girl was holding out a small glass jar covered with a square of pink and white check material.

'I brought this for you, miss. I hope you won't be offended, it's all I had. I picked the berries and made it myself. I know it's not much but I just wanted to say thank you for letting me come tonight.'

Mary stared at it for a second and then took it and examined it. Slowly she smiled. 'Thank you, Ellan. It's a lovely gesture and I don't think I've ever had a gift made especially for me. How delightful.'

Ellan smiled back as Jamie came and took her arm to lead her back to the festivities.

As she closed the drawing room door behind her

Mary turned the jar slowly round in her hand and smoothed the cheap cotton with her fingers. There were tears in her eyes. She couldn't remember when she'd felt so deeply touched by such a small trifle.

Ellan was wrapped tightly in her shawl and sat in front of Jamie as they rode back towards the croft along the lane where the gaunt hedges and trees were covered with frost and glinted like dull silver. There was a bright ring around the moon, the sky was clear and the stars shone like diamonds. Jamie let the horse pick its own way carefully as he was in no hurry for the evening to end. He held Ellan tightly against him and that protective feeling and the pride that she belonged to him, grew stronger.

'Ellan?'

'Um?' she murmured, sleepily.

'Ellan, I want to ask you something.'

'What?'

'Do you love me?'

'Oh, Jamie, you know I do.'

'Enough . . . enough to marry me?'

The drowsy euphoria vanished and she sat up and twisted round to face him. 'What?'

'Do you love me enough to marry me, Ellan?'

She touched his cheek gently and there were tears sparkling on her thick, dark lashes. She didn't hesitate, not even for a second. 'Yes. Oh, Jamie, yes.'

'I've nothing much to offer you, only the rooms above the stables and they're pretty drab. And I've not much money and I'll probably be just a groom until Will retires, but . . .' She cut off his words with her lips. Her heart was so full of happiness and love that it almost hurt as it beat. When he at last drew away from her, he started to speak again.

'It won't be for a while. I'll have to ask the master's permission for us to live there and I'll have to make the rooms decent for you.'

'I don't care, I'll wait. I'll try and save.'

'I'll have to ask your aunt's permission. Do you think she'll give it?'

A tiny dart of fear stabbed her. What if Aunt Maud refused? Oh, she couldn't. She wouldn't. She would be glad to get her off her hands. 'I don't think she'll refuse. I will be one less mouth to feed, one less to clothe.'

'But what if she says she needs you to help her?'

Ellan's chin jerked up. There was nothing Aunt Maud could do this time to thwart her desires. She loved Jamie and if necessary she'd fight with every weapon at her disposal to have him, even if it meant running away, leaving the island. 'She won't stop me with that excuse. Nor can she say Pa wouldn't approve. He would, I know he would. He wanted me to be happy and I am, and she isn't going to spoil it. She's not going to take you away from me. No-one is, ever.'

'When shall I ask her?'

'Why not now? She'll be waiting up and maybe John will still be up, too, and he always takes my part.'

Maud was still sewing and John sat by the dying fire nodding over a glass of stout and an old magazine. Maud looked up quickly and John roused himself as Ellan and Jamie entered. As soon as Maud saw Ellan's face she knew something was brewing.

'Brought her back safe and sound then, Jamie,' John announced.

Jamie nodded. Ellan stood close to his side and did not attempt to take off her shawl. If Aunt Maud refused point blank she would go now, tonight.

'Did you have a good time, Ellan? See how the other half live?'

'It was grand, John, everyone was very friendly.'

'Even Miss Mary came down to wish us all health and happiness,' Jamie added, then, seeing Maud's expression, he knew instantly he'd said the wrong thing.

'Oh very gracious, I'm sure,' Maud snapped tartly.

Jamie cleared his throat and looked at John. 'Er . . . I've something to ask you, Mrs Quirk.'

'And what might that be at this hour of the night?'

Again he looked at John and summoned up all his courage. 'I . . . I want to marry Ellan.'

Ellan tucked her arm through his and stared directly at Maud. 'Jamie asked me, on the way home, and I said yes.'

Maud looked at them both, not knowing what to say.

'And what can you offer her?' John asked.

'Not as much as I'd like to. My job is steady and we'll have the rooms over the stables, if the master agrees to it.'

Maud jumped to her feet as though the word *master* had triggered off a spring in her body. 'You want her to live there, in a hayloft above his stables? You want her to live like an animal? No! His animals fare better! You would do that to her – to us? You want to humiliate us all in front of that man who murdered her pa and my Amos? You'll not take her to live there, not while I've breath in my body.'

Jamie stepped back before the tirade of wrath but Ellan stood her ground.

'Don't you think it's time to stop hating, Aunt Maud? Pa would have approved of Jamie. He only wanted me to be happy and I'll never be happy without Jamie. I'm going to marry him, even if I have to leave here for ever and I'd live in a pigsty if I had to. It's not a hayloft, do you hear me? If you refuse I'll go now, this minute; you'll not keep me here.'

It was Maud's turn to back away. Ellan's eyes blazed and she shook with anger as the torrent of words would not be stemmed.

'You've let hatred turn your mind. You've let it eat away at you. "Love thy neighbour" – isn't that one of the Commandments? When any man strikes you, turn the other cheek – isn't that what you preach? Well, that means Thomas Costain!' she shouted.

'Calm down, Ellan! Calm down, lass! There's no need for all this talk of leaving, John intervened. 'Ma, she's right. It's time the hating stopped – it *is* eating you up. What has the lad done except ask her to marry him? What harm is there in that? Do you want to drive her away? Give your consent and be done with all this nonsense. George would have approved and you know it.'

Maud stood as stiff as a ramrod, her hands clenched at her sides, her face a frozen mask of fury. 'So, even you have turned against me! Be it on your own head, Ellan Vannin, and if there's any justice you'll never know any happiness with him in that . . . that place.'

John nodded and the anger in Ellan's eyes died.

'I consent, but you will not be married until a year has passed. I'll not have everyone saying it is a rushed affair or hinting that you have something to hide. You'll be betrothed for a year, like decent folk.'

Ellan sagged against Jamie. She'd won. This time she'd won. She was disappointed that they would have to wait a whole year but at least Aunt Maud had given her consent.

'You'd best be off now, lad,' John urged, still watching his mother closely. Lately he'd begun to doubt her sanity, and the terrible, obsessive hatred he'd just witnessed strengthened his doubts. 'Ellan, see him out.'

Maud turned and, picking up the half-finished aprons, walked stiffly towards the stairs. It was out of her hands now. In fact she washed her hands of the whole affair. Ellan's future was with the Lord, or with the Devil more like. At least there would be no unseemly rush to the altar, she'd seen to that. Maybe, given time, Ellan would come to her senses, although she doubted it.

Andrew stood at the top of the staircase, his face ashen, and when his mother drew level with him he reached out and caught her shoulder. 'You let her go. You consented, Ma,' he hissed.

'Get to your bed. She was never meant for you. She'd have brought you nothing but pain for there's a badness in her. Get to bed.'

He let her pass and leaned against the wall. Beads of sweat stood out on his forehead. He made his decision. His ma was right. Ellan was never meant for him but maybe Lizzie Killip was. He'd ask Lizzie to marry him and that would show Ellan how little he cared for her.

Chapter Five

———•———

THOMAS COSTAIN HAD POSED no opposition and Mary congratulated Jamie readily, though a little wistfully. Despite her happiness Ellan's heart sank when she first saw the rooms that were to be her home. There were two of them, reached from the outside of the building by a flight of stone steps and from the inside by a wooden ladder that led to a narrow gallery which ran parallel to the upper storeys. They were connected by a single doorway but the door itself was missing. They were clean and dry, the wooden planking floor was bare but had been swept. The few pieces of furniture were plain and decent and Jamie's personal possessions were few. The windows, although set high in the wall, let in quite a lot of light and the panes were clean, but the rooms were devoid of any homely comforts, they were purely functional. Still, she was handy with a needle now, thanks to Lizzie, and with some rag rugs, some ornaments, curtains and a bright patchwork quilt for the bed, it could be bright and cheerful, she thought. And, it would be hers.

As the spring gave way to summer Jamie worked on the improvements she'd suggested; hanging a door to give the bedroom more privacy; making shelves along one side of the living room for dishes; and cupboards in the alcoves beside the fireplace that was set against the outside wall. Because of the risk of fire, Ellan would cook their meals in the kitchen of the big house.

The long, hot days of June and July passed and in the evenings Ellan sewed contentedly. When she went to Douglas and Ramsey with her eggs she browsed around the shops buying pots, pans, the odd cheap ornament, scraps for the quilt and the rugs, and the items in her Hope chest grew.

One day in late August Jamie accompanied her on one of her excursions to Douglas and in a tiny shop down by the harbour he insisted on buying her a ring. They stood gazing into the window, through the small panes of bullseye glass, trying to discern the assortment of odds and ends displayed within. She was looking for bargains. He spotted the ring.

'We can't afford rings,' she chided.

'We can go and see how much it costs. I've not given you a betrothal ring.'

'But it's silver, or it looks like silver.' She peered closer.

'Let's go and see. No harm in asking, is there?' he urged, edging her inside the shop.

'How much is it?' he asked, turning it round between his thumb and forefinger and holding it up towards the light.

'It's silver, Manx silver. It's got all the proper hallmarks,' the owner impressed upon them.

'How much?'

'Two shillings to you. Is it for the lass?'

Ellan shook her head. Two shillings! She could think of better things she could do with that money.

'One and sixpence?' Jamie bargained. 'I can't afford any more than that and it's for a betrothal.'

The man looked at them both, shook his bald head then sighed. He envied them their youth and their obvious happiness and she was a bonny lass. 'One and sixpence and it's a bargain.'

Jamie silenced her protests, paid for it and slipped it on the third finger of her left hand.

'Oh, Jamie, it's lovely, but we really can't afford it.'

'Yes, we can. It's not a diamond or anything flashy.'

She held out her hand and admired it. It was a silver band of Manx ore probably from the Foxdale or Laxey mine, raised at the front like a signet ring, and engraved on the circle were the Three Legs of Man and the island's motto, 'Whichever way you throw me I will stand'.

'I'll wear it always,' she promised.

'Maybe one day I will be able to afford something more expensive.'

'I don't want something more expensive. Just a gold band will do, that's all I want and you.' She spoke the truth. That *was* all she wanted.

She felt so proud as they walked back to where they had tethered the horse and she kept glancing down at the ring. He couldn't have made a more perfect choice, she thought. It might have been made especially with her in mind. The symbol, the motto, the very roots of the island and its culture were linked so closely with her own name.

'What's going on in that pretty head of yours now?'

She laughed. 'Nothing much. I was just thinking it

could have been made just for me. Ellan Vannin. Isle of Man.'

He patted her hand and laughed. 'You say some funny things, Ellan. Shall we celebrate now that you have a ring for all to see? Shall we go for a sail on Saturday? The master is away and Miss Mary is visiting friends in Port St Mary and will be staying over. It's months since we last went for a jaunt.'

'Do you think that's wise?'

'Ellan, I won't try to take advantage of you, I promise.'

'It's not you I'm worried about, it's me,' she laughed ruefully.

'If we weren't standing in the middle of the main street I'd kiss you, but we are, so I can't. Harvest will be starting soon so let's have a day out before the work begins.'

When she got home she showed the ring to everyone. Maud tutted and shook her head at the waste of money. John and Mat pored over it and agreed it was a good choice and an even better bargain, for Manx silver was rare. It was the final straw for Andrew.

He'd watched her as she'd sat sewing, as she came home from Douglas with one of her bargains and his jealousy had grown. He'd started walking out with Lizzie more frequently and she'd even let him kiss her a few times, but when he'd felt her lips moving beneath his it was always Ellan's face that loomed in his mind and he'd even tried to pretend it was Ellan he was kissing. He liked Lizzie. She was a lively girl and not as empty-headed as he'd first thought, but he didn't love her. Now, seeing Ellan glowing with pride and happiness, he made up his mind. On her next day off he would ask Lizzie to marry him.

The following Wednesday afternoon he went to the Killips' home to call for Lizzie. It was a glorious day but he hardly noticed. The sunlight on the sea, the sweet smell of the hedgerows, the fields of golden wheat and the twittering of the swifts and swallows did nothing to change his mood.

Lizzie wore a pale pink cotton shirtwaist blouse and skirt and a straw boater hat trimmed with a pink ribbon, and he had to admit she looked fresh and attractive. Dora Killip smiled as she watched them walk away from the harbour, heading for the cliff path. They looked well together and she for one was happy with the situation, even if Maud wasn't.

Lizzie chattered on about how Jamie and Will were whitewashing the walls of the rooms above the stables and how it would be quite presentable when Ellan got it fixed up with her own things. Miss Mary had been very generous. She'd found some quite pretty lamps. The mantles were chipped, of course, that's why they had been consigned to the attic, and there was quite a bit of linen that was well past its best but could be turned 'ends to middle'.

Andrew felt he could take no more and stopped and leaned against a tree. 'Lizzie, I didn't ask you out so I could hear a blow by blow account of what Jamie Corlett and Ellan are doing. I get enough of that at home.'

Lizzie looked a little peeved and tossed her head. 'I'm so sorry if I'm boring you.'

He took her hand and smiled at her. 'You're not, it's just that there's something I want to ask you.' His mouth felt dry and he ran his tongue over his lower lip and swallowed hard. It was now or never. He shouldn't think

82

about Ellan but he couldn't help it. 'She's not for you!' They were words that were burned into his brain. Words that lacerated his heart and if he were truthful, his pride. 'Lizzie, will you marry me?' It was out. It was done. There was no turning back now, but a shiver of despair ran through him.

Her eyes widened with astonishment. 'What?'

'You heard me. Will you? We've been walking out for a while now – when I've been home.'

Lizzie was dumbstruck. She liked him. She liked him a lot, but marry him! Her plans hadn't included Andrew Quirk. 'I don't know what to say. I . . . I'd not thought about marrying . . . anyone!'

'Think about it now.' He felt foolish, embarrassed and annoyed.

'I . . . I didn't think you cared that much. I like you, Andrew, you know that.'

He could have shaken her and yelled, 'For God's sake say something definite!'

Lizzie was thinking quickly. They'd have to live with that old shrew of a mother of his or with her ma and pa. She wouldn't have a home of her own like Ellan. Yet she didn't want to hurt him, although she'd made such grand plans for her future. But what if she never got another proposal? A bird in the hand is what her ma would say. If she turned him down flat and her plans came to nothing . . . what then?

'I've nothing much to offer, I know that. But if you don't want to live with Ma or with your folks, maybe we could rent a cottage.'

That sounded promising but Lizzie was practical. She wasn't going to give up her job and if they rented a cottage or even a couple of rooms, she'd never be there and neither would he, he'd be away chasing the herring. 'That would be a waste of money with me up at the house and you away fishing.'

'I suppose you're right.' This wasn't how it should be at all, he thought. She should look the way Ellan had when she'd returned from the party at Glentrammon and he should feel elated. Yet all they were doing was talking about practicalities. Maybe it was better that way. At least Lizzie wasn't hanging around his neck begging for promises of undying love and devotion. They were things he could never promise her.

Lizzie had made up her mind. 'Would you mind if I thought about it? It's all too quick, I can't really take it in. I'm not saying no,' she added, seeing his brow darken, 'and I'm not saying yes. I just want some time to think about it.'

He felt the irritation rise. Why couldn't she make up her mind? Say yes or no and have done with it, but he nodded. It was the least he could do; they hadn't exactly been that close. 'How long do you want to think about it?' he asked, bluntly.

'A week?'

A week in which to torture himself with doubt but he was too deeply involved now to protest. 'A week then.'

Dora Killip had no doubts at all about what her eldest daughter should do. 'Marry him!'

'I don't know him all that well, Ma. I don't even think I love him.'

'What's that got to do with it?'

'Oh, I don't know what to do. I'm not giving up my

job and I don't think Miss Mary will want me to. She's trained me and she's very keen on women being allowed more freedom and choice.'

Dora looked horrified. 'She's not turned into one of those suffragettes?'

'No, she hasn't but I don't think she'd want me to leave. But I do have plans, Ma. Eventually I want to go to Liverpool and maybe even London.'

'And pigs might fly, Lizzie Killip! Think about now, not what might happen in the future. Take what you can, while you can. You're not getting any younger.'

'Ma! I'm only eighteen.'

'And, before you can turn around you'll be nineteen, then twenty and then you'll be on the downhill path to thirty and an old maid to boot. Miss Lizzie Killip, spinster of this parish, is that what you want? He's a decent lad and he'll make a good husband. She's brought them all up well, I'll say that for her. No drinking or gambling or squandering money on girls who are no better than they should be. So you'll be certain he's not going to beat you or desert you and he works hard. No idling about. Just you bear all that in mind, Lizzie.'

Lizzie stared forlornly out of the window. She supposed her ma was right, but would she have to live at home, for home it would be; she wasn't going to live with Maud Quirk. She really did want more from life and what was so terrible about that? She was more confused than ever now. Added to all that was the fact that she didn't love him, not the way Ellan loved Jamie. Jamie was the centre of Ellan's life and she knew Andrew Quirk wasn't the centre of hers. Oh, it just got worse. Well, she had a week to make up her mind.

*

As soon as her chores were finished Ellan changed into her Sunday dress and packed some bread and cold ham in a cloth. Aunt Maud had been particularly trying for she was going to Douglas and insisted that all the preparations for the Sabbath be done before she left. It was early afternoon before Ellan went down to the harbour.

'I thought you weren't coming,' Jamie said. 'I was just going to come up for you.'

'Oh, she was in a foul mood. She's gone into Douglas but everything had to be done before she went. You know what she's like about Sundays. Here, take this while I get in.'

He took the picnic bundle in his left hand and helped her down into the boat.

They went further along the coast than they'd done the last time, but she didn't protest. They would have less time alone together but maybe that was the safest thing. She was finding it harder and harder to keep her desire for him under control and she knew he was experiencing the same struggle.

When the food had been eaten she sat with his head in her lap and twisted the ring around her finger.

'So, that's decided, we'll make it a Christmas wedding. Is that what you want?'

She bent and placed a kiss on his forehead. 'Yes, then Christmas will always be special for me.'

'Mrs Corlett. It sounds strange . . . but nice,' he mused.

'It's better than Vannin. I've never liked my name even though Pa said I should be proud of it and that it's *L'il Daisy*'s proper name.'

'Why don't you like it? I do.'

'It's not a proper name and I feel it's unlucky.'

He laughed. 'Unlucky? You've never said that before.'

'I know, but I lost my ma and then my pa. Then I had to go and live with Aunt Maud . . .'

He sat up. 'You superstitious little fool, Ellan Vannin! It's not like you to think like that.'

'I know, but we're a superstitious people, remember.'

'In a couple of months you'll be Ellan Corlett, so you've no need to worry any more.'

She stroked his cheek. Christmas seemed an age away and yet it was only four months. She sighed. Four long months before she would really belong to him. He'd called her superstitious and she was. Sometimes it seemed that she was too happy, that everything in the future looked too bright. Aunt Maud was always saying life wasn't always what it appeared, that dreams could often turn to nightmares and happiness seldom lasted. But Aunt Maud was bitter and still wasn't reconciled to the fact that she was going to live at Glentrammon and never missed an opportunity to dampen her optimism. Well, she wasn't going to think about Aunt Maud today, she was just going to sit here, safe within the circle of Jamie's arms and indulge herself with plans for the future.

As they headed for home the breeze began to freshen and looking out to sea she saw the leaden thunderheads gathering on the horizon.

Jamie had seen them too. 'We're in for a storm, good job we started back now.'

'Do you think we'll get back in time?'

'We should just make it, they're not moving very fast.' He grunted as he pulled harder.

'Move over and let me help!'

'No, you'd have us going round in circles or you'd catch a crab!' he grinned.

'What does that mean?'

'You'd lose the oar. Just sit still, there's the harbour wall in sight now.'

Just before they reached the harbour the storm broke. Streaks of blue lightning rent the cinereous clouds and the thunder rolled almost overhead, then huge spots of rain began to fall. By the time they tied up the rain was sheeting down.

Jamie gave her his jacket and placing his arm around her shoulders they began to run along the jetty.

'You're going to be soaked to the skin soon.'

'So are you. You can't go back to Glentrammon in this.'

He pulled her towards the tavern. 'We'll shelter in here until it stops and you can dry your hair.'

She started to protest but her words were lost as a clap of thunder burst above them, so loud that the ground shook.

Maud stood sheltering in the porch of the church with Dora Killip. They'd come back from Douglas together and for Maud it hadn't been a good day. She had been horrified by the prices in the shops and the sultry weather had given her a headache. Then she'd had Dora to contend with. There hadn't been a seat backing towards the engine and she'd got a tiny cinder in her eye and smuts on her face. But what Dora had told her made all the other discomforts pale into insignificance.

She'd hardly been able to believe her ears when Dora, lowering her voice so the whole carriage wouldn't hear –

although she would have been happy to have shouted it – said knowingly, 'We could end up being related, you and I, Maud, by marriage.'

Maud shot her an openly disdainful look. 'Have you been in the sun too long, Dora?'

Dora ignored that. 'Your Andrew and my Lizzie.'

Maud raised her eyebrows but she felt as though her stomach was filled with ice-water.

'He hasn't told you then? Men! You have to drag every word out of them. He's asked our Lizzie to marry him.'

The ice-water had frozen into a solid lump. Andrew and Lizzie Killip! It wasn't possible! He'd never even hinted at such a thing! She'd have something to say about this. Why hadn't he told her instead of leaving her to find out from Dora? She seethed with humiliation.

'She hasn't made her mind up yet, though. She's got some daft notions about going to Liverpool, to London even. I told her she's a fool to even think about such nonsense! I told her . . .'

Maud wasn't listening. She hadn't made up her mind! The brass-faced little madam. Just who did she think she was, keeping her son – and he was above the likes of Lizzie Killip – dangling, waiting for her to make up her mind. And with the entire village waiting with baited breath, no doubt – she knew Dora of old. Two bright spots of red burned on her cheeks and her eyes glittered. Just what did he think he was playing at? Hanging around like a great fool. Oh, this was all Ellan's fault. She knew he cared nothing for Lizzie. This was his blind, stupid way of getting back at Ellan and he would wreck his life. She wished with all her heart that George Vannin had never asked her to have anything to do with Ellan.

Dora, now in full flight, was rabbiting on about her Lizzie refusing to give up her job at Glentrammon even if she did accept him and that added insult to injury. Maud quivered with anger and humiliation.

As soon as they left the station the heavens had opened and they had to run for shelter in the porch of the church when all she wanted to do was get home and have this out with Andrew.

'Isn't that Ellan and Jamie!' Dora interrupted her thoughts.

'Where?'

'Going into the tavern.'

Maud peered through the curtain of rain and saw Jamie and Ellan run into the tavern. A flame of white-hot anger leapt through her. The tavern! That low, common, place of sin. It was more than she could endure and eighteen or not, betrothed or not, she'd take a strap to Ellan for this. To be seen going into the tavern and by Dora Killip. She walked out into the still torrential rain.

'Maud! Maud, what's got into you? You'll be soaked to the skin. You're not going in there after her, are you?'

Maud turned and glanced at her. 'No, I'm not. I'd sooner catch a fever than go in "that" place. I'm going home.'

Dora watched her walk purposefully up the lane, head held high as though it was a fine, clear day. Well, she probably would catch a fever but that was her affair. She'd obviously not known about Andrew and Lizzie, that much was clear. Then again, if Andrew had announced he was going to marry a princess she wouldn't be pleased about that either. There was no suiting Maud. As for Ellan and Jamie, they were only sheltering from the rain like they had been, but she had the feeling that she should have kept her mouth shut on this occasion.

Maud had stripped off her wet clothes and had put them to dry over the clotheshorse in front of the range. She'd dried her hair and then coiled it into a bun. She'd put away her few purchases and had set the kettle to boil and the whole time wave upon wave of anger washed over her and humiliation bubbled up inside her. Fury that Andrew could be so deceitful and foolish and that probably the whole village had known before she did; rage that Ellan, who had already caused her so much grief and worry, had run – run, not hesitated – into that den of sin. A few steps more and she could have sheltered with her in the porch of God's house. No, instead she'd chosen the lair of the Devil. And out at sea, where the storm raged at its fiercest, were her three sons. Oh, was a woman ever so plagued as she by worry.

The rain had stopped at six o'clock and half an hour later Ellan pushed open the door.

'I'm sorry I'm late, Aunt, but we got caught in the storm and had to shelter.'

Maud turned and looked at her. The girl stood there facing her without a trace of guilt or contrition. 'I know. I saw you.'

Ellan swallowed hard. She knew Maud's opinion of the tavern and those who frequented it. 'I'm sorry, it was the nearest place and I didn't have a drink, except a cup of tea while my clothes dried. Mrs Marlin was very good, she . . .'

Something inside Maud snapped. 'Mrs Marlin! Mrs Marlin! She's no more Mrs than you are! She's little better than the whore of Babylon! How dare you say she was *kind*, that . . . that . . .'

'I'm sorry, Aunt. I am. I didn't think.'

Maud's hand closed over the leather leash her sons used to train the dogs. 'How dare you. I brought you up to be a God-fearing Christian, to walk in the way of the Lord, not to consort with the Devil and his kind. I'll beat the wickedness out of you if it's the last thing I do.'

The leash caught Ellan across her shoulder, making her scream with pain and fright. Maud's face contorted horribly as she thought of everything she had endured because of Ellan.

Ellan covered her face and head with her arms to try to deflect the blows. She did not think to try to fight back. Obedience had been strongly instilled in her. Her only thought was to get out; to get away from the blows and the curses being inflicted on her. She turned towards the door but Maud followed.

'Don't think you can escape,' Maud screamed. Her hair had slipped from its pins and was straggling around her face.

Ellan screamed again as the leash caught the side of her face but she had reached the door.

'Chastisement is the only path to repentance!' Maud raged but Ellan had wrenched open the door and had gone.

Sobbing and holding her smarting cheek she ran down towards the stile and the lane. The thunder still rumbled in the distance and the sky was dark but she stumbled on. Twice she tripped and fell, grazing her hands, but she ran on. She had to get to Jamie.

By the time she reached Glentrammon her hair was

tumbled around her shoulders, her face was streaked with tears and a large red weal marked one side of her cheek. Her clothes were torn and dirty for she'd run blindly through puddles on the track and her mud-spattered skirt hampered her as she climbed the outside steps.

When Jamie opened the door in response to her hammering he stared at her with horror and pity. Then he picked her up and carried her inside.

'Ellan! Ellan, what happened? Who did this?'

She couldn't answer him for a while, the sobs still shook her. He got a blanket and wrapped it around her, noticing how she flinched. 'Who did it, Ellan?' Anger now replaced shock.

'Aunt Maud, she . . . she saw us going into the tavern. She called me . . .' she broke down in sobs.

The woman was mad. She was a fanatic and should be locked up, he fumed. 'I'll get Lizzie to see to you. I'm going to have this out with her.'

She reached out and clutched his arm. 'No! Jamie! It will only make things worse! Please don't go. In the mood she's in nothing you can say will make any difference.'

Reluctantly he crouched down beside her. 'Ellan, she can't do this and get away with it.'

'Oh, I should have known. She hates the Marlins and all they stand for.'

He stood up. 'I'll get you a drop of brandy and some water and salve.'

The brandy burned her throat but after it she felt a little calmer and he smoothed the salve across the mark on her face. Jamie laid her gently on the bed and stroked the dark hair from her forehead. Anger consumed him and he'd have gladly taken the beating instead of her. She wasn't going to be subjected to treatment like this for any longer than was necessary.

She smiled up at him weakly. 'I feel better now, but I can't stay here all night, Jamie.'

'I don't want you ever to go back to that place.'

She held his hand tightly. 'But I'll have to. This would be nothing to what would happen if I were to spend the night with you, no matter how much we protested our innocence.'

He couldn't refute that. 'Then you can rest a bit longer and then I'll take you back.'

'Oh, Jamie. I want to stay, I really do.'

'Soon you'll be able to, it will be your home.' He bent and kissed her. 'And you'll be mine.'

She slipped her arms around his neck. That was all she wanted. She didn't want to go back to the croft. She felt ill at the thought of facing Aunt Maud, for the experience had shocked her deeply. She kissed him with a tender urgency, clinging to his lips and as his lips brushed her throat and the weal on her shoulder, the ache disappeared. The bed was soft and comforting and she gave in willingly to its solace of warmth and security. Her desire for him made her feel weak and dizzy. She no longer cared about Aunt Maud or anyone else, she no longer fought the emotions that made her body tingle and obliterated all thoughts of right or wrong. Tonight, this moment when time stood still, she felt so deliriously happy. There were just the two of them in the whole world and they were so much in love.

He was very gentle with her, caressing her breasts with his lips and whispering endearments. Beneath his hands her body awoke and responded and when he entered her, the sharp cry of pain was replaced by one of ecstasy. She loved him and now she belonged to him, heart, body and soul. She'd never experienced such wild exhilaration, such elation and yet a deep feeling of peace and contentment.

He leaned on his elbow and looked down at her. 'Oh, Ellan, I love you so much. I never meant to hurt you.'

'You didn't. Well, only a little, but that doesn't matter now.' Sanity and awareness were beginning to return and she turned her head away from him. 'Jamie, you . . . you won't think badly of me because . . . ?'

He kissed her again. 'Oh, Ellan. Ellan. You little fool! I love you even more now, if that's possible.'

'Do you really mean that?'

'Ellan, I'll love you for as long as I live, I swear I will.'

The glow of love and fulfilment remained as she coiled up her hair while he went to saddle up the horse to take her home. She was dreading going back and she blushed and bit her lip when she thought of what Aunt Maud would do and say if she knew how she had spent the last hour. Then she pushed away the thought. Aunt Maud wouldn't know and soon it wouldn't matter. She didn't feel unclean or sinful or ashamed, although she knew she should. Surely the Lord would understand that they truly loved each other and would forgive them this one transgression? Surely He wasn't the terrible, vengeful God that Aunt Maud made Him out to be. He must have some pity; He had pitied Mary Magdalene.

She was sitting in the chair by the table when she heard the voices. Jamie wasn't alone. She stood up slowly as the door opened and John stood behind Jamie, his face taut with suppressed anger. Her heart dropped like a stone but John's words dispelled her fear.

'Are you all right, Ellan, lass?'

They stepped into the room as she nodded.

John gently touched the side of her face. 'She needs horsewhipping and I told her so. The storm delayed us or we'd have been home and this would never have happened.'

'I had to get out, John. I *had* to and there was nowhere else I could think of to run to, except to Jamie.'

'You did the right thing, lass.' He nodded his thanks to Jamie, who looked a little uncomfortable. 'I'll take her home now. She can't stay here, it wouldn't be fitting.'

'Jamie was going to take me back – he went for the horse.' She, too, felt uneasy, wondering if John could sense anything unusual in their attitudes.

'I'd be grateful if you could come, too.' John turned to Jamie. 'She's in no fit state to walk and I couldn't take the animal without permission.' He lowered his voice. 'And, the less said about this the better.'

Jamie agreed and wrapped the blanket around Ellan's shoulders.

As they reached the door John caught Jamie's arm. 'You can be sure that nothing like this will ever happen again. I've made myself quite clear about that. She'll not touch Ellan again.' He said nothing of the almighty row there'd been or of the fact that he had threatened to denounce Maud publicly, even hinted of the asylum, for only a madwoman would act so viciously on such a flimsy pretext.

Chapter Six

LIZZIE HAD MADE HER decision. To all Dora's reason-ing, pleading and cajoling she was deaf. She would not marry Andrew Quirk.

Consequently, the atmosphere in the croft was terrible. Maud wouldn't speak unless it was absolutely necessary and after Andrew left, Ellan felt more isolated. Soon John and Mat would go, too, north to Stornaway and they would not return until the week she was to be married.

She knew, from the venomous looks she intercepted from Aunt Maud, that in some way Maud blamed her for Andrew's departure. Yet there was nothing she could do or say that would have stopped him. She had tried. They all had.

'I know how you must feel.' She'd started awkwardly, for she'd promised John she would try and change his mind.

'How can you? You've got what you wanted.' His voice had been harsh, his tone bitter. 'Or do you want me to stay here and be pitied by everyone or laughed at?'

'No. No, I don't and you know it. Oh, Andrew, I only want you to be happy. Maybe Lizzie wasn't meant for you. It might not have worked out, her head is so full of dreams and ambitions.'

'Just as yours is.'

'Yes, but mine are different. I don't want the things Lizzie does.' He'd started to decry her but she battled on. 'You don't have to go away. At least not that far and for so long.'

'Why?' Resentment, love and jealousy were tearing him apart as he looked down into her eyes.

'Because people forget. They do. And I . . . we all want you to stay! Go to Stornaway with the others, please? Please don't go whaling!'

He flung off her hand. At her touch he wanted to take her in his arms and tell her he loved her, that the whole sorry mess centred around that fact. But he controlled himself. He'd already made a fool of himself once and that was enough. Neither could he come back from Scotland to see her married to another man.

'I'm signing on and there's an end to it. I hate this place. There's more to life than this.' He flung his arms wide. 'The world is a big place. Who knows, I may never come back.'

That frightened her into silence. He'd never spoken like that before. What if he didn't come back? The Arctic waters were dangerous, as was whaling. She'd clutched at his arm, her dark eyes fixed pleadingly on his face, but he pushed past her and strode away. Tears slowly brimmed as she stared after him and it was then that she realized why he was going.

Yet despite the atmosphere and the void Andrew's

absence had left, nothing was as bad as the predicament she now found herself in. She was certain she was pregnant. She had told herself that first month when she had not had the curse that it was all the tension and upset, but now as the leaves were falling and the bracken on the heath was turning brown, she knew.

She felt sick and cold at the knowledge, for Aunt Maud wouldn't hesitate to turn her out. They would have to bring the wedding forward, despite the plans, and everyone would know why. She would have to tell Jamie. She didn't want to. Everything in her cried out to deny the situation but now that she'd missed a second time and October was nearing its end, she had no choice. She would have to go to Glentrammon, she couldn't wait until he got time off to meet her for he never came to the croft now and wouldn't even acknowledge that Maud existed: if he saw her, and there was no way of avoiding a meeting, he would look straight through her.

She threw the last of the fish into the basket and wiped her hands on her apron. The stench, which she had become accustomed to, was making her feel worse and she wondered how long she could carry on with this job before she publicly vomited and everyone would know.

Autumn was in the air, she thought miserably as she walked along the lane towards the big house. The trees were glorious and the slight nip in the air was refreshing or it would have been if she hadn't been so weighed down with trouble. She tried to bolster her spirits. He loved her, they were betrothed and due to be married in six weeks, so why was she feeling so guilty? She wasn't the first and she wouldn't be the last girl to hurry into wedlock. People would gossip but they would soon forget – except Aunt Maud. But what if it changed things between herself and Jamie? When she'd lain awake night after night, that question had nagged persistently. What if he didn't want bairns yet? Her stomach churned with fear. What if he wouldn't marry her now? Stop being stupid, she told herself firmly. Of course he'd marry her. If he'd have thought her cheap and easy he would never have wanted to see her again after that night.

It was Lizzie who opened the kitchen door. 'Ellan! Come in. You look terrible, what's the matter? Has she been at it again?'

'No. She still doesn't speak but that's all. Where's Jamie?'

'Didn't he tell you?' Cook said, looking up from beating a cake mixture.

'Tell me what?'

Lizzie raised her eyes to the ceiling. 'How could he have had time to tell her when he only found out himself a few hours ago?'

'Found out what?'

'That's what we want to know, don't we? He's gone to Liverpool. As soon as the post came this morning the master sent for him and then he was dashing off in his Sunday suit.'

Ellan stared at Lizzie aghast. 'Liverpool! But . . . why?' The room started to revolve sickeningly and she clung to the back of a chair.

'Quick! Cook! I think she's going to faint! You, Bessie, get a cup of water, quick!' Lizzie caught her as she swayed.

'Sit her down and push her head down, Lizzie, so the

blood can get to it,' Cook commanded.

'Ellan! Ellan! Are you ill? Do you feel feverish?' Lizzie's voice came from far away. He'd gone. The nightmare was upon her. She felt herself going again and then the swirling darkness receded.

'Here, sip this slowly. It's the shock.' Lizzie glared at Cook. 'Miss Mary was going to send for you later on to tell you.'

Ellan felt the bile rise in her throat. Miss Mary! It got worse. If Miss Mary wanted to speak to her that could only mean disaster for her in one form or another.

'I'll go along and tell her you're here now,' Lizzie said.

Cook insisted she continue to sip the water and peered at her closely. She didn't look well but she supposed it was a shock to hear he'd up and gone like that and if rumour was true, she had a terrible life with Maud. Jamie hadn't said anything but somehow the news of Ellan's beating had got around. The woman was ready for the asylum if she wasn't mistaken and she wasn't the only one who thought so. Religious mania was what Maud Quirk had, to beat the girl for sheltering from the rain. Still, she didn't like the colour of Ellan, she was so pale.

Lizzie returned. 'You're to come with me. Are you feeling better?'

Ellan nodded, getting slowly to her feet. Her world was crumbling but not by the movement of an eyelid could she show it.

'Cook's got as much tact as a regimental Sergeant-Major!' Lizzie muttered. 'Ma's always saying she never opens her mouth without putting her foot in it.'

Mary Costain was sitting in the back parlour, the room Ellan had stood in the day she'd come to refuse the offer of work and Mary was startled by her appearance. The last time she'd seen her she had been radiant, now she looked drawn and ill. 'Come in, Ellan, are you feeling well?'

'She went a bit faint in the kitchen, miss. Cook wasn't too tactful the way she told Ellan about Jamie's . . . journey.' She'd nearly said 'flit' but stopped herself in time.

'Then you'd better sit down, Ellan. I'm sorry the news gave you a shock. It was very sudden, quite a shock to us, too.'

'Is he . . . is he coming back, miss?' The words stuck in her throat.

Mary smiled. So that was it. The poor girl thought he'd up and left for good. 'Of course he is. He'll be back in two days' time. Is that what has made you unwell?'

Ellan sagged in the chair with relief.

She still didn't look well, Mary thought, but she, too, had heard the gossip and if it was true, then who would look the picture of health? No wonder the youngest of the Quirk boys had signed on for a trip to the Arctic and no wonder the other two would soon go with the rest of the boats to the north of Scotland. She leaned forward and placed a hand on Ellan's arm. 'We had a letter this morning from a solicitor in Liverpool, asking Jamie to go and see him as soon as possible.' She smiled, wondering how much she should tell Ellan. She didn't want to spoil Jamie's news but it would affect them both. 'I think he will learn something to his advantage, as they say. Something good – for both of you.'

Ellan was puzzled.

'He had an uncle in America, apparently, who has

died,' Mary explained, but Ellan still didn't understand. 'There may be a legacy.'

'You mean there's money, miss?'

Mary nodded. 'We don't know how much, and of course there's Maggie, so I don't want to build your hopes up.'

'But he is coming back?'

Mary laughed. 'I should hope so or the entire staff will expire from acute curiosity. I will probably succumb to it myself!'

Ellan was so relieved that tears sprang to her eyes. 'But he never mentioned any relatives, except Maggie.'

'I don't think he knew he had any. So, cheer up, Ellan, you've everything to look forward to.' Just a note of envy had crept into Mary Costain's voice but Ellan hadn't noticed. He hadn't left her.

She got to her feet. 'Thank you, Miss Mary.'

'You both deserve a little good luck and it won't be long before you come to live at Glentrammon, will it?'

'No, miss. Not long at all.'

Lizzie pounced on her as soon as she entered the kitchen. 'What did she say? What's it all about?'

Ellan laughed nervously. 'He's gone to see a solicitor in Liverpool. He had an uncle in America who has died and she said there will probably be a legacy.'

Lizzie's mouth formed an 'O' and young Bessie, up to her elbows in greasy dish water, stopped and stared at her.

Cook let out a long, hissing breath. 'I wonder how much?'

'Some of it will be for Maggie,' Ellan said.

'Aye, and isn't she a sly one. Never said a word about

any of it and she was up in the yard not an hour since. I wondered what she'd come for,' Lizzie said.

'Well, I just hope it doesn't go to his head, that's all. Give him ideas. Next thing we'll know is that we're not good enough for him. He'll be off to foreign parts and mixing with the high and mighty! Money isn't called the root of all evil for fun,' Cook said ominously.

Lizzie glared at her for Ellan had gone very pale again. 'He'll never change, not Jamie!'

Ellan walked slowly down the lane. She didn't turn off for the stile and the croft. She needed to think. So much had happened in one short morning that her mind was in turmoil. She needed to get away, be by herself, try to sort things out.

A few women called to her as she passed the rows of cottages and she answered automatically in mono-syllables. When she reached the end of the harbour she leaned against the wall. She was pregnant and she would have to tell him, but would this unexpected legacy make any difference to him, as Cook had suggested? Would he still want to marry her? Would he still want to live here or would he indeed want to travel? Would he want to be saddled with a wife and child? Would he even come back from Liverpool? She looked down at her skirt and rubbed her hand up and down against it. Would he now want someone more stylish than her? Would he want to mix with a better class of person? Looking down she saw Albert Killip's boat moored by the steps. She had to get away for people were watching her and someone was bound to come and speak to her soon. You were never left alone for long on your own in Peel.

Carefully she stepped down into the little craft,

loosened the mooring rope and pulled the oars towards her. She wondered for a minute if she could manage it but then she began to pull hard on them, the way Jamie had done, and to her surprise found herself moving.

She concentrated hard until looking up she saw the wall had grown smaller and that she was out in the open sea. It wasn't hard, she thought, not if you concentrated, but now she couldn't concentrate. The more she thought about Cook's words the more convinced she became that he wouldn't want to be burdened with her. She'd be left here while he became a gentleman and travelled to all the foreign cities, where he was sure to be surrounded by girls far more beautiful and elegant than she. She'd be left carrying a bairn and with no husband and no prospect of one. She'd be thrown out for even John and Mat would be shocked. And, there was only one place left then, the workhouse. Her arms became leaden and her shoulders ached. A wonderful new life was being offered to him on a plate. He wouldn't want her, a poor, ignorant islander, only fit to gut fish or work in the fields.

What little warmth there had been in the sun had gone. Long shadows thrown out by the cliffs gave the sea a dappled appearance and the breeze had become stronger. She was tired, too tired and too weary and broken to pull against it. She had been so preoccupied that she hadn't noticed that the weather was changing. Heavy, scudding clouds masked the face of the sun. The now strong wind had whipped the wavelets up into a heavy, running swell and the small craft began to pitch and lurch, and as she lifted her head there was naked terror in her eyes as she realized she was alone in a very small boat and in the path of a storm.

A cloud of white spray hit her full in the face and she screamed and tried to rise. The boat swayed dangerously as she grabbed for one of the oars that had come loose from the oarlock. She missed it and watched helplessly as it drifted away. She was bitterly cold now and soaking wet and nausea was adding to her fear. She clung to the side terrified, the salt from her tears mingling with the salt from the spray. She was going to die! She was going to drown! It was God's way of punishing her, like Aunt Maud said He would, for the badness that was in her. But never had she wanted to live more.

She looked around but could see nothing, for the spray and the huge waves bearing down on her blinded her with panic. Then with a lurch the boat was buoyed up on the crest of a wave then crashed down into the trough and overturned.

The cold sea enveloped her, causing her to gasp with the shock. Her skirts were dragging her down. She thrashed about and fought her way upwards, gasping for breath as her head broke the surface, then she was being sucked down again. She clawed the water ineffectually with flailing arms. She was drowning. Her nose, her ears, her mouth were filled with water and then she felt the blast of cold air on her face. Spluttering and coughing she tried to take a deep breath, knowing if she were dragged under again she would have no strength left to fight. Then someone was in the sea beside her, holding her up. She felt herself being pushed upwards, felt the solid mass beneath her body. Her fingers gripped the edge of something sharp and she clung to it tenaciously. She didn't know or care where she was, only that she was out of the clutches of the greedy sea.

John Quirk tossed his head back to shake the water from his dripping hair that was obscuring his already blurred vision. She was far enough up the overturned hull to be safe for a while. He took a deep breath as another wall of water bore down on him. When he surfaced he heard his brother's voice and saw the dim, spluttering light of a tarred-faggot torch.

'The life preserver's over to the right, Johnny! Over to the right!' Mat yelled.

He struck out towards the round circle of cork attached to a long rope. Then he heard other voices yelling but he couldn't see what was happening. He managed to get the cork ring over Ellan's head and shoulders and to drag one arm through. He was tiring rapidly himself. His own clothes were pulling him down, even though he'd removed his sea boots and oilskins before he'd gone in after her.

They had been nearing home when the squall had blown up and it had been Mat who first spotted the boat. It couldn't be much further now, John thought, gritting his teeth. If he could just hang on, if his strength would only last out a few more minutes.

'Jump, man! For the love of God, jump, before it's too late!'

He heard the shouted warning and borne up on the crest of a wave he saw how close they were to shore. But he was confused. He couldn't make it out. Why were they telling him to jump? Again he heard the warning and then Mat's voice and at last he felt the pull on the rope. They were pulling them in. He relaxed his muscles, his mind became clearer as the danger receded.

They dragged them both on deck and John lay on his

side exhausted. Then he heard the sound that woke him from his sleep in many a nightmare, the groaning, crashing, splintering of a ship being smashed to pieces on the rocks, like a matchwood toy hurled by a giant hand. He raised his head and heaved himself up to his knees. 'Ellan! Ellan!'

A hand pressed him down again. 'She's all right! She's safe enough. That was the *Rentray*, Davie Kewin's boat.' In Mat's voice there was a gruffness that spoke more clearly than a thousand words. John dropped his head, forehead resting on the deck.

Ellan was barely conscious when they carried her into the cottage.

'Merciful Lord! Is she—' Maud cried.

'No, Ma, she's not dead but near to it or will be if we don't get her warmed up.'

Maud stoked up the fire and ran for blankets while Mat laid Ellan on the long settle bench, propping her head with a pillow. The warmth began to spread through her and the voices buzzed in her ears but had no words or meaning.

'What happened, did she fall?' Maud was heating up a stone which she would wrap in flannel and place at Ellan's feet. John had stripped off his own wet clothes and wrapped in a blanket was clutching a mug of hot tea.

'She was out in Bert Killip's boat by herself. Bert's boat has gone and so, too, has Davie Kewin's *Rentray*.'

Maud looked stricken. What had got into the girl, going off like that? Not only had she risked her own life but John's as well and she'd cost Davie Kewin his livelihood and he with four bairns to keep. Had she gone mad? 'Why was she out alone?'

'How should we know? Have you been up to your tricks again, Ma?'

'I've said nothing to her, not a single word.' But she had wondered why Ellan hadn't come home. She knew she'd gone to 'that' house because she'd seen her in the lane as she'd been pegging out the washing. 'Maybe it's got something to do with Jamie Corlett. She went up there instead of coming home.'

The brothers exchanged glances. What had gone on between them that had made her do such a desperate thing? 'I'll go up and see him. He'll want to know anyway,' Mat announced.

Jamie's name cut through the fog of exhaustion and shock that clogged Ellan's mind and she struggled to rise, calling him. John was instantly beside her.

'What is it, lass?'

'He's gone.'

John looked at Mat. 'You'd better go just the same, there's something very wrong here. Ma and I will get her to bed. She'll be lucky to escape without catching a fever so the sooner we get her to bed the better.'

For the next day and night Ellan tossed and turned, unable to discern night from day, her body burning with fever, sometimes fighting for breath for her chest was painfully tight. Maud nursed her diligently but grudgingly, especially when Mat returned from Glentrammon, and gave the reason for Jamie's absence.

'Well, the first thing he can do with his legacy is to compensate Albert and Davie, that's if he still intends to wed her,' Maud had stated tersely.

To John it had suddenly become crystal clear. Ellan had probably been thinking the same thing herself, it was the only explanation as to why she'd taken off like that. Had she deliberately been trying to kill herself? No, she would never do that. 'If she's no better by morning, Ma, I'm going for Doctor Taylor.'

'We can't afford doctors and he always wants to be paid on the spot. No money, no treatment.'

'I reckon Jamie can afford it now and he'd not want her left like this.'

'It's only a fever and I've nursed you through fevers before. He can keep his money – if he comes back, that is. The crisis will come tonight.'

By late evening Ellan's fever broke and she looked around her small bedroom dazedly, remembering little of her narrow escape from the sea. 'Aunt Maud?'

Maud stood up, placed a hand on her forehead and nodded. No need for Doctor Taylor now.

'Aunt Maud, have I been ill?'

'Just a bit of a fever. Don't you remember what you did? I hope you're satisfied with the results of that day's work. Risking the lives of half a dozen men and the loss of two boats, to say nothing of the worry and extra work nursing you.'

Then Ellan remembered and she recalled why she'd gone off in Albert Killip's boat. She turned her head away so that she faced the wall, and the tears coursed down her cheeks. 'Has he come back?' She forced the question out although she wished with all her heart that she didn't have to ask it. But now she would have to face up to her predicament, weak though she was.

'Due back later tonight, so I hear tell. Try and sleep, I've things to catch up on.'

Sleep, she thought. How could she sleep with so much

weighing on her mind? How could she relax when her whole future depended on the next few hours? But she did sleep, weakened by the shock, anxiety and the fever, and when she awoke Jamie was sitting in the chair beside the bed. Again the tears coursed down her cheeks as he gathered her into his arms.

'Oh, Ellan! Ellan! Thank God! I've never prayed so hard as I've done this last half hour.'

'You've been here that long, why didn't you wake me?'

'The dragon wouldn't let me. It was only at John's insistence that she let me up to see you at all.'

She clung to him. 'I didn't mean to do it. I was so confused and now there's two boats lost!'

'Never mind that now. I'll sort that out. All that matters to me is that you're safe. Why did you do it, Ellan?'

She looked up at him, her eyes like two dark pools swimming with tears. 'I didn't know if you'd come back or if you'd still want me.'

He kissed away the tears. 'Oh, Ellan, you fool. Do you think I'd desert you like that? I'm sorry I had to go without telling you but Miss Mary said she'd send for you.'

He was saying he wouldn't desert her but he didn't know! She closed her eyes and prayed, prayed to God not to punish her. Not to see the look on his face, to feel him stiffen or draw away from her when she told him. 'Jamie, I've got something to tell you. It's partly why I wasn't thinking straight that day. I'm . . . I'm having a bairn.' She waited with closed eyes and the tears seeped from beneath her lashes. If he rejected her now she'd have been better off lying at the bottom of the sea, dead, or broken against the rocks like the *Rentray*.

'Ellan, look at me.' He lifted her chin and slowly she opened her eyes. 'Ellan, I love you. What kind of a man do you think I am that I'd leave you? I'm surprised but I'm glad. Yes, I'm glad.'

She was laughing and crying at the same time as he held her in his arms and rocked her to and fro. Everything was going to be fine. Why hadn't she trusted him? Oh, why had she been such a fool as to take notice of Cook?

'Our son or daughter will have the best of everything, Ellan, and so will its mother. No more living hand to mouth. No more gutting fish. You'll be a lady, Ellan, living in a house as fine as Glentrammon, dressed in silk and satin.' She drew away from him. What was he saying? Was she delirious? 'Ellan, I'm rich. We're rich. It was Pa's eldest brother who went to New York long before I was born. He never married. I have to go there to claim the inheritance on behalf of Maggie and myself, his only heirs. It's not just hundreds of pounds, Ellan, it's thousands!' She could only stare at him, too weak to take it in. 'And to think I nearly lost you and the bairn. I wouldn't have wanted the money if I had. Nothing could replace you, Ellan.'

She collapsed against him, exhausted, and just listened while he talked excitedly of the plans he had made on the crossing home. 'I came home on *L'il Daisy*, your ship, that was a good omen. She's not as fast or as fancy as the *Douglas* but I didn't care. I just wanted to get home to you. I have to go to New York, then when I've sorted everything out I'll send for you. I don't want you taking any more risks, so when everything is settled I'll book a passage for you, first class, on the finest liner there is. Mr

Costain is going to help me arrange everything. I don't understand business, shares and things, and neither does Maggie. Half the money is hers, but we'll both be rich. What money I have I'll leave with you. You're to go to Liverpool and pick a new wardrobe. If you need any advice I'm sure Miss Mary will help. We'll be married in New York, Ellan, and it will all be wonderful! A new life. A new country and a new wife and baby. Me a father!'

She still couldn't take it in. She must be dreaming, things like this didn't happen to people like them. But if all dreams were like this then she never wanted to wake up.

Chapter Seven

———◆———

THE WHOLE VILLAGE WAS buzzing with the news. Everyone wanted to shake Jamie's hand and congratulate him on his good fortune, but after the first few heady days Ellan began to feel as though they'd lost their privacy. There didn't seem to be a single place where they could be alone. And, she was beginning to feel uneasy about the inheritance. She wondered just how much it would change their lives and their relationship. At least Aunt Maud was running true to form, determined not to be drawn into the excited euphoria.

'It's unjust, that's what it is. It's sinful for one person to have so much money when there are hundreds starving.'

'We don't know how much money it actually is, Aunt, and anyway Jamie won't let it go to his head.'

'I wasn't talking about him. I meant that uncle of his and was wondering how a simple man managed to get his hands on a fortune. Not by honest means, I'll be bound.'

'It was something to do with the railways and stocks and bonds, so Jamie said.'

Maud looked triumphant. 'Sweated labour and gambling. I don't know much about bonds and the like but I do know it's a form of gambling, and as for the railways, well, everyone knows it was the poor Irish navvies and heathen Chinese that built them.'

Ellan said nothing. It showed just how much Aunt Maud hated the thought of Jamie's inheritance that she was now calling the Irish 'poor'. Her usual comments on them were scathing to say the least. She sighed, wishing the legacy had only been a couple of hundred pounds that wouldn't have caused so much speculation or the envy that was just beginning to surface.

John and Mat were two of the first to congratulate both Jamie and herself. When she felt well enough to travel they took her up to Glentrammon. She looked at the house with new eyes. Jamie had said she would have a house as grand as this one, but was that what she really wanted? Somehow she felt that she wouldn't be comfortable in a place so big. She had lived all her life in small rooms and the realization of the sheer size of Glentrammon now overwhelmed her.

John read her thoughts. 'Better get used to this now, Ellan, it will be only the best for you in future.'

'Oh, John, I'm afraid. Everything is going so fast that I feel as though I'm being hurtled along. That there's nothing I can do to slow things down or even stop them.'

He laughed and patted her hand. 'What is it you want to stop? Have you changed your mind about marrying him?'

She thought of the baby. 'No! No, it's nothing like that. I just feel that our lives have been taken over. I don't even know if I want things to change so much.'

115

'I suppose that's natural, but enjoy it, Ellan. There's not many who get such chances in life. Especially the likes of us.'

Jamie was still living above the stables and they helped her up the stairs and followed her into the room that she would now never call home. Jamie was dressed in his best suit.

'We brought her up. She said she felt well enough but just in case we thought we'd come along. Congratulations, lad!'

Jamie shook their hands then helped Ellan into a chair; she was still pale and looked tired. 'That was good of you both. I'm to see the master in a few minutes, that's why I'm dressed up like this.'

'You'd better get used to being all dressed up. Your days of mucking out and grooming will soon be over. You'll probably never get your hands dirty ever again,' John said, good-naturedly.

'Oh, come on out of that. Ever since I was a bairn I've worked. I won't know what to do with my time. I'm glad you've come – I did want to see you both.'

'Why?'

'I never really thanked you for saving Ellan's life and I want you to tell Bert Killip and Davie Kewin that I'm going to ask the master if he can do something about their boats now, not wait until I actually get the money.'

'That's good of you, Jamie. Davie has four bairns to feed and without his boat they'll all be in a bad way soon.'

Jamie nodded solemnly. 'I know. I've not forgotten. Could you tell them for me?' He looked at Ellan and then at the two brothers.

Mat nudged his brother and John nodded, knowingly.

'Aye, we'll do that. Give you a bit of time to yourselves.'

When they'd gone Jamie took Ellan in his arms and kissed her. 'This is the first moment we've had alone since I came back.'

'I know. I was beginning to feel as though I'd lost you. What will you say to Mr Costain?'

'I don't know yet. He sent for me, to discuss things I suppose but I will ask him about the boats, that's only right and proper. Davie will need his soon if he's to go to Stornaway. And, I've a few plans of my own.'

He sat her on his knee and she leaned her head against his. 'Jamie, I'm afraid. Afraid that everything will change.'

'Things are bound to change but not between you and me, Ellan. We'll have a better life but that can only be good. We'll still love each other and then there's the bairn.'

She still looked apprehensive.

'Am I making too many plans?' he asked.

'No.'

'Is it the wedding? Oh, Ellan, I'm such a blundering fool. I've just told you what I want, I haven't asked you what you want. Is that it? Do you want to be married here, before we go?'

She had thought about that and Aunt Maud's muttered, caustic comments about how she assumed it would now be the wedding of the year, with half the island invited and certain people giving themselves airs and graces, getting above themselves and flaunting their new-found wealth in everyone's faces.

'No,' she said, 'I want to be married in New York. I want to start a new life there. If we were married here people would expect a grand wedding and I don't want that. I don't want to be accused of flaunting the money and I don't want Aunt Maud to suspect or speculate about my . . . condition and she probably would because we'd have to bring the wedding forward to November, before the boats leave, and that's only a week or two away.'

He stroked her cheek. 'We'll do whatever you want. You're the most important thing in my life. All the money in the world couldn't change that. And if you want a quiet wedding, that's what we'll have.'

'And not too grand a house? I'd feel sort of lost in a huge house like the one over yonder.'

He smiled. 'We'll have a comfortable home then.' He held her against him. 'Oh, Ellan, I really can't believe all this is happening.'

Her arms tightened around his neck. She felt the same way. Sometimes when she awoke she thought it was a dream and often in the day she had to pinch herself. Her life was changing at an incredible pace. A pace she would never have believed possible a few weeks ago.

'I want you to come to Liverpool with me. There's so much to do. I have to go back and see Mr Smollet, the solicitor, and then there's the passage to book . . .'

'Why do you want me to come?'

'You'll need clothes and so will I. Didn't I promise you a new wardrobe?'

'But I thought I'd leave that until I got to New York.'

'I want you to have it now. You'll be travelling first class, you'll be a lady, Ellan. My fiancée, as the French say.'

'Aunt Maud isn't going to like that.'

'From now on she doesn't have much choice.'

'I'm still living with her, Jamie,' she reminded him.
'But not for long.'

They were interrupted by Lizzie calling up to Jamie
that he'd better get a move on. The master didn't like to
be kept waiting as he was a busy man.

'Go and sit in the kitchen with Lizzie and then I'll
take you home and I can tell you what the master said.'

The library of Glentrammon faced the lawns and
gardens and was an imposing room. Its walls were lined
with leather-bound books in glass cases and its array of
small, stuffed birds and animals beneath glass-domed
cases, heavy moss-green curtains and matching carpet
made it appear gloomy. The leather chesterfield, button-
backed chairs and dark furniture, devoid of all lace mats
and antimacassars, made it a very masculine room. On
the one previous occasion that Jamie had been there, he
had been impressed and as he glanced around he thought
with a sense of incredulous wonder that he could now
afford to have a room like this.

Thomas Costain sat at his desk hastily finishing what
looked like a letter, but he indicated that Jamie sit while
he completed the task. Jamie sat on the edge of a slippery
leather chair.

'I sent for you, Jamie, because we have a lot to
discuss.'

'Yes, sir, and I'd appreciate any advice you can offer
me.'

The older man nodded slowly. 'Have you any definite
plans?'

'I have to go to Liverpool again, sir. There are the
arrangements to be made for me to travel to America.'

'I assumed that would be the case, so I am letting you

go as from this moment. No notice will need to be given, this is an exceptional situation.' Exceptional indeed, he thought. The young man sitting facing him with such an earnest look on his face was now, or would shortly be, as wealthy if not wealthier than himself, and Thomas Costain had not made his own fortune by missing opportunities. 'So, what plans do you have?'

'I would like to take Ellan to Liverpool, sir. We are to be married in New York but she will need suitable clothes for the journey. I will go out first and get all the legal matters settled, and find a house, then she will follow me.'

'You'll need money for the fares, her clothes and suitable attire for yourself.' Jamie nodded. Thomas Costain pushed the letter across the desk. 'This is a letter to my bankers giving you the right to draw whatever sum you will need from my account. You could say it's a temporary loan.'

'Thank you, sir. It's very generous of you.'

His former employer grunted. 'You mentioned advice?'

Jamie's expression became perplexedly serious. 'Mr Smollet informed me that there were shares and bonds as well as money and property. I know nothing about such things.'

'That I can advise you on. Get Smollet to contact the American lawyers and ask them to let me have a portfolio of all the assets. Stocks and bonds are a form of gambling and the secret of success is knowing when to buy and when to sell.'

Jamie looked bewildered but Thomas Costain smiled. 'There are brokers who know all about these things, it's their business to, and I suggest you get one. Probably your uncle used the services of a reputable firm, so contact them.' He leaned back in his chair and pressed the finger-tips of both hands together, as though in prayer. 'Some of your capital you may wish to invest here.'

'Here?' Jamie echoed.

'In the Steam Packet Company. It's expanding and developing very quickly as the tourist potential grows. You may even think about investing in some property here – an hotel for instance? It would be a link with the island.'

The idea appealed to Jamie. 'I could do that, sir?'

'Indeed you could. They are investments that I could handle for you.'

'Then I'll do it. I know things will be safe in your hands.'

'Good. Now, about the American property. Once you get established, get a good surveyor to have a look at it all and ask him for his valuation and advice. It may be worth selling some of it, if it needs major repairs or renovations. Ask about its location, whether its value and marketability will increase or decrease. Too much property can be a drain on your resources, if it's not in an area where it's going to increase in value.'

Jamie was having difficulty absorbing all this. He wasn't a businessman and he didn't have Mr Costain's astute mind but he nodded sagely. 'Er, there was one other thing, sir.'

'Yes?'

'You probably heard that Ellan was nearly drowned?'

'I did. All women are capable of being fools,' but his smile belied his barbed words.

'Two boats were lost that day and I'd like to replace them. Neither of the men can afford to be without their livelihood.'

'Very commendable. Leave it to me. No need for you to worry. I'll get someone on it today. Now, what I'm going to say may appear to be a little over cautious, but that accident has made me think.' Seeing Jamie's bemused expression Thomas Costain continued, 'I think it would be wise for you to make a Will.'

'A Will?' Jamie echoed.

The older man nodded sagely. 'You'll be travelling a long way lad, across water. Oh, there's nothing really to worry about, not on those huge floating palaces like the *Mauretania* and *Lusitania*. Safe as houses they are. Unsinkable.'

Jamie remembered the size of the liners he'd seen in Liverpool. 'Can you help me, sir? I wouldn't know how to go about setting out a Will.'

Thomas Costain drew a sheet of paper towards him and began to write. 'There's no need for all the "heretofores" and "party of the third party" and all the other legal jargon. Just plain, simple and explicit. Who is to be the main beneficiary?' Jamie looked blank. 'Who do you want the money to go to?'

'Ellan. I want her to have everything.'

His former employer finished writing and pushed the paper over for Jamie to read. 'I James Corlett, being of sound mind do bequeath to my fiancée, Ellan Vannin, all my monies, property and shareholdings, unconditionally.'

'I reckon that covers it all.'

'You sign it and Mary and I will witness it. It's just a precaution, that's all. Soon you'll be a man of property and you must keep all your affairs in order, so you might as well start now.'

As Mr Costain rang for his daughter, Jamie remembered George Vannin's Will that had condemned Ellan to an austere and often miserable life. 'I don't want Ellan to know about the Will, sir. I don't want her to worry. You see, her pa left a sort of Will and if she knows she'll fret and imagine that something is going to happen to me as well. It won't but I don't want to worry her.'

Before Thomas Costain could answer, Mary entered the room and smiled at them both.

'Mary, I want you to witness this Will Jamie has made. Purely a precaution,' he added, seeing the smile fade from his daughter's face.

Mary, too, was remembering George Vannin's Will. 'Does Ellan know about this, Jamie?'

'No, miss, and I don't want her to.'

Mary nodded as she briefly scanned the few lines of writing then added her signature beneath that of her father. 'I think that's very wise, Jamie,' she said firmly, handing the pen to her father.

Mr Costain replaced the pen in the inkstand with a grunt of satisfaction. 'I'll keep it here if you wish,' he offered, thinking that should the worst happen, he would in effect be in control of both Ellan's and Maggie's share of the fortune. After all, what did two naive women know about business?

'I'd appreciate that, I really would. And thank you for all your advice, sir.' Jamie stood up. He felt uneasy sitting in the master's presence. Old habits die hard, he thought wryly. He supposed he would always think of Mr Costain as the master.

Thomas Costain also stood up and extended his hand. 'Good luck to you, lad. You've been a good servant and in that respect I'm sorry to lose you, but think on my advice and don't squander your money.'

Jamie grasped his hand. 'I will, sir, and thank you for everything you've done for me and for our Maggie.'

'Maggie will be well looked after. She's asked me to take charge of her share and to invest it as I see fit. She can live very comfortably off the interest alone.'

'That's a relief to me. I'd not want the responsibility of that, too, I've enough to contend with.'

Thomas Costain watched him leave and then shook his head. He doubted if the lad had understood half he'd said. Still, he'd the promise of investment in the shipping line and the string of new hotels that were planned and he knew young Corlett wouldn't go back on his word. He was an honest lad if none too worldly-wise. 'A fool and his money are soon parted,' he muttered as he returned to his business affairs. Corlett would do well if he hung on to his fortune for five years, surrounded as he would be by the sharks of the business strata of New York city.

It was the first time that Ellan and Lizzie had had the chance of a chat for months. Since she'd turned Andrew Quirk down Lizzie had stayed well away from the croft and the village, for her ma had been scathing in her comments and they'd had angry words over the affair. Ellan, knowing Aunt Maud's dislike of Lizzie and the entire Killip family had also kept her distance. She found Lizzie in the kitchen. Cook was doing the menus with Mrs Portree and it was Bessie's half day off.

Lizzie eyed Ellan a little warily, wondering if she'd changed.

'Hullo, Lizzie. We haven't seen much of each other lately, have we? I'm sorry about your pa's boat, I really am.'

Lizzie sat down at the table. 'I'm sorry, too. He's been like a bear with a sore head. What got into you?'

'I don't know. I just didn't think. It was the shock of Jamie going off like that . . .' She hoped Lizzie would believe her, she didn't want her asking awkward questions.

Lizzie nodded with understanding. 'What's he seeing the master about?'

'Mr Costain sent for him but I know he is going to ask about getting the boats replaced. He wants me to go to Liverpool with him, to buy some clothes and book our passages.'

'On your own? Just the two of you?'

Ellan's brows rushed together in a frown. Lizzie had a point. Aunt Maud wouldn't let her go unchaperoned. No amount of money would make her waive the strict formalities and, as she'd pointed out, Ellan was still her responsibility until she was wed. Neither would Aunt Maud go with her, she was certain of that. No matter how much she might wish to go, she would never let anyone have the satisfaction of thinking she was in the least bit interested in Jamie Corlett's windfall.

'Lizzie, Aunt Maud won't come with us, I know she won't, so it's no use me asking her. Will you come?'

'Me?'

'I'll have to have someone.'

'But how will I get the time off and where will I find the money?'

'Jamie will see to the money and do you think Miss Mary would let you have a day or two?'

Lizzie had never been off the island in her entire life and the prospect of a few days in Liverpool with its shops and theatres was a chance she wasn't going to miss. 'I'll ask her. Bessie's not too bad now, maybe she could manage for a day or so in my place. Oh, Ellan, it must be wonderful to have so much money. Just think, you'll never have to work again in your life. You'll have people to wait on you.'

'Stop it, Lizzie! Oh, sometimes I wish things had stayed the same. All I wanted was to marry Jamie and have a home of my own for when . . .' Her words petered out, she'd almost let it slip.

'You must be mad, Ellan Vannin. I'd swap places with you any day!' Lizzie's mind was racing ahead, formulating plans. She wouldn't waste her time in Liverpool. She'd have a good look round and see what kind of houses there were and she'd ask about places for parlour maids. She was glad now she had refused Andrew Quirk. Perhaps this was a new beginning for her as well. 'I know Miss Mary will agree, I just know it, once I've explained to her about your Aunt Maud. She knows what a tartar she is and what kind of a life you've had with her and she likes you, Ellan. She kept that little pot you gave her. Once the jam was eaten she had me wash out the pot, then she replaced the cover and it's on her dressing table. I dust it every day. She wouldn't have kept it if she didn't like you, now would she?'

Ellan was surprised and touched that Mary Costain had thought so much of her simple gift and an idea occurred to her. 'Lizzie, do you think it would be very forward of me if I bought her something in Liverpool? Do you think she'd take offence, think I was showing off?'

'Not if you don't buy anything flashy or vulgar, she won't. She doesn't like flashy things, she told me so.'

'Then it will be something simple but . . . genteel.'

Lizzie smiled to herself. Ellan and her big words. Well, soon she'd be in the right sort of company to use them.

Chapter Eight

I T WAS TOO COLD to stand on the deck of *L'il Daisy* for long, but both Ellan and Lizzie had wanted to watch the island grow smaller in the distance, neither of them having left it before. Mary Costain had given her permission for Lizzie to accompany Ellan and Jamie, after Lizzie had explained the situation.

Young Bessie had been elevated for two days to the position of parlour maid and was puffed up with pride and determination not to miss her chance of permanent promotion, should the occasion arise.

The choice of ship had been unintentional, it was the only steam packet leaving that day, but Jamie had laughed and said, 'There's something for you. Your first long journey on your own ship!'

'It's not *my* ship, it belongs to the Company and always has done.'

'It could be, Ellan. I intend to buy shares in the Company. Mr Costain advised me to invest and I'm going to.'

The biting north wind tugged at her hat and her hair

and made her shiver. She clung to Jamie's arm as the little steamer rolled and pitched in the heavy swell. The memory of the great walls of water that had borne down and nearly drowned her was in the forefront of her mind and she shivered again. 'Jamie, I'm frightened. Can we go down to the saloon? I don't like the sea when it's like this.'

He placed his arm protectively around her shoulder. 'We'll be quite safe, Ellan. You know *L'il Daisy*'s reputation. She always makes it to port no matter how bad the weather.' But seeing her fear-filled eyes and feeling her shiver, he guided her towards the stairway. Lizzie, he noticed, was looking rather green, despite her attempts to hide it. But the trip didn't take long and he knew they were both excited about it in their different ways.

The wind had abated a little and the sun struggled from behind ragged, grey clouds as they passed the bar light and entered the Mersey and they went up on deck for their first sight of Liverpool.

Lizzie gripped the rail and gasped as the waterfront came into view. The magnificent buildings at the pierhead, some still being constructed, were unlike anything she had ever imagined and running the whole length of the docks were ships of all sizes. Beyond them were streets and streets of houses.

'Oh, Ellan. Isn't it grand!'

Ellan's gaze was following Lizzie's and she, too, was staggered by the size and grandeur of the city and by the size of some of the ships. *L'il Daisy* seemed like a toy boat in comparison to the huge, towering hull of the *Mauretania* which overshadowed them as they weaved in and out between tugs and ferries.

Jamie smiled at them both. 'And they say New York is

bigger than all this. That there are tenements taller than the Liver Buildings.'

Lizzie looked positively envious but Ellan looked alarmed. 'Bigger,' she murmured.

'Yes, but don't forget you'll have me with you.'

She turned her face upwards towards him and smiled. Yes, she'd have him beside her and she could face anything.

They booked into a small, faded, genteel hotel on the lower slopes of Brownlow Hill and after they'd washed and had a cup of tea, Jamie shepherded them aboard the tram. He was going to Castle Street to the offices of Smollet, Smollet & Woodhouse. Ellan and Lizzie were going to Church Street, as recommended by their hostess, just to window shop. Tomorrow Ellan would buy her new wardrobe and then they would all go to the offices of the Cunard Shipping Company.

Ellan and Lizzie had recovered from the journey and as they walked down Church Street they were mesmerized by the size of the shops and the selection of goods in the window displays. They were mainly department stores but also a few select dress shops and a very large millinery establishment.

'Oh, Lizzie, I won't be able to make up my mind. There's so much to choose from.'

'And we haven't seen half the shops yet. Mrs Palin at the hotel said we should go to Bold Street for the really elegant shops; it's like Bond Street in London and the prices are just as high, too, so she informed me. Of course real ladies still have their own dressmakers,' she finished with a knowing air.

'I feel as though I've been transported to another world. I feel like Cinderella and that by midnight it will all disappear.' Ellan laughed as she remembered that John had once said something like that to her.

'Well, it won't. Oh, Ellan, I do envy you,' Lizzie sighed, and she meant it. Her fare and the hotel had been paid for by Jamie and she only had a few shillings of her own, but she would enjoy helping Ellan choose clothes.

'I'm not going to buy dozens of things.'

Lizzie was incredulous. 'Why not?'

Ellan was about to say it would be a waste of money with her waistline already thickening, but she shrugged. 'You can only wear one dress at a time, Lizzie.'

'But you'll need lots of things for the journey; day dresses, tea dresses, evening dresses. People travelling first class dress up for dinner. And shoes and hats and gloves and underwear.' Lizzie was enjoying herself, visualizing an orgy of spending.

'No I won't. Just a couple of dresses for day, perhaps a nice walking suit and one evening dress. Oh, I'll feel such a fool with all those people. I won't know what to say or how to act. Maybe it would be better if I didn't go first class.'

'You can't do that. Ellan, you've got to realize you're rich now and you can put all those long words to good use at last.'

'I'm not rich, Jamie is,' Ellan said firmly.

'It's the same thing. Shall we look for a wedding dress? I wish you were going to get wed at home. Everyone would be green with envy, especially your Aunt Maud, the miserable, old besom!'

'That's exactly why I'm not getting married on the

131

island. I don't want people to be green with envy. I feel it would cheapen the whole ceremony.'

'Well, if it were me, I wouldn't care,' Lizzie answered vehemently, pulling Ellan towards a very exclusive-looking shop called Bon Marché.

After supper they sat for a while in the comfortable little parlour of the hotel until Lizzie discreetly said she had some things to attend to and left them alone. Lizzie wanted to speak to Mrs Palin about the prospects of work in Liverpool.

The hotel had few guests at that time of year. The only other person they'd seen at dinner was a middle-aged, florid-faced man who their hostess had described as a travelling salesman, a very quiet and well mannered person who had been coming to stay with her for nearly five years. He had nodded pleasantly as they'd left the dining room and hadn't been seen since.

'I don't want you to tire yourself out, Ellan,' Jamie said.

She smiled at him. 'I'm a bit weary but don't fuss. I'm stronger than I look, Jamie. If we'd have stayed at home and lived as we had planned to then I'd have had to work, wouldn't I? What did Mr Smollet say?'

'He just confirmed the arrangements and agreed with what Mr Costain advised me to do. Tomorrow I'm going to book our passages. He agreed that it would be wise for me to go out first. I told him I wanted you to follow as soon as possible. He suggested January and I agreed.'

She looked alarmed and lowered her voice. 'As late as that! I'll be showing by then.'

He took her hands in his. 'Early January, Ellan. Mr Smollet thinks I should go about 2 December as it will take until then for his letters to reach Uncle's lawyers. Then, by the time I arrive, they should have everything in hand. I've asked them to try to find me a house.' Seeing the consternation in her eyes he added, 'Nothing too big but in a nice area. Tomorrow shall we go and choose your wedding ring?'

She nodded firmly. There had been little time to really think about the bairn until now and she wondered how she would hide her increasing girth until the New Year, but his suggestion to buy the ring somehow calmed her. It put everything in perspective and made her feel secure.

'Mr Smollet has recommended a jewellers called Browns in London Road. We'll go there first thing then I'll go to the tailors while you and Lizzie set off on your own and we'll meet up in the afternoon and go to the shipping offices.'

Ellan looked bemused. 'Everything is falling into place as though it were the most normal thing to do. I still can't believe it.'

'It *is* the most normal thing to do, now.'

'I'll miss you.'

'I'll miss you, too, but it won't be for long.'

'I'll be on my own at Christmas and so will you, and I wanted it to be so special.'

He took her in his arms. 'I know you did, but just think, Ellan, next Christmas we'll be a family. A close, comfortably-off family. We'll make up for it next year. At least you'll have John and Mat and Lizzie. That will be better than sitting in some hotel room which is probably how I'll spend the holiday.'

She was instantly contrite. 'Oh, Jamie, I'm sorry. I'm getting so selfish.'

He kissed her. 'That's something you'll never be, and I love you for that, too.'

She slept well that night, worn out by the exertions of the day, and the following morning she awoke to find Lizzie staring out of the window.

'It's raining,' Lizzie commented, morosely. 'Raining cats and dogs. We'll be soaked!'

Ellan raised herself up on one elbow and blinked. 'We'll get a tram or an omnibus, it won't be too bad.'

Lizzie brightened. 'We could take a cab.'

'We'll get the tram,' Ellan said firmly, climbing out of bed.

Lizzie pouted. No-one could accuse Ellan of throwing Jamie's money about, or Mr Costain's money as in fact it really was.

The same thought occurred to her many times during the day. While Jamie and Ellan went into Browns, which wasn't far from the hotel, she had sat in Lyon's Tea Rooms on the opposite side of the road and had watched the people hurrying past beneath a sea of umbrellas. She had been appalled at the sight of so much poverty. Poverty wasn't strange to her but the type of poverty she knew wasn't so blatant or obvious at first glance. At home there was always some token effort to try to disguise it. Here it was different. There seemed to be hundreds of ragged, waif-like children, shivering in dirty, sodden rags, their feet bare, who accosted the passers-by begging or trying to sell matches and kindling wood or offering to run errands or carry heavy bags or parcels. Nor had she seen so many public houses or taverns in her life, or so many drunks. No, Liverpool wasn't all grandeur and wealth, she thought as she sipped her tea.

The ring Ellan chose was of plain twenty-two carat gold. When she tried it on she experienced a feeling of truly belonging engulf her. He saw the look in her eyes and smiled as she reluctantly took off the ring and gave it back to the assistant to be boxed and wrapped.

The man commented on her silver ring as she slipped it back on her finger. 'That's very unusual. I've never seen one like it before and I've seen hundreds of rings in my time.'

'It wasn't very expensive but it is special,' she answered and for the first time in weeks she thought of Andrew and she wondered where he was. She would like something to leave him, to remind him of her for she'd be gone before he returned – if he returned. 'Could you copy it?' she asked the assistant.

'Yes. We have a stock of silver rings and it could be engraved.'

Jamie looked at her puzzled, but she laid a hand on his arm. 'I want to leave Andrew something. We used to be very close and I'll be gone before he comes back.'

Jamie nodded his agreement. 'Could you do that today? We have to leave tonight.'

'No problem about that, sir. It will be ready at four o'clock. What name is it?'

Jamie gave his name, paid for the rings and then escorted Ellan across the busy road and into the tea rooms.

Lizzie looked up eagerly, she had been getting bored.

'Take care of her, Lizzie, and don't go spending too much of my . . . er Mr Costain's money,' Jamie grinned.

Lizzie pulled a face. 'Fat chance of that. If it were me I'd probably bankrupt you, but Ellan is turning into a proper little penny pincher.'

Jamie laughed at them both and kissing Ellan on the cheek went back into the crowded street, heading for the tailors.

'I've been sitting here and watching what fashionable women are wearing, so I've a good idea of what you'll need.'

'You can call me penny-pinching, mean, a skinflint and anything else you can think of, Lizzie, but I'm not going to buy trunks full of clothes.'

'One trunk then,' Lizzie urged as they left the warmth of the tea rooms and went out into the cold, damp street.

Ellan refused to go into any of the shops in Bold Street, dismissing Lizzie's protests, saying she wasn't paying a fraction of what they were charging. But when they got to George Henry Lee & Company in Basnett Street, Lizzie pushed her unceremoniously through the door held open by a liveried commissionaire.

With the help and encouragement of two sales assistants she persuaded Ellan to buy a walking suit and an evening dress. The suit was made of heather-coloured tweed, its jacket single-breasted with wide revers, trimmed with black braid. The sleeves were puffed at the shoulder but narrowed at the elbow and the cuffs were trimmed with the same braid which also adorned the hem of the skirt. Ellan had dismissed one evening dress over which Lizzie had gone into raptures of joy. A dress of fine, cream wool decorated with gold brocade around its high neck and wide sleeves. The dress she settled for, and which she told Lizzie would be her wedding dress, was of pale green watered brocade. A large bow formed the only decoration across the bosom and above this rose a high-collared fichu of ecru lace. The sleeves were full to the elbow and then tightened with broad inserts of lace. A small hat decorated with a green ribbon bow and tinted ostrich feathers was bought to complete the ensemble and everyone was effusive in their praise. Ellan, however, refused to be tempted by anything else.

The remainder of her wardrobe she bought at Frisby Dyke's in Lord Street. She paid twenty-five shillings for a day dress in cornflower blue *foulé* and another of Scotch Homespun in small checks of black and white and a black Merveilleux walking costume with a long jacket. She was tempted by a cream and brown grenadine afternoon dress, but resisted firmly. With two hats, four pairs of gloves, two pairs of button boots and the underclothes, she felt she had been wildly extravagant as she and Lizzie struggled up Lord Street to meet Jamie by the Town Hall.

She looked at him shamefaced but he only laughed and kissed her. 'I think we'd better get a cab to the pierhead. We'll not get all those parcels and boxes on the tram.'

Jamie asked Lizzie to wait with the cab and the baggage while he and Ellan went into the offices of the Cunard Shipping Company. The room was luxuriously carpeted and the counter that ran along one whole side was of polished rosewood. The walls were covered with prints of the ships, past and present, and small, brocade-covered chairs were set at intervals for the comfort of prospective passengers. Jamie settled her into one of these and then approached the clerk at the counter.

Sitting watching him, Ellan suddenly realized that this moment was precious: this really was the start of their new life and nothing she had experienced over the past weeks had had such an impact on her. It was really happening: the tickets were being booked, a whole new chapter was opening up before her. It was all real, it wasn't a dream any more. Jamie turned and pointed to her and the smile she gave him was so radiant that even the bespectacled clerk drew in his breath with admiration.

With all the formalities finalized, Jamie returned to her side holding a large white envelope. 'That's it. It's all settled now. I sail on the *Lusitania* on 3 December and you sail on 6 January on the *Mauretania*, first class.'

She wanted to throw her arms around him and kiss him, instead she touched the envelope almost reverently. 'So this is it, Jamie, our new life,' she said with a catch in her voice.

'Yours, mine and the bairn's. You won't regret it, Ellan, ever!'

They collected the rings from Browns and she bought a china perfume atomizer for Mary Costain. It was pretty, decorated with hand-painted flowers but not gaudy or overly expensive. For Lizzie she bought a gold-mounted cameo brooch for, as she said to Jamie, Lizzie was the only friend she'd ever had. She gave it to her before they left the hotel to go down to the pierhead to board the *Douglas* for the return trip home.

Lizzie's eyes filled with tears as she hugged Ellan. 'Oh, it's beautiful! Beautiful! Thank you, both of you. I wish I was going with you, I really do. I'll miss you so much.'

'I'll miss you, too, Lizzie. Maybe one day you could come out and see us?'

'I may just do that. I was asking Mrs Palin about jobs

here and she said there are a lot of houses in Toxteth Park that have six or seven servants and I could really get on if I got into a good household and I could save my fare . . .'

'But I could send you the money, Lizzie. Will you write to me?'

'Oh, Ellan, you know I was never much good at that, not like you.'

'You could write a short note from time to time, promise me you will?'

Lizzie nodded her agreement as she packed her few clothes into her carpet bag. 'I've never said this to anyone before, Ellan, but now I'm glad I turned Andrew down. I knew I wanted more from life. I didn't want to hurt him and I never wanted him to go off like that, on a whaler of all things, but I felt . . . I felt he didn't really love me. Not the way Jamie loves you and I know I didn't love him. If I had I wouldn't have even hesitated, would I?'

'No, you wouldn't, Lizzie.'

'I know you were close to him, Ellan, and I think . . . I think it was you he really cared for.'

Ellan turned away. 'He didn't care for me in that way. I was like a sister to him, nothing more. I even tried to make him change his mind about going away.'

'What did he say?'

'That he wanted to travel, see more of life, I suppose. Like you do.'

Lizzie grimaced. 'Aye, but there's better ways of doing it than signing on for months in the North Atlantic.'

'Maybe when he comes back he'll decide to go somewhere warmer, more exotic. Or maybe he'll stay home. Aunt Maud would like that.'

'She'd like them all to stay home so she can keep them

under her thumb. Are you going to wear your new walking suit to go home in?'

Ellan shook her head. 'No. I'm saving it. I'm saving them all.'

'It's probably best. She'd only complain you were showing off, trying to make her look shabby. I've never met such a narrow-minded, bitter old scold and she's getting worse. Still, in a month's time you'll be packing up and leaving.'

Ellan looked thoughtful. 'In some ways I'll be sorry.'

'Sorry? What about?'

'Leaving Pa in the churchyard, leaving my roots.'

'Oh, don't be such a misery,' Lizzie cried and Ellan smiled as she heard Jamie shouting to them that the cab was waiting.

Maud looked surprised when Ellan arrived home. She had expected to see Ellan dressed up to the nines and with a ridiculous concoction of a hat perched on her head, but the girl was wearing the clothes she had left in.

'You're back then,' Maud said curtly, her eyes going to the boxes and parcels that Jamie was carrying. The finery must have cost a pretty penny just the same, she thought, judging by the fancy names on the boxes. 'Put them down there on the settle. She can take them upstairs herself,' she instructed.

Jamie did as she bade him but then he turned to face Maud. 'Everything is settled, Mrs Quirk. I will be leaving on 3 December and Ellan will follow on 6 January, from Liverpool of course.'

'Indeed! I hope it keeps fine for you both. Now I've work to do even if other folk haven't.'

Welcome home, Ellan thought. Lizzie was right, she must be mad to think she would miss the place.

She followed Jamie out into the yard. He was now living with Maggie and her husband Harry and she knew she was welcome there. 'Will you come with me to Glentrammon tomorrow? I want to give Miss Mary the perfume bottle.'

'If you like, but don't you think it might be better if you gave it her just before you leave?'

'You're right. It would be best. I'd better go inside now and help with the supper. I have to live with *her* until I go.'

He kissed her and then strode off in the direction of the stile and when he was out of sight she turned and went inside the house.

After supper was over and the pots washed and hung up and Maud had settled herself by the fire with her knitting, Ellan went up to her room. She hadn't unpacked her new clothes nor would she. She opened the lid of the battered old seaman's trunk that she called her Hope chest and drew out all the articles she had so lovingly collected over the months. She wouldn't need them now, she thought a little sadly, musing on the enjoyment and satisfaction she'd experienced when she'd bought them; remembering how hard she'd worked and saved for the few pence they'd cost individually. Most of them she would leave for Aunt Maud but a couple of the ornaments she would give to Lizzie. Lizzie would like them and they would remind her of her promise to write. It seemed discourteous to send back the lamps and linen to Miss Mary, but Aunt Maud wouldn't use them on principle. Maybe Mrs Killip would like them.

She lifted out the patchwork quilt and spread it between her hands. So much work, so much hope and love had gone into its making that she couldn't part with it. She'd keep it as a reminder of her old life, her old home. Each square of material would have a happy memory for her: days in Douglas when the sun had been warm and the narrow streets had been crowded with people; this piece of purple would remind her of the shadows of Peel Castle; this square of red, long cosy winter evenings when she'd sat and sewed by the fire, listening to the wind whistling around the cottage; this piece of bluish grey, the colour of the sea after a storm; and this one of bright yellow was spring when the common grazing was full of buttercups and the hedges were bursting with new life and the gorse had blossomed on the heathland. Every square a memory, particularly of this past year.

She held it against her cheek. She couldn't part with it, there was too much of her bound up in it. She'd probably own much finer bed-coverings; it would probably never be used for the purpose for which it was intended, but she'd keep it. Maybe she'd wrap the bairn in it, to try to impart through it some of her heritage, for her baby would be born an American citizen. Manx blood would run in its veins, but her son or daughter would be the child of a newer and younger land than this island after which its mother had been named.

Chapter Nine

⸻

THE WHOLE OF PEEL turned out to see Jamie off. Ellan, Maggie and Harry were to go with him on the train, changing at St John's for Ramsey. It was a clear crisp December evening with a moderate breeze and therefore no frost and a carnival atmosphere prevailed.

Thomas and Mary Costain sat in their carriage outside the station, a little apart from the throng, and before he left Jamie went over to them.

'Good luck, Jamie. It's a fair night, you should have a smooth crossing,' Mary said pleasantly.

Mr Costain stretched out his hand. 'Good luck, lad, and don't worry, your interests will be well served here by me. Just get yourself a good broker and surveyor.'

'I will, sir, and thank you for everything – both of you.'

'Come on, Jamie, lad. Get a move on or they'll go without you!' Harry called, and pushing his way through the crowd Jamie waved his hat to all his friends and neighbours, disappointed only that the fishing fleet was not yet home.

On the journey he held Ellan's hand tightly and although she felt dejected at the thought of being parted from him, she could feel his excitement. In five short weeks she would join him and they would all be waving her off.

There was no reception committee at Ramsey; the wind had become blustery and it was cold. Ellan shivered as the blast cut through her coat and Maggie instinctively put her arm around her.

'Don't fret, lass, he'll be all right and soon it'll be your turn.'

'I'm all right, Maggie, I'm just cold.'

'Let's walk down to the jetty, they can manage the luggage between them.'

The wind was even stronger on the exposed jetty where they were loading the last of the cargo aboard *L'il Daisy*. They couldn't wait until she sailed as they would miss the last train, but she would see Jamie safely aboard. He'd booked a cabin or berth as it was called, for it was a night crossing. She pulled her coat closer to her, gazing upwards to where the moon's face was hidden by wisps of straggling cloud, like silver-grey tresses of hair.

'That's everything stowed,' Harry said, puffing slightly. 'We'd best get back to the station. Don't want to be stranded here all night.'

Maggie hugged her brother. 'Take care, Jamie. Don't you forget to write and let us know what's what.'

'Do you think I'm going to do a flit with your half, Maggie?'

'Get off with you, our Jamie, I know you better than that. Goodbye and good luck!' She hugged him again. 'Come on, Harry, let's give them a few minutes together.'

They stood on the deck in the shadow of the wheelhouse and Jamie took her in his arms. 'It won't be long, Ellan. The time will fly, you'll see. Promise me you'll take care of yourself?'

'I will. Oh, Jamie, I love you so much!'

'And I'll always love you, Ellan. You've got your ticket and the money?'

Instantly Ellan's arms locked behind his head and she sought his lips, kissing him as though she never wanted to let him go. When he at last drew away he saw the tears on her cheeks. She nodded, the lump in her throat making speech difficult.

He caught her chin in his hand and tilted her face upwards, gazing down into her dark eyes. 'I'll be waiting for you, Ellan. I'll be on the pier when the *Mauretania* docks and then our life will really begin. You'd better go now, love, you'll miss the train.'

She clung to his lips again until he gently prised himself away then led her to the gangway and helped her off, handing her into the care of one of the deck hands.

The tears threatened to blind her and make her lose her footing and she grasped the man's arm tightly.

'He'll be all right, lass. The wind's freshening and the glass is falling but the old girl will take it all in her stride.'

She looked at him in alarm and in the dim light he saw her frightened face and was sorry he'd spoken. 'Don't you worry none. *L'il Daisy* will get him safely to Liverpool. What's your name?'

She looked back to where Jamie stood waving to her. 'Ellan Vannin.'

A deep rumble of a laugh issued from his throat. 'Well, that beats all. Named after her, were you? So why the worried face? You can't get a better omen than that. We're a superstitious people, we Manxmen, but that's an omen of good luck if ever I saw one.'

She smiled. She supposed he was right. She raised her hand in a last wave, wishing she could have stayed with Jamie until he sailed, then she turned and headed for the station.

Harry walked back to the croft with Ellan, along the dark lane where the leafless branches of the trees rustled and clicked as the wind rushed through them. She felt tired and down-hearted.

'There's a light on, she's waited up for you.'

She wished Aunt Maud hadn't. She wanted to be on her own. She didn't want to have to listen to Aunt Maud's tart comments about the foolishness of going all the way to Ramsey and back at this time of night, keeping folk up. But for once Maud didn't complain. She put a mug of hot milk before Ellan, told her to blow out the lamps before she went upstairs and retired to bed.

Ellan drank the milk, though she didn't really want it, lit her candle and blew out the lamps and went to bed. Some time during the night she awoke, drenched in sweat, the bedsheet twisted around her. She had been reliving the nightmare of the day she had nearly drowned. She'd been twisting and turning trying to free herself of her heavy skirts that were dragging her down. Salt water was in her eyes, her nose and her mouth and she couldn't breathe. She sat bolt upright and passed a shaking hand over her damp forehead. The salt on her face was from her own tears and the clothes she had been so desperately trying to rid herself of, were the bedclothes. She was shivering. She ran her hands through her tangled hair and lay down, pulling the sheet and blankets over her. It had been a dream, just a dream brought on by exhaustion and her emotions. She turned her face towards the tiny window. She could just see the stars and she wondered whether Jamie was still awake, or was he sound asleep and dreaming of the future that lay ahead for him.

As the S.S. *Ellan Vannin* ploughed her way towards the mainland with a full complement of crew, passengers and cargo, the weather changed. As the north-westerly wind increased to the force of a howling gale, there were a few jokes about how green around the gills some of the passengers would be when they reached Liverpool.

The little ship battled on as she'd always done until she reached the mouth of the Mersey. The gale had increased to force twelve, whipping the waves into gigantic combers twenty-four feet high. She passed the Bar Light at seven o'clock as the first fingers of winter dawn crept across the sky, but within sight of Liverpool and safety, she foundered. The mountainous seas broke her little back and she sank with the loss of all souls.

It was nearly noon when Thomas Costain himself came to the croft. Maud greeted him with a scowl, her hands on her hips, as he rode into the yard.

'Is Ellan at home, Mrs Quirk?'

'And why should I tell you if she is?' All the anger that had simmered over the years since Amos's death, burst forth at the sight of the man astride his horse, his hat still on his head. 'You've no right here.'

'I'm not here to argue that point. My daughter wanted to come but I thought I should be the one to bring such tidings.'

Despite her anger Maud shivered. 'What tidings?' Wherever this man went, only death followed.

'Where is Ellan?'

'Here.' Ellan stood in the doorway of the cottage, her old shawl thrown around her shoulders.

Thomas Costain dismounted, bareheaded now, and Maud moved aside. 'Ellan, I don't know what to say. How to tell you . . .' For the first time in his life he was lost for words.

Her hand went to her throat. Jamie. There was something wrong. 'Where is he? What's happened?' Dreams turn into nightmares – where had she heard that before and why did she think of it now? 'Where is he?'

'We've only just heard, Ellan. The *Ellan Vannin*, your namesake, went down in the Mersey estuary early this morning. Everyone was lost.'

He would have given his entire fortune at that very moment to be somewhere else. Her huge, dark eyes widened and the colour drained from her face. The cry formed on her lips and then, suddenly, she darted forward and before either of them could stop her, she was running across the field towards the stile.

'For the love of God, stop her! Stop her!' Maud cried, starting to run.

He laid his hand on her arm to restrain her. 'Leave her alone. Grief takes people different ways. Leave her.'

Maud turned on him like a small fury. 'You don't know her. What do your kind know about us and about grief. This is twice you've brought sorrow and despair to this house. Get out, do you hear me? Get out and leave us alone!'

He looked at her with mounting anger. This was why

148

he'd refused to let Mary come here. Well, he'd said his piece and he was truly sorry for the girl. He turned away and remounted. He was certain the poor child would get no comfort from Maud Quirk. He'd send Lizzie Killip to find Ellan.

Maud watched him go, twisting her hands together. Should she go after Ellan or should she leave her as he'd suggested. No, she'd go after her. The least she could do was to save Ellan from harming herself, that would be the worst sin of all. She wished John were here or Mat, and she was truly sorry and saddened for all the souls that had perished so close to safety . . .

She found Ellan standing at the end of the jetty, her hair blowing loose in the cold wind, her shawl clutched to her. She was taut, her face stretched in shock and disbelief, but there were no tears in her eyes.

Maud remembered those hours, years ago, when she'd felt like this, when Ellan, a child of ten, had clutched her hand. She remembered the total disbelief that preceded grief.

'Ellan, come on home now. There's nothing to be gained standing here. Come home with me.'

Ellan barely heard her. All she heard was the screeching of the gulls overhead. People said they were the souls of those lost at sea, forever drifting, crying mournfully for their loved ones. She turned as Maud pulled at her arm. 'He's not coming back, Aunt Maud. He's never coming back. He's one of them now, crying, always crying . . .'

Maud was shocked. What did the girl mean, one of them. Had the news unhinged her mind? 'Come away from here, Ellan. Come home,' she urged.

'But I'll still hear them, Aunt. I'll always hear them.'

'Who will you hear, Ellan?'

'The gulls. The wandering souls.'

Oh, dear Lord! She's gone mad, Maud thought, leading her back along the jetty. Perhaps it was only temporary, just the shock. Maybe she'd better get the doctor.

Ellan was sitting in the chair near the fire, just staring into space when Lizzie burst in without knocking. She'd been crying and her eyes were red and puffy.

'Couldn't you have knocked! What do you want? Why can't they leave us alone?' said Maud.

'She's my friend. Can't you understand that? She's my friend and he . . . was, too.'

It was the sight of Lizzie that brought the strangled cry from Ellan's throat and she rose and staggered towards Lizzie, arms outstretched, and the storm broke.

Lizzie held her tightly as the sobs shook Ellan and the tears coursed down Lizzie's own cheeks. There wasn't a dry eye at Glentrammon and when the master had returned and told them that Ellan had run off, she hadn't even waited to be told to go, she'd run straight out of the kitchen. Poor Ellan, to have so much happiness to look forward to and then to have it all snatched away. What kind of a God allowed such things to happen?

At length Ellan's sobs subsided and between them Lizzie and Maud got her to bed and Lizzie stayed with her, holding her hand as she lay with her face turned towards the wall. She couldn't think coherently, she didn't even want to think. All she wanted to do was die; there was nothing worth living for now Jamie had gone. 'I'll love you for the rest of my life, Ellan,' he'd said and now his life had ended and she wished hers had too.

When evening came Maud insisted that Lizzie go back to Glentrammon. Lizzie refused though tired and hungry but Maud was adamant, saying she would sit up with Ellan and that if she was still the same in the morning she would send for Doctor Taylor.

All night Ellan lay awake while Maud dozed, but in the morning it wasn't the doctor who came, it was John and Mat. The fishing fleet was home, but joy at their safe return was tempered by the sorrow that engulfed the whole village, the whole island.

Relief showed plainly on Maud's face. 'Try and talk to her, John, she always listened to you. She just lies there, staring at nothing, saying nothing. I know what it's like to be grief-stricken, but I've never seen it take anyone like this before!' Maud was weary and a little afraid.

'I'll try, Ma. You go and make some tea.'

Ellan was staring at the wall and John bent over and gently turned her face towards him. 'Ellan, lass, listen to me. You can't go on like this, he wouldn't want you to grieve this way. You'll only make yourself ill. Nothing I can say or do will bring him back, but you're not alone. There's grief in many a heart today, mine included. Ellan, can you hear me?'

Her head moved on the pillow and John sighed. It was a start.

'You'll have to face it, lass. Face it squarely and then, in time, you'll come to terms with it.'

'No.' The word was just audible. 'No. It's me.'

He must keep her talking. 'You, Ellan?'

'First Ma, then Pa and now . . . Jamie. He said . . . he said it was an omen.'

151

'Who said it was an omen?' He thought she was rambling.

'The man at the harbour. A good omen, he said, but it's not, it's a curse!'

'What is, Ellan? What are you trying to tell me, lass?'

She looked up into his face. 'My name, John, my name. It's not a proper name, it never has been, and it's cost me everyone I've ever . . . loved.'

'Stop that, Ellan. Don't talk such foolishness. It has nothing to do with your name. It was fate, destiny, call it what you will. Now you have to try and put it behind you. I'm not saying it will be easy but we'll all help you, lass.'

Two large tears slid down her cheeks and he felt his own heart ache for her.

'Oh, John. I loved him so much!'

He gathered her in his arms as she began to sob. 'I know you did, Ellan,' he soothed. At least this was a normal way of grieving, no more nonsense about cursed names. Best let her cry it out, but he knew it would be a long time before the pain eased.

In the days that followed she alternated between bouts of silent weeping and apathy from which no-one could rouse her. She felt dead inside and yet she wasn't, there was a new life growing within her, something they knew nothing about. She didn't care about the baby now, her bairn, as she'd always thought of it. Now it was just another burden. They all urged her to try to look forward but she couldn't, not until two days after Christmas when Mary Costain came to the croft.

John opened the door to her. 'Why, good morning, Miss Costain.'

'Good morning. How is Ellan? Lizzie tells me she is

taking it very badly so I came to see if I could help in any way.'

'Come in, miss. I think the worst is over but she just sits there. It's not been much of a Christmas.'

As Mary entered the kitchen Maud came down the stairs and her face contorted when she saw Mary. 'What's *she* come for? All they ever bring is bad news.'

'Ma, she's come to see Ellan.' The warning note in John's voice was clear for everyone to hear.

'There's nothing she can do for Ellan. If she hadn't encouraged them, letting him invite Ellan to that supper, saying they could live there, even finding lamps and things for her, it might not be so bad. I put some of the blame on you.'

'I'm sorry if that's how you feel, Mrs Quirk, but I've not come here to quarrel. May I see Ellan, please?'

John nodded before Maud had time to reply. 'Go on up, miss. You may succeed where we've failed.' Both he and Mary ignored the look Maud cast at them both.

Ellan was sitting on the bed and Mary was shocked by the change in her, although it was only to be expected. Her face was drawn, her skin putty-coloured and her eyes lustreless.

'Hullo, Ellan,' she said.

Ellan turned at the sound of her voice, and a flicker of astonishment shone in her eyes and then died.

'May I sit down?' Mary asked.

Ellan nodded and Mary sat on the bed beside her.

'Lizzie's told me how badly you've been. She's worried about you and so am I.'

'You are, miss?'

'Yes. I know it's hard, Ellan, to try to even think of

what tomorrow will bring when you've just lost someone you loved very much. I felt like that when my mother died and I was left to run a household, to cope with my own grief and that of my father and brothers. But time does heal, Ellan. What will you do now?'

'Now, miss?' Was Mary Costain so stupid that she couldn't see that her whole world lay in ruins? She had no future.

'Yes, Ellan. You still have a ticket to New York and perhaps I should have told you before, but on my father's advice, Jamie made a Will. He left everything to you. Of course none of us believed that anything like this . . . it was purely a precaution.'

Ellan stared at her in disbelief. She wasn't interested in any Will or any fortune. She didn't want to go to New York. She didn't even want to leave this tiny room. She just wanted to be left alone with her memories. 'I . . . I hadn't thought . . .'

Mary smiled. 'No, I don't suppose you have, but think about it now. You *do* have a future, Ellan, if you want it. You have your whole life ahead of you, don't waste it grieving. Jamie wouldn't have wanted that. No-one is expecting you to make such decisions yet. It's too soon, but at least try to give it some thought. Will you promise me that much, Ellan?'

Slowly Ellan moved her head in assent. She'd think about it but not now, not today, maybe tomorrow.

'Good. You're not alone Ellan, remember that. You have many friends here who care about you. Lizzie, myself, Maggie and even your aunt. She, too, has known sudden, tragic grief. Let us all help you, Ellan, don't shut us out.'

She felt weary. The world was upside down. Here was Miss Mary telling her that even Aunt Maud cared about her. 'I'll try, miss, but I'm so tired now.'

'That's all right. I'm going. I didn't intend to stay long. I just wanted to try to help, to let you know that people care. There is to be a disaster fund set up to help, and there's a Board of Trade Inquiry. The whole island grieves with you, Ellan. People *do* care.'

Ellan got to her feet. 'Thank you for coming, miss.'

'It was the least I could do, but don't forget, if there is anything at all I can do, please ask.'

When Mary had gone Ellan went and stood at the window. The bleak landscape matched her mood as did the glaucous sky and the cold, cruel sea. Did so many people really care, she wondered, or had Miss Mary only been trying to comfort her? She leaned her forehead against the cold glass of the window pane. 'Oh, Jamie! Jamie!' she murmured. She would never love again, never. He had meant everything to her and now all she had left was her grief, her memories and her child. His child. She jerked her head backwards as though she had suddenly been pulled from behind by her hair. His child! Now it would be a bastard and she would be treated little better than a whore. Despite the fortune Jamie had left her, people wouldn't countenance what she'd done. All their condolences, all their pity would evaporate when they found out. And they could be so cruel. They'd say she trapped him, that she was making certain she got her hands on that money. 'Oh, Jamie! I'm sorry, I'm sorry!' she cried softly, leaning her cheek once more against the window. She pressed her hands against the panes as though they were a conductor, forcing her thoughts inwards and they were thoughts she couldn't bear.

Her gaze fell on the ring he'd bought her. She'd never wear the gold band now. It had been in his coat pocket. She would never be Ellan Corlett, she would remain Ellan Vannin for the rest of her life.

'*Quecunque feceris stabit.*' She said the words aloud, stumbling over their difficult pronunciation. 'Whichever way you throw me, I will stand.' She straightened up and pronounced them again, more clearly, more firmly. She would stand and stand proud and his child would stand proudly, too. She'd overcome grief before. She'd picked up the pieces and gone on with her life after her pa had died. She would do it again and with more reason now. Miss Mary had been right. She *did* have a future. She knew now what she must do.

Chapter Ten

———✦———

SHE HAD LAIN AWAKE all that night and the following
morning she got up, dressed and went downstairs.
Maud was surprised but thankful to see her, yet when
Ellan reached for her coat, Maud frowned again.

'Where are you going? It's raw out there.'

'There's something I have to do, Aunt. I won't be
long.'

Maud's gaze was full of suspicion and apprehension as
Ellan closed the door behind her.

As she walked up the lane towards Glentrammon she
felt so much older, far older than her nineteen years.
And, mixed with her other emotions was shame. She
would have to tell Mary Costain about the bairn. She
didn't want Jamie's inheritance for herself, it was for the
child, so they could start afresh in a new land where no-
one would point a finger at either of them. She'd made
her plans. She'd passed the long hours of darkness
feverishly going over them in her mind. She had to see
Miss Mary and then, if all went well, Lizzie.

Mrs Portree ushered her into the small back parlour,

but there was no sign of Lizzie. Mrs Portree was kind if fussy and as soon as Ellan saw Mary's face she knew it was not going to be easy.

'Ellan! Sit down. You must be feeling better.'

'I am, miss, thank you. I've come to ask a favour of you.' She twisted her hands together nervously.

'Well, I offered, didn't I? What is it?'

'I've made up my mind to go. I can't stay here.'

'I understand, Ellan.'

Ellan hung her head. 'Begging your pardon, miss, but you don't. Not fully. Will you give me the Will for the lawyers and a letter saying who I am?'

Mary rose. 'Of course I will. I'll do it now.'

'Please, miss, let me finish! I don't want the money for myself, it's for our . . .' Oh, it was so hard. She wanted to run from the room and never have to face Mary Costain again. 'I'm having a bairn. Jamie's bairn.'

Mary sat down suddenly, her eyes widening, her cheeks slightly flushed and she appeared bereft of speech.

'If you don't feel you can give me a letter of introduction, I'll understand. I know it's a shameful thing to have to admit and believe me I am ashamed. But Jamie knew and he still wanted to marry me.' She let the words trip over themselves to cover her embarrassment and to fill the void of silence. Still Mary did not speak. 'You know what will happen to me if I stay.' Ellan was near to tears. 'I have to go. I *have* to do my best for Jamie's child. Oh, please, miss, help me?'

Mary felt the shock waves passing. She felt calmer, able to trust herself to speak. 'Jamie knew?'

'Yes. I wouldn't keep a thing like that from him. I wanted to at first. I didn't even want to believe it myself and then when he first went to Liverpool, I thought he'd gone for good. That's why I went out in Mr Killip's boat.'

Mary felt uncomfortable but she had promised her help and above all else she was practical. It would strengthen the girl's case if she were expecting. 'I'll write the letter and I'll inform them of your . . . condition. It will help if they know that there will be an heir. I'll send Lizzie down with it later – I will need to word it carefully. Have you told anyone else, Ellan?'

'No, miss. How could I?'

'Have you any money?'

'A little, but I'm afraid Mr Costain's loan may not be paid for some time.'

'Don't worry about that, Ellan.'

'Miss Mary, there's one other thing, please?'

'Yes?'

'Could the ticket be changed for a smaller ship, something cheaper?'

Mary assented. The girl would need every penny until the legalities were sorted out. She had spoken to her father about Ellan's position, should she decide to go, and he had been optimistic. She was loath to tell him of Ellan's predicament but she supposed she must. 'Shall I contact Mr Smollet, Ellan?'

'Yes, please, miss. But . . . but will you have to tell him about the bairn?'

'He is really only acting as a go-between, so it may not be necessary.' Mary hoped she didn't sound prim and disapproving. These things happened. She just wished it hadn't happened to Ellan, but then she wished that the S.S. *Ellan Vannin* had not been lost. Some things had to be borne and the best made of the ensuing misery. She rose as Ellan pulled something from her coat pocket and placed it on the table.

'I bought it for you in Liverpool, Miss Mary. I was going to save it until I left, but seeing that you've been so good, so understanding . . .'

Mary picked it up and took off the wrapping paper, revealing the perfume atomizer.

'Lizzie said you'd like it,' Ellan said shyly.

Mary smiled, a genuine smile, not a forced, formal gesture. 'I do. It's very pretty and it will always remind me of you, Ellan.'

'Thank you again for everything, Miss Mary. I don't expect I'll see you again before I go, not alone that is, but I'll never forget you.'

'Nor I you, Ellan. The day you first came here, do you remember? I thought then that you were different, that there was something about you that set you apart from the other girls in the village. You have determination, Ellan, and courage. The kind of courage I will never have. You have just proved that to me and I envy you, Ellan, strange though it may seem.'

'You envy me, miss?'

'Yes. You have the sheer guts to go out and try to make the best of your life, you always have done, ever since your father died. For that I envy you. Good luck and God go with you, Ellan Vannin.'

As Ellan turned away she saw the sparkle of tears in Mary Costain's eyes and her heart went out to her. Oh, would that she had had a mother or a sister like Mary Costain. What a terrible waste Mary's life was and the awful part was that Mary knew it, yet could do nothing to change it.

As soon as Ellan had gone Mary went in search of her father. He was in the library and about to depart to Douglas on business.

'I'm sorry to detain you but I need to speak to you urgently.'

He looked irritated. 'Make it brief, Mary.'

'Ellan Vannin has just left. She is going to New York to try to claim the money.'

'So, she's made up her mind. Everything should be straightforward, but with those American lawyers you never know. We'd better give her letters of proof of identity, just in case.'

'There's something else I think you should know.' Mary paused for a second. 'She's having a child. Jamie's child.'

He stopped shuffling the papers in his hands and stared at her. 'Is she certain?'

'Would she have admitted her predicament to me if she wasn't? She was overcome with mortification.'

'So she should be,' he pronounced, rather pompously Mary thought, overcoming her own discomfort. Why was it men always blamed women for these things, as though they had no part in the conception? She shrugged mentally. It was a man's world, always had been and probably would remain so.

'So what are we to do?' Mary asked. 'I told her I'd give her references.'

'I can't see any reason why that should alter things. It's not as if she's staying here or even going to Liverpool where people are familiar with our names. That could cause some embarrassment. She's going to the other side of the world. Oh, it's regrettable, but it will strengthen her case now there's to be an heir. Write the letter and I'll get my solicitor to draft one for me, he'll witness them both. Two letters are better than one and get that fellow Smollet to write as well. You did the right thing telling me, Mary.'

'I told Ellan that Mr Smollet might not need to be informed.'

'For God's sake, Mary! The man is a solicitor. His word is probably worth more than yours and mine put together. The time for modesty is well past.'

Ellan found Lizzie in the wash-house for Bessie had gone down with a fever and so had Mrs Webster who normally did the laundry. Lizzie pushed the damp strands of hair from her cheeks with a hand red and covered in soap suds. 'Blast that Bessie and old Ma Webster to hell and back! I'm worn out. I'm not a laundry woman. You look better, Ellan, more like your old self.'

'I am better. Much better now that I've seen Miss Mary.'

'Aye, I heard she went to see you.'

'Stop that for a minute and wipe your hands.'

Lizzie was only too pleased to oblige. 'What did she say then?'

'It was she who made me realize that I have to go on with my life. I'll never stop grieving for him, or loving him, but I'm going to New York, Lizzie.'

Lizzie looked perplexed. 'Did she tell you to go?'

'She suggested it.'

'Then I suppose she must think it's the right thing to do.'

'It's the only thing I can do, Lizzie.'

'So, you'll be wealthy then?'

Ellan shrugged. 'I suppose so but I don't really care about the money. But I'm afraid. Oh, Lizzie, I'm so afraid. Miss Mary doesn't think I am but I'm terrified. Lizzie, will you come with me?'

Lizzie was so startled that she let the washboard drop to the floor, spattering them both with suds. 'Me? Me go with you?'

'Yes. I'm not going first class now, so we should be able to get two steerage tickets.'

Lizzie was speechless.

Ellan took a deep breath. This was the final hurdle. She would have to take a chance on Lizzie's friendship. 'I'll need you, Lizzie. It wouldn't be fair for me to mislead you. It won't be long before I won't be able to manage on my own. I'm expecting. Miss Mary thinks it will help me with the lawyers.'

'Oh, Ellan! No. Not you!'

Ellan hung her head and twisted the middle button of her coat between her fingers. 'Lizzie, don't. I feel so ashamed. I had to tell Miss Mary.'

'I didn't mean to sound as though I was judging you. I'm just a bit stunned. Does your Aunt Maud know?'

'No. Do you think I'd be standing here if she did? But Jamie knew. He said we'd be a . . . family.' All her resolve broke and she began to cry softly.

'Oh, Ellan, I didn't mean to upset you, you know that.'

Ellan dabbed her eyes. 'I couldn't ask you to come with me and leave you in ignorance, could I? But I'll need someone when the time comes, Lizzie.'

Lizzie had recovered her composure. 'I'll come with

Lyn Andrews

you. We'll be all right. You don't think I'd pass up an opportunity like that, do you?'

Ellan managed a wan smile. 'You and your opportunities, Lizzie Killip. I'd better get back and tell them all.'

Lizzie hugged her. 'Oh, Ellan. Thank you for asking me. I know it's not the time to be happy, but I am.'

'I feel much better and it's me who should be thanking you.'

Lizzie smiled. 'You'd better go and tell them before I tell Ma and she goes shouting it to all and sundry like the town crier! We'll both be fine, you just wait and see. We'll both grab the opportunities!'

As she retraced her steps Ellan's heart felt lighter than it had done for weeks. There was only Aunt Maud to tell now and then this part of her life would be over. She stopped as she reached the stile and leaned on it, thinking back to that day so long ago, when she'd been ten years old and her pa had sat her on the stile and they'd watched the sunset. She dropped her forehead into her hands. Oh, Pa! Can you forgive me? Can you understand why I have to go? I'm taking your grandchild away from the island but I won't let him or her forget that they have Manx blood in their veins, I promise. And I promise I'll do my best to bring it up properly. Can you understand, Pa? She raised her head and looked out to sea and thought of Andrew. She could never face him, not in this condition. She was glad she would be gone when he got home.

Any sympathy Maud had for her disappeared when Ellan told her she was leaving.

'You've been up to see *her*, haven't you? I knew she was up to no good when she came here, all sweet smiles and sympathy. She's put you up to this. If the Lord had

164

meant you to be a wealthy woman He wouldn't have let Jamie Corlett drown.'

'Ma, that's cruel. Stop it. Ellan must have her reasons,' John rebuked his mother.

'Oh, I know her reason well enough – greed. She wants to get her hands on money that's not rightfully hers. Greed is her reason, pure greed!'

'No, Aunt, it's not,' Ellan said quietly. 'Jamie left a Will. Besides, I don't think I can stay here now, the memories are too painful. Every lane, every field, every person will remind me of him.' She felt bone weary. She had gone through so much today, but she couldn't let Aunt Maud suspect the real reason.

'Are you sure, lass? Don't rush into this,' John counselled.

She turned towards him. 'I've never been more certain in my life, John. It's best that I go, start afresh.'

'But, Ellan, you know how long all these legal things take. How will you manage?' Mat asked.

'Oh, I'll manage. I can always work. I've always been able to do that.'

'But you'll be alone and the tales you hear are desperate,' Mat persisted.

Ellan shook her head. 'I won't be alone. Lizzie is coming with me.'

Maud banged the rolling pin down on the table. 'A fine pair you'll make. A fine pair of hussies! She's as bold as brass is that one.'

Some of Ellan's old spirit returned. 'She's not. She's always stood by me. She's my friend.'

'And how, may I ask, is she going to afford the fare?'

'Miss Mary is going to change my first-class ticket, so

we'll both be able to go steerage. I've a bit of money and she's a bit put by.'

Maud felt outraged, helpless and rejected. Hadn't she looked after Ellan for years? Was this her reward? She tried her trump card which had worked before. 'And what if I won't allow it? You're not twenty-one yet and now that you're not even betrothed I could legally refuse my permission.'

'You could, but it wouldn't keep me here. You can't watch me day and night. I'd find a way to leave.'

Maud bent her head over the pastry she'd been rolling out. She'd lost and she knew it. 'Go then. Go, the pair of you and you'll both go to the bad. I wash my hands of you and your pa must be turning in his grave, God rest him!' she shouted.

Ellan fled upstairs and flung herself on her bed. She'd burned her boats now and she felt even more wretched.

'You never learn, Ma, do you? If you'd have kept quiet, maybe gone along with her, humoured her a bit, we might have been able to stop her, but not now. You've driven Andy away and now Ellan.'

Maud was smarting. 'I didn't drive him away. That brass-faced Lizzie Killip did that when she turned him down. And, that one upstairs had a part in it, too, though she didn't know it. Don't you dare tell me I drove him away, John Quirk.'

'What do you mean by that, Ma?'

'He never cared for that Killip girl, it was Ellan he really cared for. Are you both blind as well as daft? He couldn't stand Ellan mooning over young Corlett, but I'll not speak ill of the dead. That's why he went and you're both fools if you didn't realize it.'

'Of course we did, Ma. That's why you should have kept quiet. When she'd got over her grief, and she would have, she might have seen that Andy cared for her. They might even have ended up getting wed, but you and your tongue have made sure there's no chance of that. She'll be a world away from him. All you've succeeded in doing is making them both unhappy.'

Maud sank down on a chair. He was right. She was the fool, a stupid, blind fool not to have thought of that. But, as usual, her anger had blotted out all reasoning.

The news of Ellan's and Lizzie's departure divided the village. Some said Ellan should let well alone and stay in Peel. Others, and Maggie was the leader of this faction, said she was entitled to go and claim what was rightfully hers. Maud found herself joined in the opposing group led by Dora Killip who thought Lizzie had taken leave of her senses to go off to the other side of the world with Ellan. Terrible tales were told of the slums of New York and of the violence there. People carried guns, even the police had them, and there was always trouble in one quarter or another. So what would happen to two young girls alone in such a place and with all that money?

Prayers were offered up in the Methodist Chapel that God would show them the folly of their ways, but neither prayers nor dire warnings, nor Dora Killip's threats could make them change their minds. And, on 15 January they boarded the train for Ramsey.

This time there was no carnival atmosphere, no crowds of well-wishers, just John, Mat and Maggie and a weeping Dora, surrounded by the three younger Killips and a stony-faced Albert. Between them they had two steerage tickets for the *Arabia*, the Will and the letters from the Costains and Mr Smollet, addressed to Messrs Becker & Crasner, Attorneys at Law, Lennox Avenue, Harlem, New York City.

Lizzie was in tears as she hugged her sister and two brothers and then clung to her ma. Ellan embraced both John and Mat and tried to keep her voice steady as she handed John an envelope.

'Will you give this to Andrew for me, please? It's a note and something I want him to keep, to remind him of me.'

'I'll see he gets it, Ellan, whenever he comes home.'

She turned to Maggie. 'I'll write, Maggie, I promise.'

'I know you will. You're a good lass. Take care of yourself, Ellan.'

There was a piercing whistle and an outrush of steam from the engine that heralded its departure.

'You'd better get aboard, lass. Good luck and take care.' John's voice was harsh with emotion.

'I will. I'll write every week.'

'You write, too, our Lizzie, do you hear me!'

'Yes, Ma,' Lizzie sniffed.

They both sank down in their seats as the train pulled away. Ellan's emotions were mixed: sadness that she was leaving everything and everyone she had held dear for as long as she could remember, yet a spark of optimism burned.

Lizzie wiped away her tears. 'We're on our own now, Ellan.'

'Yes, Lizzie, we are, and whatever is in store for us we've got to make the best of it. I'm never coming back.'

*

Ellan Vannin

In the middle of January, Andrew Quirk stepped from the *Mona's Queen* on to his native soil for the first time in four long months. It was good to be back, he thought. Good to be away from sub-zero temperatures, ice floes, the endless days and nights at sea, the rotten food and the sickening stench of whalemeat and blubber.

He'd been a fisherman for most of his life but the barbarity of the slaughter of the huge mammals had sickened him. They didn't die quickly, sometimes they struggled for hours, even days, and the cold sea that surrounded the ship turned red with their blood. And the barbarity seemed to extend to the men who hunted them, too. He'd hated every minute of it and had sworn never to sign on again. From now on he'd stick to fishing or transporting cargo from Liverpool to more civilized places.

She'd be wed by now, he'd known that. Could he live with it? That was something he couldn't answer. Maybe his stay would be short but at this precise moment he was glad to be back.

He'd heard of the loss of the *Ellan Vannin* – news like that soon got around amongst the seafaring communities of the world – and was saddened as he always was when he heard of the loss of a ship and its hands.

He hadn't written to inform them he was coming, so when he walked into the yard he was met with shouts of delight and his ma came running from the house, smiling.

'Why didn't you let us know?'

'I wanted to surprise you, Ma.'

'You've done that all right! You look all skin and bone, haven't they been feeding you?'

'The food isn't fit to eat, Ma. Mouldy biscuits and rotten, putrid meat.'

'Never mind, I've a good stew in the pot.'

'Is this a flying visit or are you staying?' John asked as Andrew greedily gulped down the stew.

'I don't know, but I do know one thing: I'm through with whaling and whalers.'

'That bad?'

'Sickening, and the cold. Dear God there were times when I thought I'd die of the cold, that I'd never be warm again.'

'Next time take a trip to Africa or India,' Mat joked.

'I hope there won't be a next time,' Maud said, thinking that with both Ellan and Lizzie gone, there would be no need for her youngest son to go away again for so long.

At last he pushed the plate away, replete. 'How is everyone?'

'Mostly the same as when you left,' John answered, nonchalantly.

'I heard about *L'il Daisy*. God have mercy on their souls.'

'Then you know about Jamie Corlett?'

'What about him?'

The silence hung heavily, broken only by the soft hissing of the kettle on the hob. 'He was aboard her when she went down.'

Andrew stared at his eldest brother. 'Then, Ellan . . . ?'

John shook his head slowly. 'He was bound for New York, leaving from Liverpool. He came into an inheritance, from his pa's elder brother.'

170

Andrew wasn't listening, he wasn't interested in inheritances. 'So, Ellan didn't marry him?'

'No, but she's gone, Andy.'

'Gone? Gone where?'

'Gone to try to claim what she isn't entitled to, his money. And she's taken Lizzie Killip with her,' Maud answered tartly.

Andrew got up and without a word went into the yard. John opened the drawer of the dresser and drew out an envelope, then followed.

'Why did she go?'

'She had to. Too many memories here, Andy. She left this for you. A note and something she wanted you to have as a keepsake.'

John turned and went back into the house. He'd seen the bitter disappointment that had followed the hope in his brother's eyes.

Andrew tore open the envelope. Inside was a single sheet of paper and a ring, her ring. He scanned the lines. No, it wasn't her ring. Not the one Corlett had given her anyway, but a copy. 'I'll always remember you and hope you will remember me and think kindly of me and the happy times we shared.'

The paper fluttered to the ground. He'd hoped, for one glorious, joyous minute he'd hoped. He twisted the ring between his fingers. 'Whichever way you throw me, I will stand,' he murmured. She'd stand. She'd survive. She had guts, did Ellan. Should he follow her? The answer was formulated in his mind before he'd finished asking the question. No, no-one would say he'd gone after her looking for her money, no-one would mistakenly think he'd gone chasing after Lizzie. There

171

was no need for him to leave the island again, not with both of them gone.

He slipped the ring on to his little finger, the only finger it would fit. He'd wear it for her sake, for although he'd never follow her, neither would he ever forget her.

Part Two

1910

———✦———

Chapter Eleven

IT WAS ANOTHER WORLD, a noisy, hectic, bustling world, filled with a cacophony of unfamiliar sounds, inhabited by people from every country under the sun. It was huge and sprawling, with trains that ran under the ground, called subways, and buildings that rose like mountains into the sky, aptly called skyscrapers. It was a place neither of them could have envisaged and Ellan, pale from the journey, her natural optimism sapped by anxiety, was overawed. Not so Lizzie, who had found everything exciting and exhilarating and who had never stopped crying out in thankful delight from the minute the ship had sailed up the Hudson River.

They had both been seasick for it had been a terrible crossing. Ellan's sickness only lasted three days but Lizzie had been ill all the way.

The *Arabia* was not a small ship but she had been tossed and buffeted unmercifully by the cold Atlantic Ocean. Everyone had been discomforted but none more so than the five hundred passengers travelling steerage in the cramped cabins of the lower decks. The storms had died out but before the Ambrose Light had been sighted a dense, swirling fog had descended and the ship came to a standstill. Her master refused to risk his ship and passengers in a collision and although the first-class passengers objected vociferously, the second-class and steerage passengers did not. Lizzie was profoundly grateful that the pitching and rolling had stopped.

The fog did not lift for nearly three days. Finally, after a delay at quarantine when the US medical examiner had scrutinized everyone, the mail was taken ashore by tender and they had been allowed to disembark, only to be held up by more formalities at Ellis Island. They were both weary and a little bewildered as they made their way to the address Mr Smollet had given them, a rooming house in Washington Square run by a Mrs Eva Hinchey. She was a buxom woman with plain, open features and small dark eyes that almost disappeared in folds of flesh when she smiled, which was often. She always had a cheery word for all her boarders and she never appeared to be down or pessimistic. 'Life's too short,' was her favourite saying. She welcomed them warmly, although Ellan noticed that her shrewd gaze took in her thickening figure.

'Breakfast is at seven and supper is at seven sharp. My rule of "no working clothes at the table at supper time" won't apply to you. But, I don't allow gentlemen callers in rooms, only in the parlour.' She glanced at Ellan a little pointedly. 'But, I reckon that one won't apply to you either. No offence intended.'

Their room was a large one at the back of the house, overlooking what Mrs Hinchey called the yard but what was in fact a small garden. It was sparsely furnished with two narrow beds, a chest of drawers, a wardrobe that Mrs Hinchey called a closet, and an unusual and very oddly-shaped chair made from moose horns. Brightly coloured rugs covered the floor, the boards of which had been stained with varnish. It was spotlessly clean, but what delighted them most was the bathroom with its huge, white enamelled bath, blue and white patterned tiles, shining brass taps and the array of plants on the window ledge. It had been sheer luxury to soak their travel-weary bodies in the hot water that ran freely from a tap that was called a faucet.

Their first venture into this new world had been preceded by a lecture from their benevolent landlady. 'Don't take no sass from anyone, you hear me now?' she'd said, wagging a stumpy finger in their direction. 'There's some very pushy folk out there. And don't let anyone cheat you. There are one hundred cents to a dollar, work on that. Forget your sovereigns, half crowns and the like.' They learned that a tram was called a streetcar or a trolleybus, that the pavement was the side-walk, a handbag was a purse and a purse a billfold. And with the final instruction not to jaywalk across a street, they set out to take in the sights and sounds of the neighbourhood. They had returned dumbstruck, to the amusement of the other boarders and their landlady.

Within twenty-four hours Mrs H, as she liked to be called, had ascertained the reason for their voyage. She tutted sympathetically and patted Ellan's hand.

'You made a good choice if they're all so narrow-minded back there. I don't hold with young girls playing fast and loose and getting themselves into all kinds of trouble, there have got to be standards and morals, but your case is different and life's too short to be fretting and fussing.'

Ellan and Lizzie exchanged smiles.

'So, I have to go to Lennox Avenue in Harlem and see these people.' Ellan handed over the address.

'Um, it's not hard to find. Take the subway to Harlem and anyone will direct you, but I'd write and ask for an appointment or better still, telephone. These lawyers are mighty formal.'

'Telephone?' she repeated.

'I don't have one but the Malverns next door do. They'll let you use it. We'll find the number in the directory.'

'I've never used one. What will I say?'

'Just say you want to make an appointment. That's what you've come all this way for, isn't it, to see them?' Mrs H had stated firmly.

So, with Lizzie wide-eyed and open-mouthed, standing at her shoulder, she stood in the hall of the house next door and haltingly spoke into the instrument, her voice little more than a whisper until Mrs H had urged, 'Speak up, honey, or no-one will hear you, but don't shout or you'll deafen them.'

The voice at the other end sounded detached and a little bored as it asked the nature of her business. After she explained, feeling rather silly because she felt it was like talking aloud to yourself, she was told to present herself at three o'clock on Friday. The line went dead and her hand shook as she replaced the receiver.

'It's a miracle. It's nothing short of a miracle, being able to talk to someone miles away,' Lizzie cried to the amusement of both Mrs H and Mrs Malvern.

That had been a week ago and now she sat on the bed and watched Lizzie securing her hat. The weather was bleak and bitterly cold, but there had been no snow, although Mrs H had informed them that this was unusual for the time of year. Normally the sidewalks were thick with it.

Ellan felt very apprehensive. She wasn't really looking forward to the meeting. She tired more easily now and she felt none of Lizzie's delighted anticipation of going 'up' by subway train. Also, this meeting would force her, yet again, to speak of Jamie and her own condition. Both subjects she had tried not to dwell on during the journey, but it was hard and often she failed. She had felt the memories tear at her when they'd sailed out into the Mersey, past the Bar Lightship, knowing that somewhere beneath the choppy, murky waters lay her namesake.

'Ready? Have you got your purse?' Lizzie asked, using the new vernacular.

'I have.'

'Are you nervous?'

'Of course I'm nervous. You will come in with me? I don't want to have to face them on my own.'

'You know I will, but they might object, Ellan.'

This had also occurred to Ellan but she brushed it aside. There was already enough to worry about.

The freezing air made them both gasp and wrap their scarves more tightly around them. They were glad of the warmth of the subway, although Ellan was terrified by the speed of the train. In what seemed a ludicrously short time they stood outside a brownstone building whose neatly lettered sign proclaimed that Becker & Crasner, Attorneys at Law, resided there.

Inside, the office was warm and furnished with dark woods and dark colours. The woman seated at a small desk, hammering away at the keys of a typewriter, nodded her acknowledgement in reply to Ellan's announcement.

'Mr Becker is expecting you. Please take a seat.'

They sat and watched with fascination as the thin fingers flew over the keys of yet another machine that was new to them.

'Isn't it fantastic. They have machines for everything,' Lizzie whispered, her eyes darting around the room. 'There's no fire or stove, so where is the heat coming from?'

'Probably another machine,' Ellan answered detachedly, clutching her bag tightly.

One of the doors opened and a tall man with greying hair, an aquiline nose and a jutting chin, dressed in a very formal and sober suit, appeared. They both stood up.

'Er . . . Miss Vannin?' he enquired.

'Yes.' Ellan's voice was low.

'Good. Please come this way?'

Ellan hesitated and caught hold of Lizzie's arm. 'Can I . . . is it possible for my friend . . . companion . . .'

She was reassured by a genuine smile. 'Of course, Miss . . . Er . . . ?'

'Miss Killip. Miss Elizabeth Killip,' Lizzie smiled, stretching out her hand. She had confidence enough for them both.

He ushered them into his office and asked the secretary to bring in some coffee.

They both sat on the chairs indicated and while Ellan delved into her bag for Jamie's Will and the letters from Mr Costain and Miss Mary, Lizzie glanced around the room with ill-disguised curiosity. It was understandable that Ellan was nervous but she wasn't. She liked New York. She wasn't in the least bit intimidated by everything as Ellan seemed to be. That in itself was strange, she mused. At home it had always been Ellan who had been strong and resourceful, but maybe having a baby made you nervous and Ellan had had to cope with an awful lot, and she hadn't been much help or comfort on that awful voyage. Most of the time she'd wished she'd never left Peel at all.

'Mr Smollet said I was to give you these.' Ellan passed over all the documents and then they both sat in silence as Mr Becker read them carefully, frowning with concentration.

'Miss Vannin, when my secretary spoke to you and made this appointment I was puzzled,' he said at length.

'Why?' Ellan interrupted.

'I assumed you wished to obtain some advice, but now I realize that you obviously know nothing about the Forfeiture Clause.'

Ellan frowned. 'I don't understand. What is a Forfeiture Clause?'

'Miss Vannin, I really am most terribly sorry but this is going to come as rather a shock.'

Lizzie was not as reticent as Ellan. 'What do you mean, a shock? What's the matter?'

Mr Becker looked at her with his piercingly blue eyes. 'In his Will, Mr Alfred Corlett stipulated that unless the Estate be claimed by his heirs, in person, within the period of three months from his death, it would be forfeited by the said heirs and bequeathed to a number of named charities.'

Ellan just stared at him, feeling sick, unable to grasp the full meaning of his words.

'Could you please put that into simple words?' Lizzie asked, seeing the colour drain from Ellan's cheeks.

'I really am sorry. It means you are too late. The three-month period ended on 21 January. Two days ago.'

'Too . . . too late,' Ellan stammered. 'There's nothing about a date in the Will! Jamie never said . . .' she cried, losing her composure.

'No, not the Will of Mr James Corlett, the Will of Mr Alfred Corlett. Look, read the codicil at the bottom of the page.' He leaned across the desk and held out an official-looking document.

Ellan scanned the lines until she came to a short paragraph at the bottom of the page. 'But . . . but no-one has ever said . . .' she muttered.

Mr Becker looked deeply perturbed. 'Are you sure Mr James Corlett did not tell you? Did no-one from Smollet's ever say?'

'No! No!' Her voice was strangled and she heard Lizzie gasp.

'Mr Alfred Corlett was most insistent upon it. I tried to dissuade him but he was adamant. He said, "If they can't be bothered to come to claim it . . ."'

Ellan didn't hear the rest of his words. Why had no-one mentioned this before? 'Jamie and I were going to be married . . . here. It was all we talked about.'

'Miss Vannin, I don't know what to say! I'm most terribly sorry but it is impossible to revoke the Clause. You can of course appeal to the Supreme Court but that would take time and money. I can only assume that the blame for your ignorance of this fact lies either with Mr

James Corlett or his attorneys. As Mr Corlett is deceased it is impossible to blame him solely, but his lawyers have been lacking in their duty. It may be possible to sue. In fact I would strongly urge you to do so.'

Ellan stood up. She wasn't interested in suing anyone. She just wanted to get out, to go back to Mrs H in Washington Square. It was all a mistake. A terrible mistake.

It was a very shocked and subdued Lizzie who led her from the office after leaving their address with Mr Becker in case Ellan changed her mind about litigation.

It was Lizzie who pushed her into the small bar on the corner. 'We need a drink, both of us,' she stated when Ellan turned glazed eyes towards her. Neither of them had ever been in a public house of any sort before but they sat down at a corner table and Lizzie ordered two small brandies. It occurred to her that maybe Ellan shouldn't drink but she reasoned that it was purely for medicinal purposes.

She watched as Ellan sipped the drink. 'Why did no-one tell you?' she began. 'Are you sure Jamie didn't mention it and you misheard him, or forgot?'

'No. He would have told me and I would have remembered. How could I forget something as important as that?'

Lizzie tried a different approach. She didn't want to upset Ellan any more than was necessary. 'Maybe he did, Ellan. Perhaps he thought he needn't bother you with it. He knew he would be here in time. That's why everything was so rushed. Oh, Ellan, I'm sorry.'

'Lizzie, I'm positive he didn't know. He talked about us being here and being . . . being a family at Christmas.'

She couldn't go on and took another sip of brandy.

Lizzie stared at her, tears in her own eyes. How could anyone fail to make something like that known? How could they? It was so important. They were the ones who were supposed to be so clever, so learned. Maybe Mr Smollet hadn't known. Perhaps he only had a copy of the Will and maybe that copy didn't have that stupid bit at the bottom. In her opinion Alfred Corlett was a bloody-minded old fool, imposing his Forfeiture Clauses on people and ruining their lives. She hoped vehemently that he was burning in Hell.

'Oh, dear God, Lizzie, what are we going to do now?'

Lizzie squeezed Ellan's hand comfortingly. 'We could go back. It wouldn't be that bad.' She tried to sound optimistic.

'I can't! I can't! How would I face everyone? How would I manage?'

'People would help out, Ellan. Once they'd got over the first shock. Even Miss Mary might help.'

'Lizzie, I couldn't. I couldn't go begging to anyone, least of all Miss Mary. Aunt Maud would turn me away and it would be the workhouse.'

'There's Maggie.'

'Oh, I'd forgotten about Maggie. She's lost her share, too. She would blame me.'

'Maggie wouldn't do that.'

'Oh, if only we'd come on the *Mauretania* we'd have been here in time then.'

'Ellan, we didn't know! How could we? We wanted to save money. I couldn't have come with you otherwise.' Lizzie tried to console Ellan but thought regretfully that if they'd come steerage on the *Mauretania* they'd have crossed in five days. 'At least we have a little money because we economized.'

'But what will we do here? How will we manage? Oh, Lizzie, I'm sorry. I've dragged you halfway around the world on a wild goose chase.' Tears slid down Ellan's cheeks and Lizzie squeezed her hand again.

'Don't be daft, Ellan. I wanted to come. I did.'

'But I asked you. I made it sound so exciting. You would have stayed on at Glentrammon if it hadn't been for me.'

In her heart Lizzie agreed, but outwardly she was vehement in her denials. She couldn't let Ellan see how confused she was. 'I say don't be so daft. First things first. We'd better get back and try to sort it all out. Mrs H will help us. I know she will.'

'I wouldn't be so sure, Lizzie, not once she knows we haven't got an everlasting supply of money.'

'Oh, she's not like that, I know she isn't.'

'How can you be sure?'

'Because Mr Webb, that funny, quiet little man with the bald head told me that when he lost his job, she let him stay on until he got another one. He calls her an angel. He won't hear a word said against her.'

They discussed it all evening, tossing it backwards and forwards with Mrs H's help, until in the end Ellan's head was aching and she felt broken in mind and body.

Mrs H had tried at first to persuade her to go home. Then she cursed all lawyers as 'money grabbers' and 'carpet baggers' and said that Ellan being pregnant would be a five-minute marvel before folk turned their attention to something else. She then added her terse opinion of 'narrow-minded folk'. In reply Ellan had tried to convey to her the rigid moral codes that existed at home. 'We will have to stay here and work, it's the only solution,' she said wearily at length.

'Ellan, you can't work!' Lizzie cried.

Ellan passed a hand over her aching forehead. 'I'll have to, Lizzie. The money I've got won't last for ever and it's rightfully Mr Costain's.'

'Oh, to hell with him! He won't miss it,' Lizzie said.

'How far on are you, honey?' Mrs H asked.

'Five months.'

'You could work for a while. Nothing too hard.'

'Doing what?'

'Well, what can you do?'

'I was never trained to do anything, except gut fish.'

'You can keep house,' Lizzie put in.

'But I've no references like you. I've no formal training either, not to work in service.'

'You can sew,' Lizzie urged.

'Then you could work in the garment trade as a machinist. It's not easy work nor well paid, but you'll be sitting down and there's no heavy lifting and such,' Mrs H said brightly.

Ellan nodded slowly. The day's events were too much for her to take in now. She needed time, time to let it all sink in; time to try to come to terms with it, to work out a new and different future. But time was the one thing she had so little of.

'I don't think you'll have much trouble finding work, Lizzie. You're a trained English parlour maid with good references. Anyone on Fifth Avenue would snap you up. Snobby folk they are up there.'

'I'm not English. I'm Manx.'

'So you keep telling me, but it's all part of Great Britain, isn't it? So at least that's settled, Lizzie. Tomorrow take yourself up there in your best bib and tucker and I'll take Ellan to the garment district. I know a few people there, we'll get you both fixed up and then later on . . . well, we'll sort something out nearer the time, Ellan.'

Ellan began to cry softly. Never more had she wanted to go home: home with its green fields, open spaces and small houses, its peace and tranquillity, its slower pace of life. But she would never go home, not now that the fortune had been snatched from her grasp, leaving her poor, unmarried and pregnant.

Chapter Twelve

———•———

TRUE TO HER WORD Mrs H accompanied Ellan to the garment district that encompassed West 34th Street to West 39th Street, and had Ellan not been so heartsore she would have been delighted with the activities that were going on around her: rails of clothes being loaded into vans to be delivered to the department stores; more vans disgorging hundreds of rolls of cloth of all colours; the smell of freshly cooked bagels wafting from the many small bakery and coffee shops.

She followed Mrs H through a door and into a dark hallway.

'Maxie is a friend of my friend Rosa's father,' she explained, pointing to the faded gold lettering that proclaimed Max Lipman & Son to be the proprietors. There appeared to be a small office ahead. Mrs H rapped hard on the door and without waiting for a reply, opened it and walked in, leaving Ellan with no choice but to follow.

'Eva! You delight my old eyes. You've come to see me at last.'

Ellan watched as the rotund little man with the dark eyes and curly dark hair, half covered with a black skullcap, almost disappeared in Mrs H's buxom embrace.

'Maxie, how are you? You look good.'

'I may look good but I don't feel so good. I'm getting old, Eva, too old. Rosa is always saying "Retire. Retire and let Harry take all the worry." If I let Harry loose in here I have no business left to retire with! I tell her that. Oh, that Harry. I tell you, Eva, he is a fool. My own son, but a fool. But enough of me already, you have brought someone with you?'

'This is Ellan, one of my boarders. She needs a job, Maxie.'

'So does half of this city.'

'I know that, Maxie, but for me . . . I can't keep her for free.'

'You can sew, Miss . . .'

'Vannin,' she replied.

He stepped closer and scrutinized her closely. 'Vannin. Vannin. A strange name. You are Jewish?'

'No, I'm Manx.'

'What is that? In all my time here I never heard that before.'

'It's a small island . . .'

'Part of Britain,' Mrs H interrupted.

Ellan let it pass. 'I do need a job, Mr Lipman, and I can sew.'

He looked from her to Mrs H and back again. 'All right. I give you a job, but only for your sake, Eva. You can use a sewing machine?'

Ellan shook her head. He had a very unnerving manner of darting around the small room.

'Then you learn. I get Rachel to show you, she's a good girl. It's not hard. I get her now.' He opened the door, stuck his head out and shouted something in a foreign language in a voice that belied his size. A few minutes later a plump girl with large, soulful eyes and hair as dark as Ellan's, appeared. He spoke to her again in the strange tongue.

'Maxie, don't talk in Yiddish, how are we to know what you're saying?' Mrs H reproved him.

He shrugged. 'You go with Rachel,' he urged and Ellan followed the girl out.

The room she walked into, where forty or fifty girls and women were hunched over sewing machines in cramped rows shocked her. The light was poor and the noise deafening. The air was warm but stuffy and she almost gagged. She'd never seen anything like it before and the few faces turned towards her were grey with fatigue. The eyes showed no spark of interest before the gaze was dropped to their work. Conversation was impossible.

When she returned to the comparative peace of the office, the expression on her face was enough for Mrs H to speak quickly.

'I know it's nothing wonderful and neither is the pay, but you have to have something. You can't live on fresh air, honey, and it won't be for ever.'

'No. No, it won't,' Ellan answered flatly. How could she work in that inferno of a room, hour after hour, day after day? But she had no choice. It was work. And, how would she manage after the baby was born? She had a little money left and with what she would earn . . . it would just have to be stretched to keep them both until

190

such times as she could leave the baby and return to work. It was a chilling, miserable thought and the future looked as bleak and depressing as the weather. After a few details were discussed, they left and as Mrs H had predicted, large snowflakes had begun to fall.

Lizzie was in the kitchen and had the coffee pot on the stove when they got in, hats and coats covered in a layer of white, powdery snow. Ellan's mood lightened a little as she saw the animation in Lizzie's eyes.

'You must both be frozen. The coffee should be hot by now.' Lizzie bustled around getting cups as though it were her own kitchen and Ellan managed a smile as she sank wearily into a chair.

'You've got a job.'

'Indeed I have. And, only the second place I tried. The girl at the first place gave me a good tip. She said don't ask, say you've come for an interview for the vacant post and if they say "What vacant post?" tell them the agency sent you and if they say "What agency?" act confused. Say you were sure it was that address, then fumble in your purse as though you were looking for a letter or card. So, I did just that and when they heard my accent they asked for references. Then Mr Shaw, the butler, asked me some questions. He went away and came back and took me to see Mrs Van Kronin. Oh, the parlour! Ellan, you should have seen it. It made Glentrammon look small and dingy. Well, she asked me more questions and then asked if I could start next week. I'll get three times as much as I was getting at Glentrammon and with more time off.'

'You sure are a fast learner, Lizzie,' Mrs H said approvingly.

Lizzie passed steaming cups to them both. 'I was always one to take opportunities. How did you get on?'

'Ellan's got a job, too. Machinist at Maxie Lipman's. Not exactly a top job, but . . .'

'Beggers can't be choosers. I start tomorrow,' Ellan interrupted flatly.

Lizzie grinned. 'We'll manage. It will all come out in the wash, as Ma always says.' Seeing the confused expression on Mrs H's face, she added, 'Things will work out just fine in the end.'

Ellan sipped her coffee and wondered tiredly if things would ever be right again.

Through the long and seemingly endless days of February and March Ellan stuck it out, rising early and trudging in the darkness through the snow and sleet and freezing temperatures to bend awkwardly over her machine and feed miles of cloth under the drumming head of the needle. Her eyes were screwed up with concentration in bad light in the noisy, foetid warmth, until it was time to make her weary way home, back aching, shoulders aching, head aching. She was too tired to do more than eat and sleep and as March passed into April, she knew her days at Lipman's were nearing their end. She was having great difficulty bending forward to reach her machine.

She'd learned a lot in the short time she'd been there. Most of her fellow workers were immigrants, desperately poor, some unable to speak English. They'd fled from one kind of persecution or another, mainly the pogroms of Russia. To many she appeared lucky and wealthy. Rachel translated for her and Galina, a big-boned woman, the mother of four children herself, had taken Ellan under her wing.

'Rachel, Ellan should not be working like this. Her time is getting closer. You tell Maxie that,' she had shouted one day. Ellan had shaken her head vehemently.

'You take no notice of her. You tell him, Rachel. She is not like us and this is her first.'

So, Ellan had stayed at home finishing off, hemming and buttonholing by hand on the more expensive garments. But, in a few weeks that source of employment had almost dried up.

Lizzie visited as often as she could, always bringing something with her, usually begged from Cook. Lizzie was happy. She enjoyed her work and she liked her employers and had money in her pocket to spend on her days off. She bought clothes and trinkets in the smaller department stores but often ventured further afield to window shop.

On a morning in the middle of the month she persuaded Ellan to go with her to Battery Park. 'It will do you good. It's nice there, sort of quiet. Well, quieter than most places, and you can see right across the river to Statten Island. If you feel up to it we could take the ferry over?'

Ellan declined the trip on the ferry but found the park to be an oasis of greenery amidst a desert of brick and concrete.

Settling themselves down on a bench to eat the candies that Lizzie had bought, they both fell silent, Lizzie to contemplate her good fortune and Ellan to gaze at the river which had a soothing effect on her. She was so tired and weary these days and not just physically.

There were nights when she tossed awkwardly, her bulk adding to her discomfort. Nights when the baby kicked and she felt a great surge of tenderness were followed by the crushing weight of realization that every day brought her closer and closer to the time when the baby would stop being abstract and be a living child that she would have to care for and provide for. As she sat watching the sun sparkling on the water she felt embattled by the noise of the city, crushed by its towering buildings, exhausted by its ceaseless race against time.

'You're happy here, Lizzie, aren't you?'

Lizzie offered her another sweet. 'Yes. Aren't you?'

'No.'

'It will be different when the bairn is born, Ellan. You're just tired. Ma was always tired and snappy towards the end.'

'Everyone keeps saying things like that but it won't be better. I'll have to go back to work at Lipman's and pay someone to mind the bairn. So, how can things get better?'

Lizzie didn't want to dwell too deeply on the subject, yet she didn't want Ellan to think she was uncaring. 'You won't have to go back there to work. You can do something else.'

The hooting of the Statten Island ferry shattered the silence. Ellan cringed. There was never even a few minutes' peace here, just constant noise and she couldn't stand any more. She made up her mind. 'I'm going back, Lizzie.'

Lizzie choked on a humbug. 'What?'

'I didn't say "home", I said "back". I can't stand it here. I hate the noise, the traffic, the constant rushing everywhere. It's not what I expected at all. It's just noise,

noise, noise. Oh, Lizzie, I want some peace. I want to see fields again . . .'

'But . . . but where will you go? What will you do and how will you manage, for God's sake?'

'Liverpool, that's where I'll go.'

'You'll see no fields nor get much peace in Liverpool. Ellan, you're mad. Where will you live? What will you live on?' Lizzie was aghast.

'I've got enough for the fare and enough to last a few months, but Lizzie, I'd sooner have my bairn in Liverpool than here. I'll manage. I always have.' She twisted the silver ring around her finger. 'I'll stand.'

'You can't go. Not now, you're due next month. Wait, Ellan, please?'

Now she had voiced the intentions which had been forming in her mind for the last week, determination gripped her and with some of her old strength and purpose she faced Lizzie. 'You can talk until you're blue in the face, Lizzie Killip, but I'm going back and as soon as possible. I'll go and see Mr Smollet, he will find me a room.' She stood up, pulling Lizzie with her. 'In fact, you can come with me now.'

'Where to?'

'The shipping offices.' There was something in Ellan's smile that cut short Lizzie's protests. 'I'm not asking you to come back with me, Lizzie. You've got your own life to live. You like it here, you've got a good job and they say it's the land of opportunity.'

Lizzie knew it was useless to argue and besides, she didn't want to go back. She did like New York. 'Are you sure . . . ?' she said, hesitantly, feeling as though it was expected of her.

'I'm sure. In fact I'm certain and I'll need you to stay here.'

'Why?'

'To send my letters on to Aunt Maud. I don't want them to know I've come back.'

Lizzie crumpled up the empty bag and stuffed it into her pocket. 'That will be a job for life, I take it, or until you decide to go home to the island.'

They fell into step as they headed for the subway. 'I don't think I'll ever be able to do that,' Ellan said quietly.

'But what if someone, say Andrew Quirk, sees you?'

'Everyone will think I'm still here. No-one will be looking for me, and anyway, hardly anyone ever goes to Liverpool. Except the likes of Mr Costain.'

'And Miss Mary,' Lizzie added.

'It's a big place, Lizzie. Not as big as this, but big enough to hide in.'

'I hope you know what you're doing, Ellan Vannin.'

'I'm sure I do, Lizzie.'

She stuck out against all the pleading, the reasoning and the cajoling by saying flatly that she'd booked her passage and paid for it and that was that. She'd written to Mr Smollet and had posted the letter. She was going back, period, as Mrs H was wont to say. The *Lusitania* was sailing at the end of the month: she'd be in Liverpool in a week, she was a fast ship, almost as fast as her sister ship, the *Mauretania*, who held the Blue Riband of the Atlantic.

'Ellan, there's still time to change your mind,' Mrs H pleaded as they stood at Pier 27 where the black hull of the *Lusitania* towered over them and passengers and friends milled around.

'No, I have to go but I can never thank you enough for everything you've done for me. I'll always remember you, Eva Hinchey.'

'Lord above! It was nothing,' she replied, hugging Ellan, tears in her eyes.

'You'll keep your promise, Lizzie, over the letters? You won't let it slip in your letters home?'

'I promise. Oh, Ellan, I go cold with worry when I think of you alone with the bairn coming.'

'Stop it, Lizzie. I'll manage. I know I will,' she said sternly, fighting back the tears, knowing she would never see Lizzie again, trying to push aside those very fears. She'd grown up so much in such a short time. Her girlhood had gone. She was a woman, soon to be a mother, responsible for another life and she was only nineteen.

After hugging them both again she turned and walked up the gangway and after finding her cabin, which she was sharing with three other ladies, she went back on deck and waved to the figures on the dockside until her arm ached and they were just tiny dots and the watery sun was setting, leaving a sky shot with fingers of gold over the Manhattan skyline and the Hudson River.

There were fewer people travelling back, at least by steerage, she mused as she walked along the deck, trying to make some sense of her predicament and plan for the future. She'd have to work, that was a fact, but at what she didn't know. Were there places like Lipman's in Liverpool? First of all she'd have to see Mr Smollet and find a room, if he hadn't already done this for her. However, she was certain he would have, for she had written a very terse letter to him, reminding him of his failure to disclose the fact that the Corlett money depended upon a Forfeiture Clause. She would mention, when she saw him, that Mr Becker had said she could sue them and thus prodded, he might even help her to find work. But then again he might not, knowing she had no money to take them to court.

She looked up at the sky and the four, huge red and black funnels that disgorged charcoal-coloured smoke. Her attention was caught by a figure standing on the deck above which was narrower than the one she was standing on. She'd seen him there yesterday and the day before that, tall, well-built and bare-headed with the collar of his topcoat turned up. To her surprise he raised his hand in a salute then disappeared from sight. She shrugged and continued her promenade, the same thoughts and worries going round and round in her head.

When she reached the starboard side she stopped. He was standing at the bow end, leaning on the rail. He was middle-aged, she thought, noticing the slightly greying hair at his temples.

'We seem to be the only ones who have any inclination to enjoy the fresh air, or are you escaping from someone?'

His tone was pleasant and well modulated. It was also that of a gentleman. She smiled shyly. 'No, I just find it easier to think out here.'

'Let me introduce myself. I'm Lloyd Elliot. Doctor Elliot. I've been to New York for a medical conference.'

'Oh.' Then feeling very self-conscious she took his outstretched hand and shook it. The grip was firm. 'I'm Ellan Vannin.' She was careful not to include either Miss or Mrs.

His brows moved together in puzzlement. 'I've heard that name before. Have we ever met?'

'No. It will be the mail boat you've heard of. We shared the same name.'

'Ah, now I recall. The Isle of Man steam packet that sank in Liverpool Bay last year. Dreadful tragedy.'

To his surprise and discomfort he saw her face crumple and tears well in her dark eyes. God, but he was a fool at times, he thought. The poor girl must have lost someone in that shipwreck. Maybe that was why she was on this ship, and she was so very pregnant that she shouldn't be travelling at all. She was young, in her early twenties, he surmised, so it would be a first pregnancy. She was well-dressed, too well-dressed to be working class and she spoke well. Hardly a trace of an accent. She certainly wasn't American and neither was she a Liverpudlian. Nor could her condition mar the beauty of her face with those huge, dark eyes. There was a haunting quality about her that intrigued him. He had studied human nature for the past ten years in all its shapes and forms and knew instinctively that there was something different about her. He was a man possessed of a curious nature, viewed as an eccentric by many of his colleagues, but he was a caring man. He cared deeply about many things, but mostly about people. 'I'm sorry. I had no wish to upset you. Was there someone . . . ?'

'It doesn't matter . . . not now,' Ellan muttered, wiping her eyes.

'You know you really shouldn't be travelling at this late stage. Come and sit down here.'

He led her to a hatch cover and sat beside her. He envied her husband, whoever he was. She was very beautiful.

'You said you were a doctor?'

'I am an orthopaedic surgeon. I have a house in Rodney Street.'

She looked puzzled, not knowing what orthopaedic meant.

'I specialize in bones, but I do remember my paediatric training – babies,' he explained, smiling kindly.

He was so very easy to talk to, she thought, and, he looked considerate.

'When is the happy event due?'

'May.'

'I thought so, and without wishing to pry, how did you persuade your husband and your physician, as Americans seem to call their doctors, into letting you travel so far and alone? You are alone, aren't you?'

'Yes. I'm alone.' The word echoed in her head. Alone! Alone! Alone! All the fears, the doubts, the events and circumstances that had turned her world upside down crushed down on her and she began to cry.

He let her sob for a while. She so obviously needed someone to talk to that he knew in a while he could coax it all out of her. Margaret, his wife, said it was his manner that attracted so many patients. He passed her his hand-kerchief and in the chill light of the Atlantic afternoon Ellan haltingly poured out her heart to him.

When she had finished he felt moved and yet angry. Angry at fate, angry at those fools of solicitors who had caused her so much unnecessary grief, angry with a community that would shun her, making her out to be something she was not – a fallen woman, a girl with loose morals, wayward. She was none of these things. In his daily life he saw so much tragedy and she'd certainly had her share in her brief nineteen years. Yet he admired her. She had an inner strength, a certain kind of courage that he respected. An idea took shape in his mind, an idea he knew Margaret would approve of. They shared the same interests, the same compassion, and had his wife been well enough, she would have worked tirelessly for more than one charitable institution. 'So, will you contact this Mr Smollet?'

'It's the only thing I can do.'

'There is another alternative.'

'No, there isn't. I told you why I can't go home.'

'I didn't mean that.'

She raised her dark eyes in questioning surprise.

'You can come and live with us – with my wife and daughter. There's plenty of room.'

She looked at him with incredulity and disbelief.

'Well?'

'I couldn't do that. I hardly know you. I couldn't live on your charity, I couldn't impose . . . but thank you.'

'You won't be imposing and it's not charity. You could give something in return.'

'What can I give you?'

'Margaret, my wife, is in poor health. She has few friends, you would be a companion for her and it's a long time since there was a baby in the house. Selina, my daughter, is ten years old and an only child.' He didn't say that the birth of Selina was the cause of Margaret's ailments, that he knew his wife was lonely at times and that Selina was spoiled. He indulged the child to compensate for the time he didn't spend with her. And so, too, did Margaret, clinging to her, often treating her as an adult, making her far too precocious for her age.

They would both benefit from Ellan's presence.

'It still sounds like charity and you haven't asked your wife – and how can you, on this ship? Thank you, but I couldn't.'

'This ship is equipped with a telegraph. I can send a telegram, and I know she won't refuse. Margaret is a kind and caring woman.'

'But I'm a complete stranger. You just can't arrive home with a stranger and one who is . . .'

'In God's name, girl! You can't have your child alone in some squalid room and sink into the morass of the Liverpool slums.'

Ellan looked down at her hands. Why should he care what happened to her? 'Why are you taking such an interest in me?'

'Because I admire your spirit and because you've suffered far more than anyone of your age should ever have to.' He smiled. 'And because my colleagues will think I'm mad, though most of them think that anyway. Maybe it's to salve my own conscience. I work too hard. I know I neglect my family.'

She smiled. He was the strangest man she had ever met, yet she felt as though she'd known him all her life. Talking to him was just like talking to John or Mat or even to her pa. 'Maybe it's fate. Maybe I was meant to meet you, the same as I was never meant to inherit a fortune. I'm a firm believer in fate, destiny . . .'

He looked at her hard, wondering if she was mocking him, but there was no scorn in the dark eyes.

'I'm Manx and we believe in such things.'

He got to his feet and helped her up. 'So, Miss Ellan Vannin, will you accept my offer?'

202

'Only if your wife agrees.'

'I'll send the telegram right away. Now we must get you back to your cabin. You must be chilled to the bone. I am.'

That night she slept as she hadn't done for a long time and felt almost happy when she awoke. The flicker of hope that had burned so low for the last three months was now a shining light. The doctor had sent a message via a stewardess that she would be very welcome in the Elliot household. Margaret Elliot had returned the telegram. She now had somewhere to go, somewhere decent, and people who would care for her. At least, she hoped they would. She would ask him more about his wife and daughter, for she had arranged to meet him for a turn around the deck before lunch.

Throughout the morning she had backache, at least a dragging pain that came and went in the lower part of her back. But, she dismissed it. The baby had moved and was pressing on a nerve, that was all.

The weather was brighter too, she mused. The ocean was calmer, the sky pale blue and the wind only moderate. Was that an omen of better days ahead? She shook herself mentally. She would have to stop all this superstitious nonsense if she were to be a companion of someone of the same ilk as Mary Costain.

He was waiting for her, leaning on the rail. 'Did you sleep well?'

She smiled. 'Better than I've done for months, thank you.'

'Good. We'll only go as far as the bow, you mustn't tire yourself.'

They walked slowly towards the bow that cut

cleanly through the water, leaving a white-crested wake behind.

'She really said I was welcome?'

'You didn't believe me, did you?'

'I've never met people like you. You are so . . . kind.' She thought about Mary Costain, but she doubted that Miss Mary would willingly take an unmarried mother and child into her home, especially one she'd never even set eyes on. In Ellan's eyes, Margaret Elliot was rapidly taking on the guise of a saint.

'Tell me about Mrs Elliot. What things does she like to do?'

'She reads a lot. She supervises the household, most of the time, but she seldom goes out. She finds it exhausting. She has a keen mind and a sharp wit. She's intelligent and considerate. She has a great capacity to love people, people from all walks of life. She would have made a very good doctor, if circumstances had been different.' His voice held a note of guilt, his eyes were wistful. If Margaret had had a father who was not riddled with Victorian values, if she had never had Selina – and he always blamed himself for that. He should have known Margaret had been obsessed by duty, one of the 'virtues' her father had drummed into her. Yes, she would have made a good general practitioner had she been born in a different era. They were alike in the fact that they were both born ahead of their time and it bound them closer together. He realized that Ellan was staring at him.

'She takes a very close interest in Selina's education and she is interested in politics,' he finished.

Ellan looked dismayed. 'She's going to think I am very ignorant then. I know nothing of politics nor do I want to. I don't think she will find me much use as a companion.'

'She will. I know Margaret and she will find you very interesting. You as a person. In her own way Margaret is a very strong woman. Not physically, of course, but mentally and emotionally.'

'And what about Selina?'

He didn't answer for a few seconds. 'Selina is spoiled. She clings to her mother who she can twist around her little finger, most of the time. Just as she can me,' he added somewhat ruefully.

'If she's so close to her mother, won't she see me as an intruder?'

'I don't think so. You are still young enough to relate to her. I'm hoping she will eventually look on you as a confidante.'

All this sounded very daunting and very final. Ellan began to have doubts. 'I don't think she could ever think of me that way. I'm working class and I'll always be on the same level as a servant. Nothing can ever change that.'

He sighed. Maybe he was being too optimistic. What she said was true. He was too much of a visionary. He wanted to change things too quickly but the world would go on as it had always done. Change would only come slowly. True, the suffragettes were trying to speed up the cause of women's rights, but also true was the amount of opposition they faced, even from their own sex. Even Margaret didn't agree with all they wanted to achieve. But he had high hopes for Selina, they both had. If she wanted to pursue a career they wouldn't stop her, they had agreed to encourage her. Just as they would do if she chose to marry. He wouldn't be the dictatorial father.

Margaret would not be the meek, compliant wife her mother had been.

He was so lost in thought that he didn't notice that Ellan had stopped and was clutching the handrail tightly, her face white. Instantly he was all concern.

'What's the matter?'

'Nothing, just a twinge.' But even as she spoke another pain, more intense, contorted her face and almost made her double over.

'How long have you been having the pains?' His tone was clipped and authoritarian.

'For about four hours, but I've had them before. They'll go away.'

'I don't think they will. We'd better get you into the sick bay.'

'No. No, I'll be just fine. It's too early.'

'First ones often are.'

With quiet urgency he got her down the companion-way and enlisted the aid of a stewardess. He sent a passing steward racing off for the ship's doctor. 'Just take it slowly, Ellan. There's no need to panic, everything is being taken care of.' He could see the fear in her eyes as well as the pain.

The ship's doctor and nurse got her on to a bunk. The nurse helped her with her clothes and draped a clean sheet over her while the doctor and Lloyd Elliot scrubbed up, holding a quiet conversation.

Despite the reassurances of both the nurse and the stewardess who had stayed with her, Ellan was afraid. The pain was unbearable. What was going to happen to her? How long must she endure this agony? She wished desperately that Lizzie was with her or Mrs H. Another contraction tore into her and she bit hard into her lip to stop herself from screaming.

'You scream the place down, love, if you want to.' The nurse's voice was very close. 'Grip my hand and yell.'

She was incoherent; the pain was terrible and she felt herself verging on unconsciousness, dragged back to reality by the urging of the nurse and the doctor, to push as hard as she could. She was unaware that she was painfully crushing the nurse's fingers, she was oblivious to everything except the waves of agony, followed by the tremendous urge to bear down. They were telling her to hold on, stop, but she couldn't and then she heard the noise, like the mewing of a kitten at first, then louder and a sense of relief washed over her and, miraculously, the pain had gone.

'There now, love, that wasn't too bad, was it?'

She managed a weak smile for the nurse and released her vice-like grip.

'You've a fine, healthy daughter, Ellan. Look!'

Lloyd Elliot was bending over her, a small scrap of humanity still blood-stained, wrapped in a towel in his arms. Its tiny face was screwed up in rage at the way it had been forced into the world and it gave vent to that anger by protesting in a fretful wail, continuing to protest by waving small fists in the air.

Ellan took her baby in her arms. This was the life she'd nursed inside her for nearly nine months, Jamie's daughter. She held the baby close and murmured soothingly and the cries subsided. She felt so at peace, so tired, yet so happy. Really happy for the first time in months.

'We'll leave you in peace now. Feed her and then you'll both sleep,' Lloyd urged gently.

'Nurse Wright will stay with you, my dear,' the doctor reassured her.

As she fussed around making them both more comfortable Nurse Wright said, 'What will you call her?'

Ellan stroked the tiny cheek with her finger. 'Lucy.'

'Lucy,' Lloyd repeated slowly.

'Well, you've got to admit that *Lusitania* is a bit of a mouthful and you have called her after the ship, haven't you, love?' said Nurse Wright.

Ellan smiled again. 'Yes. What else could I call her?'

Chapter Thirteen

———◆———

SHE RECOVERED RAPIDLY AND Lucy thrived. Lloyd came to see her every day and examined the baby expertly.

'She's a fine healthy child, even though she's premature. And, she has your hair.'

Ellan stroked the mop of black hair. 'But she has her father's eyes.'

'All babies are born with blue eyes, they will change and she will lose all this hair.' Ellan looked alarmed and he smiled. 'Oh, don't worry, it will grow again. She won't be bald.' He stood watching her for a few seconds. 'We dock tomorrow.'

'So soon! I've lost all sense of time.'

'There will be a car waiting at the landing stage, so I'll get a stewardess to help you pack your things and get you both up on deck. I know you are not supposed to get up quite so soon, but you do seem strong enough.'

'You've been so kind. Everyone has been kind.' She was so glad she'd come back. It had been the right decision.

'That's what we're all here for, Ellan, but don't you go trying to rush around,' Nurse Wright interrupted.

'Don't worry about that, she'll be in expert hands,' Lloyd replied.

It was a short journey through the city centre, up Bold Street, past the expensive shops that she'd seen with Lizzie on her last visit to Liverpool. She thought about Lizzie then, and Jamie and Aunt Maud and John, Mat and Andrew. She was so near and yet so far.

They passed St Luke's Church in Hardman Street and then turned into Rodney Street, the Harley Street of Liverpool. From the comfort of the leather-covered back seat of the car Ellan gazed at the Georgian houses with their elegant facades, the pillars that supported porches, the glass fanlights above doors smart with fresh paint and gleaming brassware. The short flights of steps that led up to the doors were clean and whitened. Her nervousness increased as she wondered what kind of a reception she would receive.

Lloyd helped her from the car and then the driver took it to the back of the houses to park and unload. Ellan shrank nearer to him as the door was opened and a girl of her own age stood there, clad in the black dress and starched white cap and pinafore of a parlour maid. Beyond her, in the wide hall, Ellan could just discern two figures.

'It's good to see you back safe and sound, sir,' the girl said, dipping a curtsey while eyeing Ellan furtively.

'Thank you, Tilly, it's good to be back.'

'Papa! Papa! What did you bring me?'

Ellan watched from the doorway as a thin child with straight, mousy hair and pallid features, launched herself bodily at Lloyd. That must be Selina.

He laughed. 'No kiss for your poor tired Papa?'

'Selina! Where are your manners?'

So this was Margaret Elliot, Ellan thought as the woman moved slowly forward and received a kiss on the cheek from her husband. She was not as old as Ellan had envisaged, but like her daughter she was thin and had the same light brown hair, dressed in a style that was neither fashionable nor suited to her long thin face, which bore the stamp of suffering. The grey eyes were kind and intelligent and her brow furrowed as she looked past her husband and caught sight of Ellan and the baby.

'This is the girl you telegraphed me about?'

They all turned towards her and she automatically took a step backwards.

'Yes. This is Ellan.' Lloyd came towards her and ushered her into the hall.

'I'm very pleased to meet you, ma'am. I hope you won't find me . . .' She faltered beneath the steady gaze.

'You must all be tired. Come into the drawing room.'

Hesitantly she followed Margaret Elliot's thin and stooped figure, urged on by Lloyd. Selina had already disappeared into the room ahead of them.

'Tilly, bring us some tea, please,' Margaret instructed.

Tilly bobbed and nodded. Ellan felt decidedly uneasy. This was far too grand a room for her to be sitting in. She would be much happier going below stairs with Tilly.

'Selina, say hullo to Ellan. She's going to be staying here with us,' Lloyd said.

The child stared at her with open suspicion. 'Why?'

'Selina. That's very rude, dear,' Margaret reprimanded.

'Because she has no home of her own to go to and she

will be company for your mama and I'm sure you would like to help with little Lucy.'

Selina appeared to ignore her father's explanation, her hazel eyes riveted on Ellan.

Ellan felt the naked hostility and tried to counter it. 'Would you like to hold her?' she asked, holding Lucy out – rather like a peace offering, she thought.

'No. I don't like babies.'

Lloyd started to reproach her but his wife raised her hand to silence him. 'Why don't you go with Papa and help Johnson and Tilly with the luggage. I'm sure Papa has something for you.'

Following his wife's lead, Lloyd changed the subject. 'Oh, I have indeed.'

The scowl vanished from Selina's face and she smiled up at her father. 'What is it? What is it?' she cried eagerly, as he led her to the door.

When they'd gone Ellan started to speak but using the same, fluent gesture of the hand, the older woman silenced her. 'There's no need to apologize, it isn't your fault. Selina can be a difficult child. I indulge her far too much, but it's because I only have her.'

'Ma'am, I'm sorry. I shouldn't have come here. I should have thanked Doctor Elliot and firmly refused. It's so kind of you but I . . . I'm . . .'

'Not a suitable companion?' Margaret interrupted. 'Please sit down, Ellan, you must be exhausted standing. All Lloyd told me was that you were completely alone in the world with no home, no family; that you are an unusual girl, intelligent, courageous and that I might enjoy your company.'

Ellan sat on the edge of the brocade sofa, Lucy held in

the crook of her arm, fast asleep. 'That was kind of him but it's not strictly true. I do have family, of a sort, in Peel. I call Mrs Quirk Aunt Maud, but she is no blood relation. My mother died when I was four and my father was killed in an accident in the mine. I have lived with Aunt Maud and her sons until last year.' She plucked at the edge of Lucy's shawl, her eyes downcast. 'I have always been a working girl, ma'am. I'm not used to all this and Lucy is . . .' She couldn't say it. She couldn't utter the word.

'Illegitimate,' Margaret said softly.

She nodded curtly. 'But I was engaged to be married and I would have been married too. He was lost . . . the *Ellan Vannin* tragedy . . . he was on his way to Liverpool.'

Margaret could see she was on the verge of tears, she would press her no further yet. No doubt she would hear it all from Lloyd later. Ellan was another of his 'lame ducks'. He was always ready to help the poor, the sick, the desperate. Many of his patients were wealthy but he also worked free in the Royal Infirmary where those who could pay little or nothing were taken. It was little better than a workhouse in her opinion. As she watched the girl gently pull the shawl back from the baby's face she thought she glimpsed what Lloyd had seen in Ellan. She was of the working class, as she'd just reminded her, and the child was a bastard to put it bluntly, but she wasn't what could be called 'loose' and Margaret was sure by the way she spoke that she had been educated to a reasonable degree. The furthering of that education would give her immense satisfaction, if things worked out. 'May I hold her?'

Ellan looked up and dashed away the few tell-tale

tears with the back of her hand, then she placed Lucy in the older woman's arms.

'She's beautiful. You are both welcome here, my dear, and I do mean that.'

A sob caught in Ellan's throat. Margaret Elliot was a saint and in her eyes was a beautiful and gracious lady, despite her homely looks.

'Tilly will show you your room and where the bathroom is and she'll help you to settle in. You must rest now. You really shouldn't be up at all.'

Ellan was still overwhelmed and apprehensive about how she would fit into this household. 'Ma'am, would you be very put out if I were to take my meals in the kitchen? I'd feel . . .' She shrugged.

'I wouldn't be put out at all, if it makes you feel more at home, and please stop calling me "ma'am", it's so formal.'

'What am I to call you? I can't call you by your Christian name, it would be too improper.'

'Then call me Mrs Elliot, for now.'

Ellan smiled with relief.

Margaret, too, was a little relieved. It was obvious that the girl was very ill at ease. Mealtimes could prove to be awkward affairs. Besides, she always shared lunch with Selina, and Selina already eyed the new arrivals with suspicion. Dinner was reserved for Lloyd. It was the only time in the day when they could find time to converse at length and often he was too busy to come home at all and she dined alone. She, too, wondered how Ellan would fit into the household. Lloyd had placed the girl in an awkward position: she was neither servant nor equal. But only time would tell and she wouldn't turn her away to seek lodgings and work in a city where both were hard to find.

Ellan looked around the bedroom in awe. She'd never envisaged anything as fine as this. She'd thought an attic bedroom, sparsely furnished with the basic essentials, would have been her lot and she'd have been grateful for it. A carpet of dusky rose pink covered the floor. The bed had a quilt of pure white cotton. The washstand was marble-topped and pink roses embellished the bowl and ewer. There was a wardrobe, a dressing table and a tall-boy of good English oak and beside the bed was a cradle made of painted rattan.

'The cradle was Miss Selina's. The missus had it brought down from the attic,' Tilly announced.

Ellan turned to her. 'I only expected a small bedroom. This is too fine for me.'

Tilly took her carpet bag and placed it at the foot of the bed. 'I'll unpack for you. Put her in the cradle.'

'There won't be any need for you to unpack. I don't have much and I'll be taking my meals with you in the kitchen.'

Tilly pushed her white starched cap further towards the back of her head. Her copper-coloured hair was scraped back into a knot, the freckles across the bridge of her nose stood out against her pale skin and her brown eyes were frank and curious. 'Who are you? You don't look like one of *them*, so what are you doing here?'

'I'm not one of *them* and to be honest I don't really know why I'm here. They seem such good people. Doctor Elliot helped me on the ship. I barely knew him and the next thing he's telling me I can come and live here. To be a sort of companion to his wife.'

Tilly nodded knowingly. 'He's like that. Always putting his hand in his pocket for every street arab that comes along. Always finding stuff they don't need for folk who are destitute. He works free at the Royal, too. The rest of the quality couldn't care less if we live or die. I ain't never met anyone like him before and she's the same. She gave us all instructions never to turn anyone away from the door without something to eat. Cook says we feed half of Liverpool and word has got around, I can tell you. We keep seeing the same faces week in and week out, but we always get the same answer when we complain. "They must be starving, don't turn them away." What is it?' She abruptly changed the subject, pointing to the baby.

'A girl. I called her Lucy.'

'After the ship? Me brother works on the *Lucy*, he's a trimmer. You were called after a ship, too, weren't you? The one that was sunk last year.'

'No, I wasn't called after her. They changed her name after I was born. Anyway, it's not a proper name.'

Tilly leaned against the tallboy, settling down to gain as much information about the newcomer as possible. 'What is it then?'

'In the Manx tongue it means Isle of Man. I'm not a "someone" I'm a "something".'

'That's a bit daft. Whose notion was it to give you a name like that?'

'My pa. He's dead. He died when I was ten.' Ellan, not wishing to have to relate her life history yet again, sat on the bed and said, 'Your name's Tilly, that's unusual.'

'It's just as bloody daft as yours. Oh, Lord, sorry!' She clamped her hand over her mouth, but Ellan smiled.

Tilly reminded her of Lizzie. 'I know you shouldn't speak ill of the dead, but our mam – God rest her soul – had a brainstorm when she had me. Matilda Florence she called me. I don't know where she got it from, but fancy giving a poor helpless mite a name like that! No wonder everyone got fed up giving me my full title. It was me da who shortened it all. Everyone – except here of course – calls me Tilly Floss and that's just as bad!'

Ellan smiled again. It was a silly name when you thought about it. 'Oh, I don't know if it was wise to come here. It might not work out.'

Tilly gave up all pretence of etiquette and sat on the bed beside Ellan. Ellan was in a funny position but she wasn't in the least bit snooty or even remotely common as she'd first feared. 'The missus is lovely to work for. She's not well, hasn't been for years and some days she has to stay in bed all day.' She lowered her voice. 'It's something to do with her insides. You know, the curse an' all. She should never have had kids at all, that's why there's only Miss Selina. He's out all day and sometimes half the night as well, but she never complains.'

'I don't think the child liked me.'

'That one doesn't like anyone, except her ma and pa. She's a spoiled little brat. A right 'orror at times, not so as you'd notice at first. But temper! It's red hair she should have had. You should hear her when she can't have her own way. She'd get the back of me hand if she were mine. A good hiding would sort that little madam out.'

'Why isn't she punished?'

'The missus is too soft with her, that's why. She spends hours coaxing her. Maybe you coming will be a good thing for the missus. She treats that child like a grown up and it's doing no good, no good at all.' Reluctantly Tilly got to her feet. 'I'd better go down and leave you to sort yourself out.'

'That won't take long. Would anyone mind if I came down for a cup of tea? In the kitchen, I mean.'

Tilly grinned. 'Come down as soon as you're ready. Cook's going round the bend wanting to know all about you. I promised I'd give you the once-over and report back, but there's no need now. You can tell her yourself. Bring little Lucy down with you if you want.'

For the first time that day Ellan began to relax. She liked Tilly and even if she didn't fit in upstairs, she knew she would behind the green baize door that led downstairs to the kitchen and the pantries. They were her class of people.

Maud Quirk looked with suspicion at the large cardboard box tied with a fancy ribbon that Andrew had set on the table.

'Well, go on, Ma. Open it,' Mat urged.

'I told you not to go buying expensive, frivolous things,' she rejoined, gently pulling the box towards her, her work-worn fingers fiddling with the ribbon bow. 'This ribbon alone must have cost a morning's work.'

'Ma, if you are so obsessed with the ribbon use it to trim something but for heaven's sake open the damned box! The stick I've had to take from the lads about it was bad enough, but at least I didn't expect a lecture on thrift from you.'

Maud looked apologetic as she took off the lid, but her eyebrows rose instantly as she saw the contents. Nestling in tissue paper was a hat, a very expensive hat, made of rich plum-coloured velvet with a medium brim tilted up at the front and decorated with two large ostrich feathers, one plum-coloured, one pale pink. She'd never seen anything quite like it before. Not even Miss Mary Costain wore hats like this. 'You've gone and spent your wages on this?'

'I worked for them and I'll spend them, Ma.'

'You'll waste them, you mean. When am I ever going to wear it?'

'For Chapel. I know you've got a purple coat.'

'It's not purple, it's plum. Purple is . . . loud . . . and what will people think, me turning up as though I were going to a society wedding?'

Andrew sighed. There was no pleasing her at all. He'd hoped she would have been delighted. He'd expected no great demonstrative show of pleasure but she might at least have shown some interest. Instead she was about to replace the lid on the box.

'Not going to try it on then, Ma?' John asked. 'You know you're still a fine-looking woman when you're dressed up. I can sometimes see what Pa saw in you all those years ago.'

Maud looked at him hard but there was no mockery or guile in his eyes.

'At least try it, Ma,' Mat urged.

Maud lifted it from the box and ran a finger over the velvet, then placed it over her now grey hair and looked at herself in the small mirror that hung on the wall by the window. It was a very fine hat and it did make her look . . . well, almost elegant. She tutted to herself. A woman of her age worrying whether she looked fashionable, pure vanity and pride, both sins. But as she tilted her head she couldn't help but think how commanding and dignified she looked – a hardworking matriarch, strong and resourceful, someone to be respected.

'I'm looking forward to seeing the look on Dora Killip's face when she sees you in that,' John laughed. He'd seen the lift of the head and the half smile that had formed around his mother's mouth.

As far as Maud was concerned, that settled it. 'It will look well with my coat but you shouldn't have wasted your money,' she chided as she took off the hat and carefully replaced it in the box.

The three brothers exchanged looks and Andrew nodded his thanks to John.

'And talking of Dora Killip, I saw her this morning and she's had another letter from their Lizzie. That's five she's had while we've only had three from Ellan and that Lizzie was never the best of letter writers.'

'Ellan will have lots of things to do, Ma,' Mat said, ignoring the sudden, cold expression that had crossed Andrew's face.

'It's very odd,' Maud continued.

'What is?' Mat asked.

'Dora said Lizzie is working as a parlour maid in a very grand house on some avenue. A house that would make Glentrammon look like a run-down old manor house, so Lizzie says.'

'So?' Mat couldn't see where this was leading.

'So, she doesn't mention Ellan at all. The last we heard was they were living in that boarding house. And, with all that money Ellan's got, you'd wonder at Lizzie going to work as a maid.'

'Ma, Lizzie has worked all her life and so has Ellan. Maybe having money doesn't change the habits of a lifetime or maybe Lizzie was bored. Maybe she didn't want to have to rely on Ellan – she always was independent.'

'Maybe they've fallen out,' Andrew interjected harshly. 'Maybe the money has turned Ellan's head and she doesn't want to know anyone from her previous life.'

'Is that what you really think, because I don't.' John looked across at his brother and shook his head.

'Well, there's something going on. I know it,' Maud said. 'Those two were as thick as thieves and Ellan didn't mention Lizzie at all in that last letter. Money is at the bottom of it, it always is. It changes people, gives them power and if they've no idea how to use that power, they turn into monsters.'

'Ma! It wouldn't change Ellan like that. I don't believe that for a minute,' John snapped at his mother.

'She's certainly managed to cause friction in this family and she's not even here.' Andrew's tone was cutting and taking his coat from the hook behind the door, he went out into the yard. He'd go down to the tavern, maybe Bert Killip would be there and he could question him more closely about Lizzie's letter. His heart still turned over when he thought of Ellan, but he didn't really believe that she had changed so much that she would fall out with Lizzie. As his ma had remarked, they were as thick as thieves. Maybe there had been a quarrel but Ellan – or the Ellan he remembered – would never have abandoned her friend in a foreign city to fend for herself.

He bent his head against the force of the wind as he

221

walked down the lane into the village and fingered the ring she had left him. He told himself that he only wore it so that it didn't get lost and it was silver and you didn't just discard a precious metal that had been prised from the bowels of the earth by men like his father and George Vannin. He refused to even think that he wore it because she had bought it, or rather gone to the trouble to have her own ring copied.

There were long nights while he'd been at sea, taking his turn to stand watch, when he hadn't been able to put her out of his mind. She must have suffered agonies of grief over the loss of Jamie Corlett. He even wished he'd been at home when it had happened. She might have turned to him, but he hadn't been and she'd gone. She was a wealthy woman now, living a very different kind of life to that she'd known. She was still very young and very beautiful, she'd have dozens of men fighting over her, and her money. But rich or poor he'd have married her and loved her. Like so many times before, he tried to banish all thoughts of her. She had gone. She was lost to him for ever and he was a fool.

He pushed open the door of the tavern and his nostrils were assailed by the familiar smells of ale and tobacco. He needed a few drinks to pluck up the courage to tell Ma that he'd signed on for a much longer trip this time, to Australia. He smiled wryly to himself. Maud thought that Australia was full of convicts and said so, even though they'd stopped transportation in 1840. True, they were nearly all descended from felons but if anyone pointed this out she always said, 'Blood will out,' meaning the taint was still there. Nodding his greetings, he made his way to the bar and asked for a tot of rum. He spotted Bert Killip leaning against the bar in the smoke room and moved towards him.

'How's things, Bert?'

Bert Killip was a man of few words. He'd long ago given up trying to keep ahead of his wife who could talk the hind legs off a donkey and his daughters who took over when Dora left off. 'Fair to middling, Andy, lad. And yourself?'

'Not bad, Bert. Off to Australia on the next trip.'

'Place is full of thieves and cut-throats,' Bert said, gulping down his stout.

Andrew laughed. 'Not you as well. I thought it was only Ma who believed that. I hear you've had a letter from your Lizzie?'

'Aye. Dora's doing the rounds of the village with it.' His weather-beaten features screwed up in a smile. He wouldn't have minded young Andy Quirk as a son-in-law. At least he would have had another man to talk to, the companionship of someone who thought like himself. Lizzie was a bloody fool. 'She's working at some fancy house. Pages and pages of this Mrs Van Kronin and all her furniture. Must be doing her good though. It must have impressed her. Our Lizzie can only usually manage half a page!'

'Any mention of Ellan?' He hoped he sounded only vaguely interested.

'None, and the more I think of it the more bloody odd it seems. Does Ellan ever mention our Lizzie in her letters?'

'I don't think so, but then Ma doesn't read them out, and if I'm away . . .'

'If you ask me they've had some sort of bust up and

parted company. It wouldn't surprise me if our Lizzie came home.' He swigged the remains of his pint. 'Then again, she's got her pride, so she might not. But they've had a bust up, mark my words.'

Andrew nodded. It was a reasonable assumption to make.

Chapter Fourteen

———✦———

T HE FIRST TIME IT had happened Ellan believed it to
be an accident. She'd been reading to Margaret
when they'd both heard the high-pitched cries.

'I'd better go and see what's happened, Mrs Elliot,'
she said, rising hastily to her feet.

Margaret nodded and leaned her head back against
the sofa. She was having a bad day and had tried to banish
the pain by concentrating on Ellan's voice as she read
aloud from Mrs Gaskill's *Mary Barton*. The child's cries
quickly ceased.

Ellan rushed into the bedroom to find Selina holding
Lucy on her knee.

'She fell and banged her head on the chair,' Selina
informed her with a totally innocent air. 'I was trying to
hush her. I didn't want to upset Mama, I know she's not
well today.'

Ellan took Lucy from the girl and immediately the
cries subsided. 'Let me have a look at what you've done.
It's all right now, Ma's here.' She could never think of
herself as 'Mama'. A bruise had begun to appear on

Lucy's temple. 'Hush now and we'll put something nice and cold on it and then it will be better.'

Selina was all concerned urgency. 'I'll go and ask Tilly for something.'

Lucy at eighteen months was unable to tell her anything, but when Tilly came up with an ice pack her words gave Ellan some cause for concern.

'I don't mean to sound horrible, Ellan, but I wouldn't leave Lucy for so long with Miss Selina.'

'Tilly, it was an accident. Lucy fell and banged her head. Little ones often fall.'

Tilly expertly placed the cold compress against the toddler's forehead. 'She's jealous of you both. She has been ever since you came here.'

'She's got over that. Oh, she can be sullen at times, I'll give you that, usually when she feels she's been slighted or left out. And she still gets into a temper if she can't have her own way but Mrs Elliot has taught me how to deal with that.'

'Well, I'm just warning you. Why don't you leave her with me or Cook?'

'Tilly, you're always busy and so is Cook, it wouldn't be fair and there are so many things downstairs that could really hurt her. It was just an accident.'

At that moment Selina returned, a box of jellied sweets in her hand. 'Would she like one of these?' she asked, offering the box to Lucy and Ellan. Ellan took one and popped it into Lucy's mouth. She looked at Tilly accusingly but Tilly just shrugged.

Ellan had been with the Elliots for nearly two years and during that time she'd been happy. She'd felt very strange at first, unable to come to terms with both her position in the household and the sheer kindness of both Lloyd and Margaret, as they both now insisted she call them. They were special people. People who cared deeply in an uncaring world. They had money, for she learned that Margaret had inherited her father's estate and Lloyd had a very lucrative practice. But there was no side to either of them, no snobbishness. Wealth hadn't brought uncaring arrogance or derision of the poor and underprivileged. She'd seen Lloyd come home from the hospital, his face grey with fatigue, his shoulders drooping with exhaustion, his eyes haunted by the tragedies he'd seen and often angry and frustrated at the crass, callous attitude of so many people. It was at those times that she'd excuse herself and leave him alone with his wife to have one of their long conversations or silences that were companionable, even comforting.

It was on a return from one of her excursions to Tilly's home that the second 'accident' happened and made her face reality. She and Tilly had quickly become friends and Ellan often took Lucy and went home with Tilly to the tiny, cramped, back to back terraced house where Mr Rigby lived with his brood: Emily who was seventeen and who worked at Tillotsons on the Dock Road; Mary who was fifteen; and Tommy who was ten. Tilly's ma had died years ago and Mr Rigby was a taciturn man. But Tilly and her sisters made up for that fact.

Tilly's elder brother, Davie, was in the Merchant Navy and was due home and they all went down to the pierhead to see the *Lusitania* dock. Ellan had a particular affinity and affection for the ship, remembering how lucky she'd been to have met Lloyd Elliot and how she'd had the best in medical care when Lucy was born.

It was a typical April day with intermittent showers that sent people hurrying for shelter and bursts of sunlight that made the cobbled setts of Man Island gleam like polished pewter. There was a fresh breeze coming in off the river which tugged at their hats. They watched, waving madly, as the huge liner was manoeuvred alongside by the tugs and then they took the overhead railway to Gladstone Dock where she would tie up and where Davie would eventually disembark. He looked a lot like Tilly, Ellan thought as she greeted him.

'This is Ellan. She came back from America on the *Lucy* and this is little Lucy,' Tilly explained.

'Oh, it was you that we heard about then. Went and had the baby on board and called her Lucy. Caused quite a stir but you should have let us know earlier, like, we could all have had a bet on it. Boy or girl, like.'

'Davie Rigby, you hardfaced little sod!' Tilly cried, punching him on the shoulder.

'Less of the "little". I'm head and shoulders over all of you,' he laughed.

'What have you brought us this time then?' Tilly questioned openly as they all walked towards the dock gate.

Davie turned to Ellan. 'Oh, that's nice, isn't it? Hardly gorrof the gangway and all she's interested in is what I've brought her. I've got me docking bottle for Da, a few fancy bits an' pieces for our Mary and Emily. A baseball bat and ball for our Tommy . . .'

'You're as thick as a plank sometimes,' Tilly interrupted, raising her eyes to the heavens. 'He can do enough harm with a football. Mrs Murphy opposite says if he breaks her windows again she'll have the law on him, and you bring him a bloody baseball bat!'

'If yer going to carry on like that I'll give your present to Ellan here.'

Ellan felt a little embarrassed as they were drawing amused glances from passers-by.

'Suit yourself.' Tilly tossed her head in mock defiance and Ellan had to smile at this good-natured bantering.

'Oh, here. Have it, then we might get some peace.' Davie delved into his pocket and brought out a small box.

Tilly almost snatched it from him in her eagerness. 'Oh, look at this, Ellan.'

Inside the box was a watch, the kind that could be pinned to a dress or coat like a brooch. It was silver mounted but the edges and face were enamelled in different shades of blue. 'Aw, Davie, lad, you shouldn't have spent so much. You work too hard on that tub, sweating down there in the engine room.'

'There's no satisfying some people, Ellan. If I'd have brought her some tatty glass beads from the five and ten cent store, she'd have had a right cob on.'

Again Tilly punched him gently and smiled. 'Our Mary's got a good hot dinner on for us all.'

'Scouse again?'

'No, it ain't and anyway there's nothing wrong with scouse. Besides, she's done a Lancashire Hot Pot, with red cabbage an' all.'

'What's that except scouse with a crust on it.'

'Now who's being awkward.' She turned to Ellan and reiterated her brother's earlier comments. 'There's no satisfying some people, is there?'

It was a lovely afternoon. Mary had the little house shining like a palace and set a good meal before them all, carefully saving Emily's portion. The girl was delighted with what Davie had brought her, as was Tommy, but Mr Rigby echoed Tilly's words with the warning, 'Now listen 'ere, me laddo, if yer think yer goin' ter cause havoc in this street, an' upset 'er over the road again, yer mistaken. Get down the park with it an' take yer 'ooligan friends with yer.'

'Ah, eh, Da. Yer know they won't let us play footie or rounders down there. Ol' Sutcliffe, the parkie, chases us.'

Mr Rigby gave up and disappeared behind his copy of the *Echo*. 'Then go an' play ollies on the Dock Road,' he muttered, although he didn't really mean it. It was an expression that meant 'Don't annoy me'.

Ellan and Tilly helped Mary to wash up and then, reluctantly donning her hat and coat, Tilly kissed them all and they left to get the tram home.

Tilly went to help Cook and Selina offered to look after Lucy while Ellan went to tell Margaret about the outing. Margaret always liked to hear about Tilly's family and often sent things home with the girl. Nothing that could be called charity for the Rigbys were fiercely proud, but things that would save them money: a box of soaps, Margaret was trying a new brand and didn't want to waste them; she was having some new curtains and cushion covers made, could Mary or Emily possibly do anything with the old ones? There was plenty of life in them still, too good to throw away; she'd ordered some blankets for Selina's bed but Selina didn't like the colour, could Mary use them? In this way pride was not diminished. It was not a 'hand out'.

Ellan was halfway through recounting Mr Rigby's remarks about Tommy and the baseball bat and ''er over the road' when they heard a thud, followed by screams.

Ellan jumped up and Margaret slowly got to her feet.

Tilly reached the breakfast room first, followed closely by Ellan while Margaret tried to hasten her steps across the hall.

'I told her to get down, that she'd hurt herself.' Selina stood by the chintz-covered sofa. Lucy was lying on the floor crying.

Ellan scooped her up in her arms, then uttered a cry as she saw the blood on the child's face. 'Oh, my God! I'll have to get the doctor or get her to hospital.'

'She climbed on the chair to reach the brass bells and fell off.' Selina was the picture of innocence.

'You little liar!' Tilly cried without thinking.

The child's eyes narrowed but her expression remained calm. 'I'll tell Papa what you called me and he'll turn you out,' she hissed.

'And I'll tell your papa that you deliberately pushed little Lucy into the fireplace. She could have been burned!'

Ellan was oblivious to this interchange, she was soothing Lucy while at the same time trying to staunch the blood from the cut just above the little girl's eyebrow. 'Tilly, stop shouting and get Mrs Elliot or the doctor.'

Tilly glared at Selina. 'You pushed her. She couldn't possibly have climbed up on the chair, she's too small – and anyway, where's the chair? The chairs are all in their proper places and how could she drag one across the room?' Tilly was openly scornful. 'I suppose she did just that? Fell and cut her head, then pulled the chair back again. You pushed her.'

Margaret stood in the doorway, her eyes taking in the scene: Ellan, her face white, biting her lip and holding a blood-soaked handkerchief over Lucy's right eye; Lucy still quietly sobbing and clinging to her mother; Tilly, her hands on her hips, her face dark with anger; and Selina, her own twelve-year-old daughter, standing, white-faced, tight-lipped and glaring at Tilly with defiance.

'Tilly, go and call Doctor Hudson. Ellan, are you feeling all right? You look terrible.'

'I'm just a bit shaken, that's all,' Ellan replied. Tilly's accusations and reasoning were beginning to sink in.

Tilly disappeared and Margaret sat down and taking Selina's hands, drew her towards her. 'Selina, I want you to tell me the truth. You know we would never punish you for telling the truth, but if you lie, then your papa will be very, very angry and so will I. Now, tell me what happened. Slowly, in your own time.'

Selina cast her eyes down and drew closer to her mother. 'It was my fault, Mama. Lucy wanted to play with the little brass bells on the mantel. I pulled the chair up to the hearth because even I have to stand on something to reach, but when I climbed on the chair Lucy started to cry. She was pointing to the bells and saying, "Me, me," so I got down and lifted her up and she . . . she fell! Oh, Mama, I was so frightened that I pushed the chair back! I'm sorry, I really am. I shouldn't have let her climb up.'

Margaret smiled. 'You see, it is always better to tell the truth. I'm sure you didn't mean for Lucy to get hurt . . .'

'Oh, no. I didn't. I didn't.'

'And I'm sure Ellan knows that, but you must ask her to forgive you. Poor Lucy is going to need that cut stitched.'

Selina turned to Ellan, her demeanour meek. 'I'm sorry, Ellan,' she said calmly.

Ellan looked at her uncertainly. Had it been an accident? Then she remembered last time. 'I . . . I know you are, Selina,' she heard herself say, but her heart was troubled. A sinister feeling crept over her.

'That's a good girl,' Margaret murmured gently and the girl turned back towards her mother. Before she did so, she raised her downcast eyes and looked quickly at Ellan and Lucy. Ellan shrank visibly for there was pure hatred in that glance.

When Doctor Hudson had put a stitch in the cut and had given Lucy something to calm her and make her sleep, Ellan sat beside the cot with Tilly.

'It's all a pack of lies,' Tilly hissed. 'She's a cunning little madam that one and sharp. So sharp she'll cut herself one day.'

'I know. I half believed her story until she looked straight at me. Oh, Tilly, she hates me. I can't stay here any longer. Neither Doctor nor Mrs Elliot will believe me. Mrs Elliot thinks everything is fine because Selina apologized, but I can't take any more chances. She might hurt Lucy seriously next time.' Her fingers were shaking as she smoothed the end of the sheet tucked over her sleeping child. 'Yet they'll think I'm so ungrateful if I just say I'm leaving. They'll want to know why and where I will go and what I will do to support myself and Lucy and oh, they've been so kind.'

'I'll never understand why they don't see how bad that girl is, but I suppose it's because they dote on her so much,' Tilly sighed. 'And you're right. They'd be very upset and hurt if you left and they would want explanations. You could go and live with my da and my lot, so somewhere to stay isn't the problem.'

'Tilly, I couldn't do that. There's not enough room as it is, and how would I pay them?'

'We'll have to think of something and quickly. You can't leave her alone again.'

'But there's not much I can do. I'm not trained. Oh, I was a machinist, but that's all.'

Tilly was deep in thought and Ellan remained silent. Lucy was dearer to her than anything else in the world and she would beg in the streets if she had to.

'Why don't you take her home to Peel?'

'Tilly, you know I can't. She'd grow up with everyone pointing at her. She'd be shunned, made the butt of everyone's cruelty whether they realized it or not. And, when she grows up, who'd have her? I don't care about myself but I won't inflict all that on her poor, innocent little head.'

Tilly knew she was right. There had been a girl from the next street who had had a baby out of wedlock and that poor kid had a terrible life. 'Then we'll just have to think of something, and in the meantime keep her with you as much as you can and when you can't, I'll look after her. She'll be safer below stairs than left to the mercy of that lying little bitch!'

'I just don't know where she gets it from, Tilly. Both her parents are so good.'

'Aye, to others. Oh, I'm not saying anything against them, but maybe they should show some of that goodness to Miss Selina. I'm sure she feels rejected, left out.'

'But they idolize her and she spends a lot of time with her mother.'

Tilly shrugged. She was well used to the oddities of this household.

It was Tilly who unwittingly found the solution to the problem. On her next afternoon off they went down to the pierhead to take the ferry across to New Brighton. Tilly had brought some apples and some toffee that Ellan had made. Cinder toffee, Tilly called it, because it was brittle and honeycombed. Ellan had laughed at the name and told her it was carn, meaning rock, toffee.

Lucy's eye was healing and Doctor Hudson said it would leave only a tiny scar, but between them they had not let the child out of their sight for more than a few minutes.

It was a pleasant day, the river was calm except for the wake of the Woodchurch ferry boat. Two liners and two cargo ships were standing out in the river waiting to dock and the ferry weaved its way expertly between them. Ellan felt happier than she had since Lucy's alleged accident, although she doubted that she would ever feel at ease in the house again.

Tilly offered her the paper bag they'd put the toffee in. 'They don't call them sweets in America,' Ellan said.

'What do they call them? I thought they spoke the same language as us?' Tilly mumbled, her mouth full.

'They do but they use different words for certain things. They call sweets candies.'

'Candies,' Tilly repeated the word. 'Candies, it sort of rolls off your tongue. I like it. And what do they call sweet shops then, something like candy cabins, I suppose?'

'No. At least I don't think so. Candy cabins,' Ellan repeated the name and smiled. 'It sounds good. It makes you think of a shop smelling of all the delicious sweets, sweets in little boxes tied with ribbon instead of paper bags or cones made from newspaper.'

Tilly choked on another piece of the brittle toffee and when Ellan banged her hard on the back and she regained her powers of speech with tears of exertion in her eyes, she said, 'That's it. That's it, Ellan!'

'What? What's "it"?'

'A small shop selling toffees and fudges, maybe even chocolates, all nicely packed up.'

'Tilly Rigby, what are you talking about?'

'You. Your way out from Rodney Street.'

'You're mad. Where would I get the money from?'

'Doctor Elliot. Tell him you want to earn your own living.'

Ellan looked at her aghast. 'I couldn't do that.'

'You can. We can't keep Lucy under lock and key for ever. Tell him you're very, very grateful, but you'd like to stand on your own two feet.'

'But how . . .'

Tilly, now carried away with her idea, was not to be put off. 'Ask him to lend you the money, you could pay him back. Get a little shop with rooms above.'

'But suppose . . . suppose I couldn't pay him back?'

'Oh, don't be such a misery. Of course you will. If you get a shop somewhere nice, in a good shopping area, say Bold Street, you'd make a fortune in no time. It wouldn't be just any old sweet shop, it would be something different. A bit more posh, like.'

'Bold Street would cost the earth.'

'Well, you've got to look as though you are posh. Snobby folks like to think they are buying stuff from snobby places. But if we can't get something in Bold Street, there are other areas.'

'We?' The breeze ruffled Ellan's dark hair and with the flush of excitement she'd caught from Tilly, she looked beautiful and quite a few heads turned in her direction.

'It's my idea. Do you think I'm going to stay there?'

'Oh, I can't do it. What would they think? Me asking for money and you giving your notice in?'

'I wouldn't do that at first. I'd wait until you'd got another shop and then say I'm going to manage it for you.'

'Another shop! I haven't got the first yet.' Ellan chewed on a piece of the toffee that had been the impetus of this whole mad idea. 'Where would we make all the stuff?'

'Oh, we'll find somewhere,' Tilly said airily. 'Start off using our kitchen at home if we have to. I'm a genius! I'm a bloody genius! It's the solution to everything.'

Despite the optimism that was beginning to course through her Ellan shook her head. 'Only if Doctor Elliot agrees and I don't know how much I'd need.' She glanced across the water to where the ferris wheel and the tower on the opposite bank were becoming clearer. If he would agree, could she do it? She jerked her chin up and squared her shoulders. It was a good solution. It was a good idea and she'd make it work. Lucy's future depended on it.

Chapter Fifteen

———◆———

B Y THE TIME THEY returned to Rodney Street Tilly
had convinced Ellan that it would be easy to borrow
the money, rent a shop and start up in business. By the
time she'd put Lucy to bed some of that enthusiasm had
been replaced by doubt. But what else was there? she
asked herself. She couldn't watch Lucy day and night and
she was certain Selina would try to hurt her again. She
had been shocked to the core that a girl of twelve could
lie so easily and so blatantly. And to be so eaten up with
jealousy that she would deliberately harm a two-year-old
child. It was this realization that made her rap firmly on
the dining room door that night.

'Ellan, come in. Is something wrong?' Margaret's eyes
searched Ellan's face.

'No. Not really.'

Lloyd looked at her with satisfaction. How she'd
changed in two years. When he'd met her she had been a
frightened girl alone in the world, a perpetually haunted
look in her huge, dark eyes and a habit of shying away
when he spoke to her. Now she was a lovely, quiet,

confident young woman. He was well pleased by his decision and the way Margaret had handled Ellan. 'Sit down and tell us what's troubling you, my dear.'

Ellan sat, twisting her handkerchief in her hands. 'I don't know quite how to say this without sounding ungrateful . . .' She looked down at her hands. Oh, this was going to be so hard.

Lloyd sighed. He could read the signs. She was ready to fly the nest, now that the broken part of her life was mended. She looked so vulnerable that he decided to put her out of her misery. 'You want to leave us, Ellan, don't you?'

She was so taken aback that she gasped aloud. 'How . . . how did you know?'

He smiled. 'I can see the signs.'

'Oh, I don't want you to think I'm ungrateful. You've been so good to me and to Lucy, but now I want to stand on my own. I can't keep taking from you for ever and Lucy is growing up fast.'

'Have you somewhere to go? Some means of employment?' Margaret asked, her voice filled with sadness. She'd become fond of Ellan.

'That will depend on you both.' She took a deep breath. It was now or never. If she faltered she would fail. 'Could you . . . would you lend me the money to start a business of my own, please? I'll pay it all back, before God I will.'

'What kind of a business?' Lloyd asked. He'd expected her to say she'd found a position as a housekeeper. He ruled out any secret love affair. Ellan was too open to have kept something like that from them.

'Sweets. But not a shop selling just Everton Mints,

Aniseed Balls, Humbugs and Acid Drops. A sort of special shop selling home-made carn toffee and fudges nicely wrapped in boxes with ribbons. A sort of upper-class sweet shop. I'd call it a Candy Cabin. Americans call sweets candies,' she added, before realizing he would know that.

Lloyd and Margaret exchanged glances.

'How much would you need for this venture?' Lloyd asked.

'I don't know. I would have to rent a shop and refurbish it, buy boxes, ribbons, ingredients, maybe even somewhere to make things. I thought you'd be able to advise me.'

'It's a novel idea, Ellan, I must give you credit for that. But what about Lucy?' Margaret queried.

'I'd thought of that. I'd pay someone a few shillings to look after her in the rooms above the shop. I'd be on hand if she needed me.'

Lloyd smiled. 'So, this shop is to have rooms above it?'

Ellan was instantly covered by confusion. 'I'm sorry . . . I didn't mean . . .'

'I was only teasing, Ellan,' Lloyd interrupted. 'We'll think it over, Margaret and I, and then we'll talk again.'

Ellan rose. 'Thank you. I know it's a lot to ask, especially after all you've done for me.'

'Nonsense. I like to see people being enterprising, helping themselves and giving employment to others, much needed employment. That's what gives me pleasure and satisfaction, knowing I've done something to help people. It makes everything worthwhile.'

Margaret leaned across the table and placed her hand

over her husband's. 'Lloyd is right. It gives us such joy to see people getting on. We'll talk in the morning, Ellan.'

Tilly was waiting for her. In fact she almost leapt on her as she came out of the room.

'You've been listening, Tilly Rigby.'

'I haven't. What did they say? I couldn't catch all of it.'

Ellan laughed. 'They'll discuss it and tell me in the morning.'

Tilly clamped her hand over her mouth to stifle the cry that had risen.

'I think they were quite taken with the idea.' Ellan pulled Tilly in the direction of the door that led below stairs.

'I can't wait to tell Cook.'

'Don't you dare say a word until I know for certain.'

'I can tell my da and our Mary and Vi though, that's different.'

'No. Not until everything is absolutely certain.'

'You're so superstitious.'

'I'm Manx, it's born in us,' Ellan laughed, but then the laughter died and was replaced by homesickness. She wanted to tell Aunt Maud and Miss Mary. So near and yet so far. She'd have to write and tell Lizzie the news. Lizzie could tell them that she'd started up in business with her Candy Cabins. With a name like that it would sound so American that no-one would question it. As she went upstairs to check on Lucy she wondered longingly if she would ever see those green meadows again, the heaths purple with heather, the steep cliffs of Bradda Head and the sun setting over Peel Castle?

She didn't sleep much that night, wondering what she would do if the Elliots decided it wasn't worth the risk, but when Margaret summoned her to the parlour straight after breakfast, and she saw the look on both their faces, she could have cried with relief.

'We've given the matter a lot of thought and we've decided you are a good risk, although the days are going to be so long and lonely without you,' Margaret added ruefully at the end of the announcement.

'I . . . I don't know how to thank you. What to say even!' Impulsively Ellan bent and kissed Margaret on the cheek. 'You'll have Selina and I'll call as often as I can, I promise.'

Margaret held her hand. 'I know you will and I wish you every success. In fact, Lloyd is going to inform everyone he knows about your venture and I will tell all the ladies I know that they must go and buy some Manx carn candy.'

Lloyd laughed. 'It's called advertising to protect your investment. I'm not allowed to advertise myself but there's nothing to stop me advertising you. I know I'll finish up with obese patients once the word gets around.'

'Lloyd, don't tease her,' Margaret chided, seeing the look of consternation on Ellan's face.

'Sorry. I just couldn't resist it. Now, Ellan, first things first. We have to find the right premises, then we can start working out figures. Have you seen something? Got your eye on anything?'

'No. I wouldn't even think about such a thing until I'd asked you.'

'Good. We can start today.'

'I don't want to interfere with your work.'

'You won't. The one thing I don't have is time. Plenty of advice, but not time. I'll give you the names and addresses of the most respectable estate agents and surveyors, they will give you all the help and advice you need, on the spot, so to speak. After all, you know what you're looking for. You will be able to see the potential, I won't. When you decide, let me know and I'll do the rest.'

Ellan looked from one to the other, eyes brim full with tears. 'Why are you so good to me? You've treated me like a daughter.'

'Maybe that is just the reason. I always wanted the house full of children. It's a big house, there would have been plenty of room for half a dozen children. But, it was not to be and over the years I've come to look on you as a grown-up sister of Selina's.' Margaret's voice shook with emotion.

Lloyd took his wife's hand. 'Margaret is right. We've both come to think of you as ours. Lucy, too.'

'I won't let you down, I promise. You gave me a chance when you first took me in and now you're giving me another. You'll be proud of me, I swear it!'

'We already are, Ellan. Now I really must be off.' Lloyd was instantly all impatient. As he reached the door, Ellan caught a glimpse of blue and white chambray and heard Selina's petulant voice.

'You were going off without saying goodbye.'

'Of course I wasn't. I was just coming to look for you. That is a very pretty dress and you suit the colour,' she heard Lloyd say.

A smile lit up Margaret's face as Selina clung to her father, making a touching little cameo, framed by the doorway. 'She is going to be pretty, isn't she, Ellan? Don't they make a charming picture?'

Ellan nodded politely. Selina was plain and she

doubted she would ever be pretty, but that wasn't what was bothering her. How long had Selina been there and how much had she heard?

As she went upstairs, she passed the girl on the top landing. Selina didn't speak, she just gave that half-smile, half-grimace she reserved especially for Ellan. So, she was going away. Selina was glad that she didn't have to share her mama and papa with *her* any more, glad she wouldn't have to stand and watch the fuss everyone made over that horrible baby, Lucy. She hated them both and had done ever since the day her papa had brought them here. She hadn't wanted them. No-one had even asked her what she felt about having two strangers in the house. And Ellan had taken her place beside Mama. Selina had always read to Mama, ever since she'd learned to read. And, even worse, Mama had spoiled that ugly, messy baby. She told herself she would kill them both when she heard her Mama say Ellan was like a daughter. They only had one daughter, one child, and that was herself, Selina. But, maybe they had only said that out of kindness because Ellan was going. They were both so kind, so trusting, and she hated people using them. They couldn't see how people took everything and gave nothing. Not like herself. But everything was going to be better now because *they* were going.

Cook said to ask the missus for permission when Tilly asked to accompany Ellan. Margaret agreed and so, when Tilly finished her morning's work, they both walked down Hardman Street towards Bold Street, taking turns to carry Lucy.

Ellan looked with awe at the shops they passed. 'I'll never get a shop here.'

'You will – eventually.'

'They have men on the doors. I don't think they would even let the likes of you and me go inside.'

'They would if we had the right clothes,' Tilly said, eyeing her plain grey dress and short jacket with distaste.

The offices of Sykes & Maple were in Chapel Street, in the heart of Liverpool's business centre which also held the Cotton Exchange, the Corn Exchange and the offices of the big shipping companies and banks. On the corner they passed an ornate Gothic building with a polished brass plaque on the door which gave the names of various occupants. Ellan stopped. One had caught her attention, 'The Isle of Man Steam Packet Company'. Despite her effervescence a stab of longing pierced her heart. She thought of Jamie and of the wreck of the mail boat lying out in the bay. The mail was carried by bigger and faster ships than the S.S. *Ellan Vannin* now, and she'd read that the name was never to be given to another ship. She would be the only Ellan Vannin from now on. She shivered. Then she realized that Tilly was pulling at her arm and she dismissed the feeling. She was being a fool. Her future looked brighter than it had for years. She was going to start up her own business and she had Lucy. She had so much to look forward to.

'If we don't hurry up it will be lunchtime and they'll all have gone out,' Tilly urged as they crossed the road and entered yet another imposing building.

There was nothing to be either bought or leased in Bold Street, Mr Sykes informed them, but there was a small shop with accommodation behind and above in Moorfields which was quite near to Exchange Station and which would certainly be good for business with people arriving by train to board the liners.

Tilly looked him squarely in the face. 'Well, there won't be much trade from them. I can't see them carting all their luggage down to the landing stage on the tram. They'll go down to the Riverside Station.'

Mr Sykes gave her a supercilious glance and turned his attention back to Ellan. He wasn't going to deal with hard-faced little madams like that one. Probably a shop assistant or a domestic of some sort, but with far too much to say for herself. 'Look around. This is the business sector. There will be plenty of trade: managers, clerks, from the shipping offices, the banks . . .'

'We'll have a look at it. It would be better if it had somewhere to make the things I intend to sell.'

'I don't think there is anywhere in this part of town for that,' came the dismissive reply.

'It doesn't matter right now. We'll manage. Later on we'll find somewhere,' Tilly interrupted. 'Maybe we'll go and see Silver, Mackintosh and McKay,' she said, knowing full well they were competitors.

Mr Sykes glared at her again and coughed. 'I'll get the keys and ask someone to accompany you.'

'Oh, that won't be necessary,' Tilly said, getting to her feet.

'Indeed it will!' Mr Sykes exclaimed as he disappeared through a door into the inner sanctum.

'I don't think he likes me,' Tilly commented drily. 'But I don't care. Does he think we came over on the last boat, giving us all that rubbish about passengers from Exchange?'

It was a small shop halfway down Moorfields, dark, gloomy and smelling of leather.

'Used to be a cobblers,' the pimply young man with plastered-down hair informed them.

'Can we see the living accommodation, please?' Ellan asked, her mind already working on colour schemes.

The room at the back was large but murky as there was only one window that looked out into a yard. The floor was flagged and in one corner was a brown stone sink and a single tap. There was also a small pantry or store-room that hadn't seen soap and water in a month of Sundays, as Tilly tersely remarked. 'But we could get a stove in here and use it for making the stuff,' she said thoughtfully as they followed him up a flight of stone stairs.

There were three rooms above the shop, which was surprising, but all were in a similar state as the downstairs rooms.

'A sitting room and two bedrooms,' Ellan said, looking around.

'Where are the . . .' Tilly searched for the word but gave up. 'Where's the toilet and the bath?' she asked bluntly.

'There isn't a bath or bathroom. It's not flamin' Croxteth Hall.' The youth had dropped all pretence at lofty dignity. 'The privy is in the yard, do you want to inspect that, too?'

'Yes. If it's not too much trouble,' Tilly shot back.

Her comments on the small brick, shed-like building made the youth blush and Ellan dragged her back into the shop. 'We'll take it. It needs decorating and . . . er . . . things.'

'It needs pulling down and starting again,' Tilly muttered.

Ellan and the youth ignored her.

'I'll have to tell Doctor Elliot it needs improvements. It will affect the letting price or is it the buying price?'

'Letting,' he answered, consulting the file he carried. Then, locking the door, he followed them into the street.

'Tell Mr Sykes that we will be in touch,' Ellan said as they parted company on the corner of Moorfields and Dale Street.

'They've got a nerve. It's a dump! That yard is like a midden. No wonder it's still on their hands. It will have to be cleaned out, scrubbed, painted and probably fumigated too.'

'I didn't think it was that bad.'

'In prime condition and an excellent location, my foot! Did he think we were taken in by that?'

Ellan wasn't really listening. 'What colours do you think would be best?'

Tilly pulled a face. 'Brown to cover all that muck.'

'Stop it. Seriously. Colours for the decorations and boxes and ribbons. I want something distinctive. Something that everyone will recognize and say "I know where you bought those".'

Tilly shifted Lucy's weight on to her hip. The child was happily sucking a toffee apple but was covered in the sweet confection. 'Where's your handkerchief? I'm all stuck up. Ugh! I think it's in my hair.'

Ellan delved into her bag. 'You shouldn't have bought it for her then. I told you she'd get in a terrible mess.'

'But it kept her quiet, didn't it? You didn't want her acting up in old misery guts's office, did you?'

They stopped at a drinking fountain and Ellan cleaned Lucy up as best she could while Tilly bemoaned the fact that there was toffee all over her best jacket.

'Pink and white,' Tilly said as they headed towards the tram stop.

'Too prissy, as Americans say.'

'Oh, pardon me!' Tilly rolled her eyes.

'Stop that. You know what I mean. I want something . . .'

'Classy.'

'Yes, but distinctive. Cream is rich-looking and maybe rose pink. No, a plummy pink, like the carpet in my room.'

'It sounds very expensive to me. You'll have to have everything specially made – and what are you going to do for furniture? There wasn't a stick of it in the place.'

Ellan looked downcast. 'I'll manage.'

'It's a good job you've me to take care of you. We'll go round all the second-hand shops and Paddy's Market. We should be able to furnish the whole place for a couple of pounds.'

The next three weeks passed in a hectic round of visiting stationers, wholesalers, decorators, small second-hand furniture shops and the street markets. But as the hot days of June passed into a hotter July, it was finished and Ellan, with the help of Tilly, Vi and Mary, had moved in and was ready to open.

She'd draped the long counter with a skirt of cream-coloured muslin, looped up with large, deep pink satin bows. There were small tables, similarly decorated, with displays of butter fudge, chocolate fudge, vanilla fudge, packed in the small cream boxes with the words 'Candy Cabin' printed over a pink rose. Large trays, covered with butter muslin to keep the flies off, held the carn toffee and treacle toffee and toffee to which nuts and raisins had been added and yet more varieties of fudge. Ellan herself wore a dusky pink skirt and a cream high-necked blouse, the neck and cuffs of which were embellished with embroidered pink roses.

When everything was ready, Lloyd brought Margaret and Selina to become the very first customers.

'Oh, Ellan! It's beautiful! It's not like a shop at all, it's more like a very high-class milliners or fancy drapery shop.' Margaret looked around with pleasure and astonishment. 'I know it will succeed, Ellan, not that I'm an expert on shops. But I do go and buy sweets and chocolate for Selina and I've not seen anything like this.'

'I'm not trying to compete with the big firms like Fry's or Cadbury's, although I might buy some of their more expensive boxes just to give variety to the stock. But this is the way I wanted it.'

'Come along now, both of you. Choose whatever takes your fancy and Ellan will pack it in those smart little boxes.' Lloyd entered into the spirit, urging them both to try the new varieties.

'I'll have some of everything,' Selina announced.

'You'll make yourself sick,' Lloyd reprimanded but not harshly.

'I think it is a good idea, Selina. Then we will be able to pick out our favourites and recommend everything, having sampled it ourselves.' Margaret reached up and patted Selina's cheek for she was seated on one of the small chairs that had been provided for the comfort of waiting customers.

Selina didn't reply but watched Ellan move quickly

and deftly, picking up pieces with tongs and placing them neatly into the boxes, lined with greaseproof paper.

Lloyd insisted on paying for them and with his arms full of boxes, smiled expansively. 'I don't think it will be long before people are queuing up outside and you'll have to expand.'

'I hope you're right. I want to pay you back as quickly as possible.'

'Where's Lucy?' Selina asked suddenly.

Ellan shot her a glance before smiling. 'She's upstairs out of harm's way. I cringe when I think of the havoc she could wreak in here.'

'On her own?' Selina persisted.

'No, of course not. Tilly's sister, Mary, is with her. She's coming until I can find someone else.'

She wasn't certain, but she thought she saw a look of disappointment flash into Selina's eyes, then it was gone and she was her usual sullen self. 'Out of harm's way and out of your way, miss,' Ellan said to herself.

Chapter Sixteen

———•———

THE FOLLOWING JULY THE loan was paid off with the interest that Ellan insisted on paying. As Lloyd had predicted, word had got around and at busy times people were queuing up waiting to be served. It was hard work. At the end of the day when she pulled down the window blind, she had to start to clean and tidy the shop and scrub out the trays. That done, there was just time for a meal, an hour with Lucy before she went to bed and then it was back down into the confectionery room, as Tilly had christened it, to make up her stocks. To ensure that she never ran out she spent all day Sunday from first light until late at night, beating, stirring, ladling out.

Young Mary Rigby, glad to escape from the confines and drudgery at home, came as often as she could. She helped not only with Lucy but in the workroom and the shop. Tilly came on her days off but by the time Christmas came, Ellan knew she would have to have permanent help and soon.

'There's nothing for it, Tilly, I'm going to have to find

another shop and more staff,' Ellan said, easing herself down into a chair by the fire.

It was just what Tilly had been waiting for. 'I told you, didn't I? You'd better go and see the doctor and I'll give the missus my notice. I'll try and find someone else. I wouldn't leave her in the lurch, like. She's been good to me. Good to all of us. Our Mary's told Da that Mrs Murphy will come in and clean up and get his meal on the table. She's had enough of that lot, she's glad to get out. She'll come in the other shop with me, or she can help you, she doesn't mind which. Anything to get out from being a drudge. She works damned hard and they don't appreciate it. "'Er over the road" is welcome to them for a few bob a week for her glasses of port down the pub.'

Ellan managed a tired smile. 'You've got everything planned. You're a scheming, conniving little madam, Tilly Rigby, that's what you are.'

'I'm not. I'm just practical. Besides, I'll be glad to get out, too. As she gets older she gets worse, does Miss Selina. Spiteful she is and sneaky with it, but they still can't see any harm in her. God help the man that gets *that* one, I say.'

The second shop was also fitted out with money borrowed from Lloyd Elliot. It was at the corner of Bold Street and Renshaw Street but Tilly insisted it was more in Bold Street. In a matter of weeks it, too, had a regular clientele and Lloyd was joking that she'd have a chain of them all over the city and maybe in other towns as well before long.

Ellan looked aghast but Tilly looked excited. 'That's not a bad idea, Ellan.'

'Oh, stop it. This whole thing is getting too big. Before I know where I am it will be running out of control and us with it.'

Tilly sighed dramatically. 'We'll never make her a millionairess, will we?'

Ellan shuddered. 'I don't want that. I'm quite happy with what I've got. As long as I've enough for a comfortable home, good food and clothes and a good school for Lucy when she's old enough, I'll be content.' She remembered how four years ago the pursuit of wealth, in the shape of Jamie's inheritance, had almost ruined her life. If he'd never have got that letter from the solicitors, he would have been alive and they'd have been married and quietly living in Peel with Lucy and maybe other children. How different her life would have been, but she would have been content. Instead, because of the promise of money, she had lost him and the future they'd envisaged. No, great wealth held no charms for her and never would. She was happy with what she had.

The summer of 1914 was idyllic, Ellan remarked to Tilly. The days were warm and sunny, soft dawn mists quickly dispersed by the golden rays of the sun, heralded each glorious summer morning. The evenings were long, a twilight hush undisturbed by the noises of the day, a time of tranquillity, a time to sit and ponder the future, while looking back over the years and count the successes and failures. It was a summer that Ellan would often look back on with yearning, for there were darker, more sinister forces at work throughout those golden days.

She now employed two girls, one to help her in the shop and one to work in the confectionery room, which left her more time to spend with Lucy and to visit

Margaret. June was nearing its end when she took Lucy to visit for the first time in a fortnight.

'I'm sorry. I've neglected you but I didn't feel able to leave the girls until I was sure they were competent.' She handed Margaret an envelope. 'By the end of the year this should have been paid off.'

'There is no desperate rush, Ellan. We told you it was for an indefinite period of time and you've got the added expense of staff to pay.'

Ellan smiled. 'Staff to pay. Doesn't that sound grand? Lucy, give Mrs Elliot the present you've brought.'

Lucy handed over a small package, rather reluctantly.

Margaret made a great show of opening it. 'Oh, I wonder what it can be? Goodness, isn't this a pretty card and look . . . my favourite butter fudge!'

The box was a little battered and the fudge rather lumpy and the card had very childish lettering that read 'Happy Birthday, From Lucy'.

'I made it by myself,' Lucy said proudly.

'With a little help from Mary, but not much,' Ellan quickly added, catching her daughter's indignant expression.

'You are very clever and it's lovely. Come and give me a hug?'

Lucy did just that and then settled herself happily on Margaret's knee. 'After my next birthday I'm going to school,' she announced proudly.

'You've grown up very fast, Lucy,' Margaret laughed.

'Too fast, I often think,' Ellan answered.

'Will I have to leave Mary, Ma, or can she come to school too?'

They both laughed. She was an engaging child with a

sunny nature, a mop of black curls and bright blue eyes.

'Mary will take you and bring you home but she can't stay with you. I need her to help me. Besides, you'll have lots of other little girls to play with.' Ellan often felt guilty that Lucy had no friends, except Mary, who doted on her as much as she did herself.

'And before we know where we are you'll be really grown up, like Selina. She'll be fifteen on her next birthday, quite a young lady.' Margaret lowered her voice to a whisper. 'Of course she's only just had her fourteenth birthday but she does like to think she is grown up.'

As if on cue Selina appeared and they all looked up, Margaret with affection and pride at the tall, thin, plain girl whose lustreless hair was dressed in a style that did not become her at all. Ellan sensed Selina's animosity and she noticed the quick flush of anger on Selina's cheeks as she saw Lucy on Margaret's knee, but she smiled just the same and complimented her on her dress.

'Papa always likes me to wear blue. He says it suits me,' came the rather haughty reply.

Lucy looked up at Selina with trepidation. She remembered how the older girl's face had twisted up when she'd pushed her hard and she'd fallen into the hearth and cut her eye.

She also remembered Selina's laughter and the whispered words 'I'll cut you up into little pieces when you're asleep if you tell I pushed you.' She was frightened of Selina and she immediately shrank away.

'You're not shy, Lucy, are you?' Margaret coaxed.

Lucy shook her head but looked towards her mother. While her Ma was there nothing bad could happen to her.

'Show Lucy that lovely nightdress case your papa bought you. It's just like a lovely lady in a crinoline dress.'

'She won't want to see it,' Selina replied, her tone bored. What was Mama thinking of? She was nearly grown up, she didn't want to be trailing after babies.

'Don't want to see it,' Lucy said with some spirit.

'You see? She's not in the least bit interested and I'm too old to be playing with dolls.' Selina's lip curled as she looked pointedly at the doll Lucy held.

'Of course Selina's too grown up now. A young lady, you said so yourself,' Ellan intervened to break the silence.

'Then why don't you play something for us, dear? She's excellent.' Margaret urged her reluctant daughter, proud of her one social achievement.

With a smug smile Selina sat at the piano and began to play Beethoven's *Moonlight Sonata*.

She was good. She was very good, Ellan thought. She could make a career of it if such a thing were acceptable. She watched Margaret's expression and smiled. She was so proud of this plain, awkward child that it was almost pitiful. She was blind to all Selina's faults, blind to her obvious plainness, her sullen attitude, her lack of social graces – except that of music. But wasn't beauty supposed to be in the eye of the beholder? Maybe she would blossom in the fullness of time. Perhaps some young man would see something in Selina that he could love and cherish. She hoped so, for Margaret's sake.

'Is there a place that would train her? Some sort of school just for music?' Ellan asked as Selina finished and closed the piano lid.

'You mean an academy?'

'Yes, she's very talented.'

'How would you know?'

'Selina. What a dreadful thing to say!'

Ellan blushed. 'She's right. I'm no judge of these things,' she said calmly, seething at the girl's open insolence.

'I don't want to go to an academy. I don't intend to make it a career. No lady could ever appear in public, to be paid, like a servant.'

'Selina, that is enough. We both understand what you mean and I know Ellan did not mean to imply anything but praise. You will apologize for your insolence.'

Ellan had never heard Margaret speak so sharply to her daughter before.

Selina dropped her gaze and stood awkwardly. 'I didn't mean it to sound . . . that way,' she muttered, ungraciously. But I did mean it, she thought. Who was Ellan Vannin to judge whether she was talented or not? A jumped up servant, that's what she was. And, she was sitting in her mama's parlour as though she had a right to be there.

Lucy, sensing the tension, scrambled off Margaret's knee and went to her mother. 'I want to go home. Home to Mary.'

'Oh, dear! Now it's my turn. I seem to have a rather ill-mannered daughter,' Ellan said apologetically.

'She's little more than a baby, Ellan.'

'Yes, but she's old enough to know better. Lucy, it's not nice for little girls to say they want to go home. You must wait until I say we are going home.'

Lucy hung her head and tucked her thumb in her mouth, something she always did when tired or upset. Ellan removed it gently. 'Only babies do that, Lucy, and you're a big girl now.'

Selina looked away, bored and yet satisfied that the child had been reprimanded. Then she looked up and her expression changed. She smiled and it completely transformed her. She looked almost pretty, Ellan thought. The reason became clear as Lloyd entered the room.

'Ellan! It's nice to see you. We don't see enough of you these days. You know you work too hard.'

'Oh, don't take me to task, please. I love my work and I'm happy.'

'I'm glad.' He kissed his wife on the cheek and then Selina, who had become withdrawn again. Then he bent down and tickled Lucy under the chin. 'And who is this big girl?'

Lucy looked up and smiled. She liked Doctor Elliot.

As he stood up he surveyed them with a sad, wistful gaze. They presented a picture of domestic peace, a picture that was about to disappear.

'Lloyd, you look tired and worried,' Margaret said. 'It's you who work too hard. I'll ring for Daisy to bring some tea.'

'It's her afternoon off, Mama. I'll make it – for Papa.'

'Thank you, dear.' Lloyd smiled and was rewarded by the radiant look Selina bestowed on him.

Ellan felt uneasy. Was it natural that a child should love her father so much? She was being foolish again, reading too much into simple things. If Jamie had lived, he would have adored Lucy and she him.

'Have you had a really bad day?' Margaret asked.

'Not in the way you mean.'

'Then what?'

'I don't want to alarm you, either of you, but it looks as though war is drawing ever closer.'

Margaret blanched and Ellan looked at him questioningly. There had been rumours, snippets of conversations she'd heard from her customers about what was going on in countries she knew nothing about. 'I don't understand any of it. I don't read the newspapers, I don't have time.'

'Crown Prince Ferdinand has been murdered by an assassin in Sarajevo.'

Ellan looked blank but Margaret drew in her breath sharply.

'What has that got to do with us? Where is Sarajevo?' Ellan asked.

'It's in Serbia and now Austria will blame Serbia. Russia will back the Serbs, the French will back Russia. Germany will support Austria and so it will go on like a huge snowball gathering momentum and speed until everyone is caught up in it.'

'But we won't, surely?' Margaret cried.

'If the neutrality of Belgium is threatened then I don't see that Lord Asquith has any choice.'

'But King George, Tsar Nicholas and the Kaiser are first cousins. Queen Mary is from Teck, a Prussian principality. Can't they see the foolhardiness of it all?' Margaret pressed.

'Family feuds can go on for generations. They should sort it out themselves and not involve everyone else,' Ellan said tersely.

'Would that it were so simple, Ellan. There's been unrest all summer. It's been simmering just under the surface. But maybe it will come to nothing.' He tried to bolster their spirits. He hoped it would amount to nothing but the young men of all those countries were preparing eagerly for confrontation. They wanted war.

There was a strong nationalist feeling everywhere and not just within the Empire. The words 'King and Country' had a ring to them that stirred the blood.

'But if we go to war you won't have to go, will you?' Ellan asked.

Lloyd took Margaret's hand. 'I think I'm getting a bit long in the tooth. It's young men that will be needed. But it may never happen, so let's look on the bright side.' His tone was lighter than his heart. He'd fought in the Boer War and they'd need doctors all right. He'd seen the carnage, the mutilation, the agony of the wounded in the field hospitals. He knew what it was like to lie in the baking dust, sweating with fear, the rifle in your hand shaking, knowing it was kill or be killed. He also judged the temperament of the young men who knew nothing of war, who were just spoiling for a fight, looking forward to the ultimate adventure they thought war to be. But you couldn't put an old head on young shoulders. They'd have to learn for themselves. Many would learn the hard way. Many would pay the ultimate price for their brief adventure.

Suddenly, into Ellan's mind came Andrew's face. If there was a war he would go and maybe John and Mat, too.

'Ellan, you've gone as white as a bedsheet! Have I frightened you?'

She realized Lloyd was speaking to her. 'No. No. I was just thinking of someone I knew . . . in Peel.'

'A man?'

She nodded. 'A fisherman.'

'Then if it comes, I expect he'll join the Navy and he'll be wise in that choice. There's not a country in the world that can match the British Navy. The Kaiser won't even try.'

She smiled weakly, praying that nothing would happen, wishing she had taken more notice of the newspapers.

Lloyd's predictions came true as the summer wore on. Throughout July nation faced nation. Austria declared war on Serbia, Russia and France mobilized their forces. Ultimatums were delivered and ignored as the bright, sunny days of July merged into the stifling heat of early August and the inevitable seemed just around the corner.

They all went to Chapel that hot August Sunday and the minister prayed that peace might still be preserved. In the following breath he urged duty on all the men present, but that command lost some of its meaning to those men who had lived long enough to know the horrors of war. Some were old enough to remember the hell of the Crimea.

Maud had looked at her three sons and prayed harder. Dear God, You took my husband and I never questioned Your wisdom. I know this cause is righteous and good and oppressors must be dealt with firmly, but please hear me now. Don't take my boys. Leave me some peace and security for my old age. Spare my sons.

The talk was all of what would happen next.

'I don't want any of you to go until they call you.' Maud's voice was harsh with emotion.

'But, Ma, it's for King and Country. For all Christian people.'

'I know that. I'm not against it, but it looks like a European quarrel. Nothing to do with us and why we have to support France I don't know. We've fought them since the year dot but I've never been interested in politics. I don't understand half of it. I've never even heard of some of the countries. Serbia, Transylvania, what have they got to do with us? Why can't they sort it out? They're all related. It's a family squabble. Why drag us into it?' She unknowingly echoed Ellan's argument.

'It's not as easy as that, Ma.'

'I know nothing except that I may finish my days without kith or kin.'

'It will all be over by Christmas. I'm not going to miss it. I'm not going to wait until I'm sent for,' Andrew stated hotly.

'You're determined to get yourself killed then? Rushing off to join up, is that it?' Maud was sharp.

'I wasn't talking about joining the Army.'

'What then?'

'The Navy. My life has revolved around the sea and I'll go to war on it.'

Maud shook her head but Andrew ignored her. 'Look, Ma, that's the safest place to be. Our Navy is twice as big as theirs. No-one will ever challenge it. We've been masters of the seas since Trafalgar.'

She knew he had a point but she wasn't going to give in that easily. 'You'll be needed here. Food will be even more necessary now.'

'John and Mat can stay and fish and there's enough men in Peel to take the place of the younger ones like me.'

'He's determined, Ma. You'll not talk him out of it,' John said, quietly. 'And Mat and I agree with him. Our place is in the fighting line.'

'Oh, go on then. All three of you. Go on, kill me with

the worry of it all. It's a game to you, all of you. It's always the women who have to stay at home and wait and worry and pick up the pieces. If there are any left to pick up! But go and serve your King and Country, I won't stand in your way. By God! Ellan Vannin knew what she was doing when she left here. America has no quarrel with anyone.' And Maud went out, slamming the door behind her and wondering why she had suddenly thought of Ellan, in peace and safety three thousand miles away across the Atlantic.

'Now why did she say that? She hardly ever speaks of Ellan, except when she's had a letter,' Mat pondered. Ellan's letters were not a regular occurrence and contained very little of interest. Unlike Lizzie's, for although Lizzie wrote only rarely, her letters contained enough information to keep Dora going for months. Ellan's letters were stilted.

Into Andrew's mind came the picture of Ellan in the red dress she'd worn that Christmas long ago. What was she thinking about the news, if she had even heard it? Would she write? Would she wonder about him? Probably not. She'd have a new set of friends. Maybe even a husband or a fiancé, although she never mentioned anything like that in her letters. He shrugged. She probably never even gave them a minute's thought and why should she? Her life on the island had been far from happy. He made up his mind. He'd go first thing in the morning before Ma was up and about. She'd only rant and rave the way she'd done earlier on. Everyone said it would be over before it had really begun; he wasn't going to miss out. His heart began to quicken and the blood raced hot in his veins. There was something exhilarating, something noble and fulfilling in the words 'King and Country'. He'd listened to old Ben Clifton down in the tavern, relating his part in the Relief of Mafeking, stirring tales of dust and danger, heroism and valour under the blazing sun of Africa. No, he wasn't going to miss his chance. By the time the sun rose he'd be gone.

It wasn't over by Christmas and it looked as though it would go on until spring or summer with the two armies dug in in trenches that ran the length of the Belgian and French countryside. And the casualties grew daily.

September had seen the retreat of the British Expeditionary Force from Mons, the 'contemptible little army' as the Kaiser had sneeringly called them. It was a slur those men converted with humour and pride into the Old Contemptibles. It also saw the Battle of the Marne which was a tactical victory for the British and French forces. But the end of the month saw fighting along a front stretching from the Somme to the Belgian border. It was at the end of this month, too, that Lloyd Elliot announced his intended departure as a Medical Officer attached to the Liverpool Pals, the 17th Brigade of the King's Liverpool Regiment.

Margaret put a brave face on it. Ellan tried to hide her anxiety but Selina was distraught and no amount of comforting from her mother or patriotic reasoning from her father could calm her.

'You don't have to go, Papa. You don't *have* to. They have plenty of doctors already!'

'There can never be enough doctors in a war, Selina, and I have taken a sacred oath to save lives.'

'But you can do that here. There are plenty of sick

people here, people who need you just as much as the soldiers do.'

'And there are enough doctors here who are too old to go to France to look after them. War is an evil, ugly thing, despite all the bands marching and the girls throwing flowers to the troops on their way overseas. But I *do* have to go, child. You *must* see that.'

'I'm not a child and I can't see it. I won't see it!'

He shrugged helplessly as she ran from the room, tears streaming down her cheeks.

'She'll get over it,' Margaret said, trying to sound far calmer than she felt. He had said it would be too much of an ordeal to go to Lime Street Station to see him off and now she was thankful for that decision.

Ellan stood watching, feeling very out of place. This was a private time and she wondered why she was there at all. But she was there because Margaret had asked her, begged her, to be. Their farewells had been made up-stairs half an hour ago. He looked different, she thought. The uniform, instead of making him look older, had the opposite effect. He looked much younger. She was beginning to catch some of Selina's fear.

'Is it really necessary?' she asked, quietly. 'She's very upset.'

He came over to her and took her hands. 'Yes, Ellan, it is. You've seen the casualty lists, both of you. I have to go.'

She nodded, then impulsively she reached up and kissed his cheek. 'Take care of yourself. I wouldn't want anything to happen to you.'

'I will. I'll probably be sent to a field hospital which is usually far from the front line.' He saw the light of hope in both their faces and smiled. He couldn't tell them it was more likely to be a field dressing station in the thick of it, or a casualty clearing station, which wasn't much better.

Margaret clung to him for a few minutes, then detached herself, looking up into his face. 'Take care and don't worry about Selina. Write when you get a minute which I know won't be often, so I won't be disappointed.'

He held her to him once again and then he had gone, the sound of his boots on the front steps hollow.

Margaret sat down suddenly and instantly Ellan was beside her.

'You don't feel faint or anything, do you?'

Margaret shook her head, biting her bottom lip to try to staunch her tears and maintain the brave front.

'Cry if you want to, for God's sake! We're only human, both of us.' Ellan put her arm around the thin shoulders.

The two women clung together, trying to draw comfort and strength from each other.

Selina watched them from the half-open door. She'd come to cry out her own hurt in her mama's arms, but here was her mama crying and clinging to *her*, she who had no right to be in this house at all. Selina had constantly been by her mama's side, it was her own place. And now that she'd lost her beloved papa and had come to cry out the pain, she couldn't because *she* was there. She turned and ran back upstairs, alone with her grief.

Chapter Seventeen

———— ◆ ————

AT FIRST THE WAR seemed not to affect Ellan's business, but after the second battle of Ypres in April 1915, she changed the colours of her boxes, ribbons and shop decorations. The cream remained but the ribbons were now of deep purple and black. People came to buy the candies as gifts of consolation for widows and mothers and broken-hearted sisters and aunts. And every day saw more and more of them. She also provided small, black-edged cards on which messages of sympathy could be written. She didn't see it as profiting from the grief of others but as a token of her respect and concern for the bereaved.

Of course she had discussed with Margaret the future of her shops and with a sense of deep regret she realized that some time in the future she might have to close them. That would mean that she would have to return and live with Margaret and Selina, something she was uneasy about. She hoped that it would not come to that. It depended on so many things: the shortage of food stuffs, of supplies of the card and paper for boxes and bags, the event of Tilly and Mary having to leave for war work. Indeed, the possibility of being unable to find suitable replacements for them for the same reason.

At the end of their talk Margaret smiled with forced brightness and said, 'It may not come to that. Let's not look too far ahead.'

'No, perhaps it's better to take one day or week at a time,' she replied.

Margaret had had letters from Lloyd quite regularly at first but then, as the new year progressed, infrequently. In them he minimized the personal dangers but concentrated on the sheer wanton waste of life and appalling wounds. His letters to Selina were always cheerful, he mentioned none of the things he wrote to his wife about, with the result that she became more and more resentful of his absence and louder in her demands that he come home, until Margaret's taut nerves snapped and for the first time in her life she slapped her daughter and thrust under the shocked girl's nose Lloyd's latest letter with the almost screamed instruction to 'Go away and read why he can't come home, you selfish, unfeeling girl!' The fact that Ellan was present to witness this awful scene rankled deeply with Selina.

Ellan had just served the last customer before she closed for lunch and as she pulled down the blind she gazed up into the blue sky. The weather was fine for May, perhaps this evening she would take Lucy to the park to feed the ducks. The child was still a little shy and reluctant to go to school, although she was bright and intelligent. Ellan put it down to the fact that for the past eighteen months, Mary and herself had been Lucy's companions. Her gaze settled on a figure hurrying up the road towards the shop. It was Tilly. Ellan frowned. Something must be wrong. As soon as the girl was close enough she realized her assumption was correct. Tilly was crying.

'Tilly, what's the matter? Has something gone wrong in the shop?' Tilly couldn't speak. 'Come into the back and tell me what it is.' Ellan took her arm and gently propelled her to the back of the shop where Mary was stirring the huge pans of syrup and sugar. At the sight of her sister Tilly's sobs increased.

'What's up?' Mary cried.

Ellan shrugged helplessly. 'I don't know. She's so upset she can't tell me. You try.'

Tilly sank down on the bench. 'Come on, our Tilly, it can't be that bad,' Mary coaxed but Tilly only sobbed harder.

Mary became impatient. 'Oh, shurrup, Tilly! How can we help if you won't tell us what's up? Is it me da?'

'No,' Tilly choked out. 'It's . . . it's our Davie.'

'There can't be anything up with him, he's away.'

Tilly grabbed her sister's hand but her eyes were on Ellan's face. 'They . . . they sank the *Lucy*! They've sunk the *Lusitania* and our Davie . . .'

Mary drew her hand away, rocked on her heels and then slumped to the floor, a dazed, disbelieving look on her face.

Ellan blanched. 'Who? How?' she stammered.

Tilly was a little calmer. 'The Hun, with one of those bloody submarines. She sank so fast, nearly everyone was . . . drowned . . . and our Davie . . . he wouldn't have stood a chance.'

Ellan felt cold and ice-water ran through her veins. She was remembering . . . remembering the day she had nearly drowned. She knew what all those poor, innocent souls must have suffered. And the ship . . . she had fond memories of the *Lusitania*, of coming back, meeting Lloyd and having Lucy. Suddenly the hairs on the back of her neck stood up and her skin was covered in goosebumps. She'd named her child after that ship and now it had met a tragic end. It shared the same grave as the ship that had borne her name. In a sweat of superstitious fear she prayed that Lucy would not be cursed with tragedy as she had been. She looked down on Tilly and Mary, now sobbing brokenly, and bent down to them both. 'Go home, your da will need you. I'll close up. I'll go and see Mrs Elliot, then I'll collect Lucy from school.' She was surprised that her voice didn't shake and her manner was so cool.

She heard the cries of the paperboys, heard the angry mutterings of the passers-by and the sobs of more than one woman. The *Lusitania*'s crew were nearly all Liverpudlians.

As soon as she set eyes on Margaret's face she knew that she had heard.

'Oh, Ellan. Sit down.'

'It's true? I thought for a time it was a mistake.'

'It's no mistake, would to God it were! She was sunk by a submarine.'

'But she was a merchant ship, not a battleship. She was carrying passengers.'

'And a lot of them were Americans. President Wilson will have to do something about it.'

'People were shouting in the streets as I came here.'

'Liverpudlians love their ships. I fear there will be trouble.'

'Trouble?'

'People will take things into their own hands. There has already been a lot of anti-German feeling, shop windows smashed, houses daubed with paint, things like that.'

Ellan remained silent. It was a fact, but she couldn't see how taking it out on people of German origin, some grandchildren and great-grandchildren of immigrants, would bring back the souls lost.

There were riots as Margaret had predicted and it needed a strong police clamp-down to stop them. Anything with a remotely Germanic name or connection was smashed. People were man-handled and beaten up, shops were looted and set on fire and the battlecry of the avenging mob was: 'We'll teach yer to sink our ships! We'll teach yer to sink the *Lucy*!'

It was difficult to believe it was actually summer, Andrew thought dejectedly, watching the misty grey horizon merge with the cold grey waters of the North Sea. It was difficult to believe that they were in the middle of a war as well. In two years he hadn't seen any action. The entire Navy had only been involved in what could only be called skirmishes, at Heligoland, Coronel and the Falkland Islands.

Life was a boring routine of duties that he felt were often petty and unnecessary. He was stuck on the forward gun turret of H.M.S. *Lion*, with his mates, staring gloomily at the vast expanse of water. The day stretched before them, another day of watching and waiting, like the rest of the Grand Fleet, for the Kaiser's High Seas Fleet to come out and fight, something they had so far refused to do. He turned his head and the long columns of warships, wreathed and shrouded by their own smoke, crossed his line of vision. He thought of John on H.M.S. *Indefatigable* and Mat on H.M.S. *Invincible*. They were probably just as cold and bored as he was. Why they couldn't all have been put on the one ship he'd never know. But then that was the Navy for you, he mused. Maybe it had something to do with him running off and joining up. John and Mat had left it longer before leaving home.

Home . . . he often thought about the island and he often thought of Ellan. He hunched his shoulders and pushed his hands into his pockets. She would only read about the war in the newspapers, in the safety of her home. Even after the *Lusitania* had been sunk President Wilson had refused to drag America into a war that was eating up so many lives. Ma had written that the whole village was in mourning for the lads who had died in that charnel house that was Ypres. Six families had lost sons, a tragedy in such a small village. They were all lads he'd been to school with, fished with, shared a pint with. All gone. Ma said she'd written to Ellan about it for they were lads she'd known, too. He wondered if she cared now. She'd been out there six years and must have changed. But changed or not, he knew he still loved her.

'Flamin' bloody June,' Gerry Connell muttered, shifting his position.

Andrew grinned. Gerry was a small, wiry, dark-haired Liverpudlian, always ready with a quip. They'd got on well from the day they both joined the queue at the Naval

Recruiting Office. Gerry was a good mate. 'Give it a chance, Gerry, it's only the first.'

'Might as well be the bloody thirtieth. I don't think they have summer up here. All snow an' reindeer. No wonder them bloody ol' Vikings went on the rampage. Wouldn't mind a bit of pillage meself. Liven things up a bit. You've gorra admit it's flamin' borin'. God, I wish they'd do somethin'. All this hangin' about. All this hide and bloody seek. Come out, come out, wherever you are,' he intoned.

Andrew eased his cramped legs into a slightly more comfortable position. 'If you were them would you come out and fight? We've got twice as many ships as they have.'

'They've got to come out sometime or they'll be the laughin' stock of the world. Kaiser Bill an' his toy boats. He's just gorra bigger bathtub than anyone else.'

'They're not toy boats and this ain't a bathtub,' Charlie Oats reminded them dourly. 'And this ain't a peashooter.' He patted the long barrel of the gun.

'Oh, shurrup, misery guts. Can't yer take a joke?' Gerry replied, good-naturedly.

'Maybe they're out now. I've been thinking about it. Why else would the Old Man have us racing out of Rosyth?'

Gerry shrugged. 'Maybe it's a joke. Another of his bloody manoeuvres.'

'I heard a rumour that we're joining Jellicoe. He left Scapa ahead of us.'

Gerry looked more alert. 'He wouldn't take the whole bloody fleet on manoeuvres.'

Andrew peered into the gloom. 'Can't see any sign of

them. Where do you reckon we are?'

Gerry shrugged again. 'You have a wild guess, Charlie. Go on, surprise us all. Show us you've gorra brain.'

'Maybe off the coast of Norway. Jutland, maybe. How the hell should I know? You're the smart-arse around here.'

Another hour had passed and there had been no sightings of any ships, let alone the German fleet.

'Nothing. I can't see a damned thing.' Charlie broke the silence.

'You don't have to see them,' Andrew remarked darkly.

'Don't remind me, I hope we don't run into any of their submarines. Our kid's down the engine room.' Gerry often reminded them of this fact.

'I reckon we're in as much danger. They'll go for our guns first,' Charlie put in.

'That's if they ever get up the guts to come out,' Andrew said flatly, then they all looked at each other in amazement as the klaxon for Action Stations blared out.

'Christ Almighty! 'E's gone off his rocker! I can't see another bloody ship!'

Andrew, with a lifetime's experience of scanning both sea and horizon, jabbed Gerry in the ribs and pointed to where the distinctive pole masts and heavy funnels of a German battle-cruiser were visible in the distance. Then he cursed as a plume of cold spray broke over them and *Lion* turned in pursuit. The blood began to pound in his veins and his heart began to race. At last! At last there would be the chance of a fight! The chance to do the job for which they'd been trained. The chance to strike at the enemy.

With huge battle ensigns whipping out from their masts, the two lines of ships charged along, until Admiral Beatty was within range of Admiral Hipper's squadron. In minutes they were all wreathed in smoke and shell splashes. Aboard *Lion* all was action and noise. Sweat poured down the cordite-blackened faces of Andrew, Gerry Connell and Charlie Oats as the guns came into play. Between loading, firing and loading again, through eyes smarting from heat and smoke, they caught glimpses of each dull red glow that proclaimed a hit. They were all soaked to the skin by the great geysers of water thrown up by the near-misses but they hardly noticed.

Suddenly they were all flung to the deck, slipping and swearing as *Lion* was hit in her midships turret and heeled dangerously to port. Quickly they got to their feet, ignoring the small cuts and bruised bones. All Gerry said was 'God 'elp our kid' as the ship righted. They all knew that someone must have flooded the magazine, otherwise they'd have been blown sky high. Later they learned it was trapped crew members, Gerry's brother amongst them.

Lion was turning slightly to allow the fifth battle squadron to catch up and her guns were temporarily silent. Andrew wiped a hand across his streaked face and paused for breath. As he did so, *Indefatigable* steamed full ahead out of the smoke and he thought of John. The thought had barely formed when in a solid sheet of orange flame and dense gouts of black smoke, *Indefatigable* blew up. He watched in horrified amazement as the steam packet boat danced two hundred feet in the air, then she was gone. Taking a thousand men with her.

'Jesus Christ Almighty!' Gerry cried.

'Aye. He's the only one who can help those poor sods now,' Charlie said quietly.

Andrew narrowed his eyes and shook his head in pure disbelief. It wasn't possible! It just wasn't possible! He'd never seen a ship sink so fast. One minute there she was steaming full ahead. There had been that one mighty explosion, the flame, the smoke and then . . . nothing. The surface of the sea was empty. He felt physically sick. 'John. Oh, God. John,' he groaned. John, always the peacemaker, always the steady one.

'I hope it was quick,' Gerry muttered.

Charlie turned to him. 'They'd have known nothing. Felt nothing.'

There was no more time for talk. Battle had rejoined again as Beatty ran north towards Jellicoe and the main fleet, away from the main body of the German Fleet, now in pursuit. *Lion* was a crippled ship.

It was six-fifteen when they joined Jellicoe's ships and *Lion* swung her accompanying squadron into line ahead. The time, the place, the experience was to be stamped on Andrew's memory for ever. As the German Fleet steamed out of the mist he felt the hatred and bitterness rise up.

Revenge was imminent. They faced a huge arc of battleships that stretched from horizon to horizon. There would be no escape now for Kaiser Bill's Navy. The arc opened fire simultaneously so that the leading German ships were completely engulfed in smoke and shell splashes.

Some time during that summer evening of unreality, heat, smoke and deafening noise, Andrew heard Gerry yell then groan and fall silently at his feet, Gerry, who only a few hours ago had mocked Kaiser Bill and his toy boats. But there had been no time to dwell on the fact that his mate was dead. In a shocking rerun of the demise of *Indefatigable* he saw *Invincible* blow up and sink. They passed her, bow and stern in the air, her midships resting on the bottom. He saw the pathetic waves of those few who had survived and prayed that Mat was amongst them.

For two years he'd waited for this but it was no heroic adventure. It was sudden, shocking, inglorious death. It was a grave without a headstone. A burial without even a proper service.

Darkness was falling as one by one the German guns fell silent and he bent down over Gerry's slumped form while Charlie leaned against the superstructure. A last, despairing shot that hit *Lion*'s forward turret killed Charlie Oats instantly. Andrew felt as though he had been thrown into a furnace and he screamed as searing pains shot up his left arm before darkness descended on him, obliterating everything.

He came round to see the haggard, smoke-grimed face of an orderly bending over him. He tried to rise but fell back as a white-hot pain shot through his arm again.

'Lie still, mate. That arm's in a bad enough way without you trying to lean on it.'

He lay confused, bewildered and in agony until he was helped below to the hurriedly converted sick bay where he was just one of hundreds. Too much had happened in so short a space of time that he felt gobsmacked, as Gerry used to say. Gerry, Charlie, John and maybe Mat, too. It just wasn't possible. He sat, head bowed, cradling the shattered arm until a doctor finally came to him. He bit deeply into his lip to suppress the screams of pain as the makeshift splint was removed. But he couldn't hide the terror and revulsion when the doctor said, 'It'll have to come off, lad, it's past saving.'

Maud tried again to write to Ellan. It was her third attempt but the words wouldn't come. She just couldn't express in words the way she felt. Jutland was nearly three months in the past but she still couldn't believe it had happened. Her sons, her big, healthy, cheery lads on whom she'd quietly doted, John and Mat joking together, they'd never come through that door again. She thought of them every single waking hour and most of the night, too. The country might be outraged and shocked that the biggest fleet ever to sail the seas had been unable to inflict a complete and crushing defeat on the enemy, but to her it was something entirely personal. John and Mat dead and Andrew, soon to come home from the naval hospital, with only one arm. She'd always considered herself to be a Christian woman but now hatred ate away at her heart and she prayed for retribution and revenge. No matter how much the minister might preach to her, she just couldn't find it in her heart to forgive.

Half the island was in mourning, for most of the men had joined the Royal Navy and Jutland had claimed them all. For Maud the fact that she was not alone in her grief held no measure of comfort. But she *had* to write to Ellan. She pulled another sheet of paper towards her and gripped her pen determinedly as she slowly and laboriously wrote of the news that had shattered her world in a single day.

She had to go into Ramsey, not just to post the letter, there were things she would need for when Andrew came home. As she secured her black felt hat with a long pin she remembered that other hat, the one he bought her, the one that had caused a bit of a sensation the first few times she'd worn it. And, she remembered how John had said she was a fine-looking woman when she dressed up. Her features twisted with anguish at the memory. They'd been good sons, all of them.

She hated Ramsey now. It had been from here that they'd all embarked for Liverpool. From here, too, Jamie Corlett had gone to his death and Ellan had gone to New York. It was now a place of bitter memories. She took no joy or pleasure from shopping or meeting people.

Maud was coming out of the Post Office when she almost collided with Mary Costain. They stood face to face. Mary's gaze didn't falter for they both wore black. They shared the same sorrows. Maud looked old, Mary thought, old and weary, her shoulders drooping, the black coat and hat heightening her pallor. Maud was thinking the same thing. Mary Costain looked far older than her thirty-six years. The lines of sorrow were deeply etched, her eyes sad. But she was smiling, a smile that said, 'The time for quarrels is past'.

'Good day to you, Miss Costain.'

'Is it, Mrs Quirk?' Mary asked quietly.

Maud shook her head.

'I haven't seen you to express my . . . regrets.'

'Nor I you, miss. I'm sorry for your loss.'

A flash of pain crossed Mary's face. 'My father is devastated. Suddenly he's an old man. All his drive . . . his energy is gone. He's sick and heartsore, as I am. It was bad enough when we got the telegram about David, but then William, a few hours later. Fifteen years old, a boy. It was a black day at Glentrammon.'

'I know how you feel, miss. Mine went together on the same day.' Maud's eyes misted with tears. She would remember the day the news came for the rest of her life. It was heartbreaking. William Costain had lied about his age and sworn his older brother to secrecy when he joined the same regiment. They'd both died in the mud of Ypres.

'But Andrew will be coming home. That's a blessing.' Mary was fighting down her own tears.

'I wonder if he'll think so, miss. He . . . he saw them both . . . go.'

Mary wondered tiredly what Andrew Quirk's state of mind would be like. Apart from his own terrible injury, he had the awful memories of the carnage of Jutland to live with.

'It's taken me until now to write and tell Ellan. Dora Killip has probably written to their Lizzie so chances are Ellan will know, but it's not the same, miss, is it?'

'No, Mrs Quirk, it's not.' Mary looked at the older woman and for a moment she was tempted to tell her that Ellan was just a short distance away across the Irish Sea. She'd known Ellan was in Liverpool ever since the day Maggie had come to see her father. But she didn't know where in Liverpool and to tell Maud now wouldn't do any good, she thought. Maud would only think Ellan deceitful. Then there was the matter of Ellan's child. No, she couldn't tell Maud. The woman had had enough shocks to contend with.

'I pray every night that it will all be over soon. The way it's going there won't be anyone left under sixty and over fourteen!'

'It can't go on for ever, Mrs Quirk, it just can't,' Mary

said with a note of hysteria in her voice.

Maud had been right in her assumption. Ellan already knew. She'd received the news in a letter from Lizzie but in the days and weeks that had followed she'd wondered why Aunt Maud hadn't written. She'd taken her letter to work that day. Food was indeed becoming shorter and she had fewer and fewer things to sell. Margaret's predictions were coming true and she knew that soon she would have to close, until after the war. After the war! It was a phrase so full of hope. Up to the day she received Lizzie's letter, the war had had little personal effect on her.

She'd been alone in the shop. Mary had gone to lunch. Lucy was at school and there had been few customers so she'd extended her lunch break.

In her childish scrawl Lizzie had first told of the young man of whom she was becoming quite fond and who had taken her to a nice restaurant, a Vaudeville show and home to meet his 'folks', as she called them, in a remarkably short period of time. His name was Clayton Burrows and Lizzie was obviously very taken with him. Then the tone of the letter changed and after scanning the remaining lines Ellan let the sheet flutter to the floor. Poor Aunt Maud! Poor, poor Aunt Maud! She couldn't believe it. The War Office must have made a mistake. Not John *and* Mat. But Quirk was an unusual name, it wasn't like Smith or Jones. There was no error. And Andrew, alive but crippled. She tried to imagine how it would affect him, both physically and mentally. With her head in her hands she struggled with the realization that so many of the lads and men she had known had been killed. She was sorely tempted to send Aunt Maud a telegram, saying she would be home later that day, but then she thought of Lucy and trying to explain away that she hadn't been in New York for six years.

When the letter from Maud finally arrived, via Lizzie, who was now calling Clayton Burrows her 'intended', Ellan experienced the same shock, the same horror that she thought had abated a little. She also had little time for Lizzie's chit-chat about the things she was doing and the places she was visiting.

She read Maud's letter out to Margaret who patted her hand comfortingly, trying not to think of Lloyd and the dangers he faced.

'I think he'll find he can manage very well with just his right hand. Amputees seem to gain strength in the remaining limb as a sort of compensation for the loss.'

'It's not his arm I'm worried about, it's how it will affect him mentally. He was so proud and independent and this . . .' she shook her head sadly.

'Ellan, he's alive, which is more than his brothers are. You must think positively.'

'I know, but he won't look at it like that. He's always been so active.'

'And he will be again and in time he'll realize how fortunate he is. There are thousands of men who will be cripples for life. Blinded, lungs burned by gas, totally dependent on their families once they are well enough to leave the hospitals.'

'I know, but what am I going to write to Aunt Maud? I thought I'd got the worst part over.'

'Just write what you feel, Ellan, and pray it will be over soon.'

Chapter Eighteen

———◆———

THE WINTER OF 1917 BECAME known as the 'Turnip Winter'. Up to then turnips had only been fed to animals. Shortages were endemic and Ellan was forced to close her shops. Tilly and Mary had both joined the Women's Yeomanry as nurses' aids. Daisy had gone into munitions and so the household tasks were divided between Ellan and Selina. Margaret insisted on doing whatever she was capable of despite all the protests, just as she'd insisted that Ellan go back to live in Rodney Street.

'It's pointless keeping two places going, Ellan. You must come back.' So, Ellan had packed up.

That morning in late February Selina, with a very bad grace, had swept the kitchen floor and half-heartedly scrubbed it and the stairs. Since Daisy's departure she was forced to do such menial tasks and the situation between her and Ellan had gone from bad to worse. As Cook was getting on, the running of the house fell to Ellan and herself, but that fact did not stop her from venting her wrath on Ellan if she thought she could get away with it.

She stood, wrapped up against the cold, with a hemp bag over her arm, glowering at Ellan.

'Have you got the money and the list?' Ellan asked.

'Yes. I suppose I'll have to stand in queues all morning. I'll be frozen and I'm getting chilblains from having to wash dirty dishes and floors. If Papa were here . . .'

Ellan cut off the complaints. 'You've got gloves and a good thick coat which is more than many people have.'

'Why can't you go?'

Ellan placed her hands on her hips. 'Do you want to do the laundry? Do you want to spend all morning in the wash-house?'

'No,' Selina snapped.

'Then stop complaining.'

'Don't talk to me like that. I'm nearly seventeen.'

'Then act your age. Stop whingeing like a seven-year-old.'

'Why can't Lucy do more?'

'She does enough. She has school, in case you've forgotten.'

'You could keep her at home afternoons and she could take her turn with the queuing.'

'I've already said she does enough and she does it without complaint. I'm not going to ruin her education.'

Selina was scornful. 'What will she need an education for? It's a waste of time, she'll go into a factory or into service.'

'Over my dead body she will. I have plans for her and they don't include factories or other people's houses.'

Selina was about to jeer when the kitchen door opened and Margaret caught the end of this exchange. Consternation showed clearly on her features and she sighed heavily. Selina was being difficult again. She knew it was hard for her daughter who had never had to wash a dish or make a bed, let alone pick up her discarded clothes from the bedroom floor, to have to do all these things. Yet she impressed on her the fact that without Ellan's help she would have to do everything. Why couldn't she do the chores with good grace, for her sake and so she could write to Lloyd and tell him how proud he should be of his daughter who was doing her best to 'Keep the Home Fires Burning' as the popular song said. But there was a little more to it than met the eye, she was aware of that. Selina was seventeen, an age when she had expected to be in the company of young men. The war had taken them all and she knew Selina was afraid that she would never meet anyone. She also suspected that this rankled more deeply because Ellan had obviously loved and been loved. Lucy was the proof of that.

'Selina, dear, what's the matter now?'

'Nothing. I was just going out,' Selina muttered ungraciously.

'And I'm off to the wash-house or we'll have no clean sheets or underclothes,' Ellan said, ignoring the look of hatred the younger girl flashed at her. 'But let me take those from you.'

'No. I can manage.' Margaret smiled, resting the weight of the bowl filled with potatoes on her hip.

There were only four steps down into the kitchen but they were still wet and they were steep enough to cause a scream of agony as Margaret fell, scattering potatoes across the kitchen floor.

'Oh my God! Selina, go for Doctor Hudson, now.

Don't stand there like an idiot. Go!' Ellan bent down and cradled Margaret's head in her lap.

For once Selina did as she was bid.

'Should we move her?' Ellan questioned Cook who was standing twisting the corner of her apron.

'No. Best not to. Not until the doctor arrives. What do you think she's done, Ellan? Did she bang her head at all?'

'No, and she doesn't seem to have broken anything, but I can't be sure. Hush, now, it's all right. Selina's gone for the doctor,' she soothed as Margaret regained her senses and tried to rise, then sank back white-faced and white-lipped.

She had regained a little colour by the time Selina came back with Doctor Hudson. She lay with her head in Ellan's lap, clutching Selina's hand, while the doctor probed and prodded gently, shaking his head from time to time. Cook hovered in the background.

'Nothing broken that I can see but I think you may have done something inside, so we'd better get you to hospital. Just to be on the safe side,' he added, seeing the anxiety in Ellan's eyes and hearing the sharp intake of breath from Selina.

'Selina, would you get your mother's things together, please?' Ellan prodded and wordlessly the girl left the room.

'Ellan, try to be patient with her, please?' Margaret tried to smile.

Ellan smiled back. It was typical that Margaret should think of Selina at a time like this. Selina didn't deserve such a mother. 'I will. I promise.'

'And Lloyd. Don't write or send any telegrams, he'll only worry and he has enough to contend with.'

Again Ellan promised.

The days that followed were difficult and anxious and Ellan was weary, visiting Margaret at the Women's Hospital in Catherine Street where she had a private room, and trying to run the house and cope with Selina. With her mother's presence removed, Selina let her venom have full rein. She terrified Lucy, who never let her mother out of her sight and demanded to stay with Tilly and Mary while Ellan was at the hospital.

Margaret recovered slowly. The internal bleeding stopped but she had sustained cracked ribs. With her already weakened constitution she had little strength and when she finally came home Doctor Hudson took Ellan aside and told her that Margaret would be an invalid for the rest of her life.

'Do you know what that entails?'

'Yes, I know,' she answered calmly.

'Then I assume you will stay and care for her until, well, until this damned war is over and Lloyd comes home.'

'Yes. I have closed my shops for the duration and she's been good to me. They both have. It's the least I can do.'

'Good.'

'Shall I write to Doctor Elliot, now that the danger is over?'

He smiled. 'No need. She wrote herself, even though I expressly forbade her. She got one of the nurses to post it.'

'She's a very strong-minded lady.'

'It's a pity her body doesn't match her will, but then, if it did she'd be a very formidable woman, and I disapprove of strong-willed females.'

'You'd disapprove of her if she was well?'

'The situation is never likely to occur, I'm afraid.'

'I wouldn't be too sure of that, Doctor, there's a lot about her you don't understand.'

He picked up his bag and his hat. 'Perhaps it's better I don't. Good day.'

She watched him go down the steps. Sick or well, Margaret Elliot could be formidable whether he liked it or not.

Throughout the summer months Margaret improved as Lloyd's letters became more frequent. He was optimistic about coming home on leave for the first time in three years. This news delighted them all, particularly Selina, and she became easier to live with as the weeks went by. Then came the letter they'd all been waiting for. He'd be in Liverpool at the end of October.

The news had them all in a ferment of activity. Ellan washed curtains and carpets and Lucy polished everything in sight. Selina stood uncomplainingly in queues for hours and Cook planned appetizing dishes using their meagre rations. Margaret was unable to go to the station to meet him and Ellan, seeing how upset she was by this, elected to stay with her. This arrangement pleased Selina, who went off dressed in her best clothes, her face radiant.

Ellan dressed Margaret in her best dark green wool frock and had pinned a cameo brooch at the neck. She brushed Margaret's hair until it shone and piled it up on the top of her head, which made her look much younger.

'Bite your lips, it will give them some colour,' she advised, rearranging the rug over Margaret's legs and plumping up the cushions at her back. A bright fire burned in the hearth. The furniture glowed and Lucy had arranged a vase of Michaelmas daisies and put them on top of the piano. The room looked warm and cheerful.

'Do I really look well, Ellan?'

'Of course you do. You look wonderful. He'll be delighted with you.'

'I wonder whether he has changed? He must have having faced . . .' Margaret's words tailed off into silence and her features creased in a frown.

'You musn't think like that,' Ellan reproved, pulling aside the lace curtain and peering down into the street, her hand patting down the collar of her black and white checked blouse.

'I can't help it. He's such a good and caring man that what he has seen must have affected him. Oh, Ellan, I'm afraid.'

'What of?'

'What if it has hardened him? Brutalized him?'

'Never. You're just imagining things. I should think if anything it will have made him even more compassionate.'

Margaret pondered this. 'You're probably right, but that was really why I didn't want to go to Lime Street. Oh, not because I didn't want him to see how thin and wasted I've become, but in case . . . in case I saw something in his face that would make me cringe. It's stupid, I know, but I can't help it. Until I see, I can't put aside this nagging fear.'

'Then you won't have long to fret, they're here.'

They heard the clatter of boots in the hall, the quick footsteps on the stairs and then the door opened and he was there. With a strangled cry Margaret held out her arms and with a few steps he covered the distance between them and held her tightly. Selina stood in the open doorway, tears running down her cheeks.

Ellan smiled. This at least was one family that had been spared the anguish of bereavement, so far. He had changed, she thought. His skin was drawn more tightly across his cheekbones. His hair was greyer, his skin weather-beaten, but he looked no older than the day he'd gone. Lloyd looked up and smiled at her and she smiled back, but only then did she realize how false that smile was. It was nailed to his face. It never reached his eyes and in the depths of those eyes there was such infinite sadness that her heart lurched. She hoped Margaret wouldn't notice it, but it wasn't much of a hope.

'Oh, it's good to be back. Ellan, you look wonderful and Lucy, how you've grown.'

Ellan gave Lucy a nudge and she grinned and dipped a bow. She had been allowed to wear her Sunday dress: her white pinafore crackled with starch and she had a big red bow in her hair.

'You've all managed wonderfully well. Selina has been telling me how everyone has been pulling together.'

Ellan wondered what Selina had actually said but she pushed the thought away. Selina was too smart to complain to her father, yet.

'And talking of pulling together I think we'd better get on. There is always something to do and you'll want time to yourselves.' Ellan turned to Selina. 'Selina, would you help Cook and me lay the table, please?'

Selina's smile vanished and she glared at Ellan. She intended to tell her papa how hard Ellan made her work but not yet, and now Ellan was standing there as though she owned the house and she, Selina, was a servant. 'I think you can manage without me for once.'

Ellan looked meaningfully at Lloyd and Margaret but Selina chose to ignore it. She was staying put. They would be a family again, just like they'd been before the war and before Ellan Vannin had come into this house.

Dinner was a festive meal with Ellan, Selina and Margaret laughing off shortages and Lloyd saying it was the best meal he'd had for years. Ellan noticed how forced was his smile and how brittle his laughter. She wondered if she was imagining it for neither his wife nor daughter seemed to notice. Cook said nothing. She was acutely uncomfortable sitting at table with the master and missus. She'd wanted to sit downstairs but Lloyd had been adamant.

'The old order has changed.'

'Indeed it hasn't, sir! At least I hope not,' she replied.

'Just for tonight, Cook? To please me? You're one of the family, you know.' He wheedled and reluctantly she gave in. But she was not fooled by his performance and later she said so.

'There's something wrong with the master. He's covering up. I was watching him at table.'

'What do you mean?' Ellan was up to her elbows in dishwater.

'It's all an act he's putting on for the missus and Miss Selina.'

'I thought that, but then I thought surely Mrs Elliot would notice, them being so close.'

'He's been away for three years and she's only seeing what she wants to see.'

'Oh, I hope you're wrong. She was so afraid he would have changed, or that things . . . events would have changed him.'

'Well, it's my guess that they have.'

Ellan frowned and hoped that Cook was wrong.

When all the chores were done and Lucy and Cook had gone to their beds, exhausted, Ellan sank down beside the fire in the range. She'd deliberately insisted on doing everything, leaving Lloyd, Margaret and Selina together, as a family, on this night at least. Of course Margaret and Lloyd protested but she waved away the protestations laughingly. Selina said nothing.

Glancing into the flames Ellan thought how well the day had gone. There couldn't be many families in the city who had so much to celebrate. She was happy in the knowledge that her part in the preparations had been appreciated. She was lucky. She had a comfortable home with good people. Shortages didn't affect her too much and if it hadn't been for the war, everything would have been perfect. The war, there was no getting away from it, even for a few hours. How long would it go on and how many more lives would it claim? A deep sadness overtook her.

She looked up, stirred from her reverie by the sound of the kitchen door opening. Lloyd was standing at the top of the stairs.

'I knew I'd find you here.'

She smiled as he walked across the room and sat down in the chair opposite her. Only one gas jet flickered, throwing much of the room into shadow, but the light from the fire illuminated his features and her smile faded. She was shocked, for the mask of pretence had gone. She reached out and touched his arm. 'What's the matter?'

There was a heavy silence for a few seconds, as though he were trying to shape the words in his mind. 'I . . . I can't talk to them any more.'

'What do you mean? You were so happy and cheerful.'

'What else could I do? It was an act, Ellan. I used to be able to share so much with Margaret, but now I don't know what to say. Have I changed so much?'

'You haven't changed, it's just the war,' she said, feeling it was a lame explanation and of little comfort. 'It must be difficult when you come home. Especially after so long. It must be hard to put it to the back of your mind.'

'It's not hard, Ellan. It's impossible. Oh, there are so many changes here. Women working at all kinds of jobs. Uniforms everywhere, shortages, but . . .' He dropped his head on to one hand.

'But?' she probed.

'But nothing compared to . . . Oh, I just can't tell her. I just can't and it's the first time I've ever held anything back from her and she knows it. And that makes it worse.'

'Maybe in time. A day or so will make all the difference. You're worn out.'

'Time won't make any difference and I've been worn out for months.'

His tone was bitter and she was alarmed. She pulled her chair nearer to his. 'Can you tell me?'

'You, Ellan?'

'Yes. Have you forgotten that I've seen heartbreak and tragedy? Oh, not only when I was young, but recently. John and Mat were killed at Jutland. Andrew was maimed.'

'Oh, Ellan, I'm sorry.' His voice was flat. The words had been used so often they came out automatically now.

She noticed and inwardly sighed. 'Then tell me. It will help, I know it will. It's often best to share sorrow.'

'Nothing will help, Ellan. The only thing that will be of any help is to stop the slaughter and stop it now. To send everyone home, even the enemy. There's no sense, no reason and no damned glory in being killed or maimed for a few square yards of mud!'

'Will they stop it?'

He shook his head. 'No. Not until someone gives in. The generals and the War Cabinet sit in their safe, warm, dry offices and plot how many more lives they can expend with their futile offensives. They can't be called battles. My God! The poor sods are little more than cannon fodder and still they ask for more and more to fill the trenches, to feed the appetite of the Lewis guns. How long will it be before we have old men and little boys at the front?'

It was as though he were speaking to himself, she thought, and she'd never heard his tone so harsh and angry. 'So many of them lied about their ages,' she said, thinking of William Costain.

'I know. They couldn't wait to join the big adventure. Didn't want to miss anything. Brought up on tales of Mafeking, Ladysmith, Balaclava. "Into the valley of death rode the six hundred",' the lines coming from 'The Charge of the Light Brigade'. He'd read all the stories too when he'd been young. Had he ever been young, he wondered. 'They don't lie now. It's no bloody picnic and at last they know it. They found out the hard way. God in heaven! When I think of the way they marched out, bands playing, cheering crowds, young girls and mothers, too, urging them on. To what? To what?' Although his voice had risen it held a note of cold fury and she was shocked to hear him swear. But she felt she must also urge him on, cajole from him some of the anger, frustration and sorrow so that he might try to heal some of his own emotional wounds.

'Tell me, Lloyd. What is it they fought and died for?'

The embers hissed and crackled as a piece of coal fell into the hearth but neither paid any heed. In the firelight he looked so haggard, she thought, her heart going out to him.

His eyes took on a glazed look, as though he were seeing in the flames the torments of Hell, the hell that was the Western Front. He started, haltingly at first.

'There are no trees, no houses, not even a single blade of grass. Just mud and trenches and barbed wire. Shell holes like craters on the moon, ground continuously churned up by the shells. We live in mud, glaucous, clinging, filthy mud. Holes in the ground half full of stinking water. Like sewers. The noise of the guns battering the ears often mercifully drowning the screams of dying men and horses. There are rats the size of cats and just as bold. We're always wet. Always weary. Often there's no chance to get the wounded back behind the lines. No chance to get the dead back either. They lie rotting where they've fallen. It's obscene that men should be denied even the decency of a grave!' His voice cracked with emotion.

'At night, when the guns are quiet, sappers crawl out to lay duck boards between the shell holes, or at least they try. Some fall off and, unable to claw their way out, they've been drowned. Sinking into the mud, their packs dragging them down. Drowned! Drowned in mud! In the morning when another advance is tried, men slip on the wet boards or they're shot off like sitting ducks and they drown and die in the mud. There's little I can do to help them and that's the worst part of it all. Not the indignity, the senseless ignominy of all those wasted, blighted lives. The frustration and the fury that I could help, if only I had the right conditions, the right facilities, the chance to use all the skills I have. I'm a doctor, for God's sake! I was trained to save life. Sometimes I want to stand up in No Man's Land and scream for them all to stop this useless waste. Let everyone go home. Let them live their lives, not end them in man-made sewers and mud-filled craters. The youth of a whole generation is being wiped out and there's nothing I can do to stop it, nor even help.'

Ellan sank to her knees and took his hands, for tears were pouring down his cheeks. So vivid was his description that she felt she could see the battlefields, hear the noise and the cries and there were tears in her own eyes. 'Oh, Lloyd. Lloyd! Don't tear yourself to pieces like this. It must end soon if things are as bad as that. It must.'

The man who looked at her was a stranger. 'But it won't end before I have to go back, Ellan. I almost wish I hadn't come home. There I am exhausted and with that comes sleep, dreamless sleep. Here there are only the nightmares and the strain of having to put it all out of my mind for . . . for them both.' He seemed to suddenly become aware of who he was talking to. 'Oh, Ellan. I'm sorry. I swore I'd never burden anyone with . . . with all that.'

She managed a brief smile as he wiped his face with

the back of his hand. 'I'm glad you did. It may help.'

He shook his head slowly. 'No. Nothing will help, Ellan. What can erase the knowledge that fifty-seven thousand casualties were suffered in one single day? It's not war, it's genocide gone mad. Genocide that is unable to discriminate between nationalities.'

Maud Quirk scraped the dried-up food from the plate into the bowl used for the dogs. She hated to see good food wasted at the best of times, but now, when everything was so short, it was little better than sacrilege. This was the third time this week she'd given his supper to the dogs. She whipped the table cloth off with a sharp pull, the gesture yet another sign of her anger. As she folded it up she looked at the clock on the mantel. Nearly half past nine. How long would she have to sit up tonight until he staggered through the door or was helped in and carried upstairs by Bert Killip or Davie Kewin or even Dick Marlin himself. There should be a law against taverns and those who kept them. Well, this was the last time. She'd go and see Dick Marlin and tell him straight that he was not to serve Andrew Quirk any more liquor. It wasn't helping anyone to let him drown his sorrows and self-pity in ale.

The table cleared and the dishes washed, she took her knitting and sat down by the fire to wait, her bosom rising and falling the only sign of her anger now. Between rows she glanced at the clock as the hands moved slowly towards ten then a quarter past. Five minutes before half past she heard him, or she heard the dogs, which heralded the approach of someone. She flung the knitting down and went to the door. He was alone.

'Oh, so you managed to get home under your own steam tonight!' She hadn't meant to let fly like that but she couldn't help it.

'Went for a few pints. Can't . . . can't a man do that?' His speech was slurred.

'Get into the house.' Maud took his shoulder and pushed him inside. 'Is it a disgrace you want to make of us now?'

He lurched towards the ladder-backed chair and slumped into it. 'That's all you've ever cared about.'

'Stop that! Oh, dear Lord! Why do you do it, son? Why?'

His bloodshot eyes rested for a second on John's pipe, still in the pipe rack by the fire. Why did he do it, he mused. Hadn't he tried to explain it to her a hundred times? He did it to try to forget. To forget John and Mat, Gerry Connell and Charlie Oats. To forget that he only had one arm, that he was a cripple. That was a lot to forget. 'Where's my supper?' he demanded.

Something inside Maud snapped. The months of holding in her anguish, of trying to cheer him and bolster his confidence, the nights when she'd been woken by his cries: she'd tried everything and now she was drained. 'I gave it to the damned dogs! The way I've given it to them three times this week already. Don't you dare ask me where your supper is. If you came home at a decent hour you wouldn't have to ask.'

'Shut up. Can't you ever keep a quiet tongue in your head?'

'Don't you dare speak like that to me, Andrew Quirk. Don't you dare! If your pa or your brothers were here, they'd . . .'

He had dragged himself to his feet. 'Don't you talk to me about them. They're dead. Dead! I'm alive!'

'And you should thank God for it.'

He brought his fist crashing down on the table and Maud stepped backwards, her hand at her throat.

'Thank God? Thank God? I wish to God I'd gone too!'

A blast of cold air suddenly swept into the room and Maud turned her head and gasped. Mary Costain was standing in the doorway, her glance taking in the scene. Maud tried to compose herself while Andrew peered at Mary belligerently.

'I came in because you didn't hear me knocking. I saw Andrew in the village. I'd been visiting Mrs Killip, she's ill again. I wanted to see him . . . safely home.'

'He's home,' Maud stated tersely, smarting that Mary Costain should have followed her drunken son home and then witnessed a family quarrel.

Mary shut the door as Andrew sank into the chair once more.

'Mrs Quirk, forgive me. I know it's hard for you both.'

'Hard,' Maud interrupted. 'How would you know that it's hard?'

Mary didn't raise her voice. 'I know because I watch my father drink himself into oblivion every night. Because I know he's slowly killing himself with grief and whisky and there is nothing I can do about it. So, please, don't tell me I don't know.'

Maud's hostility evaporated and she indicated to Mary to sit down, while she sat at the table, her hand supporting her aching head. 'I'm sorry, miss. I shouldn't have said that. But what can we do?'

'I don't know. I really don't.'

'I've prayed. Oh, how I've prayed, miss.'

Mary nodded sadly. She'd prayed too, but it hadn't worked for her either. God didn't seem to be there any more. It was hard to believe He was ever there these days. She turned to Andrew. 'For your mother's sake, if not for your own, will you stop this?'

He looked up, tears of self-pity in his eyes. 'I don't want to stop it. Why should I? Tell me that. Tell me what I'm supposed to do. Tell me what work I can do with *this*?' He waved the empty sleeve of his jacket at her.

'You *can* work. You are crippled only in your mind. You're alive and you're young and healthy. There are men in this village who would give their few, poor possessions for that. Joe Brickhill who will never walk again with shrapnel lodged in his spine; Fred Hurst who will never sail his nobbie again, blind and his lungs scorched by gas. And the others, like your brothers, lying under the waters of the North Sea. And my brothers dead in the mud of Ypres. Neither of them reached twenty. Boys – and William still little more than a child. You're lucky, do you hear me. Stop all this wallowing in self-pity. Learn to sail with one hand, it *can* be done! Work for those who can't work any more and who will be glad of your efforts.' Mary fell silent, wondering if she should tell them about Ellan. Maud would find Ellan a comfort and Andrew might perhaps pull himself together for Ellan. She'd heard rumours that he'd been fond of her.

'Go home and leave me alone,' Andrew muttered.

Mary looked at Maud who shook her head sadly. She'd said enough for one night. It really was none of her business.

As Andrew got to his feet and stumbled out of the back door to vomit up the drink he'd consumed that afternoon and evening, Maud wrung her hands in desperation. Her eyes were bright with tears. 'What's going to happen to him, Miss Mary?'

'What's going to happen to them all, Mrs Quirk? My father is not young whereas Andrew is. Perhaps he will take notice of what I said, I hope so. It didn't work for my father and, God knows, I've shouted and railed at him night after night. But I keep on trying. I keep on hoping, it's all I can do.'

'It's got to end soon. How can it go on? Sons, fathers, brothers . . . there'll be no-one left except widows and orphans.'

'And everyone has long forgotten what it's all for. I think that's the worst thing.'

'No, miss. The worst thing is watching those who are left slowly destroying themselves.'

Andrew leaned his head against the door jamb. It was thudding but it felt a little clearer. He hadn't meant to get drunk. All he'd wanted was a pint or two, to help him sleep. But as usual the tavern was sombre. There were too many familiar faces missing, so he'd gone on and on trying to keep the memories at bay. He heard the front yard gate creak shut and then the sounds of hooves and he knew she'd gone. Interfering busybody. Following him home. What did she know about any of it? Miss High and Mighty bloody Costain. Then he remembered that she'd lost her two brothers, just as he had, just as she'd reminded him and both younger than himself. And he'd insulted her. Her words stuck in his mind. Her words about Joe and Fred and all the others.

As he walked back into the kitchen and up the stairs he thought about what she'd said. Was he only an emotional cripple? Could he work again? Work to save his own dignity and to help others less fortunate.

Chapter Nineteen

———◆———

THE QUEUES GOT LONGER as the German U-Boats took their toll on British merchant ships until at last, in April 1917, America entered the war and new hope burned. Crowds cheered the soldiers through the streets and at the stations from where they departed for the Channel and the Western Front. Others watched silently as the smiling, cheering, open-faced young American troops went off, remembering the days three years ago when British troops had gone with equal enthusiasm.

'Do you really think they will make much of a difference?' Ellan asked Margaret after Tilly and Mary had been to tell them how they'd just seen another train load of them off at Lime Street Station.

'It's bound to. They're fresh and, God help them, eager. They're not exhausted or worn out with illness. Please God it will all be over soon now.'

'Amen to that,' Ellan answered, knowing for some it would never be over. She'd had two letters from Aunt Maud. It was getting ludicrous, all this sending mail backwards and forwards across the Atlantic, but there wasn't very much she could do about it.

The first one she read with a sickening sense of despair. Maud could do nothing with Andrew. He seemed intent on drinking himself to death. Depression had him firmly in its grip and Maud could think of nothing to do to help. Ellan had been on the verge of throwing caution to the winds and going home. Only Margaret's quiet reasoning had prevented it.

Then she sighed with relief when the second one arrived. Mary Costain appeared to have talked some sense into him. He was now fishing again with the older men and had stopped drinking, but her brow furrowed when she read that Mr Costain was ill, very ill. Miss Mary was at her wit's end for she'd been unable to stop him destroying himself. Ellan had written to Mary, knowing that Maggie had told her years ago that Ellan was in Liverpool. And she received a reply, a short formal note thanking her for her concern but adding that she had nearly divulged to Aunt Maud that she wasn't in New York. That caused Ellan to catch her breath, but after she thought about it she realized Mary was not so foolhardy.

Selina stood gazing out of the window at the quiet street. She was bored. She had listened to that common pair, Tilly and her sister Mary, talking about the American soldiers and it had given her an idea. 'Do you think any of them will actually stay here?'

'Stay where, dear?' Margaret questioned, absent-mindedly.

'Here. In Liverpool.' Selina ignored the look Ellan shot at her.

'I don't think so but I believe there is a training camp

somewhere in the area. I forget who told me.'

'Oh.' Selina sounded disappointed and Margaret looked up. It was hard on all the young girls now and it would be even harder in years to come. So many young men had died that many girls were destined to become old maids.

'Perhaps I could find out. I remember now. It was Doctor Hudson's wife who told me.'

'I just thought it would be . . . well, kind, if we had one or two for tea or dinner, sometime?' Selina studiously ignored Ellan's look of surprise. It was all right for her. She had had someone who loved her. She'd had a chance, while Selina . . .

'What a good idea. They must feel rather isolated and maybe lonely and homesick. I'll enquire about it.'

Selina looked like the cat who had got the cream, Ellan thought, as the girl tossed her head and excused herself, no doubt to preen before her mirror.

'Oh, it's so hard for her, Ellan. She's just like any other eighteen-year-old, dreaming of her knight in shining armour. Poor Selina. If things had been different she would have been going to balls and soirées and to the theatre but now . . .' she spread her hands.

'Would you mind an American son-in-law?' Ellan asked.

Margaret laughed. 'Ellan, you're a gem. No, I don't think I would as long as she was happy, and there aren't going to be many young men left. But I wish she would try for a career. She's clever, she would make a good doctor and Lloyd would be so proud of her. He's always encouraged her. He's never cared much for convention though I think all that has changed with women and girls taking the place of men. Finally, they've become emancipated. But Selina only thinks of getting married when generations of young women have longed for the freedom she now has, the freedom of a choice between career and marriage.'

Ellan thought Selina would be the last person she would think of as being a 'good' doctor. She was far too self-centred and even callous. 'Was that the post?' she asked, rising.

'It certainly sounded like it. Perhaps there will be a note from Lloyd.'

Ellan smiled at her. Margaret's thin, pallid face took on an animated expression when she spoke of him.

When she got into the hall she found that Selina had already picked up the mail. 'There's three.'

'From your papa?' Ellan had to smile at the affection that transformed Selina's demeanour.

'And one for you. From America.' Selina's good humour extended to Ellan.

'Will you tell your mama that I've gone to read mine upstairs, please?'

Selina hardly heard her as she sped towards the drawing room.

As Ellan climbed the stairs she thought how much easier it would be to hear Aunt Maud's news sooner rather than later, but now was not the time to end the subterfuge. She'd read her letter then go and meet Lucy from school.

When she opened it there was only one sheet of paper and the writing was not Lizzie's. Her brow creased in a puzzled frown as she scanned the lines.

Dear Ellan,

I'm writing to you, honey, on behalf of Lizzie because she can't do nothin' just now. Mrs Van Kronin has given her a week's vacation to help her get over her shock but I reckon it will take longer than that.

Ellan smoothed out the single sheet to read it more carefully. Why was Eva Hinchey writing? What was wrong with Lizzie?

It came as a shock to us all. I guess with Europe being so far away we never thought that our boys would be killed. Not so soon anyway. But Clayton Burrows is dead. His ma got the telegram and she sent it straight round to Lizzie. She took it real bad. She worshipped him. I guess you knew that anyway, so why am I telling you? But, she's been bawling like a babe and nothing I do or say seems to help her any. She says she is planning to go home but I don't think that will help any either . . .

Ellan sat back. Poor Lizzie, she'd had such a wonderful future to look forward to. All her letters were about Clay, as she called him, and what they'd done and what they were going to do. She'd even spent a short vacation in New Jersey with him, and his folks of course. Ellan had smiled at that. Lizzie had become proud of her adopted country and had slipped easily into the vernacular. But now she was talking of coming home. Oh, she knew how Lizzie felt. Hadn't she wanted to leave the island with its memories after Jamie had been drowned? She thought of all the complications it would cause if Lizzie did come back but she dismissed them. The pain in her heart was for Lizzie and her loss.

Her mind went back to the days when they'd spent so much time together. When they'd stood in the lane that summer day and Lizzie had told her about the job at Glentrammon, the job Aunt Maud wouldn't let her take. She'd met Jamie that day. It had been Lizzie who had taught her to sew and had helped to make the red dress she'd worn the night he'd proposed to her. The hours they'd spent, heads together, chattering about her Hope chest. The visit to Liverpool when Lizzie had wanted her to buy up everything they saw. Lizzie who had gone with her to New York, Lizzie who had given her comfort and support when she'd needed it. For the first time, Ellan wished she had some of Jamie's money so that she could take the first ship to be with Lizzie. Lizzie who had turned down Andrew's proposal. That brought her sharply to reality. If Lizzie came home, what about Andrew? How would he feel? Lizzie knew about his arm and from what she'd heard from Mary Costain, he was now trying to reshape his life. Would Lizzie unwittingly destroy all he'd managed to build so far?

She got up and took paper, an envelope and a pen from her drawer and sat down to compose a very difficult letter. She had to do it now and post it, it was the best way. She'd do that on her way to meet Lucy. But how was she to beg Lizzie not to come back without sounding selfish? That was her dilemma.

She spent so long composing the letter that she had to rush the end. It was duly posted and she got to the corner in time to see the crowd of children spill out of school. She smiled as she caught sight of Lucy.

'Hullo, Ma.'

'Oh, you ragamuffin. What have you been doing?' Ellan laughed at her seven-year-old daughter's appearance. Her dark hair had slipped from its ribbons, her pinafore was crumpled and dirty and there was a hole in the knee of her stockings.

'Tommy Wear said I couldn't climb the wall between the boys' yard and ours.'

'And you did?'

Lucy looked triumphant.

'And what did Miss Fletcher have to say about that?'

Lucy looked instantly crestfallen. 'I got a long lecture about being a girl and about how nice girls don't do things like that.'

'And she's right. You are growing up to be a hoyden.'

'What's that?'

'Someone who is wild and has no manners, miss.'

Lucy shrugged and caught Ellan's hand.

'I was going to take you down to the pierhead for a treat, but I don't think I should now.'

Lucy instantly set up a howl of protest, declaring she would be the best behaved girl in the whole school. Ellan relented.

The pierhead was always busy and there was always something to see. Now it was merchant ships and their escorts, for at last the government had decided on the convoy system. They walked to the landing stage clinging tightly to the handrail for the tide was out and the roadway sloped steeply. Ellan was explaining the benefits of convoys when she saw the Isle of Man mail boat dwarfed by the other ships. A lump rose in her throat as she thought of Jamie and her namesake, lying out there in the bay. And of the *Ramsey, Empress Queen, Ben-my-Chree* and *Snaefell,* all lost in this war. All their crews Manx.

'You look sad, Ma,' Lucy observed with perception. There was a close bond between them for they spent more time together than the average mother and daughter.

'I was just thinking. Remembering, really.'

Lucy had followed the direction of Ellan's gaze. 'Because of all the ships that have been sunk?' She read the papers and she heard the boys talking.

Ellan sighed and led her to a bench. There was never a good time for things like this but she had put it off, parried all the child's questions, postponed it for too long. 'For one ship, Lucy.'

'My ship? The *Lusitania*?'

'No. It was another ship long before that one.'

Lucy looked puzzled. 'Which ship then?'

'One that had the same name as me. The S.S. *Ellan Vannin.* The mail boat.'

'Did she sink, Ma?'

Ellan nodded. 'Out there on a winter's night in a terrible storm.'

'And you were sad, the way I'm sad when anyone talks about my ship.'

'The *Lusitania* was never your ship, Lucy. Just as the *Ellan Vannin* was never mine.' Her tone was sharp as she pushed from her mind the comparison that haunted her whenever she thought about those two ships and herself and Lucy. 'I had another reason for being sad.'

Lucy gazed up at her with Jamie's eyes, her expression expectant.

'Your . . . your pa was on that ship when she sank.' She'd said it but it had cost her a great effort.

'You never told me about my pa. Even when I asked you you wouldn't tell me.'

Ellan took her daughter's hand. 'His name was James. I . . . I used to call him Jamie. He was kind and good and you look like him . . . sometimes.' She couldn't control the catch in her voice but the child seemed not to notice, she was too engrossed in her own thoughts. Ellan forestalled the question she saw in Lucy's eyes. 'He was a groom at the big house, Glentrammon, but then his uncle died in America and left him a lot of money. That's why he was sailing to Liverpool that night. He was going to New York.'

She waited for Lucy to digest this, hoping the child would not ask questions that she would find too hard to answer truthfully.

'Then are we rich, Ma?'

Ellan smiled. 'No, lass, we're not. I went to New York with Lizzie, but the uncle said in his Will . . . I wasn't entitled to the money. It was complicated, too hard for you to understand, but I couldn't have the money, so I came back.'

Lucy considered all this while Ellan sat watching the crowds on the waterfront and the ships on the river.

'Why didn't you go home? You don't come from Liverpool, Mary said so. You're Manx.'

'Yes, and so are you, even though you weren't born there. I didn't go home because it would have been too hard for me. Your pa and I were happy there and I just couldn't bear to go back without him.' It was only a half truth, she thought. The child who looked up at her so

312

trustingly was the real reason but she could never tell her that. Wild horses wouldn't drag from her the fact that Lucy was born out of wedlock, a bastard. Inwardly she cringed at the very word. It was ugly, so very ugly.

'Will we go there one day, Ma?' Lucy needed time to absorb everything but she'd think about all that later on. Now she was curious about where her ma and her poor pa had lived. Manx was a word she'd only heard a few times before. As her ma didn't answer she tugged at her sleeve. 'Will we, Ma?'

Ellan sighed deeply. 'Maybe one day, Lucy.'

'When?'

'When you are grown up and perhaps even married.' Safely married Ellan thought. Then she would not be hurt by the stigma of her birth.

'Oh, Ma. That's years and years I'll have to wait and I might not even get married. Selina said I'm too ugly for anyone to want to marry me.'

'That's a lie, Lucy. You're beautiful. Take no notice of her, she's jealous. She always has been, ever since you were a baby.' Damn Selina with her vicious tongue.

'I told her no-one would want *her* and anyway there won't be anyone left and she'll have to marry an old man, like her pa, 'cos all the young ones will be dead.'

The words sounded chilling spoken by a child of seven who had placed no special emphasis on them, nor given their meaning anything more than a casual nuance.

'That was unkind. The war can't go on for ever, Lucy. You shouldn't have said that to her.' Lucy looked confused. 'I mean, it's not a nice thing to say to anyone. It sounds as though you don't care about all the men over in France and Belgium, Doctor Elliot included.'

Lucy was contrite. 'But I do, Ma. Annie Gregson's brother was killed last week and Annie cried all the time and I cried, too, 'cos Annie was sad.'

Ellan ruffled the dark curls. 'I know you didn't mean to be nasty.'

'Oh, I did. I did when I said it to Selina,' Lucy answered with spirit. 'I hate her.'

'You shouldn't say that either. You shouldn't hate anyone. Oh, I know she's not a nice person, but Doctor and Mrs Elliot have been very good to you and me and she is their daughter.'

Lucy was rapidly becoming bored with this subject so she changed tactics. 'Do you still have friends over there? Are they Manx too?' She liked saying the word and everyone in her class would be green with envy when she told them she was different. She was Manx.

'Not really. Lizzie, my best friend, is in New York and the only other friend I had was a lady. A real lady who lived in a big house and had a lot of money.'

'Couldn't we go and see her then?'

Ellan shook her head. Mary Costain knew about her child. She was the only one on the island who did, but she couldn't just appear on Mary's doorstep with Lucy. 'No, we can't.' She waited for the question.

'Why not?'

'She's sick and she mustn't have visitors.' She prayed forgiveness for the lie. She couldn't tell Lucy about Aunt Maud or John and Mat and Andrew. 'But we have our own language,' she said brightly, to divert Lucy's interest in Mary Costain. 'I'll teach it to you.'

Lucy nodded vigorously. It got even better, she thought, a language as well.

'The toffee we used to make for the shop was called carn toffee. Carn means rock. The big house where Miss Mary lives is called Glentrammon which means "Glen of the Elder Trees" and my name isn't a name, not like Lucy or Sarah or Annie or Selina.'

'Is it a special name, like Glentrammon?'

'In a way. Ellan means isle or island and Vannin means of Man. You see? Ellan Vannin. Isle of Man.'

Lucy grinned. 'So my name is Lucy of Man?' Lucy repeated it. She liked it. It was like saying Catherine of Aragon or Anne of Cleves. Miss Fletcher was teaching them all about those ladies and bluff King Hal who kept cutting their heads off or divorcing them. Privately she thought a king who did that when they hadn't done anything bad shouldn't be allowed to be a king at all. A thought occurred to her. 'Will they call a mail boat after me?'

Ellan feigned horror. 'Isn't it enough that you were called after one ship? Don't be greedy, miss.' Then seeing the child's face fall she added, 'They might. Not Lucy, maybe *Lady of Man*.' And may she not carry the curse that haunts me, she thought, nor Lucy, she prayed as she tied the child's bonnet ribbons more tightly under her chin then bent and kissed her cheek.

'What was that for?' Lucy asked, surprised. Her ma only kissed her at night.

'That's for being my pretty, clever little love. My Lady of Man,' Ellan laughed. Neither of them was to know that it would be many years before a Manx ship bearing that name would sail into the Mersey. A ship that would play its part in another war but would eventually share the same fate as the S.S. *Ellan Vannin*.

Part Three

1919

Chapter Twenty

———— ·•· ————

ELLAN FELT AS THOUGH her back was breaking as she wearily came down the stairs. She felt light-headed and tried to remember how long ago it was since she'd eaten but the hours blurred together.

The house was in darkness so it must be late, she reasoned. As she reached the last step she clung to the newel post as the giddiness increased. A dim chink of light filtered beneath the door that led below stairs but as she stood there swaying, it got brighter and suddenly the hall was full of light. She screwed up her eyes against the glare.

'Ellan, is that you? What's the matter?'

'I'm fine. Just a little tired.'

Lloyd stood looking down at her, a lamp in his hand.

'I should be carrying that, it would be more in keeping.' She managed a tired smile.

'I didn't want to put the light on, I thought you'd gone to bed.'

'Not yet. I came down for a cup of tea. How is she?'

'Sleeping. I think the worst is over. Here, take my

arm,' he urged as she clutched again at the banister rail. 'How long is it since you've eaten, Ellan?'

'I can't remember. What time is it?'

'Nearly ten o'clock and you're going to have a meal. You can't be on your feet night and day and not eat.'

'I'll eat when I know she's comfortable.'

He propelled her firmly towards the kitchen. 'You'll eat now. I'll make you something. Cook has gone to bed.'

'She's not . . . ?'

'No, she's not ill, just tired. She's not getting any younger. What about Selina?' he asked as she sank on to a chair close to the table. 'Is she asleep?'

Ellan nodded as he moved about the kitchen.

'All I can manage are scrambled eggs. I'm not much of a cook, I'm afraid.'

She smiled again, tiredly. The war had been over for five months but in its wake had come an enemy that was decimating conquerer and vanquished alike. Nor did it discriminate between young and old, soldier or civilian, sick or well. Influenza was raging and people were dying in their hundreds every day. A whole battalion of Canadian soldiers had died from it. There had been little time to try to pick up the threads of life before it had struck.

Lucy had been the first to catch it. Most of her class had, but to Ellan's relief she got over it quickly. Just as she was on the mend both Margaret and Selina had gone down with it. Lloyd, still pale and thin after four years at the front, nursed his frail wife day and night while Ellan tended Selina, feeling that by nursing the girl she assuaged some of the guilt she felt, for it had been her own child who had brought the infection into the house.

She was especially worried about Margaret who didn't have the strength to combat the illness.

'Do you really think the worst is over now?' she asked as he placed a dish in front of her and sat down.

'I hope so. As long as it doesn't turn to pneumonia she'll be fine. It will take her a long time to get over it. Her chest sounds clear to me and she has no fever now. She'll just need building up.'

'I feel so responsible. After all it was Lucy who . . .'

'Now stop that,' he interrupted. 'I've told you a hundred times that anyone could have brought the germ in. Cook, Selina, you or me.'

She pushed the egg around the plate, no longer feeling hungry. 'I think you'd better look in on Selina. Her breathing was shallow and she's still hot and flushed.'

'I will as soon as I've seen you finish that. Eat, Ellan, or you'll be ill yourself!'

She took a few mouthfuls while he poured out the tea, adding half a teaspoon of black pepper to it.

'I thought you didn't believe in quack medicine.'

'It won't do you any harm and when modern drugs are failing you can't afford to sneer. I saw some of the soldiers do this, they said it kept colds away.'

'I'd better try it. The last thing we need is for me to catch it.'

'I think we'd both have succumbed by now, Ellan. Thank God we appear to be immune.'

He watched her closely while she finished the meal. She looked worn out. She was thin. Her dark eyes looked even larger for her face was pale. There were dark shadows under her eyes, her hair was untidy and the apron she wore was stained where she'd slopped water over it while sponging down Selina. He sighed. What did he expect? He was worn out himself. After years of dreaming about home, the first few months of peace had soon become fraught with worry as he'd watched his wife struggle against her illness. He knew only too well that Margaret was frail, but he didn't dare to even contemplate the fact that she might not recover. Selina was young and healthy and unless there were serious complications he was fairly certain she would soon be on the mend. He hoped they were immune. If Ellan was to fall ill, too, he didn't know how he would manage.

'Ellan, I've never even had time to thank you.'

'For what?' she asked him. 'After all you have done for me, a bit of nursing isn't much payment.'

'You know we don't expect any kind of payment, Ellan. You're part of the family. We're very fond of you.' He reached out and took her hand. 'I don't want to hear any more talk like that.'

She smiled at him. 'Let's hope that they both get well soon.' She started to get to her feet. 'I think I'd better go back to her now.'

'Stay there and finish your tea. I'll go.' His feelings surprised him. He meant what he said, he was fond of her, but when he caught her hand he had been startled to feel his emotions stirring. They were both tired and overwrought, he told himself. Nerves were stretched and wasn't it only natural that they drew closer together in this adversity? He refused to allow himself to think there was anything more to it. She was young enough to be his daughter.

'You go and check her, then I'll make her comfortable for the night.'

'And when will you sleep?'

'When she's asleep, I promise.'

'When they are both better we'll go out, all of us. The weather will be warmer then and it will do us all good.'

Ellan watched him go slowly up the four steps, the steps down which Margaret had fallen, and she wondered if Margaret would ever be well enough to leave the house. She herself was tired, so tired that she felt as though she were sleep-walking. She had been automatically carrying out tasks without really thinking about what she was doing. But she owed the Elliots so much.

On Armistice Day they had all laughed and cried. Selina had forgotten all her animosity and with tears of joy streaming down her cheeks, she had hugged both herself and Lucy. She'd even begged to take Lucy out to join in the celebrations and only the arrival of an equally ecstatic Tilly and Mary had made Ellan agree to the request. She and Margaret had sat sipping the last of the good sherry and Margaret had reiterated how fortunate she'd been compared to so many other women who had little to celebrate that day. Ellan had thought of John and Mat, David and William Costain and all the other lads she'd known. And Andrew. She'd wondered what it had all been for and doubted that anyone now remembered the reason why an entire generation had had to be sacrificed.

The day Lloyd came home was like Christmas, Easter and birthdays all rolled into one and on that day, too, she received a letter from Lizzie telling her that no matter how painful were her memories, she couldn't go back to the island. She couldn't go back to the life she'd led. Despite losing Clayton, Lizzie was staying. Later that day, when she left Margaret and Lloyd together, Ellan re-read Lizzie's letter and breathed a sigh of relief. Then she felt ashamed of herself. She hadn't thought of what was best for Lizzie, only what was best for Andrew, Aunt Maud and herself.

She got to her feet, collected up the dishes and put them in the sink. She'd better get back to Selina.

As she entered the room Lloyd turned towards her. 'She's cooler, Ellan. If she wakes, give her a spoonful of this. She should sleep all night then.'

'What is it?'

'Just a syrup with a tiny dose of morphine in it.'

She bent over the bed and saw that Selina did in fact look less flushed and more peaceful. She smoothed a few strands of the girl's damp hair away from her forehead. In the morning maybe she'd give her a good wash down and brush out her hair.

'You must promise to get some sleep?'

'I will,' she said as she sat down in the chair beside the bed and Lloyd quietly let himself out, again feeling confused about the emotions that Ellan stirred in him.

Ellan had given Selina the syrup, made her comfortable and was about to prepare herself for bed when the door opened. Lucy stood on the threshold.

'What's the matter? You should be asleep – you won't be able to get up in the morning.'

'When are you coming to bed, Ma?'

'Now, this very minute. Did something wake you up?'

Lucy nodded. 'A bad dream.'

Ellan pulled the child to her. 'Why was it bad?'

'I was watching the boats, Ma, like we do sometimes.

You and Tilly were with me and Mrs Elliot and there were lots of people and then it went dark and I couldn't see you any more. I was calling you, Ma, but you didn't hear me. But she was there. I saw her and she was laughing at me.' The child pointed to the bed.

'Selina?'

'Yes.'

'Oh, it was just a dream, Lucy, a bad dream. Come along, back to bed.' She took hold of the little girl's hand and led her out on to the landing, but before she could tuck her into bed she heard rapping on the front door. 'I'd better go down and see who it is. Doctor Elliot will have gone to bed and we don't want to disturb him. Snuggle down and go to sleep, there's a good girl.'

A frown creased her forehead as she went down the stairs. Who on earth could be calling so late? It was Tilly.

'Tilly! Come in. What's the matter?'

'Has he gone to bed, Ellan?' Tilly clutched her hand tightly.

'I think so.'

'It's our Mary. She's took a turn for the worse an' I don't know what to do. The old biddy next door is with her but she's driving me mad with all her old wives' tales. Do you think he'll come? I can pay him.'

'What about your own doctor?'

'He's out on a call. He's rushed off his feet, they all are. I don't feel so good myself either.'

'Wait here. I'll go and see.'

Her steps were leaden as she climbed the stairs. She hoped Mary wasn't too bad and she prayed that Tilly wasn't coming down with it. Only a week or so ago they'd been eagerly discussing when they should open for business again. She tapped lightly on the bedroom door and waited. There was silence so she tapped more loudly. After a few seconds the door was opened. 'I'm sorry to disturb you but Tilly's here.'

Lloyd was pulling on a shirt as he followed her on to the landing while she explained the situation.

'Will you get my coat and my bag, Ellan, while I finish dressing?'

'Yes.'

'Will you be able to cope? I don't like leaving you with two sick women on your hands.'

'Of course I will. Just leave everything to me. Let's hope Tilly is just over anxious. She did say she doesn't feel too well herself.'

'He's coming, he won't be a minute,' she whispered to Tilly as she took his coat from the cloakroom and went into his study for his bag. When she returned it was to find him talking earnestly to Tilly.

'I hope I won't be long, Ellan, there's no need for you to wait up. I have my keys.'

'Oh, I'm so sorry for disturbing you but I was at me wit's end, like.'

'Don't apologize, Tilly. Stay here with Ellan while I get the car.'

Ellan was asleep on the landing when he came back, her head on her folded arms, and she blinked and straightened painfully when Lloyd woke her.

'Ellan, why didn't you go to bed?'

'I couldn't. I thought if I sat here I could hear both the door and Selina and Margaret should they call out.' His appearance shocked her. His skin was grey and his eyes were heavy and hooded with lack of sleep, but there was something else. 'Mary?'

He sat down beside her on the stair. 'She died half an hour ago, Ellan. There was nothing I could do. If Tilly had come for me sooner I could have got her into hospital. It might have saved her. For God's sake don't tell Tilly that though. She's broken-hearted.'

Tears filled Ellan's eyes. 'Oh, Lloyd, she was so young. When is the world ever going to be a nice place again? If it's not war it's sickness.'

Gently he placed his arm around her shoulders. She looked so young, so vulnerable, so down-hearted. He thought he'd seen enough of death, death that struck so suddenly at people so young. He thought all that was over, that it had been left behind on the battlefields of Europe. But he had had to watch with helpless frustration as yet another young life slipped away. He was weary of it all. He drew her closer and without thinking, gently kissed her cheek.

She didn't draw away. There was comfort in his arms, solace in that gentle, paternal kiss. Perhaps that's what she had so often missed in her life, she thought, a father's love and compassion. At that moment she envied Selina Elliot and understood her closeness to her father. She did not have a pa to go to with her troubles and her joys. It was an experience that Lucy would never have either. She drew away and placed her hand on his cheek. 'Thank you . . . for just being here.'

He smiled a little ruefully. 'I'll always be here for you, Ellan, don't forget that.'

She blushed at her temerity. 'I won't.' Suddenly she

felt more optimistic and she got to her feet and stretched. 'It's nearly morning. I'll get you some breakfast.'

He watched her walk down the remaining stairs and his mouth felt dry. She viewed him as a surrogate father. He should have felt pleased and honoured but he didn't. He felt oddly hurt and disappointed, as though he'd been kicked by someone he loved and whom he had always trusted would never hurt him.

The two women recovered. Selina rapidly but Margaret more slowly until by the middle of June Lloyd declared that he thought a day out would do them all good. Selina was delighted but Ellan was a little more cautious, concerned for Margaret's health. A day trip by boat to Llandudno had been suggested.

'Won't it be too tiring?' she queried.

'I don't think so. We'll go down to the pierhead by car then find a seat in the saloon or up on deck, if Margaret would like that, and I can push her along the promenade in her chair while you young ones can go off to explore or whatever.'

Ellan thought he looked sad and that his voice was a little harsher when he said 'young ones'. 'I can push and *you* can go off and explore,' she'd said firmly.

It was a great success. They went up on the top deck for a while as it was a glorious day. Margaret laughed as Lloyd and one of the deck hands carried the wheelchair bodily up the stairs. Ellan insisted on sitting with her in the beautiful gardens on the promenade while Lloyd took Selina and Lucy on the beach and then into an ice cream parlour. Margaret was tired when they returned home but there was more colour in her cheeks and more sparkle in her eyes than she'd had for months. They were all tired at the end of the day, she said, so they'd better not try to deny it. Lucy fell asleep on the sail home and even Selina fought to keep her eyes open.

'I wasn't, Mama,' Selina had stated hotly.

'You were.'

'No quarrels now,' Ellan laughed.

'Then we'll repeat the exercise again in the near future. That's my diagnosis for better health.' Lloyd joined in the light-hearted bantering.

He was rewarded by a unanimous chorus of assent.

The next proposed outing was to be in July and Ellan doubted she would have the time to accompany them. She and Tilly had been working hard to get the Candy Cabin at the top of Bold Street ready for opening. They decided that it was the better of the two locations and it was in a decent state of repair. Vi returned which allowed Ellan more time. They scrubbed the whole place out and spent hours making the muslin table and shelf cloths and the rose-pink trimmings. The boxes were ordered as well as all the ingredients, so when Selina announced that the following weekend they were having another excursion, Ellan looked apprehensive.

'It's just that there is so much to do. I'd love to come, you know I would. Last time was wonderful.'

'Can't Tilly and Vi manage?' Selina asked.

'Where are you going?' Ellan asked, trying to ignore the pleading look Lucy directed at her and Margaret's consternation. Lloyd was flicking through his current copy of *The Lancet*.

'The Isle of Man,' Selina announced.

Ellan dropped the piece of pink ribbon she was sewing and stared at Selina. 'No.' The word was out before she could stop it and she was aware of the malicious gleam in the girl's eyes.

'Why not?' Selina persisted.

'I . . . I can't. I'm too busy.' She felt all their eyes were on her and her cheeks were flaming. She couldn't go back, even for a day trip. Not even for a few hours. Some one would recognize her and then Aunt Maud would know and Andrew would know. What if someone actually came up and spoke to her, what would she say? What would Lucy say?

It was Lucy who drew her attention to the fact that there was silence in the room. 'Ma, you've gone all quiet and pale. Why can't we go? It's where you come from, you told me. You said you are Manx and that I am, too, so why can't we go there?'

She took the child's hands and drew her towards her, knowing that both Margaret and Lloyd were waiting to hear her explanation, waiting to take their cue from her. 'You can go, Lucy. It's right that you should enjoy yourself, but I . . . I'm just too busy right now with the shop.'

'Of course you must come, Lucy. It's just that your mama is very busy just now. I'm sure she'll take you herself one day, won't you, Ellan?' Margaret looked at her with sympathy and understanding.

'Of course I will. I said I would, didn't I?'

'But you said it would be when I'm old. Married even.' Lucy was petulant.

Ellan bit her lip. She just couldn't go. Not yet.

'Didn't you like living there?' Selina persisted.

'Yes. Yes, of course I did. But . . . but it was years ago.' Ellan struggled to explain.

'What's the matter with it then?' Selina sensed a mystery and was loath to give up.

'Nothing. I hear it is a beautiful place. People go there in droves for their summer holidays.' Lloyd came to her rescue.

'Oh, wouldn't that be wonderful, Papa! Could we go for a week instead of just a day? I'm sure Mama would love it and it would be so good for her.'

Ellan felt sick. A week! If Lucy went for a week someone might notice the close resemblance she bore to herself and then there was her surname, Vannin. The first person the child gave her name to would know she was Manx and Lucy would be happily proclaiming to everyone that she was. She was bound to announce her mother's name too. Yet how was she going to explain all this to the child who was looking at her with intense hopefulness?

'I'm sorry to disappoint you, dear, but I couldn't possibly leave my practice for a week.'

'And a week would be far too tiring for me, Selina. Oh, I know you were only thinking of me, dear, but it's out of the question,' Margaret enjoined before Selina could ask why they couldn't go without her papa.

Ellan threw them both a grateful glance and sighed with relief. She patted Lucy's cheek. 'You'll have a wonderful day. It's a lovely sail and Ramsey is such a quaint place. They have some nice little shops and the fishing fleet might be in and you can buy fresh lobster and crab for your tea. You might even go and see the Laxey Wheel,' she enthused and was rewarded by the look of interest in her daughter's eyes.

Selina stared at her. She sensed there was something

wrong. There was a tense atmosphere and the glances she'd intercepted between her parents and Ellan made her sure there was some sort of conspiracy going on. Why didn't Ellan want to go back to the island that had been her home? When she mentioned a week's holiday Ellan had paled. Was there some terrible secret in her past that she wanted to hide, especially from Lucy? She'd make sure she kept her eyes and ears open in future.

'I'm sorry you can't come, Ellan,' Selina said with a note of triumph in her voice.

Ellan looked at her hard, knowing that the animosity Selina felt for both herself and Lucy was never very far beneath the surface.

Chapter Twenty-One

———◆———

THEY HAD A WONDERFUL day. On the outward voyage Selina attracted the attention of a young man who helped Lloyd with Margaret's wheelchair. He introduced himself as Charles Meadows, or Charlie as most people called him, and stayed with them for the entire day. He'd been in the Army, he told Lloyd, and had miraculously come through unscathed. He was very fortunate that he had managed to get his old job back, he assured them. He was a clerk with Shaw, Saville & Albion Shipping Line.

Before the war she would never have entertained the attentions of a mere clerk, Selina told herself, no matter how handsome and attentive he might be. It was different now, of course, because a young man who was not crippled in some way was difficult to find. He made her laugh and was very deferential to her. She was delighted when her father said Charlie must join them for lunch and that he'd brook no argument. She felt very flattered and a little embarrassed when he asked could he call on them and she was certain that when he took her hand to say goodbye, he gave it a squeeze. Of course she would have liked to have taken a walk with him, alone, but that wouldn't have been at all the thing to do. Not when she'd only just met him. She was a doctor's daughter after all. She lived in Rodney Street while he lived with his parents in Everton.

He was coming to tea this very afternoon and perhaps he would ask to take her out one evening, a concert at the Philharmonic Hall or maybe a band concert on Sunday afternoon in a park. It would most likely be the band concert, she thought. Shipping clerks didn't earn a fortune.

She jumped nervously as the doorbell rang and peered into the mirror, scrutinizing her reflection. She wore her favourite cornflower-blue dress with inserts of white lace that made it fresh and feminine and darkened the colour of her eyes.

'You've got your best dress on, are you going out?' Lucy asked, poking her head around the bedroom door, having been sent up to fetch Selina.

Selina scowled. 'No, and don't ask impertinent questions like that. You should be seen and not heard. Go away and don't you speak to me again. If you speak to Charlie . . . Mr Meadows, I'll lock you up in the broom cupboard and leave you there all night.' The last thing she wanted was for that horrible child to say she had her best dress on. Nor did she want her following her around like a lap-dog. With a quick pinch of the child's arm that made Lucy cry out, she shoved her back on to the landing and closed the bedroom door.

When she entered the drawing room she was torn between the happiness of seeing the smile on Charlie's face and the chagrin that Ellan was sitting beside the sofa on which her mother reclined. She entered into the small talk while Vi served tea, occasionally glancing at him from beneath lowered lashes in what she hoped was a very appealing manner. He was handsome in a blond way and had very blue eyes that twinkled, especially when she spoke to him. She would just have to try and manoeuvre a way to be alone with him even for a few minutes. Then perhaps he would kiss her, take her gently in his arms and kiss her. She felt her cheeks flush at the thought. Oh, she was sure it would be heaven to be kissed by him and she knew her papa liked him by the way he was smiling. It was very important that Papa liked him.

'Selina, Charlie was asking do you like military music?' her mother prompted gently and she realized she had been day-dreaming.

'Oh, yes. I love all kinds of music,' she smiled sweetly at him.

'Selina plays the piano very well. She's quite talented,' Ellan added, trying to bolster Selina's confidence and show off her accomplishment.

A shadow crossed Selina's face. She didn't need Ellan Vannin to tell him that. She knew her mama or papa would have said it, given the chance, and why was *she* sitting there at all? She wasn't part of the family.

'Then perhaps you would like to go to a concert one evening, er . . . all of us?' Charlie looked a little embarrassed.

'We don't get out much, do we, dear?' Lloyd said to his wife. Margaret nodded her agreement.

'I'm sorry. I didn't think . . . I didn't mean . . .' Charlie became confused. He hadn't thought about Mrs Elliot being an invalid.

'But if Selina would like to go we wouldn't stand in her way. I'm sure she would be safe with you,' Lloyd cut in to save further embarrassment.

'Would you like to go?'

'Yes. Yes, I'd love to.' She hoped she hadn't sounded too eager but if she had he didn't seem to have noticed.

'There is an "Evening of Strauss" at the Philharmonic Hall next Saturday, that is if you think you'd like it?'

Selina felt her heart begin to race. 'Oh, I do. I mean I love his music.'

Ellan wondered if she should mention that Selina played quite a lot of Strauss waltzes but then that was Margaret's prerogative or Lloyd's and she didn't want to usurp it. She was amused by the situation and a little sad, thinking of the first time Jamie had asked her out. She also felt sorry for Charlie. He was obviously very nervous and he was a nice young man, probably not much younger than herself. She suddenly realized that he was speaking to her.

'You didn't come on the outing, Mrs Vannin?'

'No. Unfortunately I have been very busy. I'm reopening my business in a week's time.'

'What kind of business is it?' he asked politely.

'Sweets. Toffee mainly. I had two shops before the war. The Candy Cabins.'

'Oh, I remember them. I used to buy my mother a box now and then as a treat. She loved them, especially that carn toffee and those lovely little boxes tied up with pink ribbon. Will you be having all that again?'

'Yes. It's business as usual. Pink ribbons, too. I'll give you a box especially for your mother.'

He blushed. 'Thanks. I didn't mean to sound . . .'

Ellan laughed. 'Of course you didn't, Charlie.'

Selina fumed. How dare she laugh and joke with him like that and all about her tacky sweets and ribbons. How dare she call him Charlie as though she'd known him for years and years. 'I was sorry Ellan couldn't come with us on the trip. She's Manx, you know, and so is Lucy.' Selina made sure he knew that Ellan was a matron with a child.

'How interesting. I met a man once, in the war, who was Manx. He looked like everyone else.'

Ellan laughed again. 'We do, I believe. No horns or cloven hooves. But very superstitious.'

Everyone laughed at this and Selina, hiding her chagrin as best she could, offered the plate of biscuits around the assembled group.

There was the outing to the concert, then an afternoon in Southport and another to Thurstaton Common, and by the beginning of August Charlie Meadows was calling on Selina three evenings a week. Selina became a changed person. She sang and laughed. She was pleasant to Ellan and even to Lucy, and both Vi and Cook said they hoped she would stay in love. Life was a good deal more pleasant since Charlie Meadows had appeared.

'Well, I just hope it keeps fine for her,' Tilly commented tersely as they were packing the last of the decorations to finish the shop.

They had worked their fingers to the bone to be ready for the opening, making great slabs of toffee and fudge, but Ellan's last-minute doubts were soon dispersed by the queue of people waiting for them to open up and by mid-afternoon they had completely sold out and had a waiting list of orders to start the following day. The word soon got around and Tilly commented that perhaps they had been too hasty in not reopening the other shop as well.

They had just finished a busy Saturday and were discussing whether or not to open on the Bank Holiday Monday, when Charlie walked in.

'Charlie! I've nothing left. We've sold out. I hope you haven't promised your mother a box?' Ellan cried in mock dismay.

'No. She's still eating her way through the one you gave me. You should let me pay for it, Ellan. It was bigger than the usual ones.'

'Don't be silly,' Ellan chided, wiping down the last of the trays. 'We were just wondering whether we should open on Monday for the Bank Holiday. What do you think?'

'Or would it be better to take a couple of trays and boxes down to the landing stage and sell them to people going over the water for the day?'

'Tilly, we can't do that. We don't have a street trader's licence.'

Charlie looked serious. 'I don't think that would matter, the way things are going.'

'What's that supposed to mean?' Tilly demanded.

'There's talk that the police are going out on strike.'

'They can't do that. There'd be holy murder,' Tilly cried.

'Well, it looks as if they are going to. Something to do with a union or federation or something.'

'Is that the truth?' Ellan demanded, a nagging anxiety beginning to take hold of her.

'I wouldn't swear to it on the Bible but the rumour's a strong one.'

'But what will happen?'

'What'll happen is all the villains and no marks in this city will go on the rampage with no-one to stop them. In other words, riots. Riots worse than the *Lusitania* riots.'

'Surely the City Fathers won't allow that to happen, will they?'

Charlie shrugged. 'They might call in the Army. If it does happen.'

Tilly pursed her lips in annoyance. 'Then they'll have to do something.'

'I'm sorry I opened my mouth now,' Charlie said glumly.

'So you should be,' Tilly snapped. Her feet were aching, her back was aching and so was her head and the last thing she needed was someone walking in and telling her the police were going on strike. 'It's not your idea of a joke, is it?' she asked tartly.

'Would I joke about something like that?'

'You might.' Tilly began to stack the trays.

'Then you don't know me very well.'

'I'm not the one who has to, thank you.'

'Talking of Selina, I think we'd better get home. Isn't she expecting you for supper?' Ellan was anxious to speak to Lloyd about her fears. He would know what to do.

They said good night to Tilly in the shadow of St Luke's Church and walked in silence up Hardman Street towards Rodney Street. The streets appeared normal with trams running and people going about their business.

Selina opened the door to them, her smile of welcome dimming as she saw Ellan with Charlie, but Ellan quickly excused herself and went through to the kitchen, to find Lucy, Vi and Cook poring over the evening paper.

'I've never heard of anything like it. It's disgraceful, that's what it is. Disgraceful!' Cook said vehemently.

'What is?' Ellan asked.

They all turned towards her.

'You must have heard, Ellan. The police are going on strike. In fact, they've gone on strike.' Cook passed her the paper and she glanced at the front page. Then she sat down. It must be true if it was in the newspapers.

'Ma, why is everyone so worried? What's going to happen?'

'Now see what you've done. You've put the fear of God in the child,' Vi hissed at Cook.

'Nothing is going to happen, Lucy. They will sort it all out. Now be a good girl and fetch my slippers, my poor feet are aching. What a day.'

When Lucy had left the room Ellan faced them both. 'Tilly said there would be murder, as she put it. What do you think?'

'She's right. That mob down by the docks will run riot. It will be worse than St Patrick's Day and Orangeman's Day rolled into one and God help anyone who gets in their way. I'm staying here tonight, half the City Councillors live up here and you can bet your life they've made sure their property is protected.'

Ellan jumped up. 'My God! What about the shop? I've put so much time, energy and money into it.'

'It might blow over, Ellan. There's nothing to be gained by running down there. Where are you going now?'

Ellan had reached the door. 'To see Doctor Elliot.'

Cook turned on Vi. 'You and your big mouth!'

They all looked startled when Ellan rushed into the drawing room.

'Ellan, what's the matter?' Lloyd asked, getting to his feet.

'Vi thinks there are going to be riots. What about my shop? I'll have to go back.'

'Ellan, you can't!' Margaret cried.

'Margaret is right. You can't go back there alone,' Lloyd agreed.

Selina was furious with Ellan for taking everyone's attention from herself. 'Who said there will be riots? What for?' Everyone ignored her.

'I've *got* to go! I've worked so hard. I've put everything into it!'

Lloyd crossed and took her by the shoulders and eased her down on to the sofa. 'Wait, Ellan. I'll make a few phone calls to see if I can find out exactly what is going on.'

'But then . . .'

'Let's just wait and see.'

She sat twisting her hands together helplessly until he came back into the room and when she saw his expression she jumped up.

'Lloyd!' Margaret cried, her fingers clutching the lace edge of her collar.

'It's not good, I'm afraid. It looks as though Vi was right. What police there are on duty are up at Hatton Garden. About a hundred or so. And there is a mob on the move, heading towards the docks, I believe.'

Selina jumped up as Charlie crossed towards her father. 'Oh, you can't go out there, Charlie. You just can't.'

'No-one is going out, not yet anyway,' Lloyd said firmly. 'Selina, play us something to take our minds off things.'

After Selina's musical recital in which she played every piece in her repertoire, Ellan was in such a state of agitation that she couldn't sit still. They'd tried to play crib but no one could concentrate and when a few minutes after ten, Tilly came hammering on the door, Ellan was determined that she wasn't going to sit and let events overtake her.

Tilly had been running. Her hair was untidy, her cheeks red and it was a few minutes before she regained her breath.

'Ran straight here . . . murder going on in town . . . a few police, mobs everywhere . . . fighting drunk . . . bonded warehouses, distilleries . . . looting . . .'

Before anyone could stop her, Ellan had run into the hall.

'Lloyd, stop her! Stop her, she'll be hurt!' Margaret cried.

Tilly followed Selina as the two men dashed out of the room.

Ellan already had her coat on and in her hand she had two of Lloyd's ornamental walking canes. 'I just can't sit here and do nothing. I *have* to go. I've got these. I'll be all right.'

Lloyd snatched up his coat and hat from the hallstand and so did Charlie.

'Wait a minute, Charlie.' Lloyd rushed into his study then returned with two old-fashioned but still sharp cavalry sabres that adorned one wall. Selina uttered a shriek as her father gave one to Charlie.

'Just a precaution, Selina. We probably won't have to use them. When we've gone, lock all the doors and windows and make sure the wooden shutters are fastened, too. Don't answer the door to anyone until you hear me or Charlie or Ellan call to you.'

Wide-eyed, her hand to her throat, Selina nodded as she watched Vi slam the front door shut after them and drew the bolts.

'Hurry, Miss Selina. You heard what your da said. Lock all the windows and fasten the shutters. I'll do the ones at the back of the house,' Vi shouted, disappearing into the dining room.

The trams had stopped running and the street lights threw pools of brightness across the pavements and deepened the shadows. The streets were strangely silent. There was a tenseness in the air and they were not the only ones who were rushing to protect their property. Silent figures, their faces wearing expressions of grim determination, passed them without greeting.

Ellan unlocked the door of the shop and they went inside and lit the gas jets.

'Oh, I wish I had some window shutters.'

'There are some pieces of hardboard in the yard, the builders left them,' Tilly reminded her.

'I'll get them and then Charlie and I will do the best we can to board up the windows. You drag all the movable fittings and stack them behind the door and the windows,' Lloyd instructed as Ellan unlocked the back door.

They stripped the counter and tables of their muslin frills and bows. Took down the glass shelves and laid them on the floor behind the counter while Lloyd and Charlie wedged the pieces of thin timber up against the windows.

'That's the best we can do. There's still quite a lot of glass unprotected,' Charlie pointed out.

'It might be better to smash it ourselves, save them the trouble, and us from flying glass,' Tilly said grimly.

'No need for that. They probably won't get this far anyway.' Lloyd tried to bolster their confidence.

'Doctor Elliot, I don't want to sound pushy or anything, but maybe you should go home. Just in case they need you,' Charlie said. 'I'll stay here all night if I have to,' he finished.

Lloyd looked torn between the desire to go home and defend that, if necessary, and leaving Ellan with just Tilly and Charlie.

'Charlie's right. They'll all be having hysterics without a man there. You know how nervous Selina is and Mrs Elliot . . . well, she'll need you there,' Ellan pressed.

He knew she was right. Selina was no good in situations like this and Margaret was virtually helpless.

Ellan locked the door after him and turned down the gas and they settled down to wait. Tilly was vociferous about what should be done with a police force who abandoned helpless citizens to a mob and Charlie agreed with her.

'It's breaking an oath. They take an oath when they join, same as we all did when we joined the Army. I'm not ashamed to say there was many a time when I felt like breaking that oath and running like hell, but I didn't and neither should they.'

'Will they bring the Army in?' Ellan asked.

'They may have to, it depends, but then it could turn very nasty indeed.' He launched into a complicated explanation about anarchy and bolshevism and how it had been a situation similar to this that had sparked off the revolution in Russia, but neither of them was really listening.

Ellan sat clenching her hands. This was her future. Hers and Lucy's. She'd hoped to expand maybe to other cities. She'd noticed quite a few nice little confectionery shops on a visit to Llandudno and they appeared to be doing very well. The more she'd thought about it, the less of a mad idea it had become. She could find suitable premises and a suitable woman to put in charge. She didn't want to have to rely on Lloyd and Margaret for ever. Lucy was growing up and Ellan wanted her to have all the things she'd never had. No, no-one was going to wreck her dreams. Certainly not a drunken mob of thieves and cut-throats.

Just before midnight they heard the noise, faintly at first but growing louder. Tilly bit her lip and grimaced. 'They must have got to the bottom of London Road.'

'They could have come down Copperas Hill or Brownlow Hill,' Charlie said.

Ellan remembered the little hotel in Brownlow Hill she'd once stayed in.

'Then they might not get this far. They'll have the whole of Lewis's to keep them occupied,' Tilly said scathingly.

The shouting got louder, accompanied by the crash and tinkle of breaking glass. Charlie stood up and went over to the window, sabre still in his hand. Tilly stood guard over the back door armed with a heavy piece of wood and Ellan stood behind the front door armed with another piece of roughly hewn timber that she'd found in the yard. Her heart was beating in an odd, jerky motion and her hands shook a little. They had no way of knowing how many rioters they faced but judging by the noise there must be at least a hundred. Her throat felt dry and she jumped as another shop window was smashed. The crash was followed by a cheer. It sounded as though it was right next door.

'Oh, God! It looks as though we're next,' she cried, but her words were lost in the din.

The hardboard stopped the glass from flying inward and showering them with deadly shards but her feet crunched on it as she ran to Charlie's side. Strangely she wasn't afraid now, only angry. A white-hot fury consumed her and strengthened by it she laid about her with the stave, screaming at them to keep away. The leading figures had already fallen back before the wide arc of the sabre in Charlie's hand. A few had cuts that were streaming blood. Charlie's face in the dim light looked as though it had been carved from granite. He wasn't afraid either. Four years on the Western Front had tempered him. This was a minor skirmish in comparison and like Ellan, he was filled with anger and disgust.

For fifteen horrendous minutes they stood out against the crowd that had thinned a little due to Charlie's merciless use of the sabre, but Ellan was shocked to see so many women amongst the rioters. Many of them drunk. Her shoulders ached and her hands were cut and splintered, for quite a few times the stave was almost ripped from her grasp. There had been no time to think of Tilly or Charlie or even her own safety. All was chaos. Then, from the back of the crowd came a howl followed by a sudden surge forward which almost brought the front line into the shop and on to the wicked edge of the sabre, then they were scattering, dispersed by half a dozen policemen, truncheons and boots lashing out in all directions. They were big, burly men all over six feet tall.

Their uniforms were torn and dirty, their faces grey and blood-streaked, but to Ellan they were like knights in shining armour. She sagged against Charlie as the crowd passed on, leaving a few of their number on the ground, the victims of police truncheons and Charlie's sabre.

Tilly joined them, a grey-faced, shaking Tilly. 'Oh, thank God for that! I thought the back door was going to give way. I heard them in the yard. Ellan, you look done in.'

'So do you.' But she looked around the shop with triumph. Apart from the broken glass from the window that covered the floor, there was very little damage. 'I don't know what we would have done without you, Charlie Meadows, and I mean that.'

He brushed his hair out of his eyes and grinned. 'I think I've dislocated my shoulder but it was worth it and I wouldn't like to cross you, Ellan, you wield a fearsome swipe.'

Ellan smiled weakly. 'Do you think they'll come back?'

'Not tonight they won't. I'll help you clear up and I'll board up the window. Take as much stuff as you can carry and I'll get you both back home. Then I'm going up to Hatton Garden. Those poor sods look as though they could do with some help.'

'You can't do that,' Ellan cried.

'Why not?'

She couldn't think of a convincing answer. 'You might get hurt,' she said, lamely.

'I came through the war without getting hurt,' he answered grimly. 'And I'm not letting a mob of drunks terrorize innocent people, but let's get you back first.'

The journey back to Rodney Street was quiet enough. The majority of rioters had been driven back up London Road where running battles continued all night. Rodney Street had not been disturbed but relief flooded Lloyd's face as he opened the door in reply to Charlie's shouted greeting. Behind him in the hall stood Vi and a white-faced Selina who uttered a shriek as she caught sight of Charlie.

'Everyone is safe and sound. They won't come back tonight so I brought them home.'

'We've been worried sick. Come inside, all of you,' Lloyd urged.

'Charlie's going back to give the few police still on duty a hand.'

Selina cried out again but everyone ignored her.

Charlie held out the sabre to Lloyd. 'You'd better take it. They probably won't let me use it, it's an offensive weapon. All those poor sods had were truncheons, begging your pardon, ladies.'

Lloyd took it uncertainly and Selina recoiled from the blood-stained blade. 'No-one will blame you for defending yourself.'

'I don't suppose they will but they'll only take it off me and I wouldn't want to spoil the set.' Charlie grinned and Lloyd smiled back.

'Take care then.'

Charlie turned to Ellan, open admiration in his eyes. 'By God, she can dish out a hefty clout, as a few of them found out. I wouldn't like to get on the wrong side of her. She's got a lot of guts.'

'We couldn't have managed without you, Charlie, and I'll never be able to thank you enough.'

'What everyone needs is a good, strong cup of tea,' Vi stated. 'Ellan, you'd better go and see the missus and Lucy, they're both worried sick. I'll bring in the tea.'

Tilly followed Vi while Lloyd showed Charlie out and Ellan moved tiredly towards the door of the parlour, leaving Selina alone in the hall. Despite the nervousness that had claimed her all night, she felt anger and jealousy well up in her. She'd seen the open admiration in Charlie's face when he'd spoken to Ellan. He hadn't said a single word to her. He'd never asked how she was. As usual, Ellan had managed to hold everyone's attention and had earned their admiration. Even that common Tilly had been praised for her part when they both should have stayed at home and not got themselves involved with coarse, drunken rioters. Oh, one day she was going to find a way of paying Ellan back for all the slights, she thought as she went up the stairs. She just couldn't bear to see her mama and papa fussing over Ellan Vannin.

After two more nights of rioting and looting that left parts of the city looking like a battlefield and the few policemen who had defended it battered and exhausted, the Army was called in. Tanks stood on St George's plateau, their gun barrels pointing towards London Road and Commutation Row. Out in the river a battleship and two cruisers stood at the ready but by Tuesday it was all over. Peace and order were restored. Every police officer who had gone on strike was dismissed and an entirely new force of men was sworn in. Charlie Meadows amongst them.

Chapter Twenty-Two

O N 30 NOVEMBER 1919, THOMAS COSTAIN died. The news was announced in a short note from Glentrammon written by Mary Costain and distributed to every house in the vicinity. Maud Quirk looked at the black-edged card that Andrew placed on the table.

'After a long and painful illness,' Maud read aloud then stopped and shook her head sadly. 'Drank himself to death, she means, and everyone knows it. But I suppose she has to keep up appearances, God help her!' She looked across the table at her son. 'I never thought I'd see the day when I would say I felt sorry for her, but I do. She's had a hard life with very little love or happiness in it for all her money.'

Andrew poked the fire hard with the heavy poker gripped in his right hand. There wasn't much he couldn't do with his one arm and he owed that fact to Mary Costain. His ma was right, she'd had a hard life despite all that money and creature comforts. 'So, we'll be going to the funeral, I take it?'

'We will. Not out of respect for him, for what good

did he ever do us, but to show her that we're thinking of her in her grief. Even though it will be a high church affair,' Maud added, sniffing her disapproval.

'I wonder what she'll do now?'

Maud began to put her shopping away. 'What do you mean, do?'

'Will she stay on up there in that huge house or will she sell it?'

'It's her home. Why should she sell it?'

'It must cost a fortune to run, to start with.'

'Well, that's one thing they were never short of, money,' Maud commented.

'I wonder what will happen to his business affairs? Will she take over, what with there being no male heir?'

Maud looked scornful. 'Her take over? Don't be a fool.'

'I'm not and neither is she. I bet she could handle his affairs with no effort at all. She could probably buy and sell us all.'

'She's a lady. What would she know about things like that?' Maud dismissed the subject. 'I'd better write and tell Ellan. Miss Mary was always good to her.'

Andrew got up and fidgeted with the fire. It always made him restless when his mother spoke of Ellan. 'I'm going out,' he announced suddenly, taking his coat from the peg on the wall. Maud shrugged and cast her eyes to the ceiling.

It was a raw day and he bent his head against the cold wind that cut through him as he walked along the cliff path. There was no going to Stornaway now. A man needed two good hands to keep afloat up there. He'd been bitter and argumentative when he'd first tried to handle his own boat. His efforts were punitive and futile and he'd cursed and given up and often ended the day in the tavern. But when he looked at the faces of the men who were crippled, something made him keep on trying until at last the day came when he was able to sail across the harbour without a hitch and that day, in his heart, he blessed Mary Costain.

He regained his self-respect and a certain amount of independence and he now worked for those who could no longer do so. He stopped and peered out at the darkening sky and the cold grey sea. There was hardly a day when he didn't think of John and Mat, and Gerry Connell and Charlie Oats. But the painful edge of memory had blurred now. Jutland was in the past. He'd never really thanked Mary, not openly with words. He wondered if he should call now. Perhaps it might help her to know that she had managed to stop him drinking himself into the grave, unlike her father. He turned his steps backward towards the fields beyond which lay Glentrammon.

Daisy opened the door to him, her eyes red and puffy. 'She's not seeing anyone.'

'Would you ask her again, Daisy, please? Tell her it's me.'

Daisy sniffed and nodded, indicating that he should come in while she went to ask her mistress.

He stood in the hall twisting his cap in his hand and glancing at the black drapes on all the pictures and mirrors. He'd heard that they had been there since the news came that both the Costain boys were dead. The old man refused to have them removed and he for one couldn't blame him. But it did give the house a desolate air.

Daisy appeared, beckoned to him to follow her and showed him into the small parlour where Ellan had stood years ago for the job that his mother would not let her accept. Ellan had once described the room but it bore little resemblance to that description now. The furniture was shabby, the carpet worn. The curtains and sofa covers looked dusty and faded and everything was draped in funeral black. As was Mary herself. She looked pale, tired and thin as she sat on the upright chair by the bureau.

'I was sorry to hear of your loss, miss,' he began.

Mary rose and indicated that he should sit. He did so, awkwardly, while she seated herself opposite him in a high-backed, winged armchair. She looked so old and careworn, he thought, and yet she couldn't be forty. 'I wanted to come, miss.'

'That was good of you, Andrew.'

He felt ill at ease, wondering how he could put into words his gratitude in such a way that would give her some comfort. 'I wanted to do something to . . . help. Do you remember the night you followed me home, when I was so drunk I could hardly walk?' She nodded and picked at the black-edged handkerchief she held. 'It was what you said that night to my ma that made me realize that I was lucky, that I did still have a life, though I didn't think so then.'

Mary managed a smile. She remembered the night well, it had been the first night her father had fallen down the stairs, blind drunk himself. Oh, yes, she remembered – and she remembered all the nights that followed. 'At least I had one success.'

'That's just what I meant, miss. Just what I wanted you to know.'

'Thank you, Andrew.' She paused and looked down at her hands. 'Oh, I know it is a dreadful thing to say, but at least now my poor father is out of his misery. And his life was a misery. It really ended in 1915. He lived for David and William. I was a poor substitute.'

'Begging your pardon, miss, but don't talk like that. Don't put yourself down.'

'I'm not. It is a fact. I did my duties well. I ran this house smoothly for him, as my mother had done before me, but in the end it just wasn't enough. He needed his sons to talk to, to confide in, to plan the future with. Not me.'

He knew she was right yet he was sure that given time, Thomas Costain could have built a new and better relationship with his capable, intelligent daughter. But that was the one thing he hadn't had on his side, time. 'I'm sorry, Miss Mary. I do know what it's like. My pa died in the Foxdale disaster, my brothers at Jutland. I know how it hurts and so does my ma.' He sought to comfort her.

'Yes. Yes, I'd not forgotten. In fact I remember the Foxdale disaster quite clearly. I remember the day your poor mother came up here to berate my father.'

'She shouldn't have done that, miss. Nor said the things she did.'

'Why not? I would have done in her place. We've not always seen eye to eye but I admire your mother immensely. She is such a strong woman.'

'She had to be,' he muttered, not wishing to continue with this line of conversation. 'What will you do now?' he asked tentatively, wondering if he had over-stepped the bounds of both propriety and friendship.

Mary shrugged. 'I haven't really thought.' She was too weary, too drained to think of the future. She'd sort everything out after the funeral, she told herself.

Andrew decided not to press the subject. 'Ma was writing to Ellan when I left.'

She looked away from him. Ellan, that was another secret she'd had to keep and she was so tired of all the pretence. Why couldn't she have just told everyone that her father had drunk himself to death and be done with it? Everyone knew anyway and they knew the reason. Not many had censured him. But Doctor Taylor and Mr Morley and Mr Seaton had told her she must keep up appearances at all costs. It hadn't helped and now she wondered if she was right to let Andrew Quirk and Ellan go on living with just a few miles of water between them, instead of the Atlantic Ocean. 'Do you ever write to her?'

'No.'

'Why not? You love her, don't you?'

He was so taken aback he couldn't answer. How did she know?

'You do. I know you do, don't be afraid to say it.' At that moment she thought how wonderful it would be to lay her head against a man's shoulder and let him take care of all the responsibilities and worries that plagued her. But for her it was just wishful thinking.

'Yes, I do.' His reply was barely audible. 'But what good is it? She will have her own life, her friends . . .'

Mary made up her mind. It was time to stop the pretence. 'Listen to me, Andrew. Ellan isn't in New York, she hasn't been for these past nine years. She's in Liverpool.'

He stared at her in disbelief. Grief had unhinged her mind, it must have.

She read his thoughts. 'No, I'm not mad. It's the truth.'

'But the letters . . . ?'

'Sent on by Lizzie Killip, so Maggie tells me.'

'No wonder they take so long. But why? We thought . . .'

He was shaking his head, trying to clear the confusion. Ellan was living a few hours' sail away and he'd never known. But why? Why had she refused to come back? Why couldn't she have returned home?

Mary realized that having come so far she couldn't turn back now, but she wondered how he would take the news. 'The reason she couldn't come back was that she had a child, Jamie's child. That was why they were to be married in New York.'

He felt as though she'd slapped him hard across the face. It was too much to take in all at once.

'A child who will be nine years old now. I don't know whether it is a boy or a girl. I thought it was time to stop the pretence. Life is too short.'

He got to his feet and she rose also. 'Will you tell your mother?'

'I don't know, miss, and that's the truth.'

'I'll leave it to you. She won't find out from me. I'm glad you came. Life is too short for secrets, Andrew.'

'I don't know whether I'm glad or not, miss, and that's the truth. I mean, I'm satisfied if my visit has given you some comfort.'

'It has. I was always fond of Ellan, she is an unusual girl.'

He turned as he reached the door. 'Do you know where in Liverpool?'

'No, but I can find out. It will take a while, as I will have to write to Lizzie.'

'Then could you . . . would you . . . please?'

Mary nodded her assent and with a curt nod he left her.

He walked the cliff path for hours, even though it was dark and the night was wild and cold. Mary Costain's revelations went round and round in his head. As did the questions. Questions to which there were no answers, or answers that could only be supplied by Ellan herself. When he finally turned his steps towards home he was still confused and so were his feelings. Of one thing only was he sure. He wasn't going to tell Maud. If she knew, life would be unbearable.

Charlie came as often as his duties would allow. Selina was very proud of him and thought he looked even more handsome in his uniform. He had an early shift on Christmas Eve so he was going to take her to a carol concert. She was so looking forward to Christmas this year. Everything was getting back to normal and she was sure Charlie was going to ask her father for her hand. Charlie wasn't what her parents would have chosen for her before the war but she knew they liked him. Humming to herself, she fiddled with her hair, pulling a few wisps on to her forehead and trying to make them curl.

Ellan was in the drawing room perched on a chair, draping holly and ivy above the overmantel, watched by Margaret and helped by Lucy.

'Over to the right a bit more, Ellan,' Margaret instructed.

'How does that look?'

'Fine.'

'Ma, can I put this on the windowsill now?'

Ellan glanced down at Lucy who was holding a vase filled with evergreens and Christmas roses. 'Have you filled it right to the top with water?'

'Yes.'

'Good, then set it on the little mat I've put there, then hand me another holly branch. One with lots of berries on it.'

'It all seems to have lots of berries, it's a sign of a cold winter to come, so I believe. Are you sure you're not going to fall? That chair doesn't look safe,' Margaret queried.

'I won't fall. I'm used to balancing on chairs, we've just finished decorating the shop. Did I tell you about Tilly's idea?'

'For more shops?'

'No, although I am thinking about that. She said wouldn't it be wonderful if we could get one of the big shipping companies to stock our candies in their shops? Cunard or someone like that. They have shops, I remember seeing them, not that I could afford to buy anything then.'

'Wouldn't you need to go into it in a big way? I mean you'd need tons and tons of toffee.'

Ellan leaned back to admire her handiwork then reached down and took the sprigs Lucy was holding out. 'Not at first. We could do it on a trial basis to see if it would be worth spending out on stock. If it is successful I'd have to think about getting someone to make it in bulk, to my recipe of course.'

'A big manufacturer like Barker & Dobson?'

Ellan nodded, her mouth full of drawing pins.

'Perhaps Lloyd could help you, with Cunard I mean. I think one of the directors is a patient. I'll ask him.'

'Oh, would you, please? I had thought of just writing for an appointment to see someone, although just who I don't know.' Her dark eyes sparkled as she thought. 'You know it really could be very successful. I might even be able to buy a small house of my own.' Then, seeing the consternation in Margaret's face, she smiled. 'I don't want to leave here but Lucy is getting older and I often feel we have taken so much from you and given so little in return.'

'Oh, Ellan, don't talk like that. What would we do without you? I'd miss you so much, you've become like a daughter to me and so has Lucy.'

'We won't talk about it any more. It's all just wishful thinking. No-one may want to spend the whole time sailing across the Atlantic munching away on my toffees. Lucy, go and open the door, there's a good girl,' she added as the door bell echoed through the house.

Lucy did as she was bid and returned followed by Charlie.

'Is that the time already?' asked Ellan. 'I promised Cook and Vi I'd give them a hand with the last-minute baking.'

'I'm sure Selina won't be long, Charlie. She's looking forward to this concert. In fact I think she is really looking forward to this Christmas. I've never seen her so happy,' Margaret said brightly.

Charlie looked a little embarrassed. He did like Selina but he felt she clung to him far too much. Her affection was overpowering. She hung on his every word, often reading more into them than there was. She was very immature and spoiled whereas Ellan . . . He looked at her perched on the chair, her dark eyes full of vitality, her cheeks flushed with the warmth of the fire and her exertions, the light playing on her shining dark hair. She was so easy to talk to. She wasn't over-eager to please and he admired her courage tremendously after the night she'd stood beside him and fended off the mob. 'Here, let me help you down,' he offered as Ellan prepared to vacate her perch.

She laughed and let him catch her around the waist and lift her down. 'Isn't he a true gentleman?' she joked looking at Margaret who, she realized, was looking beyond her to the doorway. Turning round she saw Selina, her hands clenched, her lips set in a thin line of disapproval, her pale face clouded with silent fury. 'Oh, dear, I hope I'm not going to be the cause of a quarrel,' Ellan said, turning to Margaret for support.

Her mother and Charlie had smoothed down Selina's outraged feelings but the evening was spoiled. She joined in the carols without much enthusiasm and she was quiet and off-hand with Charlie. Oh, he explained that it was just courtesy, there was nothing in it at all, hadn't her mama been present? Somehow she didn't believe him. She had noticed the look in his eyes even if no-one else had. She was miserable as she closed the front door on him, just nodding when he said he would call on Christmas Day, in the evening of course, he wouldn't intrude on the family festivities. Now all her dreams were blighted. He said nothing about calling especially to see her father. He was coming to see them all, Ellan included. Christmas was ruined and she felt like crying and scratching Ellan's eyes out. She was older than

Charlie, too. Why, she must be nearly middle-aged.

Selina crossed the hall silently, unable to face her parents and explain why she was back so early. As she reached the foot of the staircase she stopped. The drawing-room door was slightly open and she caught a few words of their conversation. They were talking about Ellan. She moved closer, holding her skirt down with her hands so it wouldn't rustle and give her away.

'So, do you think it is a feasible proposition?' Margaret asked.

'It could be. It could be a golden opportunity if it is successful,' Lloyd replied. Selina leaned closer. What would be a golden opportunity?

'She did say if it was successful she might buy a small house for herself and Lucy, but I begged her not to think about that. I'd miss her so much. She's been like a daughter to me.'

Selina jerked her head back, her mother's words cutting her like a knife.

'Yes, she has.'

There was a note of bitterness in her father's voice. Did he resent Ellan, too? Selina wondered. But resentment was too feeble a word for what she felt for Ellan. She bit her lip to stop the tears of rage that blurred her vision.

'When I think back to the day she first came here, bowed down with grief, pale and thin and so bewildered by life,' Margaret reminisced. 'But I suppose it was only natural. She'd had such a shock losing her fiancé, then losing the security that the money could have given her. No home to go to and with a baby to care for. I would have been prostrate with despair but she had such courage . . .'

Selina didn't hear any more. One word had stuck in her mind: *fiancé*. Ellan hadn't been married! She wasn't Mrs Vannin, she was Miss Vannin. And as for Lucy . . . a slow, cruel smile spread across her face as she went quickly up the stairs.

Ellan had finished decorating the tree and Vi brought in a tray of cocoa and biscuits. Ellan leaned back on her heels to admire her handiwork. 'How does that look?'

'It's lovely, Ellan. You've got a knack for dressing things up,' Vi replied, handing a cup to Margaret.

'She has, hasn't she? I would be all fingers and thumbs.'

Ellan laughed. 'You made all the bows, don't forget, and they're fiddly. Don't put yourself down.'

Margaret smiled then looked questioningly at Vi. 'Did Miss Selina go straight to her room?'

'She did, ma'am. I took her a drink and an aspirin. She said she had a headache and I said I hoped she wasn't getting a cold but she told me she was tired. All the excitement, I suppose.'

'You're probably right, Vi. This week has been so hectic. You get off home now. Doctor Elliot has only just come in but we'll go up shortly. Good night, Vi, and Happy Christmas.'

'Thank you, an' the season's greetings to you, ma'am.'

Ellan stood up and placed her hands in the small of her back. 'I'm exhausted but there is one last thing I have to do and that's take Lucy's stocking in. I just hope she's asleep. She's so excited I could hardly get her to bed.'

Margaret smiled. 'Christmas is really a time for children, isn't it? I remember when Selina was small it was wonderful to see her face on Christmas morning. It's not the same somehow when they grow up.'

Ellan thought of all the Christmases spent with Aunt Maud. They had been sombre occasions with visits to Chapel, small gifts always of 'useful' purpose, never frivolous like the red satin ribbons Lizzie had once received and which she had coveted so much. She also remembered Christmases with her pa and they had been happy times. Oh, she'd never had much in her stocking, an apple, an orange and a bright, shiny halfpenny, but it had been wonderful to walk with him in the cold, frosty air to Chapel and then to the harbour in the afternoon to see the fishing fleet decked out in evergreens.

They were both so lost in thought that neither of them heard the door open until Lucy's quiet sob made them turn towards her.

'Lucy, why aren't you asleep?' Ellan cried but the tone of mock consternation turned to real concern as the child ran sobbing towards her. 'Lucy! What's the matter, love? What is it?'

It was a few minutes before the little girl could speak. 'Ma . . . is . . . it true? Is it?'

'What?'

'That you . . . you were never married to my pa, that . . . that I'm . . . I'm . . . a bastard?'

Ellan recoiled at the word. All the colour drained from her cheeks. 'Oh, my God!' she cried.

'Lucy, who told you that?' Margaret demanded quietly but firmly.

Lucy sobbed harder. 'Selina said I was. Is it true, Ma?'

Ellan felt her heart lurch sickeningly. How could Selina say such a thing? How had she found out? 'Come

Lyn Andrews

on, back to bed and I'll explain it all to you.' Ellan picked up her child and held her tightly, praying she would be able to find the right words to explain away the accident that had made Lucy fatherless. She couldn't use 'that' word, she just couldn't.

As she carried Lucy across the hall, Lloyd came out of his study and saw the tear-streaked face of the child and the tears that threatened to spill from Ellan's eyes. Ellan didn't speak, she just continued on up the stairs.

He went straight into the drawing room. 'What's wrong with Ellan? Is Lucy ill?'

Margaret bit her lip. 'I think you'd better go and speak to Selina, dear. Something terrible has happened.'

Lloyd instinctively knew what she meant. He raced upstairs and didn't pause to knock on his daughter's bedroom door. He threw it back with such a force that it crashed against the wall. Selina sat bolt upright in bed, her eyes wide with fear. She'd never seen her father so angry.

'Get out of that bed this minute, miss, and get downstairs. Your mother and I want to talk to you.'

She pulled the bedclothes up to her chin as though trying to shield herself from his anger. 'I . . . I don't know what . . .'

In two strides he was across the room and had gripped her by the shoulder. 'Don't come the innocent with me, Selina. You told that child something that should never have been said and don't deny it. It's not something she would make up. Get down those stairs!'

She fled before him, not even pausing to reach for her dressing gown, and ran to her mother for protection. She'd always been able to count on her mama. 'I didn't mean it. I didn't!' she cried.

'Then why did you say it and how did you find out?'
Lloyd thundered.

'I . . . I heard you talking . . . tonight, when I came in.'
All the resentment she felt for Ellan burst out. 'She's
turned Charlie against me. She has. It's her he comes to
see, not me. She's taking Charlie away from me!'

'You jealous, spiteful little madam. Is that any reason
to brand a child a bastard, even if it were true? Do you
know what effect it will have on her? On the whole of her
life? Ellan is no common slut, as you well know. Do you
think I would have brought her into this house if she had
been? All these years we have never condemned her, she's
a good girl and only an accident ruined her life and
Lucy's. What you've done is unforgivable, Selina. I don't
know what Ellan will tell the child, but whatever it is
you'd better go along with it, do you hear me?'

'Selina, you've undone years and years of happiness.
Your papa and I have done everything to make certain
that both Ellan and Lucy were happy and respected. You
will not breathe a word of this to anyone, do you
understand? Not to anyone!'

'And you will apologize to Ellan first thing in the
morning,' Lloyd added.

Selina nodded miserably. Her mama had failed her.
They were all against her. Didn't they know that she was
the one who had been hurt and now they were banding
together against her.

'Now, go back to bed.'

She scuttled across the room and through the door,
tears of self-pity pouring down her cheeks.

Margaret reached up and took Lloyd's hand. 'Oh,
where did we go wrong with her, Lloyd? I never thought

she could be so . . . so cruel and vindictive. She's always had so much.'

'Maybe she's had too much. Maybe it's our fault,' he answered, but his thoughts were with Ellan.

Chapter Twenty-Three

CHRISTMAS WAS MISERABLE FOR everyone. Ellan sat up half the night trying to explain to Lucy until, in the end, the child had fallen into a deep sleep. She filled her stocking with the things she'd bought but her heart was heavy, her tears bitter.

Selina cried all night and spent Christmas Day with swollen eyes and her lips clamped together, vowing silently that she would never, ever speak to any of them again, especially Ellan Vannin. It was a sombre day for both Margaret and Lloyd. Margaret felt ill and tired and old. Lloyd found an excuse to go out for an hour and he spent it walking up and down the deserted pierhead in an attempt to try to control his own feelings. He, too, had spent a sleepless night. More than once he had been tempted to get up and go along the landing and see how Ellan was coping. His heart had gone out to her. He relived the days he'd first met her and the unquestioning trust she'd placed in him. He could have cut Selina's tongue out. He was furious and hurt that his own daughter could be so vicious. All because of some trifling incident concerning Charlie Meadows.

He liked the lad and he hoped that something might come of it, but more than once he'd seen how Charlie looked at Ellan and it disturbed him. He also knew why it disturbed him and it was nothing to do with Selina's hopes and dreams. He knew there must be times when he looked at Ellan like that and prayed that Margaret had not noticed. He was finding it harder and harder to quash his feelings: telling himself he was a fool and an old fool, berating himself for even thinking such things, betraying Margaret and all the years they'd spent together. As he turned his collar up against the cold wind coming in from the river, he told himself such thoughts must stop and stop now.

Charlie couldn't fail to notice the terrible atmosphere in the house and he felt uncomfortable. They were all obviously trying to cover something up and he wondered if it had anything to do with him. He said as much when Lloyd saw him out.

'Only indirectly,' Lloyd answered. 'But . . . well, maybe it would be best if you didn't call quite so often. Selina is a rather fanciful and impressionable girl, if you understand me?'

Charlie thought he understood. Her father was trying to tell him in a roundabout sort of way, that he didn't want him to encourage Selina's hopes if he didn't mean to ask for her hand. He didn't. He realized that night that he didn't love Selina Elliot. He loved Ellan.

Lucy, thankfully, seemed to have forgotten the incident though sometimes Ellan thought she saw a questioning look in her daughter's blue eyes. She was very careful never to leave Lucy alone with Selina. In fact Lucy was spending more and more time at Tilly's, as she was herself, discussing the 'Grand Plan' as Tilly had named it. Lloyd promised to speak to Mr Jarvis as soon as possible, and the man himself came to see her one bleak day early in the New Year.

Business was not too brisk now that the Christmas rush was over and Ellan and Tilly had been discussing the possibility of opening another shop when he entered.

'Morning, sir. Can I help you?' Tilly had put on her best welcoming smile and manner.

'Are you Mrs Vannin?'

'No. I am.' Ellan put down the list she'd been reading.

He raised his hat. 'I'm Benjamin Jarvis from Cunard Shipping Line.'

'Oh! Oh, how good of you to call. I wasn't expecting to hear so soon.'

Tilly's mouth dropped open but she quickly hid her surprise and started leafing through the notes Ellan had made.

'I'm sorry there's nowhere . . . suitable to discuss . . . things,' Ellan apologized, wishing she had some sort of an office in the back.

'I think this a very suitable place, don't you?' He looked around at the neat but decorative counters and displays.

Ellan pulled forward a small gilt chair but he waved it away. 'Now that I've seen things myself I'm impressed. Your product is very well packaged and it looks tasty.'

She took a box from the shelf and filled it with an assortment of her most expensive fudges. 'Perhaps Mrs Jarvis . . . ?' she said.

He smiled broadly. 'She particularly asked for the nut toffee. We're both very partial to it and it is excellent.'

She quickly filled another box and placed them both on the counter.

'What quantities did you have in mind?' he asked abruptly.

'Oh, I just thought I'd start with something small, as an experiment, then if it is successful, I'd approach a large firm to use my recipes.'

'Good. I assume you can cost everything out, deal with the invoices et cetera . . . ?'

'Oh, yes. Doctor Elliot did the books when I first started but now I do them myself and his accountant audits them for me. I can assure you everything is done in a totally professional way. I have good contracts with all my suppliers and everything arrives on time and is promptly paid for.'

'Indeed. I wish there were more businesses as efficient as this. Yes, I'm very impressed. You have excellent references and an equally excellent reputation. We'll try it on the cruise liners first, I think. Then, if all goes well, we'll extend it to the other ships. Could you have a hundred and fifty boxes ready and delivered to the chief steward of the *Mauretania* by the end of the week?'

She heard Tilly gasp. 'Yes. Yes, of course.' She'd never expected an answer right away or a request for a hundred and fifty boxes.

'Good. The office will deal with all the necessary paperwork and see that you are paid. A sale or return basis?'

Ellan nodded.

'Then if you'll excuse me, I'll leave my card and thank

370

you on behalf of Mrs Jarvis.' And pressing a stiff, white embossed card into her hand and picking up the boxes from the counter, he left.

Tilly shrieked. 'We've done it! We've done it!' and grabbing Ellan by the waist, she swung her around.

Ellan laughed. 'I don't believe it. I just don't believe it. But let's not get too carried away. They might not sell.'

'Of course they will. He wouldn't have come here if he didn't think so. He's not that much of a fool, even if he is a friend of Doctor Elliot, he's a businessman first. How do you think he got the money for that overcoat? I swear it was cashmere.'

'Calm down. We've work to do. That's a big order on top of what we need for the shop, so we'd better get busy.'

Business picked up in the afternoon so there was no time to think about the future until closing time. And, just as Tilly was about to put the Closed sign on the door and pull down the windowblind, a shadow fell across the threshold. She uttered a little scream.

'God! You gave me a fright, Charlie Meadows, creeping up like that. Ellan, look who's here. PC Plod.'

Ellan smiled as she came in from the back room. 'Charlie, we haven't seen much of you lately.'

He looked a little uncomfortable. 'I thought I might get a quick cuppa, it's going to be a long shift.'

'Wouldn't you know it, he's on the cadge. We were just closing up,' Tilly tutted with mock annoyance, trying to lighten the atmosphere. She'd seen him look at Ellan like that before and she was certain the last thing on his mind was tea. There had been some sort of bust up over Christmas, that was all she'd been able to get out of Ellan.

'Tilly, go on home. I'll finish up and make him a cuppa.'

'Well, if you're certain. I'll send our Tommy home with Lucy, she's bound to have come down after school.'

Ellan threw her a grateful look. Even though it was still early evening she didn't like Lucy walking home on her own.

Charlie followed her into the back room, taking off his helmet. 'I'll be disciplined if the sergeant sees me,' he explained as his reason for following her.

'Sit down and when you've had your tea you can walk me home. I'll be glad when spring comes and the nights get lighter.'

She busied herself with the kettle and teapot while he watched her.

'You're very quiet, Charlie. Is something bothering you?'

'Yes.'

'Oh, I know it's none of my business, but has it got something to do with Selina and your now infrequent visits?'

'Um.'

She passed him the cup and leaned back against the scrubbed table. 'You're not serious about her and you're afraid to say so, is that it?'

'Partly.'

She could have shaken him. He wasn't his usual chatty self tonight. 'You know Doctor Elliot doesn't expect you to say you are passionately in love with her if you're not. He's a reasonable man. He won't take offence.'

Charlie sipped his tea. 'I know that. He . . . well, it was he who said maybe I shouldn't call so much at the house.'

'Did he?' She was surprised.

'He said that she, Selina, was a bit fanciful.'

'Desperate' was the word that came into Ellan's mind but she nodded slowly. 'She's very young for her years.' She had been a mother at Selina's age, she thought. And, she'd been on her own. Not surrounded by the love and secure comfort that money afforded.

'But it's not that, entirely.'

'Then what is it, Charlie? It's not like you to be so reticent.'

He put down the teacup and got up, towering over her. 'It's you, Ellan . . .'

'Me?'

'I never loved Selina. It's you I love.' At last he found the courage to reach out and take her hands.

She was astounded. She liked him. If she was truthful she would say she was fond of him, but love? 'Charlie, that's the nicest thing anyone has said to me for a long time.'

'Ellan, I'm serious. I mean it.' He drew her towards him and she stiffened.

'Charlie, please!'

'Ever since that night, the night of the riots, I think it started then.'

She cast about looking for something to say that would not hurt him. 'But I'm so much older than you and then there's Lucy . . .'

'Don't worry about Lucy, she likes me and I like her. She's a good kid. You're not much older than me, Ellan, and anyway what does age matter?'

She knew she must put a stop to this, now before it got out of hand. She withdrew her hands. 'Charlie, I'm

fond of you, I really am. But that's all it is. When . . .
when Lucy's father died I swore I'd never love another
man and I meant it. I could never love anyone the way I
loved Jamie. You're a good man and I don't want to hurt
you by letting you go on thinking . . . that would be
cruel. I'm humbled and touched by the fact that you love
me, but it wouldn't work. I'm sorry.'

'Won't you even try?' he pleaded.

'No. I can't, Charlie. I don't believe that love comes
after marriage. It just wouldn't work.'

He looked so defeated and miserable that she almost
relented. She pulled herself together. 'You'll find
someone else. Not Selina, someone nicer, kinder.' She
wished she could tell him how cruel Selina was.

'No, I won't.'

'You will. You don't believe me now but one day you
will see it's the truth.'

He straightened up as though realizing where he was
and the fact that he was on duty. He owed some dignity
to the uniform he wore, he thought bitterly.

She laid a hand on his arm. 'Don't be bitter. I don't
want you to leave vowing never to speak to me again,
please?'

It was a lot to ask, he thought, especially at this
moment in time. He shrugged.

Ellan realized that that was all the confirmation she
was going to get, for now. 'Good. Then let's part friends
and you don't have to walk me home. You need time to
think. Time to be on your own.'

When he'd gone she sighed deeply. Did she mean
what she said about never loving anyone again, or had it
just been a way to let him down gently? There were times

when she was lonely, even though she was seldom alone. It was possible to be lonely in the middle of a crowd, that was something she'd learned. As she looked up she felt a great wave of homesickness break over her. Would she ever be able to go home again, she wondered. Or would she have to stay here for ever? She shook herself mentally. After that awful experience at Christmas she couldn't expose Lucy to yet more speculation and gossip. It wouldn't be time to go back for many years to come and she'd better get used to the fact.

'You're very quiet, Ellan,' Lloyd remarked over supper. He knew Jarvis had intended to go and see her and wondered if it had anything to do with that.

'Sorry. I was day dreaming.'

'What about?' Margaret asked.

Ellan smiled at her. 'How things come unexpectedly out of the blue. Things you never dreamed could happen.'

'Like what?' Lloyd probed, smiling.

She had been thinking of Charlie but pushed the thoughts away. She knew what he meant. 'I had a visitor today. Mr Jarvis, from Cunard.'

'And?'

'And I have to have a hundred and fifty boxes delivered to the chief steward of the *Mauretania* by the end of the week.'

Margaret clapped her hands. 'Oh Ellan! How wonderful!'

Ellan looked across at Lloyd. 'And I have you to thank for that, I know I have.'

'Nonsense. I just happened to mention . . .'

She pealed with laughter. 'Oh, just listen to him.'

Margaret joined in the laughter. Selina remained silent. She felt left out of this conversation. 'Will you make a lot of money?' she asked, ungraciously. She remembered what her mother had said about Ellan buying a house of her own and hoped she would. Selina hoped Ellan would go out of their lives for ever and take that brat, Lucy, with her.

'I don't know. I suppose I might, if I get a contract.'

'And I'm sure you will. So, let's raise our glasses in a toast. To your success!'

Ellan laughed as they raised their water glasses to her. 'I couldn't have done it without you, both of you!' It was an exciting prospect and she was looking forward to the future, but thoughts of Charlie still bothered her. She'd speak to Lloyd about that later.

As she tucked Lucy in bed the child's thoughts were running on the same lines as Selina's and for the same reason. 'Will we be rich, Ma?'

'I don't know. Why?'

'If we will be, can we move away? I don't like it here any more.'

Ellan smoothed back the dark hair from her daughter's brow. 'Why not?'

'Selina hates me.'

Ellan sighed. 'No, Lucy, she doesn't hate you. You see, it's hard for her. All she wants is to get married and have children of her own and now . . . now there's not much chance of that.' She held up her hand to stem the imminent outburst. 'I know she's been horrid to you in the past and I'm not asking you to like her. I'm just explaining.'

'But if we had our own house . . .'

'Oh, Lucy. Do you think Mrs Elliot would like us to go? She'd miss us both terribly and I feel sort of responsible for her. She's not getting any better. Some days she is in terrible pain. I couldn't leave her. You know that. Now let's not have any more talk like this. I might not even get a contract.'

She met Lloyd on the landing and he stopped when he caught sight of her.

'Ellan, you look worried.'

'Oh, it's nothing. Just Lucy being difficult.' She smiled. 'Wanting to know will we be rich.'

'I'm beginning to regret I spoke to Jarvis – it seems to be causing a lot of concern. Margaret was looking worried, too. You won't leave us, Ellan, will you?'

'Of course not. How could I after all you've done for me?'

'We want you to feel that this will always be your home.'

'I know that.'

'Is anything else bothering you? You were very preoccupied over supper. You hardly said a word.'

She sighed. 'Charlie Meadows came to see me at the shop just before we closed, on the pretext of a free cup of tea.'

'What did he really want?'

'Oh, it sounds foolish.'

'Tell me. It can't have been that foolish otherwise you'd have dismissed it from your mind.'

'He doesn't love Selina.'

'That I already know. I think I've always known it, but I hoped.'

'He . . . he said . . . he said he loves me.'

Lloyd didn't speak. He couldn't stop the force that was surging through him, a force so alien that it almost unbalanced him. He was jealous. Jealous of Charlie Meadows and the freedom that gave him the right to declare his love for her. 'What . . . did you say?' he managed to get out at last for she was staring at him.

'I let him down as gently as I could.'

He felt relief course through him.

'I told him that I could never love anyone again. Not after Jamie.' She seemed hesitant.

'And do you mean that?'

'Oh, I don't know. I honestly don't. It's so long ago now, I was only a bit of a girl. Who knows?'

He was grimly hanging on to his self-control. Could he tell her now? But what would she do? Would she run straight to Margaret?

'Lloyd, what's the matter? You've gone quite pale and you're sweating.'

Quickly he wiped away the beads of sweat on his forehead. No, not now, not ever, his commonsense told him. 'I'm just a bit run down. Nothing to worry about. Did Charlie seem satisfied with that explanation?' The words almost choked him.

'Yes, I think so. He'll get over me in time. I told him that, too. He'll find someone else. He wasn't too sure about that but I think we parted friends. On speaking terms anyway.'

'He'll come round, give him time. His pride's been hurt.'

'I suppose you're right. This has been a very odd day in so many ways. I feel quite exhausted myself.' She smiled up at him and then turned towards the head of the stairs.

His gaze followed her hungrily but the dim light on the landing threw his face into shadow and for that he was grateful.

Chapter Twenty-Four

IT HAD TAKEN HIM nearly five months but at last he had come to a decision. He would go and find her. Part of the delay was due to not having her address but, true to her word, Mary Costain had obtained it. Mary had sent for him and in answer to Maud's questions, he said he had gone to do a few jobs for her as old Adam Helsby was stiff with rheumatism these days – Mary refused to pension him off.

He had spent days and nights thinking about her and about her child, a girl called Lucy, so Mary had informed him. She'd been born on the *Lusitania* during Ellan's voyage back, hence her name. 'Carrying on the family tradition,' he'd remarked to Mary. She looked puzzled until he reminded her of the mail boat that had borne the same name as Ellan.

Could he accept the child? Jamie Corlett's child. That was the question his decision had foundered on so many times. The answer was that he didn't know. He just didn't know. Rodney Street was the Harley Street of Liverpool, so Mary had told him. A doctor and his wife had taken her in and been very good to her, so Lizzie had written to Mary. He'd spent many a sleepless night wondering what she looked like now. Had she aged? Was she still as beautiful? Until in the end he knew he had to see her. He'd get no peace otherwise.

To Maud's demands to know why he was going to Liverpool, he replied truthfully that Miss Mary Costain wanted him to do something for her, something she didn't want the entire board of directors of the mines or the shipping company to know about. Maud was curious but in response to all her hints and even outright demands, he refused to enlighten her. So, on a windy but bright April morning, he went to Ramsey to take the mail boat to Liverpool. It was the first time he'd been off the island since coming home from the naval hospital.

As always he found the city noisy and hectic and to his country eyes, dirty. Crossing the street was taking your life in your hands, dodging between trams, omnibuses, carts and more cars and motorized lorries than there had been before the war. He asked the directions from a policeman and as he strode up Hardman Street he felt his doubts returning.

On the corner of Rodney Street he stopped and looked at the houses, the Georgian houses of the wealthy, and he wondered what sort of reception he would receive from this Doctor Elliot. His clothes were those of the labouring class even though they were his Sunday best. Would he go to the back door? He had no way of knowing what kind of a position Ellan had in the household. Was she a servant? Or had she been elevated to a status similar to that of a governess? There was only one way to find out.

He pressed the bell and heard it echo through the house. His right hand was thrust in his pocket, clenched tightly into a fist. The empty sleeve was tucked into the other pocket. Although it was chilly he felt warm, uncomfortably warm.

The door was opened by a young woman in the black and white uniform of a parlour maid. 'Tradesmen round the back,' Vi snapped, annoyed at having to run up from the kitchen.

'I'm not a tradesman.' His tone was equally brusque.

'And hawkers.'

'I'm not selling anything. I've come to see someone. This is Doctor Elliot's house, isn't it?'

'Yes.' Vi looked him up and down. She'd never seen him before.

'I've come to see Ellan. Ellan Vannin.'

'Oh. What's your name then?'

'Quirk. Andrew Quirk.'

Vi stared at him. She'd never heard Ellan mention anyone of that name. 'Can you tell me what it's in connection with?'

He was losing his patience. 'Look, if it's not convenient just say so. I'll come back later.'

'Don't get all aereated with me. I'm only doing my job. I suppose you'd better come in while I go and ask does she want to see you. Wipe your feet.' Grudgingly she indicated that he step inside and wait in the hall.

She made him feel very inferior and this wasn't the way he wanted to see Ellan again, standing, cap in hand, like a servant in someone's fancy hallway. And it was very grand. It reminded him of Glentrammon. It seemed an age before the door at the end of the hall opened slowly and Ellan was standing there. His heart leapt. She was still beautiful and until this moment he hadn't realized just how much he'd missed her. She was smiling at him and coming towards him, her hands outstretched.

'Andrew! Oh, Andrew! Is it really you?'

'Yes. It's me, Ellan.' He took both her hands in his one hand. Despite her smile he could see she was troubled. 'Miss Mary Costain told me where you were.'

Her heart was racing. When Vi had told her she hadn't believed it. He couldn't have found her. He didn't know where she was. Only Lizzie knew that. Lizzie had written, saying she'd had a letter from Miss Mary, telling her that Thomas Costain had died and asking for her address. Mary knew she was in Liverpool, she'd known that. Maggie had had to tell her years ago. But she never dreamed that Mary would tell anyone. She was lost for words. 'I . . . I don't know what to say.'

He looked around uncomfortably. 'Ellan, I can't talk to you here.'

She grasped at the straw. 'Wait here, I'll get my hat and coat. There are some little gardens in the square not far from here.'

As she went for her things she met Vi on the landing.

'You look as though you've seen a ghost. Who is he?' Vi whispered.

'Someone I know from home. I'm going out, will you tell Mrs Elliot? Tell her I won't be long.'

They walked in silence to Abercrombie Square and not until they sat down on the bench in the small, enclosed garden in the middle did she speak.

'It's good to see you. I really do mean that.'

'Then why couldn't you tell me you were here?'

She looked down at her hands folded in her lap. 'I have my reasons.' She didn't want to have to explain everything. 'Lizzie has kept me informed about things at home. I was sorry to hear about John and Mat and all the others. It was a terrible time for everyone. How is Aunt Maud?'

'Older and sadder but not much changed.'

He was studying her closely. She wasn't the girl he remembered, she was a woman, a woman of poise and beauty. There was an air of tranquillity that she'd not had when she'd been younger. He longed to reach out and touch her.

'I was sorry about you, too, but at least you came back alive. So many didn't. Lloyd . . . Doctor Elliot was with the medical corps, we knew all about the conditions.'

He held her gaze. 'Ellan . . . why?'

'It was all so long ago, Andrew.' She dropped her gaze, her thick dark lashes making shadows on her pale cheeks.

'Ellan. I know about Lucy.'

She sucked in her breath. Oh, why had Mary Costain done this to her? She never expected Mary Costain to betray her like this. She didn't stop to think that Mary might have had a good reason. 'That's why I couldn't come home. You must understand that, you know how I would have been treated. I just couldn't go back. It wouldn't have brought respect or standing for me or Lucy. I hated deceiving everyone but I had to. I met Doctor Elliot on the *Lusitania*. He and his wife offered me a home and they have been so good to me. They've treated me as a daughter.'

He felt a barrier between them, a barrier that had not been there all those years ago and it had nothing to do with Jamie Corlett or even the child. It was a wall built by years of change, changes of personality, of circumstances and experiences, and he was confused and lost for words. She seemed to understand his predicament for she smiled sadly.

'We've both grown up, Andrew.'

'Will you stay here?'

'Probably. I have a successful business.'

'Doing what?'

'Selling sweets or candies as I call them. I did learn something in New York. I've just got a trial concession for the Cunard Line.'

'You've done well for yourself then,' he said quietly, his admiration for her rising, yet tinged with regret, for what could he offer her? A home with his ma? A standard of living that bordered on genteel poverty? He wasn't a whole man.

'I've had my fair share of disappointments, too, Andrew. It hasn't been easy.'

He looked at the rich Burgundy melton coat and the hat with curled feathers. Her gloves were leather as was the bag over her arm. He seemed to really see her for the first time and what he saw was a lady, a lady with confidence and refinement and no trace of the island burr in her quiet, well modulated voice. He felt foolish and annoyed. He shouldn't have come. What had he expected to find? The sweet, helpless young girl he'd known? Now she was successful and she didn't need him. He stood up, ignoring the look of disappointment in the dark eyes.

'Must you go so soon?' she asked.

'I've things to do.'

She laid a hand on his arm. 'I could always tell when

you were lying. You haven't come all this way for a few errands. Oh, Andrew. I know you so well.'

'You used to, Ellan.'

'No. You haven't changed much. Why did you come? Tell me the truth.'

'Just to see if you needed anything. Maybe to see if you were . . .'

'What?' she urged.

'If there was anyone special . . .' He hated himself for saying it.

'No, there isn't. There never can be, because of Lucy. I couldn't keep a secret like that from someone I cared about.'

'You kept it from me and from John and Mat.'

'Because I didn't want to hurt or shame you. You must believe that. Do you think it's been easy for me living here? A few miles away from home and yet unable to set foot on Manx soil? There have been times when I've yearned so much to go home that my heart felt as though it were breaking. But I love Lucy too much.'

'So you'll never come home?'

'Is that really why you came? To ask me to go back?'

'In part.'

Her dark eyes searched his face. 'And the other part?'

He shrugged. 'It doesn't matter now. I can see you've outgrown us. You've become a lady. Independent too. A businesswoman.' He hadn't meant to sound bitter but his feelings were so confused that he no longer cared.

Anger flared. 'How dare you judge me. What was I supposed to do? Come crawling back begging forgiveness? Live with the insults hurled at both me and Lucy?

Having to watch her grow up an outcast, pitied or reviled? Be forever on Aunt Maud's charity or someone's charity? You should know me better than that.'

'I'm sorry, Ellan. I just meant that you've changed.'

Her anger died. 'Yes. I've changed. Too much to go back and face all that. Do you remember this?' She took off her glove and held up her hand on which she still wore the silver ring.

He nodded.

'I've *had* to stand and stand alone, Andrew. Or go under and I won't do that. I can't do that.'

He managed a smile. 'You always were plucky, Ellan. I suppose I shouldn't have come.'

She let her hand fall to her side. 'Can't we part friends?'

'I seem to remember you said that once before but no matter, it's water under the bridge now.' His smile was wintry. 'Your secret is safe with me, Ellan. No-one will know unless you want them to.'

'I don't. Maybe one day I'll come home. I've promised Lucy I'll take her there. When she's safely married.'

He looked down but he wasn't seeing her. He was seeing a future that stretched away emptily.

'Will you come back and see me, Andrew?'

'If I ever come back here it will be to take you home, Ellan, so let's say no more. I'll go now. I can find my own way back into the city.'

He kissed her cheek and then turned away. She stood watching him, her fingers curled tightly around the iron railings, her eyes bright with unshed tears, wishing she could go with him.

*

In the days and nights that followed she couldn't get Andrew out of her mind, nor could she dispel the longing in her heart for home. She was silent and preoccupied, her mood noted by everyone, until Margaret at last asked what was troubling her.

'He was like a brother to me. I was very fond of him. Oh, people said he loved me, but I never believed it. He asked Lizzie to marry him but she turned him down.'

'And why do you think this Miss Costain took it on herself to tell him you were here?'

'I wish I knew. She must have had her reasons, I don't think she is a person who acts rashly. Unless she's changed.'

'Did he want you to go back? Did he ask you to?'

'Not in so many words. He seemed angry and hurt that I'd become a businesswoman.'

Margaret saw it all clearly, very clearly. 'Oh, Ellan, my dear. He loves you. I think he has always loved you, that's why he appeared to be angry. I think he wanted to find that you couldn't cope, that you'd jump at the chance to go home, with him.'

'Do you really think that's why he came?'

'I'm almost certain of it. How do you feel about him?'

'I don't know. I really don't know.'

'Then I suggest you think about it as I've a feeling that we've not seen the last of him.'

'He won't come back. He's too proud and that's something I'm certain of.'

Margaret's words stayed with her day and night and she even found herself listening for the doorbell. But the weeks went by and he didn't return. It was futile to think like that, she told herself. She couldn't go back. She was just using him as an excuse to hope and that wasn't right nor was it fair for either of them. But she still couldn't get him out of her mind, though she had plenty of other things that should be occupying her.

The sample candies were a great success and she went with Tilly and Lloyd to see Mr Jarvis to discuss the expansion of her business. Meetings were arranged with Barker & Dobson, prices and contracts were discussed and when everything was finally settled, Lloyd suggested that a party should be given to celebrate and to launch her new venture.

'Launch being a very apt word in the circumstances,' he'd finished.

'What kind of a party? Where?' she laughed.

'Nothing too grand and where else but at home? It will cheer Margaret up no end and Selina, too.'

And so the invitations were sent out and Ellan spent hours discussing the buffet and the decorations and what she would wear with Margaret. Even Selina began to take an interest and the surly look left her face. The only thing she complained about was the fact that Tilly had been invited.

'But she just won't fit in, Mama. That's all I'm saying.'

'We can't possibly have a party without her. She's been wonderful and I'm thinking of promoting her.' Ellan came to Tilly's defence and as Margaret agreed, Selina was forced to keep her own counsel about Tilly and her manners.

Tilly herself echoed those doubts. 'I can't stand chatting to all those nobs, Ellan. I won't know what to say or even what fork to use. I'm bound to spill something I'm that clumsy and I don't want to show you up.'

'Now stop that. I couldn't have carried on without you and you know it. I don't want to hear another word. You're to go and get a really nice evening dress. I'm paying. Go to George Henry Lee's or Henderson's.'

'I'll never get past the bloke on the door.'

Despite her trepidation and at Ellan's urging, she bought a dress of pale lilac challis inset with bands of ecru lace. The skirt was shorter than anything she'd had before and she felt very daring.

'I just hope me da doesn't throw a fit and forbid me to wear it, not at that price. It's nothing short of daylight robbery the prices they were charging. You'd think it would cost less, the skirts being shorter an' all, less material.'

Ellan laughed. 'You're paying for the style and workmanship and the lace.'

'Paying for the name more like. They'll all think I've come into a fortune when I walk down our street with this box.'

Ellan smiled, noting the self-satisfied expression on Tilly's face. 'I suppose you could say we have.'

Tilly grinned. 'Not "we", *you*.'

'No. I mean "we", *us*. I have been talking to Lloyd and I've decided to make you a partner.'

Tilly stopped and stared at her. 'You mean . . . me . . . and the shop?'

'Yes. Once all the papers are signed you'll be a part-owner. We'll share everything, debts as well,' she laughed.

'But, Ellan, I can't.'

'Tilly, you've worked damned hard for me and this contract with Cunard was your idea. It's only fair that you should become a partner now. I couldn't have managed without you.'

Despite the fact that they were in the middle of a crowded street, Tilly threw her arms around Ellan and hugged her. 'Oh, Ellan. Me dream's out.'

Ellan disentangled herself. 'People will think we're mad.'

'Oh, let them. Wait until I tell me da and 'er over the road. I'm glad now you bought me this dress, it's going to be a really special do.'

The evening was very successful. Tilly, though tonguetied and nervous, had stayed firmly by Margaret's side and Margaret, realizing the girl felt out of her depth, made every effort to make her feel at ease. Quietly and subtly she drew Tilly into conversation with people who came to sit with her.

Lucy, allowed up late for the first part of the evening and resplendent in a sapphire-blue velvet dress with lace collar and cuffs, helped Vi pass around the canapés.

'What a charming child and what lovely manners she has,' Mrs Jarvis remarked to Ellan after thanking her for the boxes of fudges and toffee that Ellan sent each week.

'Thank you. I do my best with her,' Ellan replied. She knew Margaret had made sure that everyone thought she was a widow. It certainly wasn't unusual these days, there were hundreds of young women who were war widows.

'And such a little beauty. You'll have suitors fighting their way to your door in a few years' time, you mark my words. My Barbara was just the same. I lost count of the broken hearts she left in her wake.'

'I'll cross that bridge when I come to it. Thankfully it

will be years before I have to cope with suitors.' At Lucy's age she had lost her pa and gone to live with Aunt Maud and there hadn't been much joy after that, which made her all the more determined that Lucy would be happy. She'd come a long way from that little croft in Peel, she thought, as she listened attentively to the older woman's instructions on how to cope with future hordes of male admirers.

Behind them, Selina stood engaged in conversation with Dr Swinton, a colleague of her father's, but she wasn't listening to his views on women in medicine. She heard everything that ghastly, overweight woman said about Lucy and she clenched the stem of her glass so tightly that it was in danger of snapping, a fact Dr Swinton pointed out. She smiled and relaxed the pressure. The woman's voice grated on her nerves as she prattled on about suitors. She really hadn't wanted to attend this awful gathering, although at first she thought it would relieve the tedium of her life. It was just an excuse for Ellan to lord it over her, to emphasize the fact that she was still very attractive and that Lucy was her pride and joy. As much as it hurt her, Selina had to admit that Lucy was beautiful, but she still hated the child. She wanted to shout out that Lucy Vannin was a common bastard and that in her eyes Ellan was little better than a whore. Oh, they'd soon change their attitudes then. The stupid smiles would turn to looks of horror. Ellan's face would become twisted with humiliation and that precocious little brat would burst into tears the way she'd done on Christmas Eve. For a few seconds she was sorely tempted but then she remembered her father's anger.

Lloyd found himself watching Ellan. She looked a

vision in her cream lace evening dress. The soft, ivory guipure seemed to drift around her and the peach satin under-dress made her skin glow. He'd never seen her look so beautiful. All night he'd been fighting down the surge of emotion he felt when he looked at her or caught her gaze and she smiled at him. For the first time he realized how much he wanted her, for the first time he admitted it to himself and that admission just didn't bear too close a scrutiny.

Eventually everyone left and Margaret insisted that both Vi and Cook leave everything until morning. It had been a great success but everyone was worn out. Selina went up early, pleading a headache. Margaret and Lloyd retired and Ellan wandered over to the window and gazed out into the deserted street. It had been a wonderful evening and well worth the hard work. She was too excited to sleep for Mr Jarvis had offered herself and Lucy a short cruise to New York, all expenses paid, and she'd had trouble getting Lucy to sleep. Oh, it would be wonderful to see Lizzie again and Mrs Hinchey. She'd take Lucy to see all the sights and this time she would be going first class.

She picked up a rose-pink satin bow that had fallen, with two of its companions, from the large floral arrangement in the wide bay. It had become her trademark and she smiled as she twisted it between her fingers. Life was almost perfect. If only . . . if only Andrew could have been here to share her happiness and success. A shadow flitted across her face. The shadow became a frown. He would have felt out of place, ill at ease, and would have resented her. But the more she thought about him the more important it became that he should accept her for what she was, or rather what she had become. If only she could win his approval. If only he would come back. If only he could understand about Lucy – if, if, if. There were too many 'ifs'. She would be wise to put all thoughts of him from her mind.

'Ellan, why haven't you gone to bed?'

She looked up and saw Lloyd standing in the doorway. 'I knew I wouldn't sleep so I thought I'd stay down and clear up a bit.'

He smiled as he came towards her. 'It was a great success, wasn't it?'

'Oh, I was so nervous.'

'No-one would ever have thought it. You looked so calm, but then you always do.' He stood close to her, looking down into her upturned face. He'd known she was down here and hadn't been able to stop himself. He knew he was mad but he couldn't help it. He took her hands in his. 'I've never seen you look so beautiful.'

She felt uneasy yet it seemed churlish to pull away. 'Thank you.'

'Ellan, you know how fond I am of you.'

She smiled at him. 'I know, and in my heart you've taken the place of the father I lost. Did you know that?' she said gently, her eyes misting. Oh, how proud her pa would have been of her. The tears blurred her vision so she didn't see the look of pain that flashed across his face.

'Oh, Ellan! Is that how you think of me?'

'Isn't that what you want?'

'Yes, but I had hoped . . . for more.' Cold reason fought with wild infatuation and longing.

'More?' she queried, her uneasiness deepening.

Infatuation won. He could deny it no longer. Before

she could stop him he gathered her into his arms and was kissing her passionately.

She started to fight him, twisting her head away and crying his name in an attempt to make him stop, but his lips only burned the flesh of her throat and shoulders.

'Lloyd! No! No!' With a wrench she jerked herself away from him but he still encircled her waist with his arms.

He began to remember where he was. The room stopped spinning and the enormity of his actions began to dawn on him. 'Ellan, I'm sorry! I'm so sorry! I didn't mean . . .'

She was trembling and there were tears in her eyes. 'Oh, Lloyd! Why? Why? I've never done anything to make you believe . . .'

'It's not your fault, Ellan. I've been a fool. I couldn't help it. I . . . I love you, Ellan.' He tried to draw her to him but she pushed hard against him. Then she felt him stiffen and release her, muttering to himself. She turned around and her hand went to her mouth to stifle the cry that leapt to her lips. Selina was standing in the doorway.

Chapter Twenty-Five

———— ◆ ————

S HE KNEW SHE MUST have tried to explain, she knew she had. Lloyd caught Selina's arm and pushed her into the room as Ellan fled upstairs. She sat on the landing for what seemed a lifetime, hearing the muffled voices from the drawing room. When the door opened at last she crept to her room and lay down on the bed, but she didn't sleep.

She would have to leave. There was nothing else she could do now. She would have to take Lucy and go. They could stay with Tilly until they found a house of their own. But what about Margaret? Oh, dear God! Margaret! The kindest, gentlest, most trusting woman she'd ever known. Oh, it hadn't been her fault but that's not what Selina would say. Selina had always hated her. Oh, she couldn't bear to see the look on Margaret's face.

She got up and dragged off the lace dress, throwing it carelessly over a chair, heedless of its cost. She sat down at the dressing table and began to take the combs from her hair with trembling fingers. She looked at herself in the glass and shuddered. She was cursed. All the men she'd ever known she'd hurt in some way and she'd lost them. There was Jamie. Had she not been expecting Lucy, would he have been in such a hurry to claim his uncle's fortune? Would he have taken a later ship? Very probably and then he would have missed that last tragic voyage of the S.S. *Ellan Vannin*. Andrew she'd hurt because she loved Jamie and she'd lost him because Lucy and her success stood in the way. And Lloyd. She'd never encouraged him yet somehow he'd fallen in love with her. He'd forgotten, at least for those few fateful minutes, the best wife a man could ever have and now he'd lost them both for she doubted that even Margaret's heart was big enough to forgive such a betrayal. Ellan would have to leave this house. But what would she tell Lucy? She lay down on the bed again and sobbed into the pillow until she fell into a fitful sleep.

Steeling herself to face them, she went down the next morning: inside she was shaking, she felt awash with ice water. But Margaret's smile was the same and Lloyd greeted her pleasantly as he did each morning. Of Selina there was no sign.

'Ellan, you look worn out, dear.'

She smiled bravely at Margaret. 'I didn't sleep much last night.'

'Neither did Selina. She has a migraine.'

Ellan felt as though a great burden had been lifted from her. Whatever Lloyd had said to his daughter she must have believed him, but she couldn't look him in the face.

He folded his newspaper. 'There's been too much excitement all round. You look a little washed out yourself, my dear. I think a day's rest for you all would not go amiss. Now, I have patients to see to.' He kissed his wife on the cheek and nodded to Ellan.

So, there was to be a reprieve, for the moment, Ellan thought gratefully. But now she must seriously think of leaving them. She couldn't trust him or Selina and she would die rather than hurt Margaret.

'You're as bad-tempered as a weasel these days. What's the matter with you?' Maud demanded when Andrew had come down and slammed every door in the house.

'Nothing. You know I get these black moods. Doctor Taylor said it was a result of the war.'

'And you know what I think of him and his theories. Other men don't make everyone's life a misery. You've only started having these black moods as you call them, since you started going up to Glentrammon and running errands for Mary Costain.' A thought occurred to her. 'If you've got any ideas about you and her, forget them. Oh, she's not as high and mighty as she used to be and I feel sorry for her, she's lonely, but don't think any of that makes any difference.'

To her surprise he threw back his head and laughed. 'Me! Me, entertain hopes of Miss Mary. Oh, Ma, you're a card.'

Maud bristled. 'I was just warning you, that's all.'

'There's no need to, Ma.'

'Well, where are you going now?'

For the first time in months she saw him smile without cynicism. 'To a secret meeting with Miss Mary.'

She smiled back. 'Oh, be off with you. And take that dog with you.'

The smile vanished as he crossed the fields, climbed

the stile and walked up the lane to Glentrammon. His ma was right about one thing: Miss Mary was lonely and she had very little in life to look forward to. She was good to him and there were occasions when she talked to him for hours, just as if he was one of her own brothers. He had been emboldened to discuss with her things he never mentioned to Maud. But the one thing he could never tell her was how much he loved Ellan. She never questioned him about his trip to Liverpool, except once when she asked if it had been successful. 'Fairly,' he answered evasively and they'd not spoken of it since.

The weather was much warmer, he thought, but the beauty of the early spring morning only made him feel depressed. He nodded to old Adam and to Daisy who was pegging out the washing. There was only half the staff now at Glentrammon, compared to the days before the war. There was an old heavily carved bookcase in Mr Costain's study that was in need of some minor repairs, Miss Mary had told him. He was very adept at using just one hand these days, there were few things he could not do.

She came out of the small back parlour to meet him and he thought about what his ma had said. She looked sad and somehow frail.

'Morning, miss.'

'Good morning, Andrew. I'll show you which one it is. It's not really bad enough for me to call the cabinet maker. Daisy noticed it when she was dusting in here.'

The room was dark and smelled musty and he shivered as though surrounded by ghosts. The furniture was mostly covered by dust sheets.

'It's always been a dark room. I never liked it,' she said, noticing the shiver.

'Why don't you sell the house, miss, if you don't mind me speaking so forthrightly?'

Pulling aside a dust sheet she sat down on a chair. 'Oh, I've thought about it many times. It's far too big for just me and it costs so much for the upkeep. Not that I mind that,' she added hastily in case he should think she was crying poverty. 'But it's my home. I do have some happy memories, and besides, I can't throw the servants out of work, not with things as bad as they are. Sometimes I must admit I would like to have a nice little cottage. I sometimes feel so . . . alone.'

'We all do at times, miss.'

'You have your mother, your friends and workmates.'

'But sometimes that's not enough, miss.'

She looked at him with compassion and understanding in her eyes. He was eating his heart out for Ellan. Oh, he'd never said as much but she was a perceptive woman. She quickly noted the signs. 'Andrew, why don't you go and bring her home?'

He dropped the small hammer he was holding. 'Who?'

'Andrew, I'm not a fool. Ellan. You love her. I know you do. Never mind what people will say, go and bring her home.'

'I can't, Miss Mary. It's not as simple as that.'

'You mean the child?'

'Not just that. Ellan's changed.'

'We all change, Andrew.'

'She's got her own business. Some fancy name for sweets. She sells them in a shop and on the Cunard liners. And then there's the house. It's as grand as this. What can I offer her?'

'Your love. Don't you think that would be enough? It would be for me,' she mused softly.

'No, miss. I don't.'

'Did she say as much?' she probed.

'She doesn't know.'

'Oh, Andrew! Then how can you be so sure she wouldn't leave all that for you?'

'Because . . . because . . . Oh, I don't know. I don't even know if I could take on the child. It's not as if she's a bairn that I could grow to accept. She's already ten.'

Mary sighed. 'Lucy, isn't it? A pretty name. Is she a pretty child?'

'I don't know. I didn't see her.'

'Don't you think you could at least try? I know it's none of my business, but life can be lonely. I have very little to look forward to but you have. Don't waste your life being stubborn, Andrew. Don't squander your happiness and Ellan's. You could be a family. You could all be happy.' She wanted them to be happy. She wanted to feel that she had achieved something. They would be the family she no longer had. She would always remain on the fringe, she could never be an integral part of such a family, but she'd settle for that.

He just stared at her, not knowing what to say or what to think.

She smiled. 'I'm just being selfish. It will make me so happy, you see. I always wanted Ellan to do well. I knew she was different from the other village girls. In a way she has done well but success in business isn't always everything. Oh, take no notice of me. I'm becoming an interfering old maid. I'm sorry.'

'No, you're not. You're one of the kindest, most thoughtful people I know.'

'Will you think about what I've said?'

He smiled. 'Aye, I'll think about it.'

As the weeks slowly passed and the spring days lengthened and became milder, with daffodils nodding in the warmer breezes, Ellan spent longer and longer in the shop, trying to think of some concrete reason for leaving and finding a home of her own. The strain was beginning to tell on her. She would not stay in the house any longer than was necessary and made use of the lighter evenings to take Lucy for walks to the park or down to the river to watch the ships. She was very tense and nervous in both Selina's and Lloyd's presence. Lloyd spoke to her in a detached, mildly distracted way which often prompted Margaret to look puzzled and say he was getting very absent-minded. Apart from the occasional look of hatred Selina flashed at her, the girl seemed withdrawn and preoccupied, and more than once Margaret had voiced her concern over her daughter's state of mind.

'She's withdrawing into herself, Ellan, and I can't reach her. We used to be so close. I know she is terrified of becoming an old maid but there is little I can do about it. I've tried to interest her in a career. Not medicine but music, it's the one thing she really enjoys and is good at, but each time I mention it she clams up.'

Ellan hadn't paid much attention to Margaret's worries. She was just glad the girl seemed not to notice her.

The beginning of July was very hot and oppressive, as Vi remarked. 'Though it probably won't last and we'll have a terrible storm,' she added. 'Maybe the master will take you all out on Sunday for the day, like he did last year.'

'Do you think he will, Ma?' Lucy cried, looking up from the table where she was doing her homework.

'I don't know. He's very busy these days. You know he's working more days at the hospital now. Maybe we could go – just you and me and Vi and Tilly.'

'The furthest you'll get me is New Brighton. I don't like ships,' Vi said.

'Then can we go there on Sunday? Can we go on the ferris wheel and up the tower?' Lucy pleaded.

Ellan smiled. It would be a change and she was sure Margaret wouldn't mind them going alone. It wasn't really far enough to warrant the exertions of the whole family. She would be able to relax for a few hours at least. 'Yes. All right. As long as Vi can get the afternoon off.'

'Will you ask the missus, Ellan?'

'Yes. I'll ask her.'

Margaret agreed readily. 'It will do you all good and you should make the most of the weather. It's really very warm, and it may not last. I'm afraid it's too much of an effort for me now, Ellan. I'm not even as strong as I was last year. You all go and enjoy yourselves.'

'Cook will be here and Vi will leave a tea tray ready.'

Lucy agreed wholeheartedly about the weather. Each morning and evening she scanned the clear sky, uttering the old rhyme, 'Red sky at night, sailor's delight. Red sky in the morning, sailor's warning.' And each night there was a spectacular sunset and on Sunday it dawned clear and warm.

'It's going to be a scorcher, don't forget your hats and sunshades,' Margaret urged when Ellan and Lucy went into the drawing room to say goodbye.

They all looked fresh and cool, Ellan thought, as they boarded the tram for the pierhead. She, Vi and Tilly wore cream cotton dresses with wide straw hats to shade their faces from the sun. Vi's and Tilly's dresses were shorter than Ellan's, revealing legs encased in white stockings. Lucy wore a white sailor-style dress, edged with navy. A straw boater trimmed with navy ribbons was perched over her dark curls.

It was a lovely day for a sail and it would be cool on the river, Ellan mused. But obviously they were not the only ones who thought so. The landing stage was crowded.

'Oh, damn! Half the city's had the same idea. We'll be crushed like sardines and I was looking forward to a lazy day,' Tilly said irritably.

'We're not going back, are we? Oh, please, let's go,' Lucy pleaded.

'We've come this far so we're definitely not going back,' Vi stated.

'It won't be all that bad, Tilly. There will be plenty of room on the beach,' Ellan urged.

Tilly looked pained as they pushed their way towards the gate for the New Brighton ferry.

'Lucy, keep hold of my hand or we'll get separated,' Ellan instructed.

'It's not so crowded over there, let's move,' Vi suggested and after a bit of pushing and shoving and elbowing from Tilly, they stood just behind the chain that separated them from the edge of the stage.

The *Royal Daffodil* was making her way slowly towards them, leaving a grey-flecked wash behind her, and Ellan began to explain to Lucy how the Mersey ferries had earned their title 'Royal' for their service during the war. She heard a scuffling behind her and turned around to see what was going on. That was the last thing she remembered and those few seconds were always to be a blank in her memory.

All she could remember was falling, then the shock as she felt the cold waters of the Mersey close over her head, the blind panic as she clawed and fought her way upwards, spluttering and gasping for air. Then hands reaching out, the blurred faces and then coming round to find herself lying on the ground surrounded by people. Tilly was bending over her, sobbing hysterically.

She struggled to rise and through the gap in the crowd saw someone being hustled away by two police-men. 'Tilly! Tilly! What happened?' She coughed and sank down again.

'Stand back and let her breathe, get back!' she heard a man's voice shouting and then she retched violently and vomited up the dirty water she'd swallowed. She felt slightly better as a policeman helped her into a sitting position.

'That's right, luv, get it all up. We'll take you to hospital just to make sure you haven't hurt yourself. The ambulance is on its way. You had a lucky escape.'

She stared at him in confusion. What had happened? 'Did . . . did I faint and fall in?'

'No, luv, you didn't. This lady here saw it all. You were pushed.'

It still didn't make any sense. She reached out and clasped Tilly's arm. 'Tilly! Who?'

Tilly managed to stifle her sobs. 'Selina. It was Selina Elliot, I saw her as plain as day.'

Ellan shook her head in disbelief. Then she remembered Lucy and Vi.

She lay in the hospital bed too shocked, too weak to care about anything. Tilly had been with her for a while, she remembered that. Tilly who had just sat and held her hand and wept. Lloyd, too, had visited her and she thought how old and broken he looked, his face haggard, his eyes tormented. There had been nothing she could say to either of them. The police sergeant told her she'd been lucky, not many people survived the strong undertow of the river at the landing stage. Lucky! Lucky! How could he say she was lucky? Lucy hadn't been lucky, and what was her life worth without Lucy? He also told her that Selina Elliot was to be locked up in an institution for the criminally insane, for Vi had drowned as well. When he'd gone she stared around her at the bare, white walls and thought she wouldn't care if she ended up in a place like that. There was nothing to live for now.

They were all worried about her, the nurses and doctors. She would eat nothing and lay most of the time in a semi-comatose state. When Tilly came on her next visit she was escorted into the matron's office.

'We are very worried about Mrs Vannin,' Matron began.

After that visit Tilly went in desperation to see Margaret Elliot. Cook opened the door to her. 'Come in. I'm glad to see you. Maybe you can do something . . . anything to help her. I hate this house now. It's awful, what with the doctor so quiet and strange and Miss Selina screaming and saying terrible things . . . until they took her away. And the missus. Oh, God! I feel so sorry for her!'

Tilly sighed heavily, thinking she would get little help here.

Margaret looked paler and thinner since the last time she'd seen her. The hands that gripped the coverlet were transparent and skeletal.

'Mrs Elliot, please can I talk to you?' Margaret turned her head in Tilly's direction. 'It's about Ellan.'

'Oh, yes. Poor, poor Ellan. She is taking it badly.'

Tilly nodded.

'I know . . . I know how she feels. Oh, Tilly. Say it's all a nightmare!'

'Oh, ma'am. I wish I could, believe me.'

'I blame myself. I should have given Selina more time, more love and attention. I should have begged Lloyd to give Ellan a house of her own. I was so selfish!'

'No. No. You're not.'

'Lloyd is a broken man. His career, his life is in ruins.'

Tilly took her hand. This woman deserved none of this. 'What will you do?'

'Move away. There is nothing else we can do. I . . . I can't stay in this house now.'

Tilly understood. 'What can we do about Ellan? I'm at me wit's end.'

Margaret looked past her, towards the window. 'It's so very hard to lose your child.' She spoke slowly, every word an effort. 'But she is young and healthy, not like me.'

'She won't be for long, unless someone can do something,' Tilly cried.

Margaret knew what she had to do. One last act of kindness was all she was capable of, before she closed her mind to reason. 'In the drawer . . .' she whispered to Tilly.

Tilly went to the writing table, opened the top drawer and brought out a small, leather-bound book.

'Look in the back. In the back, Tilly,' Margaret urged.

Tilly leafed through the pages and suddenly her thoughts were on a plane with Margaret's.

The days and nights slipped by but they were all the same to Ellan. People came and went. Some she recognized. Some were strangers. Some urged her to eat, to drink, to make an effort to get well and look forward. But only the dark and empty void stretched before her. Then Tilly was at her side again.

'Oh, Ellan, Ellan. Please get well,' she sobbed.

'What for?' They were the first words she had spoken for a week and through her tears Tilly smiled.

'Because . . . because there's someone here to see you.'

Ellan turned her head and then rubbed her hand across her eyes. Andrew Quirk was smiling down at her and behind him was Mary Costain.

He took the wasted hand. 'I've come to take you home, Ellan, and to change your name to Quirk, if you'll have me?'

Her fingers curled around his and for the first time she felt the fear and the darkness fade. She caught sight of the silver ring on his finger. The one she'd given him. 'I can't . . . stand. Not . . . not this time.'

'You won't have to. You'll have us both to help you. We're going home, Ellan, and we'll start afresh. At home.'